BLOOD LUST

David tried to stop, but Monique pulled him along as if he were a reluctant puppy on a leash. They grabbed the Brookens boy, then shook him. His eyes fluttered open. "It is better when they are awake," Monique said, then sank their teeth into his bare, exposed throat.

David felt the flesh part underneath his lips, then blood rushed into his mouth. He tried to scream but couldn't, as the viscous, iron-tasting fluid swelled within his mouth, then poured down his throat.

David vaguely sensed the Brookens boy struggling in his grasp. His pulse hammered within David's head, within his very soul, as though a blacksmith were working. Pound, pound, pound . . . then the pulse slowed, the thundering weakened, and Benny Joe's resistance grew even more feeble. David was expanding, growing larger than a giant, filling up the world.

"No!" David screamed, and pulled himself free of Monique's grasp. "No! No! NO!" David pounded on the keyboard. He could still taste the blood, still felt larger than life, as though this room could barely contain him.

"No!" David cried again, trying to regain control of himself, to push away the seductively alien feelings. He murmured a heartfelt prayer as he grasped his crucifix and the locket.

When he opened his eyes, the computer screen read:

Was it good for you too, David? Mmmmmm . . .

GOT AN INSATIABLE THIRST FOR VAMPIRES?
LET PINNACLE QUENCH IT!

BLOOD FEUD (705, $4.50)
by Sam Siciliano

SHE is a mistress of darkness — coldly sensual and dangerously seductive. HE is a master of manipulation with the power to take life and grant *unlife*. THEY are two ancient vampires who have sworn to eliminate each other. Now, after centuries, the time has come for a face-to-face confrontation — and neither will rest until one of them is destroyed!

DARKNESS ON THE ICE (687, $4.50)
by Lois Tilton

It was World War II, and the Nazis had found the perfect weapon. Wolff, an SS officer, with an innate talent — and thirst — for killing, was actually a vampire. His strength and stealth allowed him to drain and drink the blood of enemy sentries. Wolff stalked his prey for the Nazi cause — but killed them to satisfy his own insatiable hunger!

THIRST OF THE VAMPIRE (649, $4.50)
by T. Lucien Wright

Phillipe Brissot is no ordinary killer — he is a creature of the night — a vampire. Through the centuries he has satisfied his thirst for blood while carrying out his quest of vengeance against his ancient enemies, the Marat Family. Now journalist, Mike Marat is investigating his cousin's horrible "murder" unaware that Phillipe is watching him and preparing to strike against the Marats one final time . . .

BLIND HUNGER (714, $4.50)
by DarkeDarke

Widowed and blind, pretty Patty Hunsacker doesn't feel like going on with her life . . . until the day a man arrives at her door, claiming to be the twin brother of her late husband. Patty welcomes Mark into her life but soon finds herself living in a world of terror as well as darkness! For she makes the shocking discovery that "Mark" is really Matt — and he isn't dead — he's a vampire. And he plans on showing his wife that loving a vampire can be quite a bloody affair!

Available wherever paperbacks are sold, or order direct from the Publisher. Send cover price plus 50¢ per copy for mailing and handling to Penguin USA, P.O. Box 999, c/o Dept. 17109, Bergenfield, NJ 07621. Residents of New York and Tennessee must include sales tax. DO NOT SEND CASH.

VAMPIRE'S KISS

WILLIAM HILL

PINNACLE BOOKS
WINDSOR PUBLISHING CORP.

PINNACLE BOOKS are published by

Windsor Publishing Corp.
475 Park Avenue South
New York, NY 10016

Copyright © 1994 by William Hill

All rights reserved. No part of this book may be reproduced in any form or by any means without the prior written consent of the Publisher, excepting brief quotes used in reviews.

If you purchased this book without a cover, you should be aware that this book is stolen property. It was reported as "unsold and destroyed" to the Publisher and neither the Author nor the Publisher has received any payment for this "stripped book."

The P logo Reg. U.S. Pat. & TM Off. Pinnacle is a trademark of Windsor Publishing Corp.

First Printing: March, 1994

Printed in the United States of America

Prologue

Waiting for the Sun

As though powerful sorcery were being worked, the study held an eerie ambiance. Bathed in blue radiance, David sat before his computer, electronically crafting his latest creation. The shadows along his crowded, sprawling wall-to-wall desk were pitch-black. Their allies near the file cabinets and by the bookshelves appeared to be fathomless, shadowy gateways into unknown reaches of imagination. Displayed in fresco fashion near the top of each wall, the artwork from his book jackets took on depth, if not life, from the screen's eldritch glow.

There were nearly a dozen covers, all with an air of danger and urgency—eyes in the dark over a gleaming blade; a couple running away from a looming shadow; a torch-carrying mob; a creature crawling from a moonlit alpine lake; and more. Below the titles *Razorsharp, Hellbent, Witchhunt,* and several others, was the author's name—DAVID MATTHEWSON.

Sighing, David quit typing and sat back, slowly stretching his long limbs and lean frame. It was time for a break. He was tired and worn, and looked worse because of his unnatural pallor and wild, ink-black hair. The screen's azure glow had set his eyes strangely alight, while giving a ghostly luminescence to his skin.

Since his most recent book had become a surprising bestseller, his publisher was pressing him to expedite his latest manuscript. Even before that he'd been writing relentlessly, night after night, obsessed. He'd worked too long and too hard to turn out a personally unsatisfying read, no matter how impatient the public might be or how high the monetary incentive. And the pressure affected him; the fatigue was evident in his face.

All in the name of art, David thought, or therapy. He rubbed his eyes, then reached for a cup of iced coffee. The night air was hot, but he still needed something to help him stay awake. Even after a decade of being an unwilling night owl, he still had trouble adjusting to the graveyard shift.

"OUCH!" David suddenly clutched the back of his neck. He'd been scratched! "SHADY!" David accused angrily, and whirled around expecting to find his most playful cat. He was alone. Even Shadowcat didn't move that fast or soundlessly.

But David could have sworn he wasn't alone! He sensed another's presence as surely as though somebody were staring silently at him. But nobody was visiting, and he lived by himself. Maybe paranoia and unexplainable physical discomfort were his rewards for writing about Native American shape-changers.

Earlier David had wondered if it might be another symptom of his illness, then discarded the idea. Paranoia and hallucinations were not related to porphyria. His treatments wouldn't be causing this.

But now there was no doubt in his mind that something strange had been happening to him all night. Several times he'd felt as though he were being spied upon. At first he'd shrugged it off as a quirk of creative jitters, his mind playing tricks on him. It liked to help him procrastinate, when he was getting close to presenting something for critical review.

The presence had changed over time. Later, he had felt uncomfortably crowded, and swore somebody was breathing hotly down his neck. Several times he'd imagined smelling a musky scent, then it disappeared as if a gentle breeze had blown it away. With the windows open, a perfumed aroma was the last thing he expected to emanate from his ranch.

"Hey!" something pricked his neck again, then nipped his ear playfully. He grabbed his ear. For a moment, the perfumed scent was cloying, overwhelming . . . then it was gone. Nothing had changed about the room, but the presence had departed, leaving him alone.

"I'm going—" David glanced at the screen, thinking he had seen it blink. "Hey, that's not right!" he muttered as he read the text. Why in the world had he incorrectly described Danielle? She was a honey-hued blonde with crystal blue eyes, not raven-tressed with indigo eyes. And . . . and he'd named her Liselle! His mind was gone; it was time to quit writing.

But good Lord, he hadn't thought of Liselle in a long time, and then only after having vivid dreams. He re-read the text. The description reminded David of a woman he'd met over a decade ago in Austria. Why had he thought about her tonight? Simply doing so made his pulse race.

Suddenly David sensed amusement—it was the only way he could describe it. Confused, he whirled around, seeing nothing, but wanting to flail about until he hit it—hit something! Suddenly, it was gone again. What was gone? And where? He pressed the save key on the computer and began to hunt for whatever it was that had bothered him.

As David searched the upstairs, he almost didn't bother to turn on any lights, but found he needed to. He had excellent night vision, and could usually see fine in the ebony world—better than in the daylight, in fact—but tonight was different. The darkness was murky, as if a misty curtain had been drawn.

David checked the bedroom he used for storage. All was

as it should be. The sensation of another presence drifting about was maddening; it felt just out of reach. Sometimes it was at his side, then ahead of him. Often times, it was behind, stalking him. David kept rubbing himself to remove chills and goose bumps. He wasn't sure if he believed in ghosts, but somebody else was in the house. He'd lived by himself for too long not to notice the difference—company gave the place a different feel, an active air. He checked the guest room and the bathroom. Nothing. The attic was secure, too.

Wait! David cocked his head as he heard a swish of cloth and light footsteps from his bedroom. David pushed open the door and reached for the light switch.

Slowly blinking eyes stared back at him from his bed. "Oh, it's just you. Hi, Shady," David told his cat. The black feline looked at him as though he'd interrupted something vitally important. Since Shadowcat didn't seem unduly agitated, there wasn't any need for him to check this room. And yet, the sensation of amusement continued to haunt him. Shadowcat looked at him, then her gaze flicked to something behind him.

David whirled. Nothing. But he felt the presence move downstairs. David followed, heading down the steps, walking through the entry hall, past his dusty high school trophies and into the sparsely furnished living room. There weren't any plants, and neither the stereo or television looked used, coats of dust thick on each. He checked the dining room. Clean and deserted.

David came back and checked the front door. Locked. As he walked past the stairway down the short hall to the back of the house, a cool breeze slipped by him, as though somebody had run toward the kitchen. David shivered, then sprinted ahead. There was somebody in the house! He knew it! They'd just left by the back door!

David raced into the kitchen and slid to a stop. The back door was closed. Nothing and nobody! Just to be sure, he turned on the overhead light and winced. The back door was locked. He quickly turned off the light. Despite feeling silly, he checked the closet, pantry, and even under the table. How come he had the feeling he was being toyed with? This had to be fatigue, combined with his attempt at going cold turkey. He'd read about D.T.'s; hallucinations were a possibility. He probably should just go back to writing and forget about this. But he couldn't. He was restless and curious.

Maybe he just needed some fresh air. David used that excuse to head outside. He opened the back door and stepped out into the muggy Texas night, full of the odors of hay, manure, and grass. As he walked through his garden, then past the silent chicken coop, he barely noticed the late night heat, typical for the middle of June in Temprance.

David looked across the green-brown field at the sleeping cows and then over the slow rise of the pasture, to where the earthen dam held Cedar Creek Lake. He could imagine the placid waters he loved. The light was pale and colorless, touching the land with gray. Dawn was still some time off.

David sighed with exasperation. He still sensed somebody lurking about, sometimes in front of him, sometimes behind. He set off toward the barn. The two-story structure was painted beige; the lower half had been repainted, while the upper was still faded and flecked. He'd started work on the house and barn in April, but hadn't finished the barn, becoming consumed by his latest creation.

David walked through the corral gate and around the barn. The presence was here; it was everywhere. He glanced inside the door and saw his horses asleep. He opened a second gate and entered the pasture. As he passed the pigpen, none of its occupants stirred. David paused at the side door, struggling with his feelings. He reached for the handle, then pulled back his hand, unsure if it was wise to enter. David knew there was danger inside—not because of his imagination, but of his own making and weakness. He'd been resisting the growing urge to come here for a few days, because he was sure that if he got too close, he might not be able to control himself; and that would lead to death.

David stepped back, wiping the sweat from his brow. The horses were fine. If there had been an intruder, they would have made noise or left the barn. Sure. That made sense. There wasn't any need to check the barn . . . to go near the closet.

David felt the air of amusement swell toward laughter, then the presence was suddenly gone. David was relieved; he felt truly alone. He hated having to tell Dr. Katyu that he was imagining things, but it was probably wise.

As David climbed the pasture fence, he glanced at the sky. It was almost dawn. David ran to the house and grabbed a lawn chair, carrying it to the edge of the front porch and facing east. Whenever he could, he would watch sunrises and sunsets. They never grew dull. Because of his illness, the indirect and diffused light was all the sunlight he could handle. He desperately missed the sun's warm caress, its golden radiance in blue skies.

All this because his body had betrayed him. David clenched the arms on the chair and cursed. Damn his weakness! Damn his wild times—his drunken despair and debauchery! They had ruined his life!

David glanced at his reflection in the window. He rarely studied his face, having removed all the mirrors in the house but one for shaving and trimming. Being honest, he concluded that he was looking better, despite his albino appearance. His long hair was as dark and lustrous as his skin was pale and translucent. His last tan, as well as some of his handsomeness, had begun to fade over a decade ago. His sad face was lean with finely boned features, strong cheekbones, and a bearded jaw. His red eyes and teeth were both by-products of porphyria. Fortunately, the treatments were working, and the lesions had healed. His hair no longer grew as though he were lycanthropic.

But was it the medical treatments or his own folk remedy that had triggered the improvements? Several days ago he'd actually watched the sun set, tolerating direct light for a moment.

Well, he would soon know, for he had forsaken his home brewed remedy, and he hadn't tested himself since stopping. Now was as good a time as any. It had been three days, and oh, how he'd longed for the warm caress of the light of day!

As David stared into the window at his reflection, the grayness had given way to purples, reds, and pinks. He looked eastward and thought that the scattered clouds resembled party streamers and shredded crepe paper. Soon the sun would be rising over the lake, a great, red blazing ball heading for the heavens. David couldn't wait!

Orange was added to the dawn's light, setting the clouds afire and strafing the land. David glanced about and squinted. It was as though he were seeing his ranch through an amber lens. The light grew brighter, changing to a peach hue. It felt wonderful. His attentive gaze became riveted on the brightening horizon.

The top of the wavering, crimson orb became visible. David squinted, wishing he'd worn his sunglasses, then had to turn away. Suddenly, David grew feverishly hot, breaking into a cold sweat and trembling. He'd regressed. His recovery hadn't been natural, but due to his home remedy—the elixir.

David tried to stand, but his legs buckled. He staggered backward, falling over his chair and collapsing on the porch. He had to get inside! Too much exposure could cause him to pass out; then he might die. He was already dizzy.

David crawled across the front porch toward the front door. Each second he felt as though he were growing heavier and heavier, feeling hotter and hotter. His back was afire, the flames spreading across his body. Blistering hot . . . then suddenly cold. David shivered as he began to perspire profusely, streams of chilling sweat running down his face, back, and legs. Something was very wrong.

He kept crawling and finally reached the front door. He clawed his way up the wall to stand, then tried the handle. It was locked. He shoved his hands into his pockets. He didn't have a key.

Tears streaked down his face as he staggered across the porch toward the shaded side of the house. He stepped off and fell into the shadows, crashing to the ground. The grass smelled wonderful, sweet and rich, and he wondered if it would be the last thing he would remember.

For a few minutes, David lay there reveling in the cool darkness and regaining his strength. Finally, he felt well enough to sit. He couldn't wait too long. Soon, even the diffuse light would be too much to endure. If he was to make it to the back door, he must try now. Damn, what a fool he'd been! What had gotten into him?

David used the wall to help him stand, then trudged to the back corner of the house. He took several deep breaths, then raced toward the back door. As soon as David stepped into the sunlight, he felt as if he'd been struck by a sledgehammer. His body ached, his head spun, and he tripped over something. Staggering forward, he threw himself at the steps and collapsed just within reach of them, his hands grazing the rough concrete. Gasping, he crawled forward, growing increasingly weaker, the sun draining him of life. He wanted to cry out in frustration, but couldn't spare the breath. Instead, he prayed.

Suddenly the world went black. And yet, he still felt the steps under his hands. Keep going! Come on! He bumped headfirst into the screen door. With scrabbling fingers, he pulled it open and dragged himself inside, away from the beloved and poisonous sunlight.

The kitchen linoleum was cool underneath him, and David wanted to simply lie there, but knew he shouldn't. He crawled further inside the tightly shuttered house and its cradling darkness, then kicked the back door shut. Exhausted, David slumped, then began crying in frustration and anger. Would he ever see the sunlight again?

Part One:
The Pack

One

Phantoms

The five teenagers were hiding behind an old, faded blue tractor and attached bushhog parked between the barn and ranch house, outside the fences near the woods. The boys were a mixed batch: two tall, healthy-looking blond brothers; a portly cowboy complete with hat and boots; a curly-haired bean pole; and a lean, restless one who appeared older than the others. Each of Grimm's Reapers was appropriately dressed in dark shirt and jeans. Surrounded by the boys was a small cooler of beer already half-empty. Four of the boys were sitting, but not Kevin Grimm. He couldn't. It was going to be a special night—the first of summer—and there was electricity in the air.

Kevin was tall and lean, with shoulders that might have been constructed from hangers and joints stolen from an erector set. The dark clothes matched his curly hair and bushy brows, but made him appear unhealthy. Skin so white, he'd once heard a classmate whisper that he must have been strained through a bed sheet at birth. In the twilight, his eyes were colorless, and his gaunt face tight, but expressionless.

Kevin stared over the seat of the tractor at the writer-dude's ranch house. It was set among a cluster of tall mesquite trees and at the bottom of a long, sloping pasture. Something about it mesmerized him. As it caught the last light of day, the simple two-story structure appeared hauntingly aglow . . . the off-white paint holding an odd luminescence. The trim and shutters were dark. The chimney was huge and centered, stretching into the fiery sky. Along the front was a full-length, covered porch, where the twilight failed to reach. A hedge and fence surrounded the front yard, and a gate led to a walkway beyond the bushes which ended at the dark porch.

Perched on the barn off to their left was a bent, rooster weather vane, standing starkly atop the corrugated metal roof. The hayloft door was open and gently swayed back and forth. A soft lake breeze brushed by, and Kevin could smell hay, cow dung, grass, and a mingling of other natural odors that hung heavily in the air.

Kevin searched but didn't see any livestock. Besides the coop, there appeared to be a pigpen on the left side of the barn near the corral. But where were all the animals? Hiding in the barn? Did they sense trouble? Reaper trouble?

Suddenly, Kevin felt as though chilled fingers were lightly sliding along his back, and he shivered. There was nothing wrong—nothing he could see—but Kevin sensed something odd in the air. He tried to shake it off, blaming the excitement and his imagination.

Wait. Did something move? Couldn't be. The writer-dude—Dick Matthews was it?—was a night owl, and it wasn't dark yet. According to the article in the *Times,* the writer-dude suffered from some kind of blood disease that disfigured him and made him allergic to the sun.

There really seemed to be something odd about the shadows around the house, as well as those by the barn. They shifted and writhed, as though chained and silently tortured.

"Where the hell is Skeeter?" JJ drawled, interrupting the silence, then he took a swig of beer. Jayson James Tubbs's cowboy hat was pulled down tight, its shadow hiding most of his face, except for the outline of wire-rimmed glasses and jowls. JJ was thick everywhere, through the face, neck, and shoulders, with a barrel chest and a prelegal beer gut. He was hairy and built much like his older brothers, a furry tree stump with a cowboy hat and boots. He slapped at his neck, muttering, "Damn mosquitoes."

"I always thought Skeeter was a pussy," Jim Bob Brookens offered in slow, eastern Texan, then scowled. Just like he always does, Kevin thought. As far back as anyone could remember, Jim Bob always wore a look of displeasure, distaste, or impatience. It went along with the stiff walk that led Benny Joe to joke that Jim Bob had sat on a corncob. Still, his hair was white blond and wavy, his eyes blue, skin fair, and he was well built—easy on the eyes according to what Kevin heard from girls at school and church. Jim Bob claimed that he only did one thing without his hat—it was black felt banded with leather and two hawk feathers—and that absolutely, positively, nothing scared him.

"I'm bored," Benny Joe muttered. He wore a hat identical to his older brother's. Physically, there was no doubt he was Jim Bob's sibling, except Benny Joe was taller, wore rounded glasses, and had straight hair that might have been cut with shears and a bowl. But the main difference was his expression. Benny Joe's face was unlined, and could project so much innocence that JJ claimed the sight made him sick. "Bored, bored," he repeated and made snoring noises.

"I got something that will make the wait fun," Kevin told him. He reached underneath his shirt and pulled out a dark, squarish bottle.

"What's that?" Jim Bob asked.

"Jaegermeister, buddy boy. It's hot," Kevin said as he unscrewed the top. "Hunters drink it to stay warm. It's better than Mad Dog 20/20. Jaegermeister," Kevin grandly pronounced, "is imported from Germany. Heard it has codeine or some such drug in it. Makes you see things." With that, he took a slug, then licked his lips. "And it's part of the initiation, if Skeeter ever gets here. But we can start without him."

"I'd like to try some," Jim Bob drawled. He took the open bottle from Kevin, chugged a belt, then burped and smiled. He sniffed, then quickly blinked his watering eyes. "Killer!" JJ's smile was huge, and he followed suit. His eyes were dangerously steady, and his smile unchanged.

"Hey, know why Louisiana has niggers and California earthquakes?" Kevin asked. He loved telling jokes, knowing thousands of them. He could keep people rolling for hours. Jim Bob shook his head. "California had first pick!"

Jim Bob laughed, then took another drink. After a belch, he handed his brother the bottle. "Go for it, Benjo." His brother hesitated. "You're old enough now, Benjo. You gotta start drinking some time. Be a man." He nodded, and Benny Joe tentatively put the bottle to his lips.

"Hey, why ain't cowboys circumcised?" Kevin continued. "So they got someplace to keep their Skoal, when they're eating lunch!" He laughed. Sometimes he really cracked himself up.

Benny Joe choked, then coughed. "Quiet!" Jim Bob and Kevin whispered harshly. Benny Joe tried to control his fit, but couldn't and tried to muffle it with his hands. Smiling, Jim Bob took the bottle from him. "Give it a shot, preacher boy," Jim Bob taunted, as he handed the booze to Patrick, who was sitting quietly.

Patrick's face, usually placid, became defiant. Patrick was as tall and thin as a willow and had no chest, but his biceps looked similar to Popeye's, hams developed from helping out on needy farms, hauling hay and splitting wood—good deeds his father required. For a fleeting moment Patrick looked doubtful, then he shrugged and took the bottle from Jim Bob. "I . . . I . . . I'm doin' this n . . . not because you guys are, b . . . b . . ." he had to spit the word out, "but because I've always wondered what r . . . real alcohol tastes like." He took a sip. Suddenly it looked as though Patrick had swallowed a handful of fire ants.

Kevin snorted, then said. "Good shot, PP. This is another step in getting you out from under your old man's thumb. Be your own man, I always say." This was fun, but where was their new initiate, Kevin wondered? All was ready, but Skeeter was needed to put it all in motion; and take the fall if necessary.

Kevin glanced skyward. Above the lake, the red sun was muted, enshrouded by thin clouds as it sat upon the flat horizon. It was teasing him; it knew he was waiting for darkness. The higher clouds were red, angry, and serrated—giant crimson fronds pasted against a golden twilight. All around them the amber light barely touched the land of indistinct shadows thrown by the pine, oak, and mesquite trees. As the light weakened, a veil of low fog appeared off to his right, thickening near a small stream. There'd been days when he'd seen the fog get thicker than the smoke from a chili cook-off.

Kevin wiped the perspiration from his brow. It was early summer, and already he was tired of sweating like a pig. The evening air was like a wet blanket, so heavy that it drained life. The humidity was as suffocating as the quiet, and everything was dead calm, as though holding its breath. Even the crickets and frogs were unnaturally silent, the night air devoid of furtive, shuffling movements.

The silence was abruptly shattered. Everybody could hear a loud thrashing noise, as though a herd of elephants was trampling the forest. It had to be Skeeter. Kevin stepped next to a tree near the edge of the forest and waited. Skeeter burst out of the woods, and Kevin grabbed the skinny redheaded boy about the head and shoulders, pulling him to the ground. "Quiet!" Kevin said harshly and shifted his grip, clamping one hand hard along the back of Skeeter's head and another across his mouth. "You're late, Skeet boy. Not a good way to start, if you still want to join the Reapers."

"I do!" Skeeter mumbled under the hand.

"Shut up!" Kevin spat as he shook Skeeter. The boy nodded. Reluctantly, Kevin removed his hands. "Good deal. That writer-dude ought to be going out for his early evening stroll any time now."

"Good. I'm sick and tired of waiting," Jim Bob drawled.

"Well I'm ready." It was obvious Skeeter Marshall was nervous. He'd forgotten the instructions and dressed incorrectly, in shorts and a green tank top.

"Soon, Skeet. First you slug and chug, then we get on with it. It's all part of being a Reaper." Kevin gave Skeeter the green bottle. Trying to appear cool, Skeeter casually took a swig. He gasped, then choked. JJ pounded on his back as Skeeter kept coughing. Everyone shushed him. He finally got his hacking under control.

"Anyone know why farts smell? So deaf people can enjoy them, too," Kevin snorted. JJ laughed.

"Another shot, Skeet," Kevin told him. "It'll make you brave." Skeeter took a smaller sip this time and survived, although he looked a bit green.

"All right! Party! Let's do shots," Jim Bob suggested. Kevin agreed, and they took turns passing the bottle back and forth. Jim Bob gargled, then burped.

"Wish I had some tequila," JJ said.

"Wild Turkey," Kevin countered.

"Speaking of wild," Jim Bob said. He pulled something from his waistband.

"A . . . a g . . . gun!" Patrick squeaked.

"A .38 special."

"Radical," JJ laughed. "You're ready to create your own excitement." His eyes were shiny from inebriation.

"Just don't point it at any of us," Kevin admonished. Then he looked at Skeeter, and smiled as he asked, "You ready?" Skeeter nodded. "This is all you gotta do . . ."

* * *

Just before David awoke with a start and a terrible thirst, he could have sworn that Liselle was looking down at him. Arrestingly beautiful, she stared at him, the hunger obvious in her eyes, and passion painting her face. Behind her, he thought he saw his beloved Tina look away, her disappointment in him evident on her face.

David forgot all about both of them when his stomach clutched, knotting and forcing him to double over. He knew what was wrong. His body needed the elixir he'd been denying it. David refused to give in, trying to ride out the searing pain in his gut, but it started to swell. David's chest and abdomen burned; he was light-headed; and his vision was blurred.

David crawled out of bed and staggered to the bathroom. Collapsing against the sink, he turned on the water, splashing his face and gulping down handfuls of the cool liquid. But it didn't quell the inferno. David retched.

Maybe going cold turkey wasn't such a good idea. David slipped to the floor. The pains continued, and he began to tremble and shake. This was worse than his exposure to the sunlight this morning. Or . . . maybe this was because of his overindulgence—his foolishness—at sunrise. Maybe it was just an attack of porphyria. Might the elixir help? He had to try it while he could still move.

David grabbed the sink and hauled himself up. He felt ancient, bent crooked and as fragile as an old man. He didn't bother to dress and, clad only in black sweat pants, he staggered to the stairs. With each step, as though the elixir were summoning him, he felt a little stronger and more determined.

Somehow he stumbled downstairs and into the kitchen, knocking down several pictures in the hallway. A wobbling juggernaut, he made his way toward the back door, sweeping a chair and small stepladder to the side. "Get out of my way!"

he shouted, and feebly kicked at Midnite, who was entangled with David's feet. The black cat skipped away.

David collapsed against the door, resting for a moment, then shoved it open, and burst into the twilight. The back door slammed against the wall with such ferocity that the boys froze with surprise at David's abrupt appearance. He moved so quickly the teenagers barely glimpsed him.

In the fading light, David was an odd figure, appearing disembodied, feet and upper torso racing across the barnyard without legs. His skin had taken on an odd, wetly gleaming appearance in the peach and lavender twilight.

Teetering and gasping, David reached the barn door. He couldn't wait. He had to drink before the pain burned a hole in his gut. But what if it didn't work? He couldn't think about that. David snatched open the door and darted inside, slamming it shut.

He hurtled across the barn past the stalls, and crashed into the closet door. Fumbling around his neck, he pulled a cord holding two keys over his head. His hands were shaking so badly he couldn't get the key in the first lock. He took several deep breaths, then used one hand to hold the other as he inserted the key and turned. The second lock was less troublesome. David yanked open the door, rushed to the refrigerator, and pulled it open.

Inside, row after row of unlabeled bottles waited. All were opaque—some dark green while others were brown—and each one was filled with a dark liquid. David grabbed a bottle, unscrewed the top, and began chugging. After draining the bottle, David immediately felt better. "Ahhhh . . ."

Suddenly, he sensed the presence again—the amusement—and then it was gone just as quickly as it had come. David didn't care. His stomach no longer felt as though it were a boiler ready to blow.

David removed another bottle and closed the ancient Frigidaire. For a moment, he stared at the case of Jack Daniels next to the refrigerator, then left the large storage closet. Although he desperately wanted a drink of booze, he knew it would only exacerbate his illness, and that he didn't need. He already had enough troubles.

Bottle in hand, he left the barn and stepped back out into the night. He stopped after a few feet and put the bottle to his lips. This time he sipped. He was feeling better, almost giddy. Oblivious to his surroundings, he staggered around as he worked on the second bottle, weaving in the direction of the tractor, and then back toward the barn.

David sighed happily and stared skyward. High clouds had swallowed the moon, which had been in the sky even before sunset. It was then that he noticed smoke. Or was that just early evening fog? No, he also smelled—

Suddenly, a mournful wail echoed throughout the barnyard, carrying through the woods as a second cry started. David's eyes widened as a white form swirled in front of the barn, twisting as though a thick cloud of fog had been caught by a dust devil. Suddenly, the tendrils coalesced, taking on the shape of a golden-tressed woman clad in a flowing white robe.

David whirled about, staring at the apparition with a gaping mouth and wide eyes, then yelled, "Tina!" Could it be? Had she returned? Is that what he'd felt earlier? Tina calling him? Their love was strong enough to bridge any distance . . . even the afterlife.

"Tina? TINA!" David rushed toward the door. He reached for the ghostly apparition and found himself within it. The image and colors, darkness and light, swirled across his pale flesh as though an ethereal being caressed him. Spinning around, his hands grasping only air, David began yelling, "No . . . No . . . NO!" He couldn't touch Tina.

David clenched his empty hands, turned, and attacked the barn with frustrated fury. "NOOOOooo . . ." He hammered blow after blow against the door, each strike shattering wood and shaking the front wall. In moments the door was devastated, and David stopped, his body heaving as he slowly lowered his bloody hands. He slumped, feeling hopeless as well as helpless.

David's mind slowly cleared as his rage ebbed. Sulphur. He smelled it in the smoke. And there was warmth and light like . . . like a projection. Suddenly he knew he'd been duped. David straightened and slowly turned. Light was coming from the tall grass near the fence. He cocked his head. Sound was also coming from there. He squinted. Were those really stereo speakers? How . . .

Then David heard some chuckling and a hushed voice or two. He closed his eyes and concentrated. He smelled sweat and beer. He was being spied on! He'd been tricked.

In the white light of the projection, Kevin could see Matthewson's face. It had been transformed into something horrible, contorted and twisted. The flesh appeared to take on a brighter, unholy illumination, as did the eyes, which were now amazingly bright.

"He looks crazy," Benny Joe whispered, nervously pulling at his hat. David's head was cocked as though he were listening to them speak.

"I don't know about this," JJ said in a low voice, the words thick. He rose and took a step back. Skeeter nodded, his eyes wild-looking as his gaze met Patrick's. They thought alike: Run! Suddenly, David sprinted toward them. Skeeter and Patrick bolted. "Shit!" JJ dropped his beer.

"The bikes—" Benny Joe gasped. Holding their hats, the brothers went right, and JJ crashed left.

Except for Kevin, the others scattered like a handful of tossed marbles. Kevin watched. His sneer was fleeting, his expression growing doubtful. "To the pickup," Kevin breathed, and fled. For the first time in a long time, Kevin was scared. He didn't know what it was, maybe the speed of the writer-dude or the way he hurdled the fence, but Kevin pretended he had wings on his ankles and sprinted through the woods as though his ass was on fire.

"L . . . Lord, p . . . please help me," Patrick prayed as he ran, holding his forearm across his face to protect him from the ripping branches. He could barely see Skeeter ahead of him, darting in and out of the trees with surprising agility and lots of noise. He would get to the bicycles first.

What about us? The slowest one was always caught first, Patrick thought. At least JJ Tubbs was with them; he was the slowest. Patrick was immediately mortified by his cowardly thought. Still, he ran as though the devil's hounds were on his heels. "R . . . Run! G . . . Go, Skeeter, go!"

"Man, oh man, oh man . . ." Skeeter breathed, running even faster than he had earlier, and starting to easily outdistance the others. Unless he was lost, the fence should be coming up soon. Suddenly, Skeeter thought he heard something behind him, the crack of a stick. A shuffle. Crunching. Worried about his friend, Skeeter glanced over his shoulder. "Patrick?" There was nothing there. As he turned, Skeeter's world abruptly turned to black.

Still running, Patrick thought he heard something fall. He couldn't see or hear Skeeter any longer. The silence was heavy, sounds cushioned by the quickly thickening fog. It had cropped up everywhere, and was almost waist deep in some places. What if he stepped in a hole?

What if something had happened to Skeeter? Patrick heard a soft swishing noise and then a slow intake of breath. Patrick's gasp was sharp, his fears thrown into overdrive. Clutching his crucifix and praying for forgiveness for being a coward and deserting his friend, Patrick sprinted full tilt.

* * *

Somewhere behind everybody else, Kevin and JJ moved through the woods. Kevin was as light on his feet as JJ was heavy; the dry sticks and leaves cracked under JJ's big boots. JJ clutched his hat in his left hand. "I left the beer!" JJ breathed. "I gotta—" Kevin came to a halt, and he almost bumped into him. "What was that?" JJ asked.

"I don't know," Kevin replied. Nobody had cried out. Kevin couldn't see or hear anybody. Should he use his flashlight? No, it might give them away. Let someone else take the fall. "Here!" Kevin exclaimed. "Here's a shortcut. We'll beat everybody to the truck." He turned to look at JJ.

Huffing and grunting, JJ gave him thumbs up. He wanted to get out of here. He was scared, and almost nothing scared a Tubbs.

All around them, the darkness swirled through the fog. It seemed to hang about them, pulled along as though tied to them by a string.

Elsewhere in the woods, Jim Bob grabbed Benny Joe by the arm. "No, the bicycles are this way." Benny Joe thought he was wrong, but let himself be dragged on anyway. "This way." They quickly moved toward a copse of trees. They heard the hooting of an owl, but no other sounds from their pursuer or their friends. "Where's everybody?" Jim Bob drawled.

"We're lost! Damn fog! Damn you!" Sweat ran down Benny Joe's nose, and he shoved his glasses closer to his face. They kept sliding down his nose, and now they had fogged. He took them off to dry them. "You have a crappy sense of direction." Jim Bob ignored him and kept moving in the same direction. "I think I saw something over there," Benny Joe pleaded, stopping and grabbing Jim.

"Bullshit. Ya don't even have your glasses—" Jim Bob began, then he, too, thought he saw something move. The fog drifted, then grew darker. It moved forward, reshaping, almost taking on a human form. The brothers ran in the opposite direction.

For a few minutes they stumbled along in the darkness, missing trees but tripping over rocks, fire ant mounds, and stumps. The fog was hip deep and rising, as though a pool were filling. "I wish the moon was out," Benny Joe muttered.

"I wish you hadn't left the flashlight!"

"It's foggy. Wouldn't do any good. And you know what? All you ever do is complain," Benny Joe snapped. They had come to a railed fence. It should have stretched left and right, but instead, it immediately disappeared into the mist. "Since first I remember, you've bitched and moaned. Hey, I don't recognize this. Ain't we going the wrong way?"

"I can't tell. It wasn't foggy when we came in."

"Let's walk . . ." Benny Joe said, then looked along the fence. As though a wind touched the mists, something slid along the rails, billowing and slowly crawling closer. They bolted, caring little about what they ran over or stumbled through.

This is invigorating, David thought as his outrage fueled him. With his heightened senses, he wasn't having any trouble following the boys. Not only could he hear their clumsy attempts to escape, but he also heard their hushed voices and rasping breath. David wondered if he could hear their hearts pound, if he really concentrated?

Why had he believed Tina had returned? Was it because of that odd, phantomlike presence loose on the ranch?

Regardless, he would show these troublemakers. He would scare the crap out of the boys so bad, they'd never do anything like this again. As David continued to stalk the two brothers, he felt the haunting presence return. This time it was no longer amused, but angry . . . and thirsty. David tried to push away those feelings, but they wouldn't leave. Suddenly, he found that he was enjoying the hunt.

Now David noticed that he could hear the thudding, machine-gun-quick hammering of their hearts, and he smelled blood.

Both brothers' breath was much shorter, and their shirts completely soaked with sweat, when they burst out of the woods and into the barnyard where the fog was thinner. The equipment was still on, and the image of burned film—brilliant light with browned edges—projected along the front of the barn. The destroyed door hung limply from one hinge. "Should we break for the lake?" Jim Bob asked.

Then, as though the projector had been turned toward the house, a white image appeared near the porch. It wavered for a moment, then drifted in their direction.

"Uh, run!" Benny Joe mumbled, and turned around. Both of them suddenly saw what looked to be a figure, something solid in the fog. It darted among the trees along the barnyard line, shuffling in and out of the tall grass that whispered without the aid of a breeze.

"Finally, we're here," Kevin said, as he reached the fence. His blue Chevy pickup was in sight, parked next to an abandoned house. He rubbed his head, and now that he'd stopped, realized that his vision was blurred. "Must've hit my head," he mumbled. Kevin didn't really remember. Oh well, he had a hard head. He'd been hit there before and survived; the metal plate helped.

"Let's burn rubber. JJ?" Where was he? Even Tubbs wasn't this slow. Kevin turned about. "JJ?" The fog had grown dense, thicker than the smoke from a wildfire, and an opaque darkness had overtaken everything. Kevin grew even more wary and left, slipping through the rent in the wire fence. JJ's a tough boy, he thought.

"Now where'd Grimm go?" JJ breathed heavily. He was lost, so he slowed down. "Fucking fog." He cupped his hands and called, "Kevin? GRIMM?!" As though a slice of winter had been hiding and waiting, it now sprang free. He shivered and rubbed himself, warming away the goose bumps. "Weird," he chattered.

Suddenly the darkness ahead parted to reveal beauty unlike any JJ had ever seen . . . only dreamed. His jaw dropped, his mouth opened wide. He couldn't believe his eyes or his luck. Finally he managed, "Howdy, my name's JJ." Smiling, he paused, then stepped forward as beckoned. The bittersweet darkness descended as though a curtain fell. He sighed with pleasure, then a coldness gripped him, followed by intense, riveting pain. JJ tried to scream, but failed, gurgling instead.

Mocking laughter drifted through the night.

David staggered to a stop. Suddenly he was dizzy and light-headed. He tasted blood and spat. "Odd," he muttered. "I must've bit my lip." Again a wave of confusion and imbalance overwhelmed him, then he suddenly felt stronger—much stronger. Yes, he was going to enjoy taking his revenge. First these two boys, then he would catch up with the others.

Jim Bob and Benny Joe arrived at the thicket that led to the creek. Now the visibility was severely limited, worse than trying to see into a muddy river. "Let's keep going this way," Jim Bob mumbled. Then he saw the fog swirl and puff, as though something massive approached. The boys sprinted away, although they were beginning to slow and tire. Sweat stung their fear-widened eyes, and their mouths were agape and gasping for air.

"The fence again!" Benny Joe cried, his voice desperate.

Jim Bob thought he saw something out of the corner of his eye. "Somebody's playing us for fools, trying to scare us. Let's stand and fight!" He pulled the .38. They both were sure they heard a quiet, mocking laughter. Jim Bob hesitated, unnerved and unsure of where to fire.

They looked at each other and ran again. Benny Joe was behind his brother when he tripped. Benny Joe fell forward, head over heels, arms outstretched. "YEAARrrgh!" Pain rocketed up his arm as something snapped. Rolling onto his back and writhing in agony, Benny Joe grasped his left wrist and moaned, tears rushing to his clenched eyes.

"Benjo, Benny boy?" Jim Bob called, stopped, then retraced his steps. He couldn't see his brother. "What's wrong! Come on!" Suddenly, he stopped again. Not far away, the white mist whirled and roiled. A cold breeze rippled Jim Bob's shirt and hair, then something dark took shape within the fog. Red pinpoints of light burning like coals froze Jim Bob for a moment, then he raised his .38. He began to feel cold and dizzy, then disoriented. Something rushed toward him, the darkness sweeping forward and shoving the mist aside.

KABLAMM! KABLAAM-BLAAM! Jim Bob fired until the .38 clicked empty, then turned, and fled.

Benny Joe heard his brother flee. "Owww, Jimbob. Jimbob? JIMBOB! Don't—" Suddenly a coldness reached him, sweeping across him and chilling his sweat-drenched body. Panic surged through him, and he tried to clamber to his feet, but slipped and fell. The fog around him seemed to dissipate, but the darkness grew even heavier.

A tall, long-limbed figure appeared, looming over Benny Joe. "Oh, God, no," Benny Joe managed. "Jimbob!!"

* * *

David smiled wickedly. Revenge was sweet. He watched as the boy tried futilely to rise; he looked scared shitless.

Suddenly the clouds cleared, and the moon shone down upon them. The boy's expression was one of mortal terror. David laughed, inundated with feelings of raw power and violence. He reached for the boy, then stopped. His hands! What had happened to them? Not only were they badly torn and bloodied, but preternaturally long with sharp, red fingernails. Bloodied claws!

Gripped by horror, David screamed and ran, believing he was truly damned.

Two

Official Visit

"Ross! Look alive and open the gate!" Deputy Sheriff Logan Candel snapped as he stopped the black and white Mustang at the ranch gate. The car's headlights shone weakly through the fog, illuminating the mail box, which read "The Matthewsons." On an arch atop the gate and above the mist's reach was another sign, "MX Ranch." It was the last structure near the end of Cedar Dam Road, a stretch of oil-sprayed dirt and gravel that went from Temprance and wandered along the southern end of the lake until it came to the dam.

Logan checked his watch. It was one o'clock, late by most people's standards, but he knew that David would be awake. Logan hoped this wasn't a waste of time. He knew David was reclusive and not appreciative of surprise visits. But he'd tried to call, and all he got was an answering machine. He hated those things. You didn't know if somebody was home or not.

"Come on, Ross, there's work to be done. Ten years or ten minutes extra beauty sleep ain't gonna help either one of us."

"I'm on my way," the massive man replied as he hauled himself out of the car, leaving it shaking.

Logan was disgusted; Donald Bricker had left his nephew's training to him. Bubba was over six foot and three hundred pounds. His shoulders had once been broad and his chest massive, when he played tackle at Athens High and served his country in Desert Storm, but now he'd gone to the training table without training. Ross—Logan refused to call him Bubba—resembled a massive pear with large legs. Bricker claimed Ross was experienced with a gun and always ready for trouble; doubtful unless he meant with a fork.

It had been a short drive from Temprance to the MX Ranch, after a stop at Ross's apartment. The huge man had come running out with his shirt unbuttoned and hanging out, his belly flapping. To say Ross was unkempt was an understatement.

Their military background and current employment with the Temprance Sheriff's Department ended the two lawmen's similarities. Logan was very tall and wiry, a whip of a man with long arms and a stiff back. He dressed neatly, his boots always spit-polished. His hair was dark, cut short, and slicked back. Except for a thin mustache, he was usually clean-shaven, but not at this hour.

At the gate, Ross turned around and spread his hands apart, in a gesture giving up. Logan searched the glove box and came out with a set of master keys. He climbed out of the air-conditioned squad car and walked to the wide metal barrier. Beyond it, the gravel road led into fog-choked woods. Logan didn't see any signs of recent traffic. "Strange weather," he said, as he examined the keys in the headlights' glare.

"Fog gives me the creeps," Ross drawled. "It's either a bad start to a day or a bad . . . end." Ross whirled, thinking he saw something out of the corner of his eye.

"Jumpy, eh?" Logan asked, and Ross nodded. "Well, any day is a good day, as long as you're not being shot at." Logan stuck a key in the lock. It fit and turned. As he pushed the gate open, the fog swirled around them as if alive. "Damn dog days," Logan grunted. Already beads of perspiration had appeared on his forehead. It was that time of the year when each day would be a carbon copy of the previous scorcher. He hated to wish for rain after months of spring flooding, but Logan was already tired of being steamed. Or he was just feeling testy because he'd been awakened from a deep sleep. Surprisingly, his senses weren't dulled, rather they were hypersensitive, leaving Logan with the feeling that he was being observed. Maybe it was the way the fog's coiling tendrils and slowly shifting walls moved that made him uneasy. All shapes were indistinct, the world amorphous.

"Yeah, it's creepy all right," Ross said, rubbing his holster. "Makes me feel like I'm being watched." He tilted his head and asked, "Did you hear, uh, heavy breathing?"

Logan shook his head and smiled wryly. "Did you see action in Kuwait?"

"Nope."

"I did in Nam. Often we'd feel watched. I learned to trust that instinct. It was the only thing that kept you alive sometimes. We'll just be real careful." Then, as now, he felt as though the woods were full of piercing eyes and danger, a sniper's cross hairs lined on your back. Logan watched Ross fondle his holster and hated to admit that *his* gun hand was also itching.

A little brusquely, Logan said, "Let's get going. Close the gate behind me, but don't lock it. We'll secure it on the way out." Logan got into the Mustang and drove through slowly.

Ross joined him, looking around once more before getting in. Again his head jerked about, his gaze darting as he thought he saw movement. And yet, how could he be sure? The fog was thicker than the smoky aftermath of last July's fireworks stand fire. Ross shrugged, then finally climbed inside, nearly engulfing the front seat.

Logan drove on. Rocks pinged underneath, imitating a haywire pinball machine, and Logan slowed. The fog mingled and whirled with the gravel dust, and evanescent, ghostly shapes slid by the slowly moving car and whirled in its wake.

The phantoms of mist danced with the high, unattended grass and weeds along the road. Except for soft static, Logan's radio was as silent as the back roads had been deserted. Just as everything should be in Henderson County at this time of night.

"I know I'm still three-quarters asleep, Mr. Candel, but what are we doing out here again?"

"We are answering a complaint call," Logan explained, trying not to curse Claire Brookens. He'd been dreaming about fishing along the Trinity River—catching a big one—when the phone rang. As usual, Claire had been frantic and demanding.

"And what did the woman—"

"Mrs. Brookens."

". . . Say?" Ross asked.

"She asked if I knew who she was, then told me she had an emergency. Something terrible had happened to her boys at the Matthewson ranch. Said Benny Joe was hurt bad. His wrist was all swelled up."

"Ought to see Doc Katyu."

"He will in the morning. Claire demanded that I immediately check into this dangerous situation we have here in Henderson County. You'll learn, Ross, that when you're a sheriff, people frequently tell you how to do your job."

"And were they attacked?"

"That's what she claimed. About two hours ago. Of course, she wouldn't let me talk to the boys. Said they were finally asleep like they should be, and that I could talk to them in the morning." Logan rolled his eyes. "You can bet I will."

"A real pain?" Ross asked, and Logan nodded. "What were they doing at the Matthewson ranch?"

"Another unanswered question," Logan snorted. "She accused me of accusing her boys of doing something wrong. Then she told me not to get huffy, that I was supposed to provide help and protection to the residents of Henderson

County and Temprance, particularly those who are taxpayers and registered voters."

"Did she accuse Matthewson of anything?"

"No. She claimed they were so scared, even Jim Bob could barely speak."

"This isn't the first time the Brookens boys have been in trouble, is it?" Ross pulled a chocolate-frosted donut from the paper bag he'd brought along.

"No. They used a mail order inflatable doll to frighten Thelma Weaver," Logan said, and Ross grinned. "She thought it was some kind of stalker. Nearly drove Mrs. Weaver crazy. Thelma Weaver and Claire are two of a kind, except Claire has kids. Those ladies are live wires, bold, opinionated, and outright pious pains in the butt.

"Except for maybe the Tubbs boys—who are criminals—no family compares to the Brookens when it comes to causing trouble. James Robert and Benjamin Joseph have a history of mischief. I think they inherited it from their father. Thomas disappeared several years back. They screwed up the fireworks show two years ago by faking a bridge-jumping suicide. The people with weak hearts didn't appreciate that," Logan said, and Ross chuckled. "One time they glued closed all the locks of the shops on the town square. The boys are probably making up the story to cover for something stupid they've done."

"Sounds like crying wolf to me," Ross said.

"Yes."

"You called Mr. Matthewson?"

Logan nodded. "Yes. No luck."

"Then why are we here?"

Because it's in my blood, Logan started to reply, and it was part of the job. A job he intended to do well, following in the footsteps of his dad and grandfather, who had set good examples. Even without that bit of history, Logan might have joined the department. When he'd been in school, the kids had nicknamed him Logan DoRight, after he'd returned some money he'd found.

"We can't afford to assume it's a cry-wolf situation. The best thing you can do during an investigation is to be thorough. Part of the process is getting up and investigating at odd hours. If you were in Dallas, it would be worse. Temprance is sleepy and thankfully quiet. Just remember, without someone to enforce the law, citizen's rights would constantly be infringed upon by those who think themselves special, better, or above the law."

"Do you know this David Matthewson?"

"I know his mother, Penny, and knew his father, Kennedy. I met David long ago. We're members of the Temprance Presbyterian Church. The Matthewsons have had more than their share of tragedy." Logan briefly thought of the times he'd been fishing with Kennedy at the pond they'd just passed.

"Isn't David a writer?" Ross asked.

"Yeah. A damn good one."

"I read about him in the *Temprance Times*. Article said he was sick."

"Porphyria."

"What's that?" Ross scratched himself.

"A blood disease. It causes skin problems and makes you allergic to the sunlight. Some kind of breakdown in creating hemoglobin."

"Oh oh, are you sure . . ."

"It's safe. Doc Katyu says there's no worry of contagion."

"Uh, Mr. Candel, pardon me for asking, but aren't you on vacation? Why didn't you refer Claire to my uncle?"

Logan smiled. "Even if Claire were desperate, she might not call Bricker, not after the run-in they had last year. Claire is sure that Donald has it in for her boys, especially after the stalker prank, and he probably does. After two weeks investigating the incident and watching Mrs. Weaver recover in the Athens hospital, he had no sense of humor left. Donald attempted to put the boys into a juvenile home, but failed. It was a nasty scene."

"Sounds like Temprance isn't quite so sleepy."

"We have our share of hell-raisin' boys," Logan admitted. "Youth gives us job security."

The Matthewson place came into sight. There weren't any lights on in the house or the barn. Nothing appeared amiss. If this was a wild-goose chase, he was going to spank some Brookens' butt, Logan promised himself. He pulled next to the front walk beside some hedges, parked, and then killed the engine. "Wait by the car," Logan said, as he grabbed a flashlight and got out. He pushed through the gate, then followed the walkway to the front door. With each step, he felt as though imaginary sights were being focused on him again. Logan rang the doorbell and waited.

It was so quiet, deafeningly so, that he could hear Ross shuffling around behind him. Even the crickets were taking the night off. After a minute, Logan rang the doorbell again. Still no response. "No answer," Logan called to Ross. "Let's look around. You take the barn. Call out if you see anything strange or find David." He turned on his flashlight.

"Sure thing." Ross turned on his light and ambled off.

Logan watched him go, then started his own search. With his flashlight constantly probing, he walked around the corner and along the side of the house. The fog wasn't nearly as bad in the yard as it was in the woods. He found the back door with his search light. It was open. No surprise. Out here, people didn't worry about locking their doors every time they went outside. David was here somewhere; his Blazer was parked next to the garden.

Curious, Logan approached the open door and unconsciously unstrapped his revolver. "David?" he called through the screen door. "David, is everything all right?" What if something was wrong? Maybe David had had an accident or had been attacked. There might be some truth to the Brookens boys' story. Wouldn't that be a change?

And David's health was questionable. He might have collapsed or something. Logan tried the door and heard a soft thump inside. "David? It's Logan Candel, from the Sheriff's office." No response. The door was unlocked, so Logan warily entered.

As soon as he walked into the kitchen, darkness seemed to engulf him within its cloak. All the shades had been drawn, leaving the room as pitch-black as a deep cavern. The house was deathly silent. His flashlight's beam danced over the counters, floor, and kitchen table. A chair and stool ladder had been knocked over. A fight perhaps?

"David?" he called out once more. Dead silence. Logan crossed the kitchen and headed further into the house. The hallway had been decorated with enlarged photographs of Texas landscapes, sunsets, and the lake. Several were on the floor, with shards of glass scattered about. He entered the main foyer and looked up the stairs. Again, he thought he heard something move quickly, then silence.

Logan noticed a strange odor in the air. Something that reminded him of the lingering scent of death—a smell he'd become all too intimate with in Vietnam. There had been a time when . . . Logan shook away the memory. Live in the present.

He was certain there was something wrong with the house. It wasn't the smell, or even the sight, but the feel. It wasn't something he could explain except to another in his line of work. A sixth sense—his survival instinct—always kicked in when there was danger afoot. His guardian angel had saved him many times over. Logan began ascending the steps. Again he heard something softly padding around upstairs.

* * *

His nightstick shaking in his unsteady hands, Ross approached the barn. With a ghostlike eeriness, the barn wavered in the fog, as a small breeze whispered across the fields.

I don't like this, Ross thought. It reminded him of a bad movie. Wait, did I hear something? Ross broke out in a cool sweat. He advanced, his flashlight probing through the mists in the direction of the barn's front door. Ross listened carefully. There! Sobbing? Was somebody crying inside the barn? His light illuminated the door; barely hanging from a hinge, it was shattered, battered, and bloody.

He dipped the beam. "Logan!"

Almost at the top of the stairs, Logan heard Ross's call. He was tempted to continue the search for whatever was moving through the house, but he couldn't ignore his partner's call. Backtracking quickly, he descended the steps and ran outside.

Logan could see that Ross was all right. His partner was standing at the front of the barn with his light shining on somebody who was hunched over, ravaged hands over his face. Blood was all over his shoulders and chest. The ground was littered with dark green liquor bottles. The man shifted, then took his hands away from his pale, tear-streaked face. "David!"

David couldn't believe somebody had found him in this condition; ashamed, he wanted to hide. He knew he must look pitiful. He'd grown to hate that type of sympathy. His expression changed from agony to bitterness. His face was gaunt, and the skin around his red eyes sunken. The light made them glow reddish in a feline fashion, and his skin was slightly phosphorescent. His hair was unruly.

"David, are you all right?" Logan asked. He didn't look all right. David shrugged. "What happened?" David was silent. He never looked at Logan, just stared at his hands, then closed his eyes, and slumped against the door. "Ross, is he hurt?"

Logan noticed the smell of liquor and something else he couldn't identify.

"Not badly. I think the blood's from his hands," Ross stated. Logan stared at David's hands. They were scratched raw, bleeding in several places. A few parts of the hands were already scabbed.

Finally, David pointed into the foggy field and toward a fence. "Look around," Logan said. Ross nodded and moved off. "Obviously, this warrants coming out here." Logan knelt, looking closely at David. Although distraught, the author's condition was better than Logan remembered, his face smooth and unmarred. He even appeared younger than Logan remembered.

Logan took in David's streaked cheeks, quivering chin, and slack jaw. There was pain, but he also thought he saw anger. "David, what's wrong? What happened?" David continued to point. "Ross," Logan called, "find anything over there?" He guided the light in the direction to which David still pointed.

A moment later, "Holy spit!" Ross said. Logan waited. "Trashed equipment. Looks like somebody tore apart a projector, stereo, and speakers. And there's blood."

"Probably David's, but we'll check. Anything work?"

"Demolished."

"We'll check for fingerprints, too. David?" he turned back to the motionless man.

David didn't trust himself to say anything. The rage that had consumed him earlier felt barely in check, on the edge of his awareness, but ready to pounce upon him like some wild beast.

"What happened?" Logan asked. "Please, I want to help you, but you have to tell me somethin'." Nothing. "We'll need to drive you into town—"

"No," David whispered harshly, his eyes open. "I don't ever go into town anymore."

"Then tell me something!" Logan licked his lips. He was

uncomfortable under David's raw stare. He tried to shake off the sensation, but it kept returning. It didn't help that David's teeth as well as eyes were blood red. He knew it was the disease's fault, but it was still unnerving.

"You'll find a cooler of beer behind the tractor. It's not mine," David said hoarsely, then sighed heavily. "I'd been drinking," he began, his words choppy and halting, "and doing my evening walkabout, checking the ranch and the animals."

Logan nodded. "And?"

Ross returned to stand beside Logan.

"And I thought Tina appeared," David began. "I know it sounds crazy. But she hadn't. It was just a lie—a projection that reminded me of her," David finished sadly.

Logan's shoulders slumped. Ross's expression asked who Tina might be. Logan shook his head, silently saying not now.

David put his head in his hands and continued, "When I discovered the truth, I went . . . berserk, out of my mind. I don't ever remember being so mad. I chased the perpetrators, six boys, into the woods. I was ready to punish them, but I couldn't do violence, not even in anger. So I let them go."

Logan looked again at David's hands. "What happened to your hands?"

"I vented my frustration on the door, then later my rage on the equipment."

Logan looked at the door and nodded. There was dangerous strength in anger. "Can you describe them?" David did. Logan nodded. "Sounds like the Brookens boys all right, and maybe a Tubbs. We'll have a long talk with them tomorrow and get the truth," Logan told Ross, "with or without Claire's help. David, you ought to come into town and see Doc Katyu."

"No! Doc Katyu comes out here," David replied. He held up the bottle and looked at it. "A lot of good it does. Ironic isn't it? First my life was destroyed by a drunk; now I am one."

Despite knowing the facts surrounding the tragic accident, Logan didn't know what to say. He wanted to be sympathetic, but felt words were inadequate. "Would you like to file a complaint?" David didn't answer. "I'm willing to reprimand and punish the boys, if you'll pursue the issue. They already admitted to being out here. And we have their fingerprints on file."

David said nothing. Logan stood. "Ross, pull the car over here and let's load up the evidence. Don't forget to wear gloves. And check near the tractor." He tossed his partner the keys. "David, think on it. You can call me tomorrow. I'm going to need a statement. In my opinion, you shouldn't let this go. If there were others, they may come back. I'm sorry I had to bother you."

"It's your job," David said. Somewhere in the barn a horse neighed. David had his own work to do; cows to feed, hay to change, chicken nests to check, and more. Maybe chores would snap him out of his self-pitying mood. He hated this feeling!

"Sometimes I wish I was a writer instead of a law enforcement officer, especially when I read your stuff," Logan said, suddenly conversational. He was trying to think of something pleasant to say to change the tone, so he latched onto David's recent success. Logan smiled and held out a hand to help David to his feet.

"You've read my work?" David said, sounding surprised. His smile was wan.

"Almost everybody in town who can read does, now anyway. *Witch Hunt* is a big, big hit. Did I see that it made the best-seller list?" Logan asked. David shrugged. "You don't know?"

"Michael would know. He keeps up with all of that. I just write."

"Well, I think I read, or maybe heard, where it broke the top ten. My sister loved it. She saw your interview on the show "Tales of Texas" and taped it for me. Unfortunately, I haven't seen it yet."

David's gaze suddenly sharpened, and his face hardened as he asked, "Do you think that's what caused this attack? The publicity?"

"Well, history shows us that success can bring unwanted attention and adoration. Unfortunately, there are plenty of sick people in the world. When you're prominent, you can become a target. Hell, even when you're not, you can be in the wrong place at the wrong time."

"Do you really think the publicity encouraged the vandals to invade my privacy? Destroy my peace?" His voice was loud and his tone sharp enough to disturb the animals inside the barn, eliciting moans, whinnies and grunts. David's rage was building; he fought to keep it in check.

"Possibly. I'll try and find out." Logan glanced over at Ross, who had pulled the car over and was loading the trunk. Since he dwarfed the equipment, Ross wasn't having any problems.

"Thanks," David managed, holding in his anger.

When Ross was finished with the equipment, Logan said, "All in a day's . . . and night's work. Well, I'll let you have your peace back," and he began walking toward the car.

David stared off into the woods, wondering if he'd ever know peace again. Dejected and silent, he wandered back toward the house. He needed to find someplace where he could think things out.

Feeling very sad, Logan drove off, promising himself that he would discover the truth about tonight. No matter what.

Three

Grimm Musings

"Sweet!" Laughing, Kevin Grimm drove his blue pickup at high speed on the fog-shrouded roads. He couldn't see where he was going, but it didn't matter. He was driving fast just for the hell of it. And it was fun—dizzying and heady at the same time—with the wind whipping through the cab and the radio blaring. Kevin never worried about being stopped; there were advantages to being the mayor's stepson.

And for all Kevin cared, he could have ended up in Seven Points, Gunbarrel, or Malakoff. The final destination didn't matter, as long as there was fun to be had. He spotted a sign reading Highway 274. Good! He was on his way to Malakoff.

Very early on this wild drive, the beer cans had blown out of the open bed and onto the road. And who gave a shit? Over the roaring of the wind and the rumble from the hole in the muffler, the Little Ole Band from Texas was jamming on the radio, looking for some tush. Kevin hummed along with the song and dragged on a cigarette.

"What a bunch of chumps!" Kevin smiled broadly, still riding high. Who would have believed that Benny Joe's wondering if that writer-dude was as smart as his fictional dude—

the Psychic Detective—would have led to such a great trick! Kevin laughed.

The writer-dude had been furious, the maddest Kevin had ever seen anyone get. And his buddies had been scared shitless, like chickens running with their heads cut off. Speaking of heads, Kevin gingerly touched his. It wasn't the first time he'd been hit there and not remembered it. He checked himself in the rearview mirror. No abrasions, just a welt. No biggie.

Anyway, it was history now. Kevin puffed up, proud of himself. It had been his idea to create some kind of ghost, some kind of floating thing to surprise the writer-dude. Then Benjo had jumped on the idea, adding wild thoughts about stereo equipment and projectors. That boy was really smart, and devious, too, even if he looked innocent as hell. It was just too bad that Benjo had absolutely no common sense.

A great bunch of puppets, Kevin smirked. They would help him stir up plenty of fun this summer, and take all the heat. He was good at selecting the type; reading people was just one of his many special talents.

Jim Bob Brookens was arrogant, mad at the world and himself. He was anti-authority and thought he was bullet-proof. Perfect. All you had to do was tell him he couldn't do something, dare him, tell him he was afraid, and he'd do it. And Benjo would go along with anything his older brother did, just so that Jim Bob wouldn't call him a pussy or an Okie.

And JJ was a piece of work—a great guy—and in many ways a lot like himself. JJ had a keen mind for mischief and he had plenty of experience for sixteen. He was the youngest of four, and his brothers had all had a lot of fun in their time, when they weren't in jail.

Kevin wasn't quite so sure about the other two. They were probably just along for the ride, in hopes of doing something cool. Patrick was looking for some excitement and freedom, since his parents were religious nuts. Kevin rolled his eyes and took a drag off his cigarette. Was there anything worse than being a preacher's son?

And Skeeter, well, he was just a lonely guy looking for friends. He would be easy to manipulate, especially if he became hooked on the excitement.

Kevin drove past a worn sign reading, "Malakoff Mall— HITCHIN' POST waterin' hole". Kevin thought about it briefly, then spun the wheel, quickly turning around and pulling into the dirt lot. He stopped and parked near a bunch of other pickups in front of the coin laundry, video store, and auto parts shop. The front walk, made of wood and whitewashed like the rest of the building, was flimsy and warped. Much of the mall had been repaired with plywood, and two vacant stores were adorned with rental signs.

Just the right hole-in-the-wall that might lead to fun. There might be some tush or new jokes. And just because he was seventeen, didn't mean that he couldn't buy a drink. He'd had a fake ID since he was fifteen. As a Texan, it was his right to drink underage. Hell, it was expected of him.

Stiff-backed and confident, Kevin walked inside past the Red, White, and Blue and Miller Lite beer signs. The Hitchin' Post was jam-packed and blue-clouded as though somebody had tossed in a couple of smoke bombs. Just inside the door, Kevin waited, taking it all in. He preferred scoping out a place before getting comfortable.

The four pool tables were crowded, and used for both playing and dining. The bar stools were scattered, and several had been knocked to the floor. A loud, twanging country tune that made his ears curl came from the jukebox to his left, which was surrounded by three women in snug jeans, cowboy boots and hats. Kevin smiled. Quite a party.

Through the maze of people, posts, and tables, the bar was all the way across the room and beyond a regular set of small round tables covered with beer bottles. Behind the bar, the wall was a massive set of mirrors. In the corner was a television set showing a soundless ESPN rodeo contest. Hanging from the ceiling was the Texas flag. Surrounding it were promotional beer posters covered with scantily clad babes.

Kevin nodded. Yes, there were a few okay honeys in attendance. The ones at the juke box were all right. To his right, the short-haired blonde with the long, willowy figure, and her sister, both playing darts with a short, stocky guy, were okay, too. There was potential, so Kevin decided he'd stay. Too bad Jim Bob and JJ weren't here. They had fake ID's too. He would just have to tell the boys what they'd missed.

Kevin squeezed his way through the crowd and sat down at the nearly deserted bar next to a heavy-set blonde clad in jeans, black high heels and a blue tank-top. Kevin figured he could have some fun with the chick. With shoes like that, he thought, she was undoubtedly in heat.

"Can I see some ID?" the bartender asked, drawing each word out. Her name tag read "Peg"; she was a lean woman in her early forties with sleepy eyes but hardened features, made more severe because of her ponytail. Kevin read the doubt in her gaze.

"Sure," Kevin slowly removed his wallet and handed her his fake driver's license.

Peg examined his license. "Twenty-three?"

"My parents never looked their age either."

"What will it be?"

"A brave bull."

"Tequila and Kahlua?" Kevin nodded and Peg moved off. A handwritten sign on the mirror read "Drink all 94 of Hitchin' Post's beers and get a free commemorative T-shirt." Not tonight, Kevin smiled. His gaze wandered to the mirrors, and he touched the welt on his head. Things didn't seem quite right. The glass had begun to warp and looking in the mirror reminded him of being in a funhouse, back when such simple things amused him—before the accident. Kevin studied himself in the mirror. No one could ever tell that he'd been kicked by a horse nearly six years ago, nearly destroying half his head. Now he had a metal plate where there had once been bone.

Kevin noticed that the heavy-set woman next to him was glancing at him when she wasn't staring at the rodeo on the tube. But then, how could she not? Man, she must be at least thirty pounds overweight. Where did she get jeans to fit, Emilio the poncho-maker? With a cruel smile, Kevin said, "Hello. Do men wrestling with animals get you hot?"

"Excuse me! "

"Oh, I'm sorry, you're a blonde, right? Hey, know what you get when you turn a blonde upside down? No? A brunette!" Kevin smiled. She was speechless. "Do you know what the similarities are between a moped and a fat woman?" He thought he saw her flinch. "They're both fun to ride, but you wouldn't want your friends to see you on one!" he laughed.

"That'll be two-fifty," Peg said as she set his drink before him. Without a word, the blonde moved to the far end of the bar.

Kevin gave Peg a five spot. "Bring me a Bud and keep it."

"Gotcha. Thanks."

As Kevin sipped his drink, he studied the other patrons through the haze. To his left was a Hispanic man who was alternately doing shots of Cuervo and trying not to fall asleep. On the bar, there were four full, butt-jammed ashtrays. "Hey, Ernesto," Peg called to him, "you can't sleep here. *Comprende?* Go on and pass out in your car!" Ernesto feebly raised his head and waved. Kevin couldn't really see his face, except for a prominent nose and dark mustache. Probably an illegal alien. They flooded across the border into the land of opportunity, the home of the free and the brave. Where there was one, there were a dozen more riding in a pickup and pretending to do yard work. Just in case, Kevin always carried a knife in his boot, but tonight he had one in each, and a switchblade in his pocket. He was itching and well prepared for trouble. Something he'd learned over the last few years without ever being a Boy Scout.

The guy to his right appeared respectable enough. He was pepper-haired, thin, and wore rounded glasses. His gray suit was slightly rumpled, with an open shirt and loosened tie. Kevin figured the man was slumming when he noticed his companion, a wild, red-haired woman dressed in red and black. She was certainly a whore. Her makeup was caked on with overly large red lips, streaks of blush, and huge eyelashes. Her top was made of spandex that strained around her busty figure and tucked into painted-on jeans that were cinched with a thin black belt. Grimm thought that she might be all of twenty. She was leaning on the old guy pretty good, and Kevin suddenly noticed the geezer was tipsy.

As was his nature, Kevin listened to their conversation. "So, you haven't any plans this evening?"

"Not scheduled, I'm a woman on the loose tonight, but that doesn't mean I'm free," she replied, as she exhaled and flipped cigarette ash near a tray. Her drawl was thick, even for around here—thicker than Cajun coffee, Kevin thought.

"I have a cabin near here," he slightly slurred.

"I like cabins, they're cozy, and there's something about being in the woods that makes me feel wild." She stretched to give the guy a good view. "Is it on the lake?"

Kevin chuckled to himself, then almost bought the old guy a drink. She was probably going to roll him.

At the closest billiards table, a pot-bellied, bearded man wearing a torn flannel shirt, jeans that hung too low, and a Pearl Light cap, was playing pool with a woman even larger than himself and dressed in a white tank top and massive jeans. "Get it together, June!" he'd tell her each time she missed a shot. Thank God I'm a country boy, Kevin smirked.

The slimmer women were still messing with the jukebox, dancing, jiggling and shaking. All decked out as if it were ladies' night out, and they were ready to cheat on their husbands. Maybe he should hang out with them, buy them a drink; for a long time he'd wanted to roll in the hay with more than one heated bitch at a time.

The curly-haired blonde with the hawkish nose and slightly hairy upper lip might be interested. Actually, the bustier one with straighter, strawberry-colored hair—the one that could be the first's sister—looked even more willing. She was constantly casting her gaze about the bar to see if she'd land something, frowning when she looked at the foursome of truckers, but smiling at the two young harddicks dressed in button-down shirts with rolled-up sleeves. Probably imports from Dallas. The third woman was short, dark-haired, and dark-eyed. She looked nervous and constantly chewed her lip. Kevin decided that she was kind of cute, in a timid sort of way.

The song changed to the Little Ole Band from Texas asking for someone to give it up. More people danced.

Another pool table was occupied by four truckers whose rigs hauled Shaeffer, Bud, Lone Star, and Pearl to Henderson County. Beer drinking was an important part of being a Texan. All the truckers were smoking cigarettes, and they probably also ran drugs, Kevin decided, knowing that anyone who used drugs couldn't deal with the twisted humor that life threw at you. He, on the other hand, just twisted it back.

The door opened and again Kevin was disappointed. It wasn't a babe. Damn! It was a third city harddick. The new studly guy joined the two others. All three had slicked-back hair. Harddicks, Kevin thought again. Dallas, definitely.

Kevin finished his first drink with a big gulp, and told himself that they wouldn't get the best of him. If they bothered his action with a honey, he'd just have to cut one. City boys were pansies.

The front door opened again, and Grimm smiled. My, my, my, it was definitely his lucky night. It was Becky, the receptionist from TU Electric. And she was alone. His pulse raced. Becky was so beautiful, so sexy, she could have walked directly out of *Playboy*. Kevin could barely breathe. Becky was in cowboy boots, skintight, stonewashed jeans, and a green shirt that was pulled taut. Long, wavy, auburn hair streamed from under her hat, over her shoulders, and a long way down her back. She smiled as she gazed about the place. Yes, Kevin thought, ride 'em cowboy. Mustache rides for free! He'd even grow one for her.

Becky sat down at the other end of the bar, past the geezer and the whore discussing payment. Becky gave no hint if she noticed Kevin. She probably doesn't remember me, Kevin thought. Well, nothing ventured, nothing gained, he decided and stood up. Taking his Bud with him, Kevin walked over to Becky and sat next to her.

Peg set a Miller Lite before Becky, then frowned at Kevin. She started to say something, but instead, picked up the money and went back to watching television.

Becky glanced at him, then ignored him.

"Buy you a drink?" Kevin asked.

"No thank you, please go away," she said brusquely and turned coldly away.

"Just one drink?" he asked. Someone increased the volume on the jukebox as a George Strait tune began.

"I don't spend time with customers," she said loudly without looking at him.

Kevin knew she was lying. Everybody used electricity. Why would she lie to him? His temper started to boil. "Why won't you have a drink with me?"

"Because I don't drink with men that follow me, that's why," she replied without looking at him, then sipped her beer.

"I wasn't following you! I was here first!" Then, "Will you have dinner with me?"

"No. Go away. Lou, my boy friend, is coming."

54

Sure, Kevin thought. "Why won't you have dinner with me?"

"Because you're not my type."

"What do you mean?" he said petulantly.

"You're not the . . . outdoors type."

"I'm not manly enough for you?" Kevin asked, puffing up his chest. "You know why there aren't any real men anymore? Because real men jump out of airplanes without parachutes." Becky didn't respond, so Kevin touched her on the shoulder.

Becky jerked away and slapped his hand, "Don't touch me! I'll have the owner kick your butt out of here." She looked about, but no one was watching them. The music was loud. She started to call out to Peg.

Not only did Kevin hate to be hit, but he despised being threatened. "I'm sorry," he apologized. Her eyes widened with surprise. Before she realized what was happening, Kevin pressed the handle of his switchblade against her ribs. "I really am sorry." Her eyes were suddenly pleading and aglow with fear. "Listen."

Kevin quickly twisted the handle to lay flat against her side, then the blade shot straight outward with a *snikt*. Just as quickly it retracted. Once again the dull end with deadly potential poked into her ribs.

"Come with me," he said quietly. "And laugh at my jokes, will you? You lead, I'll follow . . . hand on hip." Kevin smiled. "I like to watch you walk. Go ahead and strut. Okay?" No response. "Okay?" His voice was low and menacing.

Becky's voice shook. "Okay."

They stood up together and began walking out. Becky's walk was exaggerated with swaying hips. No one gave them a second glance, except for the amazed harddicks, wondering what a babe was doing with him. They wouldn't know a real man if he hit them. "You know why the Aggie snorted Saccharin?" Becky's shake of the head was jerky. "Because he thought it was diet coke!" Kevin laughed. "Why did the cops in Dallas take the 911 emergency number off the back of their cars? The Mexican's kept stealing them—thinking they were Porsches!" Becky said nothing. Kevin poked her. "Ya can laugh." Over her shoulder, she gave him a tight smile. "What's the difference between a coyote and a fox? About five drinks." As though she'd been struck in the stomach, Becky's laugh was forced. Some nearby players turned at the odd sound.

Kevin smiled at them and quickly ushered her outside. He looked around quickly. "All right. It's just the two of us. You and me, babe. No more beating around the bush, if you know what I mean. I'm goin' bushwhacking." Kevin guided her along the building and toward his pickup.

Suddenly a tall, dark, mustached man wearing a tan cowboy hat, a blue cotton shirt and jeans rounded the corner and saw them. "Becky Sue!" His tanned face was a mixture of confusion, hurt, and growing anger.

"LOU!"

"You just bought yourself a mess of trouble, boy." Lou rushed forward with fist balled, ready to kick ass.

"Damn cowpokes," Kevin muttered, and quickly slammed Becky's head against the wall. "Bitch." She crumpled to the ground. With his other hand, he smoothly raised the switchblade to meet Lou's charge. *Snikt,* it snapped open.

"Holee shit," Lou cried and dodged, throwing himself aside. Kevin lunged forward, slashing and missing. "You're crazy, boy," Lou said, slowly backing up. There was a hint of fear in his expression, but he said. "I'm really going to kick your ass. You'll be pissin' out of your ears." He started to dart forward, but quickly stepped back as Kevin's blade slashed before him. Lou's eyes widened when he looked down to find his shirt, ripped open. Red slowly stained the cloth. Wary now, Lou continued to back up, no longer looking calm or confident.

Eyes glittering, Kevin forced him backward, the blade cutting the air, whistling through where Lou had just stood. Kevin smiled confidently and followed him around the corner of the bar and toward the woods. "Beg, and I'll only leave you scarred, so a babe like Becky will never want you." Lou continued backward, his eyes locked on the slashing blade. Then he stumbled into a garbage can and almost fell as it clattered onto its side, rolling.

Kevin lunged forward, "Clumsy, bud. Gonna cut you bad, you'll bleed sweet. Just like Julio showed me."

Lou staggered around the trash can, then shoved it between them. Kevin stumbled, but still lashed out. Lou ducked once, desperately reached for the lid, and missed. Kevin slashed and Lou leaned back, then struck at the passing arm, knocking Kevin off balance.

Snatching the fallen lid, Lou defended himself. Kevin recovered and attacked again. Lou parried. The blow clanged off Kevin's wrist, and he screamed, dropping the blade and clutching his hand. "This is for Becky Sue," Lou slammed the metal lid into Kevin's head. Seeing a flash and stars, Kevin collapsed, stunned. Lou kicked the knife away, and it skipped across the dirt. "And this, too." He stepped around and kicked Kevin in the ear.

As a blinding flash of white overwhelmed Kevin's vision, he heard a ringing, and blood flew from his mouth. "Dad! Stop! Please," Kevin whispered. Not this. Not again. Not ever again, I killed you. "You're dead!" He began to move, then Lou kicked him between the legs. Kevin tried to scream, but only screeched hoarsely. Paralyzing pain—as though something had ruptured—twisted his stomach and knifed into his chest.

Kevin couldn't breathe. All he could do was watch Lou's face. It appeared huge, bloated and twisted in a strange mixture of anger and pleasure. Lou slowly moved to Kevin's side, then kicked him once, twice, then again and again. Kevin thought he heard something crack and rolled onto his side. Lou kicked him in the back. "Pull a knife on me, will ya!

You're gonna need a body cast, and when the sheriff comes, it'll be self-defense." The kicking continued. Kevin blacked out and met his long-dead father; paybacks were hell.

Four

Sanctuary

Awakening with a start, the Rev. Cooper Page bolted upright in bed, trembling and sweating profusely. Something was wrong with Patrick! He could feel it! Rubbing his eyes, Cooper wondered whether it was just a dream, or possibly providence?

He would find out. Trying not to disturb his wife, Cooper slipped out of bed, put on his slippers and robe, then left the bedroom. It was dark, but weak moonlight shone in through the windows, turning everything murky indigo with faint outlines, instead of pitch-black and night-blinding.

As Cooper quickly walked down the short hall to Patrick's room, he passed a mirror and glanced at himself. Even in the dim light, he could tell he needed more rest. His face looked more lined and his jowls puffier than his fifty, God-blessed years warranted. His hair was turning gray, as well as sparse. Dark circles sank his eyes deep into their sockets. Even his mustache was drooping.

This was the third night in a row Cooper hadn't slept well. Last night, he had awakened believing something was wrong with Martha, then he'd found her gone. He'd been frantic until she returned from the bathroom. And he didn't remember anything from two nights ago, except for the feeling of cold terror which had jarringly awakened him.

Cooper carefully opened his son's bedroom door. Tonight was probably just a repeat of last night, needless worry and alarm. Patrick would be there.

The moonlight came through the open window and cut across the empty, untouched bed. "Patrick?" As he stepped within, Cooper thought he heard something outside. He glanced out the window just in time to see a shadowy figure dart through the light surrounding the porch, then into darkness as the side door of the nearby church opened and shut. That was odd, Cooper thought, that door was locked; he'd locked it himself. Could that have been Patrick? He had keys, but why would he be up and going to the church?

Cooper moved to the window and peered out. A dim light flickered in the chapel windows, slowly growing brighter as though candles were being lit. This warranted an investigation. Cinching the robe's belt beneath his belly, the reverend headed out the front door, down the steps, and toward the church. Cooper hoped that no one would see him attired in his night clothes, then that silly worry was replaced by a very real one. He prayed there wasn't a thief or vandal loose in town. Well, the Lord would protect him. The Temprance Presbyterian Church was a good and devout place to worship the Lord, learn His words of wisdom and their meaning. The place was inviolate, as long as one believed in the wonders of the Lord God Almighty and the Savior.

Cooper tried the side door and found it unlocked. He entered, calling Patrick's name as he walked down the hall toward the wavering light shining from the chapel. Cooper stopped and peeked in through the antechamber's door windows. "What's this?" There were candles burning in the candelabra in front of the pulpits. Even stranger, the smoke was dark and oily, creating a low, ugly cloud, reminding him of big city pollution.

Out of the corner of his eye, he caught a furtive movement. Cooper immediately pushed the doors open and rushed in, not even thinking about facing an antagonist while clad in his slippers and robe. Even stronger now, he felt that Patrick was in danger.

The chapel was silent except for the swinging of the two-way doors, once, twice, three times . . . The candles flickered, then fluttered, as though kissed by a breeze from an open window. Between the tapers and the faint moonlight filtering in through the tall arched windows along the far right wall above a row of doors, the shadows appeared to take on texture and depth, sometimes even shifting impatiently. The two rows of pews appeared unusually distinct, until fading to nothing in the blue haziness halfway toward the back of the chapel. The foyer and front entrance were indistinguishable.

Cooper walked along the front aisle toward the pulpit. Nobody. And nothing appeared wrong. But it felt wrong, as though something were hiding, waiting to pounce. And what was wrong with the candles? He shook off a shiver and moved closer.

"This is silly. I have to quit reading King," Cooper chuckled. He stopped at the steps which led to the altar, then, as though drawn, looked down to find several dark stains. He touched one and gasped. Blood! In the church! In the Lord's house! The trail led to the altar and the cross! Trembling, he walked toward them.

Before Cooper reached the altar, he discovered a pool of blood. It saturated the carpet in all directions. Lord Almighty, what had happened? He checked the altar. Nothing was amiss. The Bible and candles were still there. They and the cross above them were undesecrated. The reverend breathed a sigh of relief, then winced as though a dagger bit into his back. Cooper whirled around but saw nothing, except the bloodstains that marred the carpet of the center aisle. He followed the trail toward the back of the chapel. At the tenth pew on the right, the stains stopped.

Cooper caught his breath when he saw a motionless form prone in a pew, blood dripping onto the tile floor underneath. A pool filled the pew, and his son's clothes were soaked where he lay. "Oh Patrick." He whispered a quick prayer as he rushed to his son's side. He touched Patrick, and his son's head lolled to the side to reveal the gaping wounds in his neck. "De'ah Lord!"

"It is too late for prayers, preacher," something hissed, sounding as if each word were a monumental effort.

Cooper's attention snapped to the rear of the chapel. Three pews back, a blackness was growing in the dark, gray haze. The amorphous shadow coalesced, taking shape as it expanded and mutated.

The reverend stood frozen, his face pallid and his white-knuckled fist grasping his crucifix. At first, the shape might have been a huge, winged creature with wild hair, but then it slimmed. The pinions became long, oddly jointed arms with thin hands and long fingers. Despite the mingling of candlelight and moonlight, none of its features were illuminated; whatever it was absorbed light as though it were a black hole. Steady crimson eyes stared at Cooper, who sensed a cold hate that killed the weak. "In God's name, what *are* you?"

"God has nothing to do with me. I am beyond His powers," the figure hissed. The words were heavily accented. With spidery and undulating movements, it crawled over a pew and toward him. Clawed hands reached out, snatching nervously at the air in anticipation. "I am here for you!"

Repulsed, Cooper took a few unsteady steps backward. It kept coming, reaching, talons clicking. The reverend stumbled, grabbed a pew, and stood defiant. He would not be threatened in the Lord's church! "Leave this place of God!" Cooper held forth his crucifix.

The creature laughed and kept advancing. "Do you believe

that will work?" Cooper simply held the crucifix steady. The creature might have blanched. Halting, it said, "It matters not. Turn and see."

Cooper wasn't going to do so, but he heard something move— a rustle of cloth and the creaking of the pew as it shifted under weight—and turned to face Patrick. His son looked neither alive nor dead. Patrick's mouth worked as though it hadn't been used in a long time, and he'd forgotten how. His blinking was slow and measured, making him appear addled and simple. And his face! It was bone white, as if all life had been harnessed into his crimson eyes, no longer blue! His left cheek twitched, and Patrick smiled. The flesh on his face cracked as he did, ichor oozing out, and his teeth had become fangs, lengthening even as Cooper watched.

"T . . . This is for all the s . . . smothering, Father! All the sermons! All the p . . . passages and rules!" Patrick shouted, and leapt forward. Staggering back, Cooper fell . . .

And awakened from his nightmare. Cooper stifled a scream as he bolted upright and stared forward, blinking rapidly. His heart was racing, matching his gasping. All had changed. He was still in bed. Cooper chuckled quietly with relief, forcing his breathing to slow down.

He'd been dreaming. Oh Lord, what a nightmare, but now he was awake! Truly awake! Thank you, Lord! Cooper prayed, then reached for the glass of water on the nightstand. As he drank, he noticed that his hand was shaking, and he was sweating.

What was causing these terrible dreams? Was it a premonition, or just a simple nightmare based on guilt? Could it be both? Cooper felt he was losing his son to the temptations that taunted teenagers. Believing in the Lord didn't make you immune to having unruly children.

"Dear?" Martha mumbled sleepily.

"Bathroom," Cooper mumbled, and climbed out of bed. On the way out of the room, he grabbed his robe. Between the moonlight and his familiarity with his home of a dozen years, Cooper moved confidently. Shrugging off the strange feeling of déjà vu, he walked toward Patrick's room.

Maybe he'd quit drinking coffee so late, Cooper thought as he rubbed his fingers through his thin, gray hair. As he'd gotten older his hair had gone its own way, unless it was kept very short. He patted his stomach and thought maybe he should quit snacking late, too. He didn't mind being stout, but Martha drew the line at portly. Ah, but she could cook and sing! That woman was truly a gift of love and strength. Better to give up coffee and watching the late news, Cooper thought, than stop eating Martha's cooking or quit reading Stephen King's books. For a moment, Cooper was disoriented, knowing that some of that thought had come from his nightmare, the dream merging with reality.

Cooper shivered, still feeling uneasy about Patrick. Cooper opened the door to his son's bedroom, and found the moonlit bed was empty! But he'd been here earlier! Cooper started to enter. "Patrick?"

Immediately Cooper glanced out the window and thought he saw a fleeting movement at the side door of the church, but there wasn't the sound of a door shutting. However, there was a wavering light in the chapel windows.

Cooper shivered as remnants of his dream came back to him, then he chuckled uneasily, and headed outside, walking toward the chapel at a brisk pace. Not surprised, he found the south door, a side entrance, unlocked. Cooper entered, then peered down the hallway past the closed office doors. There was a dancing light coming from the chapel through the door windows.

Cooper peeked in, somewhat surprised to see several tapers burning in the candelabra. This is odd, he thought as he pushed his way in through the swinging doors. "Patrick?" The place was silent.

Cooper stepped inside and shivered, the sensations from

his nightmare flitting by. He pushed them away, getting annoyed with himself. Wait, the chapel wasn't silent! What was that sound?

The reverend moved toward the pews. Was that crying? He didn't see anybody, even though there was plenty of candlelight. The soft sobbing seemed to come from everywhere. Cooper walked down the center aisle, searching. He could tell he was getting closer; the sound grew louder. Somebody was definitely crying.

Halfway toward the foyer, Cooper found the late night visitor. Patrick was curled up in a pew, face in hands and weeping as though he'd lost his best friend. For a moment, Cooper saw the streaming tears change to blood, as though the nightmare was trying to reassert itself, then all was normal. The abrupt transformation was jarring, and made Cooper dizzy. He grabbed a pew, steadied himself, then approached his son. "Patrick, are you all right, son?"

Patrick started, staring at his father with wide eyes. "W . . . W . . . Wh . . . What!" His face was ashen and tearstained. "Oh, hi, Father." Patrick relaxed, the tension slipping from his expression. He slumped back into the pew.

Cooper's expression reflected his usual feelings when dealing with his son—a combination of love, worry, and bewilderment. "Patrick, is everything all right?" He sat next to his son and put his arm around him.

"Y . . . Yes. No. I . . . I . . . don't know, Father."

"Oh, I see." Talking to his son these days was always an enlightening experience. "Why are you lying in a pew and crying?" Cooper suddenly realized that Patrick had been badly frightened. Having just experienced a terrifying dream and seen his own reflection in the mirror, he recognized the signs.

"I . . . came to ask for f . . . forgiveness," Patrick mumbled, hanging his head. "I g . . . got scared and ran, leaving Skeeter alone in the woods and in t . . . trouble."

"I think you should start from the beginning," Cooper suggested, his drawl becoming more pronounced as his speech slowed.

"Oh, Father, please, not another lecture. N . . . not tonight."

The reverend sighed and shook his head sadly. Where was he going wrong? When had they lost their ability to communicate? "Patrick, have you done something you're ashamed of?"

Unable to restrain himself, Patrick began weeping again and nodded. "I was s . . . so scared. Afraid I was going to d . . . die."

Cooper hugged his son again, cradling him and stroking his head as though he were much younger. "Tell me about it." And Patrick did. When he mentioned David's angry reaction and transformation, Patrick's words raced and blended so that his father had trouble understanding him. Cooper tried to soothe him. "Don't worry. I'm sure Skeeter is all right, but to be sure, I'll call in the morning.

"As we've talked about, and you saw tonight, hate and anger can transform someone strongly, almost as strongly as love. Now do you understand what I meant, when I said by hurting someone else, you can hurt yourself?"

"Father . . ." Patrick didn't want to go into this. He felt badly enough already. Why rub his nose in it?

"Why did you hassle David? He is a fine man and a longtime member of this church, although it has been quite a while since he visited us. What did he do to deserve this invasion of privacy?" Cooper asked. Patrick shrugged. "Is it because he's different? A recluse? Handicapped? A celebrity?"

"F . . . Father, you don't understand. You n . . . never d . . . do," Patrick stammered, heading for his last refuge when things got confusing.

"Now listen, Son. I understand better than you think. You have just bothered somebody for the sheer fun of it. That's wrong! I have never understood why people make judgments on differences. It's not the differences that are important, but the similarities. We are all sons and daughters of the Lord. It is not right or proper to judge and stereotype someone, just because they're black or white, Jewish or Gentile, fat or thin, short or tall, healthy or handicapped, beautiful or plain, dumb or smart. It's not the physical attributes or labels that are important, but the person's actions and deeds upon which he or she should be measured, as you are measured by yours tonight.

"You are who you are, my son," Cooper continued to preach. "You are more than just a preacher's son. You are an individual, and will be judged as such one day as an adult, citizen, and possibly parent." He could see Patrick's thoughts spin on his son's face. "The Lord will judge truly, judge the quick and the dead." Cooper looked at his son. Once again he had the feeling that Patrick's ears had shut down before he'd reached his conclusion. He needed to find a way to get to his point more quickly, and yet, some words of wisdom could not be compressed into a sound bite. Still, he was a minister, and sermons had a long history of putting some to sleep.

"Okay," was all Patrick said. "I think I can sleep now. Can we go?"

Cooper wanted to say more, talk about his son's friendships. He didn't like Kevin Grimm or the Brookens brothers, let alone the Tubbs boy, but now wasn't the time to mention it. Patrick wouldn't hear a word. If Cooper had been lucky, Patrick might have heard and understood half of what his father had said tonight. If he remembered half of that tomorrow, it was a victory. "All right. But I believe you owe David Matthewson an apology." Patrick shrugged. Cooper decided he would press the issue tomorrow, then continue to do so until Patrick agreed and apologized.

They stood together and walked out the front door, arm in arm. Cooper loved his son so, and wondered what to do. His son was drifting farther and farther away. If he couldn't help his son, how could he expect to aid others in trouble?

His mind elsewhere, Cooper never saw the figure in their path as they exited the church. "W . . . whoa!" Patrick stammered. Cooper blinked and saw a slim woman, her jet black hair swirling in the soft breeze. She was very beautiful, with dark eyes and a tanned complexion. He noticed that her makeup was streaked, as though she had been crying, too. She looked very familiar, but Cooper couldn't place her.

"Hello, Reverend, I didn't mean to startle you," the woman said. "I . . ." She paused and then shrugged. "Um, don't you remember me?"

Suddenly Cooper did. "Jana! Jana Perrin! What a pleasant surprise. What are you doing in town?" He paused, wondering why she was at the church so late. "Uh, may I be of service?"

Jana smiled brightly, but Cooper could tell it was a little forced. "Not tonight. Maybe soon. I was out wandering and ended up here. I just rented the Alvera house on Fifth."

"You've moved back to town?" he asked, and she nodded. "You're not staying with your family?"

"No," she said and sighed. "Too crowded. I came back to get away, but also to spend some time by myself. I got tired of Dallas, tired of the big city and bright lights. Tired of all the troubles it caused. And . . ." she paused, "I've changed my name back to Martinez."

"Oh, well as you know, the church and my door are always open. In fact, why don't you come by for lunch Monday?"

Jana laughed, "I love how you never change, Reverend Page. How about a rain check? I start a new job Monday, working for Michael Woods as his legal assistant. It doesn't pay as much as I was making," she sighed, "but it feels good to be back to a simpler place."

"Of course, we shall see you Sunday."

"Count on it. Good night, Reverend."

"Good night." Wondering if everyone was having as much trouble sleeping as the three of them were, Cooper watched her turn and head down the sidewalk. He had an uneasy feeling it was going to be a long while before he slept soundly.

Five

Hallowed House

Feeling confused and miserable about what had happened earlier that night, David stared across Third Street at the church. He could usually go to the lake and find peace, but not tonight. David sensed something terrible in the air, and something horrible inside him waiting to get loose—or worse, grow stronger. If there was ever a time David needed the comfort and forgiveness of the Lord, it was now.

Despite what his mother had always said, David felt the Lord could indeed give you more than you could handle. As he leaned against the tree and fingered his tarnished copper crucifix, David wondered if he would be able to enter the church. It had been a long time.

Could the cursed enter without permission? Would he be struck down by lightning? Or would he disintegrate when he touched the door? Were the damned allowed another chance?

David shuddered. A crushing weight sat upon his shoulders, as though he were being observed and judged. Every time David closed his eyes, and even sometimes when they were open, he relived his stalking of the fallen youth. David saw the terror in the boy's face. It should have told him that something was wrong, but he had ignored it. Then, as if a sign, the clouds had parted, and the moonlight had shone on his hands. They were mangled and torn, transformed into the claws of a demon. David winced and looked away from his ravaged hands.

He studied the brick, L-shaped building, hoping to come to some revelation just by staring at the church. Temprance Presbyterian was the largest and oldest place of worship in town. It stood just off Main Street at the central square. The solid-looking church was simple in design, and at this hour, all was peaceful and dark except for the back-lit cross above the front entryway.

Resolutely, David straightened and began to walk across the street. As soon as he stepped out of the shadows and into the light, his skin took on a luminescent quality. *"Warten—* wait! Dis is futile," coming from behind David, a silken voice switched to English. "You cannot enter." Her voice had an odd, Germanic accent.

"What?" David whirled to face the woman and caught his breath. She was beautiful and wild, radiating a powerful sensuality. Her eyes were dark and shiny, almost glowing, as though lit by an inner fire. Flushed, David could feel her heat. The woman's hair was long and lustrously dark, almost matching her sheer outfit, which stretched to the ground. A cape had been thrown over her shoulders, but her creamy skin was visible through the thin, clingy material of her dress. The neck of her dress was high, covering her throat; the outfit was seductive, not prudish. There was something strange about her, intoxicating and mysterious, dangerous and wanton.

Lust welled within David. He fought the urge—the compulsion—to take her in his arms. He bit his lip and tasted blood. The pain helped him remain strong, and he somehow resisted his dark urges.

Once he'd been consumed in such a fashion. A decade past, he'd been aroused beyond control. And yet, it couldn't be the same woman! She couldn't be Liselle! Again, thoughts of

Liselle! She would be older than this stranger, and an ocean and more away. This woman had to be a vision, something to remind him of what he'd done—of why he needed redemption. "Liselle?"

The woman's smile was perfect, and remained for a moment when all else disappeared as she stepped back into the shadows. "Because of what you are—*die Dunkelheit*—you no longer have a place dere." Her words were clipped, harshly shortened. "You are *Gottverdammt*. Look at it and see dat I speak the truth."

David tore his gaze from her—from Liselle—and looked longingly at the church. He didn't believe her words. In the Lord's House, there could be redemption and forgiveness, even for a damned sinner. He was just one of many prodigal sons—or was he? He didn't see what she saw. "I don't understa—" David began, as he turned to find her gone.

His mind must be playing tricks, but it didn't matter. His heart was heavy and set, as was his mind. He knew in his soul what he must do, no matter what the vision claimed was impossible. There was still a place for him in the church. His mother had often told him that no matter what happened, you could come home to the Lord.

Without another glance to where the vision had faded, David walked across the street and up the steps. He was growing warmer, starting to sweat. Well, it was hot out tonight, but usually he enjoyed the heat. Hesitant, David stood at the double doors. He wiped the sweat from his brow, then his palms on his pants. He was growing more and more uncomfortable. It is just fear, he told himself. Or was it something more?

His expression was grim and determined, but his hand shook as he reached for the handle. Inches short, he stopped. What if Liselle were correct? What if he burst into flames or turned into salt, when he touched the door?

Did it really matter? He no longer cared whether he lived

or died. Life continued to turn sour. David reached for the handle and prayed.

He clutched it, but nothing happened. Relieved, David sighed, then pulled one of the front doors open. Cool air poured out. With a glance over his shoulder and half-expecting the vision to wave goodbye, he entered the foyer.

David felt a sense of victory! No longer did he feel watched and judged, just accepted. With a newfound sense of wonder, David walked into the foyer, past the coat closets. There was a dim light in the chapel, coming from the front where a few tapers were burning. Long shadows were everywhere, stretching from the pews, the pulpits, the cross, and into every nook and cranny.

The chapel expanded once he stepped through the narthex and out from under the small balcony. As always, David felt a sense of simplicity and taste in the little hall. There were two sets of wooden pews, maybe twenty on each side, with an aisle down the center. David noticed that sometime during his absence they had added carpet. Along each side were open doors leading into two long meeting rooms that could also be converted for the overflow, when the church was jammed during the holidays. Moon and street light came through the doors and arched windows above them.

David walked down the center aisle. He paused at the first pew, then kept going. He felt he must get closer. Finally, he knelt at the prayer rail, bowed his head, and began to pray.

When he finished, David felt a little better, but weak, draping himself over the rail. "Almighty, please forgive me, for I have sinned. I've lost faith, and I've cursed you, failing to keep you in my heart. I've wined and wenched, letting myself become immersed in debauchery. I've lost my soul and my health.

"Please lend me thy strength. I ask for your love, your light to touch me, take me, reshape and mold me, as you will to do thy will. Purge me of my past and help me start anew!" He waited, impossibly hoping for a sign.

In his mind's eye, David suddenly saw that which he had tried to banish. Liselle the dark and beautiful, so arresting that she consumed his attention. She beckoned, her smile promising pleasures. Her fiery eyes revealed the spirit that would willingly deliver. She was a contrast of light and dark—pleasure and pain—a true temptress.

David knew that it was his own frailty that had led him to the darkness. He had paid for stepping way from the Light. And the illness still gripped him. It seemed to be incurable, and kept him out of the sun. Whose fault was it? Liselle's? His? Somebody else's?

NO! He was his own responsibility, but he needed help. "Please!" he whispered desperately. "I will do whatever's necessary for redemption!"

"May I be of help?" drawled a gentle voice.

"Lord?" David hoped.

"No," the Rev. Cooper Page replied wryly as he walked toward David. The minister, unable to sleep since putting his son to bed, had been staring out the window of his house and had seen David enter. "Just his humble servant, and a very surprised one. David, I'm so glad to see you here!" The reverend helped David stand and gave him a hug. It was a night for homecomings! "A miracle. Thank you, Lord!" He held David at arm's length. "Yes, you are a fine sight for tired eyes. I have often prayed that you'd return to us."

"I wasn't sure that I could come back."

"We must always be the first to take a step in the direction of God Almighty. Come sit. You've been missed." The reverend led him to the first pew. David was exhausted and collapsed. "Is there something I can help you with? Something you'd like to talk about?" The reverend knew about the incident at David's ranch and felt an apology was in order on Patrick's behalf, but only when the time was right.

"You know, when Tina and Timmy died, I no longer believed. I couldn't believe that a loving God would ruin my life. I ran away to Europe. I drank and stayed drunk, because it made it easy to use many women. I don't remember their faces, let alone their names. And I've paid the price. Ever since the accident, my life has been pointless, worthless."

"David," Cooper said gently. "Your life isn't worthless. It has great value—value you don't see. It's true that God knows the number of hairs on our heads, as well as what is in our minds and hearts. His creation of you means you are special and unique. Our Lord certainly doesn't look down and say 'Today I'm going to ruin David Matthewson's life'! He has a plan—a grand design. This is something we'll understand when we are with him in heaven."

"I hear you," David said, his voice weary, "but I can't make myself believe there's reason behind all the agony and sorrow. Why is beauty and innocence taken, when the unworthy and sinners are spared?"

"Belief in God doesn't necessarily come from empirical reasoning or understanding," Cooper told him. "Faith comes from somewhere deeper, the soul, and a feeling that there is something more, something greater than we. Something all-powerful, glorious, and loving, with a benevolent purpose. Faith helps us believe in the things common sense tells us not to. You must help the Lord rekindle whatever is already there. You must reach out your hand and ask for help."

"I am ready. What must I do?"

"Good. There is always room for a God-loving man in this parish. The Lord judges us from this time forward, when we are cleansed anew, but cleansing doesn't come just by praying and wishing it so. We must live the Bible."

"Would you bless this for me, Father?" David asked, holding out his crucifix. The reverend nodded, praying aloud as he touched the cross. "Please, Reverend Page, tell me how I can live with the Lord and myself again."

"Well, a good way to start is by re-reading the Bible. Start with the New Testament."

"I will."

"Good. And you should come to church at least once a week."

"You know I can't stand the light or . . . the crowds. They would stare."

"David, you look fine. Neither the Lord nor his flock judge by appearances. But if you're uncomfortable with coming to Wednesday night services, then you may come whenever you wish. The front doors of the church are never locked. You can come and go as you please, or simply make an appointment. You may meditate, read, or speak with me or the Reverend Wright. Then after you grow more comfortable, we can see about integrating you into some of the church's activities and services. If you wish it, that is."

"Sounds wonderful. I'm willing to do whatever is necessary to start fresh," David proclaimed. Cooper smiled. "Who is Reverend Wright?"

"Daniel Wright is—"

"Right here," the tall man entered the church from the direction of the offices. His stride and expression were purposeful. His young face was stern and narrow, his features sharp, and his blue eyes hard. The Reverend Page was obviously surprised to see Wright at the church at this late hour, but before he could speak, Daniel drawled heavily, "I couldn't sleep, so I came to work on Sunday's sermon." The assistant minister's eyes narrowed for a moment, as though he recognized David. "I am Daniel Wright, the assistant minister. Are you Penny's son?"

"Yes."

Wright turned to Reverend Page. "Cooper, why is this blasphemer here?"

"Blasphemer? David comes seeking forgiveness and refuge."

"Oh, really," Wright said a little sarcastically, "then he'll have no problem publicly stating that what he wrote in *Witch Hunt* was irresponsible, wayward, and sinful!"

"I don't understand," Cooper said. Neither did David.

"Haven't you read his latest piece of heresy? Well, I have! It was damaging to the faith and could warp fertile minds." Wright turned to face David and took a step closer, as he raised his finger and said in an accusing tone, "Witches and warlocks certainly weren't people of God. They were pagans and sinners. They weren't good people, nor people to be tolerated. They got what they deserved. They were punished by the Lord, when they broke his commandments!"

David started to say something, but Reverend Page interrupted. "Daniel, I'm surprised at you. We don't judge a man on fiction. It's a story that is told, not to be believed. We must get to know the man, not his trappings."

"One writes from experience and the soul," Wright countered. "Art is a reflection of the man."

"I know David," the Reverend Page continued. "He is a good man and needs our help. We're not to judge, but assist those who want to find Jesus."

"I don't debate that, even though he doesn't seem penitent. But you're right, all deserve a chance. Will you do as I ask, and publicly denounce your writings?"

Suddenly, David's shock and disappointment changed to rage, as though a switch had been flipped, releasing years of anger and frustration. His face was livid, and his fist balled and white-knuckled. Not only was this censorship, but also prejudice! He tried to maintain control as he found himself wanting to smash Wright's holier-than-thou expression from his face. Ready to strike, he raised his fist.

"See, Cooper! He'd hit a devout servant of God on hallowed ground!"

At the last second, David held back, fighting his emotions. He couldn't let himself be carried away again. Already he'd committed an unpardonable act in anger. No more. "I apologize," David managed through gritted teeth. "I am not well. Reverend Page, I will be leaving." Without looking at Wright, David began to walk out.

"David! Wait!" the Reverend Page called out. "Daniel, we must talk!"

"Let 'em go. Can't you see it? He doesn't belong here! Come back when you're sincere, not just placating!"

"Your actions are out of place, Daniel."

"Matthewson! Unless you change your ways, you will face the Lord's justice. We all do. The Lord trieth the righteous," Wright yelled, "but the wicked and him that loveth violence, his soul hateth. He shall rain snares, fire, and brimstone and a horrible tempest; this shall be the portion of their cup. For the righteous Lord loveth righteousness; his countenance doth behold the upright!"

Fighting a last urge to turn and face Wright, David stalked outside. The words seemed to follow him into the night, where he suddenly felt free and unencumbered.

Six

Reminiscing

As David stormed out of the church, he was so furious he could barely see straight. Fighting with himself, he was tied up in knots. He knew it would have been wrong to hit the assistant minister, but he certainly wanted to. David gritted his teeth and shook his head. What had possessed him? He could barely control himself, ready to erupt at any moment with volcanic fury. How could that be? He wasn't a violent person, but this was twice tonight! And the second time was in church! Maybe a walk would help him clear his head and cool off.

David passed his Blazer and headed toward the Temprance town square. Without a glance, he quickly walked by venerable homes, built long before air-conditioning became standard, and some even before central heating was put into operation. Many were constructed of brick, a few of stone, and several were sheathed in aluminum siding. Two-story structures were uncommon, most being a single level.

Almost all of the houses and yards were in good shape, as though appearance was important. The hedges had grown tall, showing they'd been around a long time, and gardens were in bloom. Vines and flowers covered the fences, adding a lush, almost jungle quality to the community. The trees in the neighborhood were of good size, well established, and providing welcome shade from the sweltering summer sunshine. The scent of roses and gardenia dominated the warm night air. In several yards, sprinklers were running, watering the sidewalks as well as the lawns. David got wet once or twice. Head down, he just kept walking past the small metal mailboxes along the curb and sometimes atop fences. Next to each of them was an orange rectangular box with *Times* painted in black.

Why had Wright been that way? There had been instant antipathy between them, as though they were arch enemies. That was crazy; he'd never met the man. Obviously narrow-minded and judgmental, Wright hadn't even given him time to defend himself.

David wrung his hands. Did Wright really have such a negative reaction to him because of his writings? Or was it because of his appearance? Even in his prime, he certainly wouldn't have been confused for Kevin Costner, but now he could easily be cast as a freak or villain. His pale flesh, red eyes, hairiness, and oddly colored teeth had elicited strong reactions from people, which is why he hadn't been into town in a long, long time. Even people he had grown up with had adverse reactions to his countenance. Now his sister or mother did all his shopping, and sometimes even the selling of produce and livestock. David had no desire to interact with people that thought he might infect them with just a look. Besides, no one took advantage of his mother; Penny was a cattle baroness and veteran horse trader.

Town? David looked around and suddenly realized that he was standing in the middle of one of the streets which comprised the small town square. In the center stood the administrative buildings, all very old and made of brick. A statue of Gerald Alvin, the town's founding father and first sheriff, stood in front on a pedestal. The trees were huge, almost concealing the courthouse. The giant clock was still visible between two of them, and pigeons were sleeping on it. The flagpoles were bare, and would be until the morning.

David looked around with an awkward feeling of déjà vu. He hadn't been to the town square in at least seven or eight years, and nothing had changed! Well, almost nothing had changed. The Tastee-Freez was gone, replaced by a Dairy Queen in a refurbished building. And he noticed that the hardware store was now affiliated with True Value. He wondered if old Larry Kinard was still alive. He'd owned the place and was at least fifty when David had been in high school. Curious to see if anything else had changed, David began a tour of the square, his raging anger quickly forgotten.

David crossed the street and passed the tiny, white stone building with a large waiting area and a worn sign reading "Greyhound." Next to it was Tom's Deli, a dim light inside revealed a single row of glass coolers across from a row of benches. The floor was wooden, and the ceiling fan was spinning. David vaguely remembered eating lunch at Tom's once or twice with his father. Tom had been very nice to him, usually giving him a free Fudgsicle for dessert.

Funny what stuck with you through the years, David thought. That's the way he'd remembered the town, friendly, neighborly, or at least it had been until the accident. And some of that change was as much his fault as theirs. He'd grown distant, unable to stand their pitying looks, or even their overly kind words. When they reached out to help, he'd shied away. Pride, mixed with anger, was a terrible virtue. Things had only grown worse after his return from Europe, when his affliction became well known.

Trudging on, David continued around the square. He passed a defunct savings and loan. Texas had taken the worst of the scandal. He hoped the locals hadn't been hurt too bad. The post office was next, and a poster displayed the latest philatelic collector's kit. David heard a slight flapping noise and looked up.

The banner exclaimed that Summerfest was coming late in June. Thoughts of the festival brought back good memories of booths, games, ice cream, and lively music. In comparison, Wright's accusations faded away, just a bad memory. A small smile touched David's face as he continued on, his steps even slower, bringing back his childhood.

Frank's Autoparts followed, with a couple of overturned chairs out front—a place to slowly watch the world go by. The interior of Bigby's drugstore was back-lighted, and David wondered if Jerome had taken over from his father. They had played football together. David passed the hardware store, then came to Zane's Barbershop. The red and white pole brought back more memories. He'd been fascinated by it as a youngster, watching it whirl for minutes at a time. How mundane it now seemed, the magic gone with the passing of years. Still, David remembered balking at having to have his hair cut, especially in a crew cut. Now he let it grow long. Nobody saw it, and it helped hide his face. The only good thing about the trips to the barbershop was being able to look at the latest edition of Sports Illustrated and listening to the man talk. There were never any women in the shop, and it made David feel as though he were a part of something special, a secret society like "The He-man Woman Haters Club."

Almost smiling, David walked past the two-story, brick building that held Annie's Antiques and State Farm Insurance. The hanging sign over the door was weathered, probably the same one she'd opened with over a quarter of a century ago. The Temprance beauty salon run by Katie Rasmussen was next to it, and then the Paperback Peddler operated by old man Kessler. It was the only place David had been allowed to shop. They couldn't afford new books, so when he wasn't playing football or basketball, he'd spent hours sifting and searching through them, looking for something different. All his Dad had were some old EC comics and a few ancient pulps without covers. David peered in and sighed, wondering if his books would be found in there. Surely they would be. Or maybe, David smiled, they were so good that people didn't turn them in for trade, but kept them. He laughed at himself.

For a moment, David thought he heard the soft whisper of a scraping footstep, then felt eyes on his back. He turned around, but didn't see anything out of the ordinary. The town square was deserted except for an occasional piece of drifting trash. Suddenly he felt a bit chilled, despite the heat of the night. David had an odd thought and wondered if the woman Liselle might be following him. He listened, stretching out his senses, but didn't hear anything odd. Still, he felt disconcerted.

Off to his right, a green lit sign caught his attention. Something new, a travel agency had been put in town. That almost made David laugh. For some reason, he never envisioned the town people needing one. He got the impression that everything they needed was right here. Even after he'd been to college and done some traveling, he'd discovered that most of the people around here had never left the state—and didn't desire to. After all, it took at least four hours just to get out of Texas.

Shaking his head, David passed Spencer's Jewelers, several small fashion stores with full window dressings—one of them new—and Dr. Connors's office, the town dentist. David shuddered. He'd hated going to see Connors, hated the fluoride treatments. And he still had bad teeth, but now they were red instead of white!

On the bench at that corner, before crossing the street to the First Bank of Texas, David noticed someone sitting and watching him. The observer's head was cocked sideways, entangled hair dangling in front of his worn face. Maybe this was the cause of the spying sensation he'd felt. The man was dressed in a ragged shirt, pants that were much too large and held up by a utility belt empty of tools, and working boots. For a second, David wondered if it were Ronnie—"the village idiot" they had cruelly called him as kids. He looked old enough. Ronnie had moved from shop to shop, working odd jobs that paid quarters, enough to keep him alive and out of trouble.

"Who's that?" the figure mumbled.

"Uh, Ronnie," David began. "Sorry, I didn't mean to disturb you."

"Not Ronnie," he said with slurred speech. "Ronnie stays with Kathy. Sister in town. Got a job sweepin'. Name's Bob." He reached for something on the bench, then put on a hard hat. "I'm inspectin'."

"Bob?" David asked, not sure he'd understood correctly. The man nodded. Then David remembered something his sister, Carolyn, had said. A new vagabond, another kind but dull-witted fellow, had replaced Ronnie. This fellow entertained the locals by dressing up as something different from day to day. Sometimes he was a policeman, other times a fireman or doctor, and today a construction worker. The Salvation Army on Second Street kept him supplied and fed, as did the church.

David felt sorry for this fellow who didn't have any place to sleep—didn't have a home. His own life could be worse, David told himself. At least he had a home and a family. That should balance out his tragedies at least a little bit, but it didn't. Still, it was terrible to feel better about yourself by finding somebody who was more pitiful than you. "Sorry to disturb you."

"Ya didn't. Cool breeze did. Somethin' funny about." Bob scratched himself, then spat.

David noticed it again—the feeling of being watched returned, growing stronger. He was suddenly hungry and realized he hadn't eaten yet today. "Didn't feel like summer?"

"Nope," Bob replied wide eyed. "Got work I could do? Spare change?"

David's heart went out to Bob, and he forgot all about his troubles. He reached into his pocket and pulled out his money clip, then also pulled out his business card. "Here," David gave Bob two twenties and some change, then his business card. Bob's jaw dropped. "Do you know who Michael Woods is?"

"Lawyer? Black?"

"Yeah, he might have some cleaning that needs to be done, or trash moved. Stop by and see him, but don't be drinking, or he won't help you. I didn't give you money to buy booze. His office is on Fourth. How's that sound?"

Bob's smile was huge, his stained and crooked teeth resembling miniature wickets. "Don't drink. Thanks. Lord bless ya mister," he looked at the card. "Whut's say?"

"David Matthewson," David said. The man's head bobbed up and down. "I'm . . . Uh, look him up tomorrow and give him that card, tell him you met me tonight." Bob nodded again.

Feeling better, David turned to leave the square and headed for his Blazer. He'd seen enough. Things in Temprance had changed, but hadn't really changed much at all. Ronnie was gone, but Bob was here. Mom and pop were still there, just sometimes affiliated with big corporations. He guessed that nothing ever seriously changed in Temprance. From the looks of things, they still had home milk delivery. Yep, the metal boxes were still on the porches.

David was thinking of chores to be completed and food, when he heard a short, slashing scream. It was agonizing, as though ripped from the soul, and froze David's heart. Muggers in Temprance? David sprinted to see if Bob was in trouble. As he ran, he heard a soft gurgling noise, as well as a sliding-dragging sound.

The bench was empty, except for Bob's helmet, still rocking back and forth. David listened, hearing nothing but the soft sweeping of the wind. What had happened to Bob?

Seven

The Gathering Place

Reading and waiting his turn, Logan sat gunslinger style, with his nose in the newspaper and his back to the wall of Zane's Barbershop. He was dressed casually in khaki pants and a white cotton shirt. The shop was cool and hazy, and sunshine burst through the front window. Golden dust—bits of fuzz, dust, and hair—drifted in the light. A wall of mirrors behind the barber chairs made the place bright, except the corner where Logan sat. The furniture and design of the shop were anachronisms, throwbacks to the sixties. Pictures of the local high school football teams from 1952 until today lined the wall above the mirrors.

In the first chair—Alvin's chair—Michael Woods was basking in the sunshine and reading the sports page. Temprance's well-respected lawyer and David's agent came to escape the honey-do jar, too. Despite it being Saturday, there was only one barber working, the owner Zane Harkness. He was a huge Irishman, clad in a bulging white shirt and brown pants. Alvin was on vacation. Zane was trimming Leo Peters's thinning hair, while the insurance agent was talking about the effect of last year's Summerfest on rates.

The third chair and closest to Logan never had a barber.

Ernie, their postmaster, sat next to the television reading *Field and Stream*. When he wasn't working or drinking, he was here with Zane, his best friend, telling tall tales. A retired old coot and sports fanatic, Old Man Watson, chimed in with the television's commentators covering the Rangers' game. Fortunately, Jack Huntington, who also enjoyed hanging around the shop, left when he saw Logan. Jack was a fishing guide, "retired" member of the KKK, and troublemaker through and through. He might as well have been related to the Tubbs boys.

Logan snapped the *Morning News* and turned the page. He planned on reading every page. He wasn't in any hurry, and it would be fine with him if nobody knew he was here. He was still on vacation—trying to start his vacation—so his wife thought him fair game for the job jar, a fact he'd shared with the other men. He and Michael briefly commiserated. Michael wholeheartedly agreed that Logan wasn't at the barbershop. Everybody else said it was dandy with them.

And he did need a haircut, the type that might take the rest of the day. He'd already had to work this morning, talking with Judge Marshall about Skeeter, who was badly bruised after a face-first run-in with a tree on the Matthewson Ranch, then Reverend Page about Patrick's involvement, and finally Donald about the entire Friday night matter.

Logan was wondering about the message David had left on the department's answering machine about Bob, when the deputy heard trouble. "Well, hello Claire!" Leo said. Logan glanced over the top of his paper, then raised it. The portly insurance agent had tipped his hat and was holding the door for Claire Brookens. She was a stern-looking woman in expression and form, with red hair and a temper to match. Logan was sure that raising the boys alone was a handful, and assumed that was why she looked older than her forty-plus years.

Her boys were behind her, armed with the usual teenage expressions and carriages. Benny Joe wore a fresh cast on his wrist, and was bent over as though it weighed a ton. Logan wanted to question them, but not when Claire was around. He didn't want to talk with her; he wouldn't learn anything. Logan raised the paper to completely hide himself. Besides, he was on vacation.

"Thank you," Claire nodded. "In you go, boys." Logan imagined her waving them inside. Benny Joe would be looking around with wide-eyed interest, while his brother wore an expression that said the barbershop didn't rate.

Several men called out greetings to the boys, as Leo said, "How are you doing, Claire?"

"I'm in a hurry, Leo."

"Have you changed your mind?"

"I've said no at least a thousand times, Leo." Logan heard her sigh. "Leo, the body is a temple to our Lord, and I believe how we care for ourselves tells us a lot about the caretaker of that temple. Good day." She moved into the room.

"Morning, Claire," Zane said. "The usual for the scamps?" Logan imagined his wide, toothy smile that was more than a bit crooked.

"Come on Rangers. Beat them damn Yankees!" Watson sighed heavily. "You'd think after twenty tries—twenty years—they could win a pennant." His voice shook with age. "Lord help us, with Canseco, Franco, Gonzalez, Palmiero, Brown, and Ryan, maybe it's our year. You a fan, Claire?"

"No," she said coldly. "Zane, give them a summer cut, short, real short. It's plenty warm outside, and I'm tired of them looking like rag mops." Both boys groaned, as though they were barred from eating ice cream. "Jimbob, take off your hat!" Logan thought he heard reluctant movement.

Zane laughed and so did Ernie. "Won't that sap their strength, like Sampson?" Ernie snickered, probably from behind his magazine. Claire must have glared, because Ernie continued, "Now don't be that way, Claire, I'm just funnin' ya."

Logan could feel Claire bristle. "Mister Woods," Claire began, her drawl prominent and thick, "can't a fine, upstandin' man like you do somethin' about public drunks? The ones that are roamin' our streets and adversely influencin' the young of Temprance?"

Michael Woods removed the pipe from his mouth before he spoke. His tone was serious, "Only if you or I want to make a citizen's arrest, Claire."

Claire laughed. "I think I'll pass today. Maybe the sheriff will be by." Zane coughed.

"Probably will be, since Jimmy Bob and Benny Joe are in town," Ernie snickered. "Hey, hear that? Insurance rates just jumped again," Ernie laughed loudly.

Claire was ignoring him. "Now, Jimbob, and you, too, Benny Joe, I want you boys to behave while I run a few errands. Show them that you know some manners, unlike some people. Okay?" Silence. "Zane, I'll be back soon. You have my permission to paddle them, if need be."

"Don't hurry back on my account," Ernie said. More glaring, Logan imagined. He knew Claire thought that Ernie was a sinner—full of himself, as well as being a drunk and a rumored Peeping Tom. Nothing proved yet. With a huff, Claire finally departed. "We can breathe again," Ernie laughed. "So, Michael, do we have extra police for this year's Summerfest?"

"I believe so. Logan mentioned it."

"And I thought the roads were supposed to be fixed. After the spring rains, it feels like four-wheelin' on the moon," Ernie complained.

"You should know," Watson cackled.

"And what are they filling the potholes with anyway—mud and sugar? Washes away when it rains," Zane began. The boys groaned.

"What else is new," Ernie said.

"Ernie, will ya pipe down? I'm trying to watch the game," Watson finally groused.

Zane was using a spray bottle on one of the boys. Logan thought it was Jim Bob. "Well, what's new, boys? Looks like you've been up to something, with Benny Joe having broke his arm and all. Jim Bob, I swear your hair has a mind of its own." The brothers were both silent. "So, nothing new?"

Benny Joe finally managed, "Nuthin'."

"Shit no! You boys are angels," Ernie said with a laugh. "We all know that, don't we, Zane?"

"Ernie," Michael said sharply, "please watch your language." Logan smiled. He could picture Ernie's expression—a kid caught with his hand in the cookie jar.

"Something strange going on. They ain't yakking their heads off. So, Benny Joe, how'd you break your arm?" Zane asked, as he began clipping Jim Bob's hair. Logan imagined he was constantly having to recorrect Jim Bob's head position.

"I was running through the woods and stepped in a hole," Benny Joe said. He paused, then continued, "And some scaredy cat left me there!"

"Running from something?" Zane drawled. Neither boy said anything.

"Was it dark?" Ernie asked eagerly, always hungry for a story.

Logan thought this would be a good one. The boys were well-practiced liars. He peeked over his paper to observe them. They hadn't noticed him yet.

"Foggy," Benny Joe finally said. The younger Brookens looked out of sorts, almost depressed. "Reminded me of winter."

"Winter! This time of year! Bah!" Ernie reacted. "This time of year it's air-conditioning all the way. Where would civilization be without it?" Ernie was a short wiry man, who reminded most people of a weasel with his thick sideburns, full mustache, beard, and pinched face.

"Where'd ya get hurt?" Zane asked. He had thinning red hair, ruddy cheeks, and was in his early fifties.

"Out of town," Benny Joe said.

"Near the lake," Jim Bob added.

"Near the dam?" Michael asked. Neither boy said anything, the silence thick. Michael puffed on his pipe. He was a handsome black gentleman with prematurely silvered temples. His features were chiseled and distinctive, giving those who opposed him in court the feeling he was hewn from stone. He'd made the community proud by graduating from SMU's Law School, then returning to practice at home.

Logan concluded that the boys weren't going to reveal anything, and he'd skulked long enough. He wanted to question the boys, not eavesdrop. "What a surprise, Benny Joe and Jim Bob Brookens," Logan announced. "I was going to come out and see y'all today. You saved me a trip." He stood up. Logan preferred asking questions while on his feet.

"There goes the ball game," Watson breathed.

"This won't take long," Logan assured him. "I'd like to talk with you boys about last night," Logan said, then waved at Michael, "and you even have an attorney present." Both pair of eyes shifted quickly from Logan to Woods, who simply smiled.

"Not much to say," Jim Bob replied. "Ow, watch my ear!" He glared over his shoulder at Zane.

"If that nose gets big," Ernie laughed, "go ahead and trim it, too!"

Logan ignored him. "Now, your mother called me last night and claimed that you'd been attacked on David Matthewson's property. Is that correct?" Both boys nodded without looking at each other. Michael Woods leaned forward and put down his paper. "Is that correct?" Logan asked again.

"Yes," they said.

"Is that where you broke your arm?" Logan asked.

"Yes," Benny Joe replied. "I was running and stepped in a hole."

"Running away from . . . somebody?" Logan asked.

"Uh-huh," Benny Joe replied.

"Do you know who?"

"Nope, didn't get a good look at his face." Both Michael and Logan glanced at each other. It was obvious by his expression and the look in his eyes that Benny Joe was lying about getting a look at his assailant. Before Logan could ask another question, Benny Joe continued, "And Jim Bob didn't see them either. He was too busy running," he said and imitated a chicken's squawking.

"Hey!" Jim Bob rose to leave the chair. "Your face is gonna meet my fist!"

"Stop that," Zane said, grabbing the apron strings and pulling him back into the chair. Jim Bob sulked.

"Were you hit?"

"N . . . no," Benny Joe managed. "At least I don't remember. My wrist was hurting mighty bad."

"Jim Bob, did you see anything?"

"No man . . . I mean, no sir," he managed. Benny Joe was looking away from his brother, and Jim Bob was trying to burn holes in him with a laser stare.

"Were you hurt?" Logan asked Jim Bob, who shook his head. "And why were you two out there?"

"In the *Times,* Benjo read about David Matthewson being a local author," Jim Bob said glibly. "He's a fan. We rode out for autographs."

"Is that right, Benny?" Logan asked. This was farfetched. Logan couldn't imagine either of the boys reading for fun.

Without looking up, Benny said, "Uh-huh. I've read all his books, starting with *Hellbent* to *Witch Hunt*. I didn't know Matthewson was a local author until I saw the article. I . . . I didn't think he would be bothered by our visit. We weren't going to stay long. But we never even saw him. We saw somebody else, and he chased us." He hoped that his thick-headed brother would follow his lead.

"Did you see anything out of the ordinary?" Logan asked.

"Uh, not really. Why?" Benny asked.

"Jim Bob?"

"Couldn't see much of anything, because of the fog. I wasn't sure Benjo was even close sometimes, fog was so thick."

Michael was shaking his head. This was another wild-goose chase perpetrated by the Brookens brothers. It was then that he noticed someone outside the shop, listening. All he could see was a shadow.

"Did you hear anything odd?" Logan asked. They both shrugged. "Then you didn't hear music, see a stereo system or some kind of light, maybe a projection?"

"Nope," Jim Bob said. Logan stared at Benny Joe. As though he had absolutely no idea what anyone was talking about, Benny Joe looked totally innocent.

"Then you don't think y'all's fingerprints will appear on this stolen equipment?"

"Stolen equipment?" Benny Joe asked. He looked surprised, but refrained from looking at Jim Bob, whose hair was being blown dry.

"So tell us, Benny Joe, my boy," Ernie encouraged, "what was really chasing you? Freddy Kruger? Now don't try fooling me. I can spot a liar a mile away, and I'm closer than that."

"Ernie, stay out of this," Logan said and glared. "This is an official investigation. Mr. Matthewson has filed a complaint, naming these two and several others."

"David filed a complaint?" Michael asked, surprised.

Logan nodded. "We'll discuss it later. Now, who was with you boys?"

"Nobody. I told you, we were by ourselves. It must've been that guy who chased us that Mr. Matthewson thinks is us. It was dark and real foggy, pea soup stuff," Jim Bob claimed. "Maybe Mr. Matthewson is confused."

"I don't think so," Logan said, "But I would be more than glad to take you boys out there, so he could identify you." Jim Bob swallowed hard, but said nothing. Benny Joe acted as though he wasn't part of the conversation, but Logan could see small signs of fear: immediate fidgetiness, tightening around the eyes, and licking of the lips.

"You'd have to talk to Ma," Jim Bob said.

"You're positive that nobody was with you?" Logan said. They both nodded. "Okay, now why do you think someone was chasing you?"

"I have no flamin' idea," Jim Bob replied.

"Come on, Benny Joe, you're next," Zane motioned to the younger Brookens's brother to come sit, then he pulled the sheet from Jim Bob and brushed away the loose hairs.

Ernie snorted, then laughed at his own thought before speaking.

"What?" Zane asked.

In a conspiratorial tone, Ernie said, "What if our favorite writer and local hero is pulling a fast one on us? Here we think he's a quiet, shy fellow, and he's actually the violent type!"

"That's hogwash!" Michael said, standing up. "You are slandering a very good friend of mine."

Ernie paled and took a quick drink.

"Well, I guess that's all for now," Logan said. "I'll be talking to you boys again real soon. And your mom, too." He started out, then paused, and asked. "Anyone seen Bob today?"

"No. I've been wondering where he was," Zane said.

"Yeah," Ernie added. "He never misses a Saturday bull session. Strange."

"Oh well, he probably found something to entertain him," Logan said. "Have a good day, gentlemen." And as he headed out to find a peaceful place to continue his vacation. He'd call Bricker later. If he went close to the office again, his wife would maim him.

"So this Matthewson, the local writer, might be a child molester?" a short, haphazardly dressed man asked, as he entered the shop on the coattails of Logan's departure.

"Oh, look what crawled in," Michael began, "the King of Yellow Journalism, straight from the National Inquirer School of Writing."

"What's this about?" the unshaven man asked, unfazed by Wood's comments and looking around at everyone as if he'd just walked in on the greatest cover-up ever engineered. The reporter was dressed in a stained white cotton shirt, a loosened plaid tie, and light brown pants with his threadbare dress coat over his arm.

"Well, if it isn't our new *Times* reporter, straight from Houston—" Zane began.

"Via boot-in-the-pants airways," Ernie cackled.

"Mr. Corey Stones. Welcome to my shop," Zane said jovially, ignoring both Ernie and Michael. "Shave and a haircut, Mr. Stones?"

Still wearing his sunglasses, Corey Stones sat in the last unattended barber chair and rubbed his stubbled, chipmunk cheeks. "Yeah. Be careful, I bleed easily." Stones flipped a quarter and caught it. "So what's this about this author guy, Matthewson, being a child groper?"

"I'm warning you," Michael said. Something about Stones made Michael want to punch him.

"Maybe he deserves slandering," Stone said coolly. "We can find out. That's a big part of being an investigative reporter, you know. Now," he looked about, "who exactly is this Matthewson? What's his history?"

"He's a proud product of Temprance," Zane began, "And a fine, upstanding citizen. He donated money to help build the new gymnasium, he and Mr. Woods here. I used to cut his hair, when he was just a kid. Way back when, watched him play football. He was a hell of a halfback." He pointed to several pictures on the wall. "Could really run, too, until the ranch accident."

"Ranch accident?"

"Fixing a tractor. It slipped off the block and broke a bunch a stuff. Was several hours until his mom found him. He never returned to the football field," he sighed. "Would've hooked them horns." He made the UT hand sign with forefinger and pinky extended. "Maybe been a Cowboy. Anyway, studied finance and journalism at UT, then went to work in Athens for the phone company."

Stones nodded. "And now he writes, right?"

"Yeah," Ernie said. He looked at Zane. Neither one mentioned the car accident.

"And he's allergic to the sun?" Stones continued.

"Porphyria," Zane said. "A blood disease."

"And now he's a recluse and writer?" They both nodded. "What's your name, boy?" Stones asked Jim Bob. There was something about the two that screamed to his reporter's sense; he could smell something hiding.

"Jimmy Bob Brookens, and that's my younger brother, Benny Joe."

Michael could see where this was going and didn't like it, so he intervened. "Jim Bob, Benny Joe, this gentleman here— and I use the term loosely—creates news, instead of reporting it. That's the same as making things up or starting trouble, say an incident at a ranch," he stared at them for a moment, "so he can write a paper on it. Stones was kicked out of Houston for paying—"

". . . Allegedly . . ."

". . . Allegedly paying people to do illegal things, so he would have a story. Remember, if you tell him something, and you know it's a lie that will do damage to David Matthewson's reputation, then that's slander, which is against the law and a punishable offense." Michael glared at Stones, and continued, "And if he reports it as the truth and it's printed, that's defamation of character, sometimes known as libel. That, too, is a punishable offense and against the law."

"Maybe it would be good publicity," Ernie laughed. "Any publicity is good for a book."

"Not molesting," Zane said. "Remember what happened to Rafael Septien, the Cowboy's place kicker."

Stones smiled. The sight was an unpleasant and oily sensation. "I always research my stories, Mr. Attorney."

Looking from Benny Joe to Jim Bob, Michael continued, "Boys, I know you've a penchant for causing mischief. I have known David for a long time. Think of this: would you want your brother or one of your friends to tell false stories that you thought were innocent enough, but caused him lots of trouble, suffering, and grief, because it ruined his private life, his reputation, and maybe even his livelihood?"

Benny Joe shook his head no, while Jim Bob just shrugged.

"Yeah, yeah, Mr. Attorney, just sue me when the time comes, okay, and give my ears a rest. Jeez, what a bleeding heart," Stones said. "I guess I should interview this guy, this David Matthewson."

"I'm his agent," Michael said.

"Really? So when can I talk to him?"

"When it snows in July," Michael said with a smile.

Stones stood, stretched, and then smiled. "I guess I'll just talk to Sheriff Bricker, see if he knows anything. But don't worry about the truth, Woods, because I only report the truth. And I'm gonna see if this is worth reporting. See ya!" He left, tossing Benny Joe the quarter.

"Jim Bob, Benny Joe," Michael said. "Follow your conscience. Good day, everybody." After Michael left, Ernie and Zane started laughing.

Claire walked in on them, the adults laughing and her sons stone-faced, but their eyes worried. "And what's so funny?"

"This town is gonna be hoppin' soon," Ernie said. "I can feel it!"

Eight

Uninvited Visitors

"This is the life," Michael Woods said to David. Michael was clad in a Houston Rockets tank top, dark brown slacks, and loafers—since he was loafing. He stretched his feet out onto the ice chest, leaned back in his lawn chair, and flick-released hook, sinker, and bobber into the quiet pond. Michael gave David a big smile, pulled out his pipe, and lit it. He had a Corona sitting on another cooler next to a Coleman lantern that gave off a dim glow.

Michael had arrived during twilight with poles and a tacklebox. Still unnerved by last night's incident, David was more than happy to have company. He had offered to take Michael out on Cedar Creek Lake, but his friend swore he would catch more fish in the MX pond. "Yep, you know everything is all right, when you have time to kick back and fish," Michael finished.

"Definitely," David replied, and reeled in one of his lines. He still had three poles standing on the shore with lines in the water. As usual, he was dressed in a white shirt, Dockers, and tennis shoes. In the dim illumination, his skin made him stand starkly white in the darkness. "I just enjoy getting outside and spending time with a good friend."

"You have that right, buddy," Michael smiled largely.

David smiled as well and looked around, staring at the small lake and the woods. The outdoors was both intoxicating and refreshing, relaxing but invigorating. Since he couldn't enjoy the daylight, he frequently went out at night, reveling in the brush of the wind across his skin, the scent of water, and the sound of its unrest. The sky was clear, and only a little of last night's fog nestled in among the trees. Above, a crescent moon was low in the west. With the soft breeze and lower humidity, it felt cooler, making it a very pleasant evening.

David was surprised that it was so quiet. There was an occasional bullfrog, but no crickets. Of course, both men smelled of Cutters, so the bugs would leave them alone. The MX pond was famous for its mosquitoes. "You know," David began, interrupting the silence, "I believe you love fishing more than basketball, maybe more than Lydia."

"Now, I wouldn't go quite that far." Michael removed the top off another beer. "I just felt fishing-lucky tonight. I have the feel, just like I have playing hoops sometimes. Some days you have it; some days you don't. I've always had good luck in this pond. Caught four keepers already!"

David suddenly grew melancholy. "Mom always says Dad caught more fish than Carter had pills—meaning a bunch. You know, I don't remember fishing here much with my father, but Mom said we often did." David's expression grew long.

"You all right? You've been quiet all night."

"Just nostalgic. Somebody once said, 'Nostalgia: I didn't like it then and I don't like it now.' And yet, I always get nostalgic around my birthday. This is number 40 and no big deal, except that I'm outliving those I've loved. My sister Lisa, my father, Tina, and Timmy. And soon Mom. She's getting up there."

"Parents aren't supposed to outlive their kids."

"I've already outlived Timmy. Some days I'm still not sure I can continue," David admitted.

"But you're looking great. And you still have your mom, and Carolyn and her unruly clan," Michael reminded him. David just nodded. "David, I'm a good attorney, a fine basketball player, but only a fair philosopher at best. I believe there's a good reason for almost everything that happens, just not always one we understand at that moment; maybe not for a long time. I think when we're finished with this life, we give and get an accounting. We aren't immortal, so we'll find out soon enough. All we can do is try our best: to learn, find guiding principles, adapt, and enjoy our time no matter what we step in and what gets dropped on us."

"That sounds pretty folksy," David almost managed a smile.

"Shucks, ain't nuthin'," Michael exaggerated the drawl he'd lost in college. He got a nibble and jerked the pole, but the hook was picked clean.

David checked his poles. "I can't think of anything worse than being immortal. Life hasn't been that pleasant."

"David," Michael grimaced, "let's try another subject. How's the ranch coming?"

"Fine, though I don't really ranch much anymore. I spend more time writing. And to tell the truth, I don't miss messing with the tractor. It's temperamental. The garden, though, is going hog wild. I guess I've developed a green thumb after all. Would Lydia like some tomatoes, cucumbers, or squash?"

"Sure. What about livestock?"

"I've cut it by more than half. There was too much to handle by myself, and I didn't feel like hiring help," David shrugged. "It wouldn't work out. Anyway, I slaughtered a couple of pigs, filled my freezers, and sold some others just last month. I still have the goats and their offspring. I have a few cattle left, and I'll probably sell most of them come fall. I'll make sure I keep

Tessy. Neither Midnight or Shady would forgive me, if I sold their favorite cow."

"You and your cats," Michael smiled. "And Trigger?"

"Still as ornery as ever. He nipped me when I was brushing him the day before yesterday." David held up his left arm. The mark was obvious, but not serious.

"Why do you keep such a mean horse?"

"He's beautiful and obeys me, most of the time. He's been easier to put up with since I bought Hazel last year."

"Ah, something to soothe the savage beast."

"Yes. It seems like eons since I delivered a horse. I'm not really looking forward to it."

"You might call Al Cochrane. You know, I hadn't even noticed that there were less animals around. I did notice less hay in the fields."

"It's been three-months since your last visit."

"Has it been that long, since I've been out here?" Michael asked and David nodded. "Gosh, I'm an awful friend. Maybe I should scrap my fax machine, then I'd have to visit."

David chuckled, "Oh well, we've both been busy."

"Prosperous, partner," Michael smiled. "Financially, creatively, and in health. Speaking of which, how's treatment coming? You look great."

"Thanks. Things are good. I only have to travel to Dallas every other month now, instead of every week. I still see Doc Katyu once a week, though."

"A fine man and an excellent doctor. I trust him with my life. Is he still drawing blood?"

"Occasionally."

"Tried being outside?"

David laughed. "I was out yesterday morning, and it didn't go well. I can't stand direct light. Fortunately, I didn't blister."

"Well, you do look a whole lot better. Have you cut down on the consumption?"

"Mostly."

"Good work, keep at it. That's probably why you're better."

"You sound like my doctor."

"I'm better. I'm your friend, no matter what."

"Even if I write dogs instead of best-sellers?" Michael nodded vigorously. "So tell me, Mr. Woods, how prosperous is prosperous? How well is *Witch Hunt* selling?"

"Beyond our wildest expectations."

"I have very high—"

". . . Wild, I said . . ."

". . . Wild expectations," David commented.

"*Witch Hunt* has cracked the top ten of the best-sellers list, and should hit at least number five. Not bad."

"It only took ten books," David said with some sarcasm.

"Some people never make it. It's just a dream they have."

"Well, at least one dream came true," David said.

"Undoubtedly. You're going to be a wealthy man. And you're guaranteed good exposure on your next book, maybe the next two." David didn't look very excited. "Hey, what's wrong?"

"Nothing. Really. Well . . . last night it was really strange."

"Want to talk about it?"

"I was the butt of a twisted joke," David said, then told him about exiting the barn.

"I didn't know you believed in ghosts."

"I believe in miracles."

"What did you do?"

"I chased them through the fog, trying to put the fear of God in them."

"Did you attack Benny Joe Brookens?"

"Is that who it was?" David asked. At Michael's nod he responded, "No, I didn't touch any of them."

"Good. How many boys were there?"

"Six boys. You know, I'm afraid of what I think."

"What's that?"

"That my privacy has been shattered because of my success. Now that I think about it, I probably should have written under a pseudonym. I never dreamed that something like this would happen. It was terrible, Michael. I felt as if it almost cost me my soul."

Michael stared at him for long moments. He didn't understand, but said, "You're stronger than you believe, my friend. Listen to what I witnessed at the barbershop this morning," and Michael proceeded to tell him about the boys, Logan, and Stones.

"Great. I really don't want publicity. I don't want attention. I just want to write."

"Yeah, I know. Your writing success might be part of your healthy recovery, although it could also be attributed to taking some of my advice and eating better and drinking less."

"You want to live forever," David accused, "but you smoke."

"I don't inhale. And I only have a beer or three when I fish. I don't want to live forever. I want to die gracefully and with dignity. David, are you okay?" David seemed to be lost, staring at the ground abstractedly.

"Yeah. I've always thought it would be nice if you could sort of choose how and when you die, but I guess we'd all get greedy. Hey!" He cocked his head, listening intently. "Did you hear that?" David asked. Michael shook his head. "It sounds like several cars coming down the driveway. I wonder if it's the sheriff, or who knows who. A few days ago I didn't have this problem. I may have to install a security gate."

"I don't hear anything," Michael said. He opened another beer. "Don't electrify the fences yet."

"Michael, my hearing is very good." David could hear the pinging of the gravel against metal and the crunch of the rock. His hearing had heightened since he'd become ill. It was one of the few positive by-products of his new treatment. "I want to check this out. It could be more," he grimaced, "fans."

"But your poles . . ." Michael said. "Hey! You have something on your line!" He jumped out of his chair and rushed to it. David found himself standing next to Michael, who handed him the pole.

Catching the sunfish occupied him for a moment, then David handed Michael the pole, and said, "And now to attend to my visitors." David moved quickly up the knoll, not expecting Michael to follow, but he could hear him do so. Yes, my hearing is very sharp tonight, David thought as he topped the rise. And so was his sight. Below and through some trees was the driveway. David saw streaks of orange, signs of heat, along the wide gravel road, disappearing around the bend and into the trees. He also smelled car exhaust.

Suddenly, David had the feeling that he wasn't the only one watching. Again, he felt observed and judged.

"Nothing?" Michael asked, coming to stand next to him. He had the stringer of fish in his hand.

"No, there are at least two cars, maybe more. I'm heading back to the house."

"I'll go with you." They jogged back to the road. After putting the fish in a cooler, they climbed into Michael's silver Forerunner. It refused to start. "Damn!"

"I'll run," David said and before Michael could respond, he hopped out of the car and sprinted along the road.

"I hated to do that," Michael said and watched him go. He was amazed at how fast his friend ran in the dark. Michael hoped they'd had enough time.

David was now sprinting. Who could it be? He had a bad feeling about this. When he topped the hill, his house came into sight. There wasn't any sign of other cars. He looked carefully, finding a faint luminescence behind the house on the lake side. David remembered the gunshots last night. His expression grew grim.

David heard a car coming along the road behind him. He stepped off the road as headlights came over the knoll and shone past him. Michael's Forerunner stopped next to David. "Get in." David climbed inside, and they drove to the house.

"Somebody's in my house!" David cried, seeing the front door open. David leaped out and pushed through the gate, rushing up the sidewalk. Angrily, he yanked open the screen door.

The house was dark, but that didn't bother David. There was no one in the living room, but he could hear nearly a dozen heartbeats filling the house, in the hall and dining room. He smelled paper, paint, and plastic, as well as perfume.

"SURPRISE!" they shouted as the lights came on. There was a camera flash as family and friends poured out of the hallway and living room to his right. David had no trouble looking surprised and pleased. He saw his mother, sister Carolyn, and her family—husband Stan and three little ones; Carol, Suzanne, and Doug. All carried presents. Behind them were several men he thought he recognized, as well as a very attractive lady. She looked familiar.

The woman's long hair was dark with auburn highlights. Her eyes were large, round, and dark, while her smile was friendly. She was dressed in a simple, white sun dress with a black belt, the outfit highlighting her deep tan as well as her trimly fit figure. Wait. Could it be Jana?

"HAPPY BIRTHDAY!" they yelled, this time not so in sync.

"Wow!" Nearly speechless, David smiled broadly as he stared at their decorating. White garlands were draped all over the place, with blue streamers stretching across the wall and crisscrossing the ceiling. Balloons of both colors floated around, while the signs read, "Happy Birthday, David" and "BIG 4-0!" They had done a lot in little time, the decorations filling the abundance of empty space.

"Wonderful!" David hugged his mother, who looked ready to cry. Penny, a short, solid woman, hugged him firmly in return.

"Happy birthday, Son." Penny's round face flushed, and her sunburned nose glowed even brighter. She sniffed, "I'm always thankful that the good Lord has seen fit to let you stay another day." She finally broke down and cried.

David hugged his mother even tighter. "Me, too, Mom," and he meant it, despite what he'd said to Michael. Family made it worthwhile. "How was the checkup with Doc Katyu?"

"Fine," she said, without meeting his eyes.

"Happy birthday, big brother!" Carolyn came forward all smiles and hugged both of them. Carolyn was well-endowed and just under six feet tall. Her blond, permed hair touched her shoulders and contrasted with her dark brown eyes. She and David didn't appear to be sister and brother, especially now when she was tanned and glowing with health. Still, their faces were both finely boned. Her husband Stan Hanson, a mad-scientist-looking type—somewhat balding with wild hair, brows, and large ears—stood back watching with a Polaroid in one hand and waving an instant print in the other.

Carol age ten, Suzanne age eight, and Doug age six, came marching with their arms full of presents. All three were blond, but only Doug was a blue-eyed cherub. The sisters were young saplings. "Open your presents!" Doug shouted, his face aglow as he jumped up and down. In her best big-sister tone, Carol shushed him.

"David, you remember Matt Derkins and Harry Price, don't you?" Michael motioned to the two tall men who stood with Allan Jones, the high school principal.

"Matt! Harry! It's been a long time," David moved forward with both hands outstretched and a wide smile. "I didn't know you guys were in town."

"You never did have your ear to the social scene," Harry told him. "I just moved back here about two weeks ago from Little Rock." Harry could have been the Hardy of the pair, over six feet tall, but a bit plump and full-faced, with short dark hair and a beard.

"And I'm visiting him, mixing business with pleasure. Harry's managing the Walmart, and I'm a regional manager. I'll be here for several weeks," Matt added with a slight Texas accent. He was built more in the mold of Laurel, even taller than Harry, but thin, with long facial features that were always relaxed. His hair was short, straight, and dirty blond. They had always been close, hanging around with each other as well as with Michael and David.

"Forty, are you? You don't look a minute over thirty," Harry told him.

"I would agree," Jana said with a dazzling smile that said more than words.

"David," Michael said with a smile, "meet my new legal assistant, Jana Martinez. Desiree moved to Dallas, and the next day, Jana dropped by looking for advice on a job. What good luck I have! You do remember Jana, don't you?"

"Of course, I do," David replied. "But we haven't seen each other since our ten-year reunion. Jana, you look marvelous."

Jana smiled broadly and curtsied, "Thank you, kind sir." David thought she blushed. She didn't look forty either. David remembered her well, although he didn't think of her often. They'd had the kind of friendship that might have developed into something more, if he hadn't met Tina. He'd met Jana during a futile attempt at school theatre. David had thought that she loved the country, the outdoors, and riding horses, but then she'd gone off to Dallas to work for a Big Eight firm after graduating from Stephen F. Austin College. A pretty country lass learning the ropes and politics of the corporate world, she was a good Texas gal, a stand-by-your-man kind of lady, or so he had thought. There was no ring on her finger, and last he'd heard, she had been married. David couldn't help but wonder what might be different, if he'd become more involved with Jana.

"You look very surprised," Stan said, as he showed him the Polaroid. "I love candid shots."

"Good but pale," Matt added, as he peeked at the photo, then David. "You look like a gym rat. Or maybe a lab rat," he laughed. So did David.

"You been playin' any hoop?" Harry asked. David nodded.

"You look healthy and fit," Jana said.

"Thanks."

"Is your basket behind the barn still good?" Matt asked, looking suspiciously devious. David nodded. "How about a little game of two-on-two after the party? We can work off the calories. And we all brought our shoes," he said conspiratorially. "Harry and I say we can take you and Michael in a game to twenty-one."

"Oh, oh," Michael rolled his eyes. "Twenty bucks!"

"I could referee," Jana offered, to their surprise. "I've seen many an illegal use of hands."

"That's football," Harry said.

Matt elbowed him. "You're still dense. Anyway, Jana, thanks but no. We enjoy arguing over the fouls."

"Open your presents," little Doug yelled, repeatedly bumping into David's knees.

"Great idea!" David scooped him up, presents and all. "I need your mom's permission though." Doug yelled to his mom.

"Hold your horses, Doug!" Carolyn had an ice cream cake in her hand and was following Allan, who was carrying a huge bowl filled with lime green punch from the kitchen hallway. The candles were brilliant, lighting up her lean face with a warm, golden glow. They set the cake and punch on the coffee table in front of the couch, then joined in the singing of *Happy Birthday*.

"Blow 'em out, Uncle David!" Carol and Suzanne called.

David leaned over and made a big show of blowing out the candles. A cloud arose. Everyone cheered. The kids and their uncle posed for a picture. "How about everybody!" Stan called out. They crammed in and several shots were taken, getting goofier with each following take. "Say best-seller," Stan said, and everyone smiled broadly.

Several times, David glanced at Jana and found her staring back. She was using her maiden name, so he gathered she was divorced. Is that why she'd returned to Temprance?

"I'll cut the cake," Carolyn told David. "You open the presents." That announced the festivities. Penny poured the punch, while Carolyn and Jana doled out the ice cream cake. David, with much help from the kids, opened his presents. He received a new set of the Webster's Basic Reference Collection, since his was in tatters, as well as plenty of blank diskettes, from Carolyn's crew; a new folding fishing pole along with lures, sent by his Uncle Albert; a leather basketball from the guys, and a transcriber setup and microcassette recorder from Michael, who suggested he might try dictating his next manuscript.

"Well, one present left, and it reads 'From your loving mother.' " David turned the red package over to remove the white bow. The box was about the size of a hardback book. David tore into it, and pulled out a large, silver cross and a copy of the Living Bible. The cross was beautifully engraved and crafted. "Thanks, Ma," David said, standing to hug his mother.

"It's been blessed. We need all the help we can get sometimes," she said. "And I won't always be around to offer unwanted advice." David nodded. In spite of Wright's accusations, David felt better for having been to church and talking to the Reverend Page. David wanted to ask his mother more about her checkup, but now wasn't the time.

"Hey, I found another one!" Carolyn cried. She was kneeling next to the huge china cabinet and pulling something out from underneath. She held up a blue box with gold ribbon. By the expression on everyone's face, David could tell that no one recognized it. "It must have fallen from the stack. Open it!" Carolyn handed it to him. The package was about the size of a box of earrings.

David tore the ribbon off, then the paper. Within was a purple felt jewelry box. With some trepidation, David opened it to discover a magnificent silver locket on a braided chain. "That's beautiful!" Jana crooned, her hands going to her throat. Inside the locket was a picture of Tina, a young beauty with golden hair and shining green eyes. Her smile was loving. The room was quiet and the kids were confused, looking around at everyone.

"Mommy, more cake!" Doug demanded with his plate held high over his head.

"I'd like a brandy," Stan said to David, then, "Would you like one?"

David was sorely tempted. "No, thanks, but I will take more cake," he said, and everyone appeared to relax. His mother quietly asked him where the locket had come from. "I don't know. It was Tina's. I thought I'd lost it." David put the locket in his pocket. The urge to put it on was strong, and later he did, after excusing himself to go to the bathroom.

Michael's expression was curious, while Carolyn's was pitying. Stan came out of the kitchen with coffee, a bottle of brandy, and Kahlua. Blissfully unaware, the young ones romped about and played. Carolyn was quickly caught up by their mood, as was Penny. Soon, they were all laughing and talking about the Brookens boys' visit. After listening to Michael and David's accounts, everyone was glad that David had scared away the boys; maybe it would teach them a lesson.

Next came a discussion about the kids, then the status of the ranch, and finally about David's upcoming books and ideas. Sheriff Bricker's phone call briefly interrupted them; David told him what had happened with Bob at the town's square. Bricker hadn't found any signs of blood, but he'd look into it.

The chatting continued and before they knew it, it was after midnight and now Sunday. Church services loomed in the very near future, not many hours away. Doug had fallen asleep in mid-stride, while Susan was dead to the world in Stan's arms. It was time for Carolyn's brood to head home. With a hug and a kiss, Penny prepared to go with them. Before she left, she asked, "Do you need groceries or any shopping done?"

"Not yet."

"See you tomorrow night?"

"You know I wouldn't miss a Sunday night with you," David said with a smile. She would love to hear he'd been to church. And there were questions to ask. If she didn't answer them, he'd ask Doc Katyu. They hugged again, and Penny headed out to the station wagon.

"You positive you don't want me to referee?" Jana asked.

David was thinking it would be nice to have her stay a little longer, when Matt said, "It might get ugly, real ugly. It's been a while since we played. Then there's the grudges."

"Okay, maybe some other time. Happy birthday," she said, and kissed David lightly on the cheek. "It was good to see you again. I hope it won't be twelve years until the next time."

David nodded, "It won't be, I assure you." Jana smiled, her gaze lingering before she left. Now only the basketball players remained.

"Time for some midnight madness hoop," Matt exclaimed. The foursome changed clothes, and the barn floodlights were turned on over the asphalt half-court.

"Let's kick some tail," Michael said, then smiled at David. "I hope you play better than you used to." Matt and Harry jumped out to an early lead, keeping it until Michael and David caught them at nineteen with their fourth point in a row.

"No blood, no foul," Harry proclaimed.

"Yeah, his arm's still intact," Matt agreed.

"Hey, I made the basket," Michael said. "Our ball. Here

comes the finish, boys. We are going to make it six in a row, and beat your butts." He fed the ball to David, who faked into the middle, then reversed. Harry was there, so David shot a fadeaway jumper that caught all net. "String music!" Michael cried.

"Whoa!" Matt said. "I may be slower, but I think David's gotten faster at forty." Harry nodded. Both looked tired.

"He's just playing over his head," Michael said, then, "David, just keep doing it for one more point."

"Hey, you were the superstar," David countered. "You're supposed to make the money points, like the guy in Chicago."

"I think I'm more magical," he said with a huge smile and rubbing his hair. "This is it, for all the marbles and twenty bucks," he said, as he walked to the top of the key. He dribbled, faked, then passed the ball to David. Michael followed the ball as David set a pick, planning to screen and roll. Both defenders followed Michael, so David dunked.

The three were surprised. "You could hardly do that in high school," Matt claimed.

"Not true," David defended himself. "You guys have just gotten slower, while I'm aging like a fine wine." Fermenting came to mind.

"Well, that's it. That was a lotta fun, and I'd love a shot at revenge, but I've gotta go," Harry said. "It's gonna be an early mornin'." Matt agreed.

"Twenty bucks," Michael said to them.

As they toweled off, the deal was done. "Should give most of it to the football player," Harry commented, as they walked to their cars.

"Welcome back to Temprance," David said.

"I knew there was something good waiting for me in Temprance," Matt laughed, waved, and drove off. Harry followed.

"Got enough energy for one more?" Michael asked.

"You think you can take me tonight?" David asked. "I got

the feel. I'm in the zone, as they say. Maybe its the new basketball."

Michael chuckled. "Come on halfback. To eleven."

Suddenly, David had the sensation that he was being watched again. It was unnerving, and the sense was so overwhelming, so distracting, that he quickly found himself down five-zero. "Seven is a skunk."

David concentrated and blocked Michael's next shot, took it past the free throw line, and scored on a jumper. "Rally time." He focused, blocking out the watchful sensation. With several very agile moves and one dunk, David was suddenly up six to five.

"No more," Michael stated. David drove the ball and put up a shot. "Eat this!" Michael yelled as he forcefully rejected it. The ball rolled into the woods. David trotted after it. He'd only taken a few steps into the trees, when something stepped from the shadows and scooped up the ball.

The pale woman's hair was a cascade of midnight waves, and she was stunningly beautiful, dressed in a black silk shirt with a red scarf about her neck, a black skirt with a crimson sash, lacy hose, and high heels. With a crooked, mildly amused smile and the ball in her arms, she approached David, then tossed him the ball. "I shall return tomorrow night. *Auf Wiedersehen!*" Then she turned, stepped into the shadows, and melted away as though she had never been there.

"Liselle?" David whispered.

"You lost?" Michael called to him.

"Uh, no, just planning my strategy." He had to finish with Michael quickly, so he could find out what was going on! Was it the same woman he'd seen earlier outside the church? Was it Liselle? It couldn't be! And yet there was something powerfully magnetic about the woman, just as there had been about Liselle. Her presence had immediately evoked sexual tension. And it was something more than just her beauty.

"I'm wearing you down," Michael puffed. "I can tell."

David methodically scored five points in a row with an array of moves, two jumpers, a scoop, a dunk, and a banked hook. Michael was flabbergasted. "Amazing. Are you in a hurry to get rid of me?" he asked pointedly and with a smile.

"Of course not," David lied. He was always amazed at how acutely observant his friend could be. "I was just striking, while the iron was hot."

"I've never seen you play this well."

"It's the healthy living you recommended," David joked, as they walked away from the court. He glanced over his shoulder.

Michael groaned. "You mean it's my own fault! Maybe it's the shoes," he smiled. "Well, you're certainly not the same old David." With some goodbyes and promises, plus a time set for next Saturday, Michael drove off.

As the car rounded the hilltop, David sprinted into the woods. "Liselle! Liselle! Where are you?" David listened. He noticed that the crickets had returned, and he no longer felt watched.

David looked for footprints, but found nothing. How could that be? She had been in high heels, for Christ's sake. Stubborn, David continued searching. Was he going mad now? Maybe he was hallucinating; there had been plenty of excitement, laughing, and exercise to throw him out of kilter. He wasn't used to all the attention. And Jana . . . she had grown more beautiful with age. And Tina's locket. He touched it through the fabric of his shirt. Where had this come from?

It had certainly been a very strange twenty-four or so hours, and David had a feeling things would only get stranger. The mysterious woman had said she'd return tomorrow night. He would be waiting.

Nine

Promises

"Patsy, I don't care how old he is—seventeen, six, or thirty," the man's drawl carried through Kevin's bedroom door to where he was lying, barely on the edge of awareness. Kevin could hear and understand, but he didn't open his eyes; it hurt too much. Still, it was better now, merely painful instead of the sheer, blinding agony of a few hours ago. "As long as he's livin' under our roof, he should be goin' to church," Kevin heard his stepfather, Mayor Maynard Campbell, say to his mother.

"But he isn't feeling well," his mother said. "He's had an accident."

"Probably because he was drunk," his stepfather blustered. "He needs to get a summer job. It would keep him out of trouble. And he wouldn't have his hand out, askin' for money all the time."

"Maynard," his mother's tone was defensive. "He fell off JJ's motorcycle." Good, Kevin thought, she believed him. Even if she didn't, she should protect him, as he'd protected her from Dad. His father couldn't hurt her any longer. It was just too bad she hadn't done better with her second marriage, but then, Maynard didn't beat her to within an inch of death.

"Should we call Doc Katyu or take him to Athens Hospital?" Kevin was amused. His stepfather actually sounded concerned. That effect must have been for his mother, Patsy, because it certainly wasn't for him.

Maynard Campbell, barrel-bellied mayor of Temprance, Texas, didn't give a dime for his stepson—didn't give a cent of concern or a dollar of care. Kevin could tell. He could read people, judge them, and almost instantly know what they would do and why. He knew Mayor Campbell's type; votes and control were important to him. The family was just a showpiece, something to help him reach voters.

"I don't think so. He's just badly bruised all over. Nothing seemed broken. I was going to let him sleep another day, and see how he is tomorrow morning."

"He might have a concussion," his stepfather said. Kevin thought he was starting to lay it on a little thick, but then it might be hard to turn off once started.

"Maynard, just let him rest, okay? Come on. We're going to be late for church ourselves."

Kevin heard shuffling, then the front door closed. Shortly, he heard the sound of a car starting, then it drove off. Good! He was alone.

Kevin still wasn't sure how he'd managed to crawl to his pickup, while Lou went to check on his lady—the BITCH!—and call the police. But he'd been able to get the door open and drive off, even made it home to the mayor's mansion. In the process, he'd bled from his mouth, ears, and nose, all over the upholstery of his beloved pickup.

At least that was over with, Kevin thought. He still ached all over and throbbed with varied pulses of pain, but the bleeding had stopped, as had the vomiting. Mom's painkillers had helped some, but he still tasted bile—the taste of hate.

Oh no, his body was beginning to awaken! Please no! Kevin tried to relax. Physically, he was in terrible shape, but his mind was sharp, better than ever. There'd been another white event during the beating—a flash of light and a step higher toward brilliance—to genius! Kevin now realized and understood things which had never been clear before. "You're smarter than ever, Kevy," said the voice, and Kevin knew it was true. Since being kicked by the horse, he'd had a slight buzzing in his ears—static in his head—but now it was gone, and the voice was very clear. "Give it time, you'll heal." Kevin knew that was true, but it was taking too long, much too long.

Kevin rolled over and groaned. Arrr . . . Despite the medication, he still hurt so bad that each time he moved, he cramped, and white hot knives sliced into him.

"Oh no!" Kevin whispered, and his eyes snapped open. Even so, Kevin could see Lou punch him in the face, kick him in the balls, then hammer him again and again. Down and on the ground, he was being kicked over and over, his body threatening to rupture. As though he were being beaten again, the intensity of the pain returned to shake Kevin.

He closed his eyes. Lou would pay. He . . . Kevin Grimm WOULD MAKE HIM PAY! "We'll make him pay, Kevy," he heard the voice say.

"Yes, yes, they'll . . . pay," Kevin managed through clenched teeth. The pain heightened. "Oh no!" Kevin cried. His father, a huge, bony man with mallets for fists, had joined Lou, and they were both hammering him.

Mercifully, Kevin passed out.

"Don't git even, Kevy, git ahead," Kevin heard, as he awakened. "We'll pay back Lou and Becky, and even that author-guy, David Matthewson, just like we repaid your dear ole dad. I've been thinkin'. Next time we go back to Matthewson's during the day. He won't bother us then. And I wonder what we'll find?"

Although it hurt, Kevin laughed and laughed. He would get the last laugh, no matter what it took. No matter what!

Ten

Strange Ties

"Well, that just about finishes today's checkup," Doc Katyu said to David. Despite over thirty years in America, the frail-looking Dr. Nails Katyu spoke with a clipped accent held over from his native India. The doctor was in his early seventies, brown-skinned, and balding. He wore old-fashioned, dark-rimmed glasses with big lenses. As always, his expression was placid, and his manner reserved, giving the impression that he'd seen it all. But he never looked bored or disinterested.

"Just about?" David asked. He was sitting on the living room couch, staring out the window into the night. Was Liselle out there? She did say tonight. "What's left?"

"A blood sample," Doc Katyu said. "We haven't done one in almost a month. Roll up your sleeve."

The phone rang. Saved by the bell, David thought. He got off the couch and answered the phone. "Hello. Oh hi, Mom. No, Doc Katyu is still here, putting me through medical gymnastics. Did the same to you, too, did he?" David laughed softly and smiled at Dr. Katyu. "Yes, I was still planning on coming over tonight. You know I wouldn't miss—What? They are? Then maybe I shouldn't come over tonight. Okay. I'll call you soon. 'Bye." David hung up. "The kids have the flu."

"The afflictions of the young are many," the doctor said.

"As are those of the old," David added. "Speaking of which. I forgot to ask my mother about her physical. How is she?"

"I'll have the test results later this week."

"Which means?"

Doc Katyu didn't think it necessary to needlessly worry David. "She looks fine. I'll let *you* know when *I* know. Now, the blood sample. Don't worry. I'm not concerned. You're doing well. Just stay away from drinking. That's self-destructive behavior." He reached inside his black leather satchel, which looked several decades old, and pulled out a large syringe.

"Right." David was edgy.

"I'm just a cautious old man. I want to make sure you stay on the path to recovery," Doc Katyu told him. "We need to constantly stay abreast of your heme, as well as porphyrin levels, in case we need to perform a phlebotomy. Is that all right with you? I know you've tried to become somewhat of an expert on porphyria."

"Let's get on with it," David said reluctantly. "I'm just tired of being poked and prodded."

"I can understand that. I'll try to make it gentle," the doctor smiled. "I must say, the change in the last six weeks has been dramatic. You no longer shave twice a day?" David shook his head. The doctor felt along his face and neck, then checked his hands. "And the lumps are gone! Totally vanished. That is wonderful. Be thankful." He inserted the needle. "There, that doesn't hurt, does it?"

David shook his head, but his teeth were still clenched. He forced himself to relax, but he was having trouble—Liselle had said tonight! Just the thought of seeing her made his breath quicken and his mind reel. She was mysterious and beautiful. But why was she here? Where had she been? How had she found him? Too many things were happening to David after years of seclusion; he was beginning to feel out of balance—sensory overload. He preferred his privacy to all the commotion.

"That's it." Doc Katyu removed the needle and capped the blood-filled syringe, then he dabbed David's arm with a cotton swab. "I'll call you about the results in a week or so. Call before then, if your status begins to change or you don't feel well."

"I promise." His attention went back outside.

"David, is anything wrong? You seem a bit preoccupied."

"I probably am. I've had a lot of visitors, because of the recent success of my novel. And I celebrated my fortieth birthday last night."

"Well, the way things look," Doc Katyu said with unusual humor in his voice, "you're probably at the halfway mark, and that's not what they mean by middle-aged. David, in many ways your health is better than before you returned from Europe. Have you tried exposing yourself to any sunlight lately?"

"Yes. Friday morning. It was going wonderfully," David began, his gaze faraway as he remembered, then he frowned bitterly, "until the sun peeked over the horizon. After that I felt feverish and weak. I had to crawl into the house," he understated.

"But you look fine. No blistering," Doc Katyu said. He didn't appear concerned. "That is still an improvement. Diffuse light is progress. Before, any type of sunlight made you ill," he reminded David, who nodded. "Well, I should be going." Dr. Katyu began packing, putting his stethoscope in his bag.

"Thanks for coming out, as usual," David said.

"I've been your family's doctor for a long, long time. I hate to admit how long. And one of the reasons I enjoy practicing in Temprance, is that I can still make house calls. I get tired of staying in the office all the time. It's nice to get out, drive, and think, as well as help people. This way I avoid all the pharmaceutical sales people who drop by." He laughed. "What a business. Besides, if you're going to be a celebrity, I need to get adjusted to your reclusiveness, irrational demands, and of course, to charging higher fees." His smile broadened. "I'll be a celebrity doctor then."

"I don't think writers get that kind of celebrity," David said with a laugh. He walked the good doctor to his car.

Doc Katyu was glad to hear the levity in David's voice. While he might be somewhat distracted, he appeared to be full of vim and vigor. They said their good nights, and Doc Katyu got into his red Jeep Comanche.

David watched him drive off, cresting the hill, then disappearing. He listened carefully, searching for any sign of Liselle. Could he really have felt her presence? That was absurd. Still, David couldn't help hoping, and concentrated, looking for Liselle. Then the phone rang. He was beginning to get very irritated by all the interruptions.

He'd almost decided to let the answering machine do its job, when he turned and jogged inside. David picked up the receiver just as the message began to play. He hit the stop button, and said, "Hello. Oh hi, Jana! This is a pleasant surprise! No, this is morning for me. Not really. Doc Katyu came out here to poke and prod."

Suddenly, as though she had reached out and touched him, David knew that Liselle was here! He didn't know how or why, just that she was there. There was an electricity in the night, where it was usually calm. David glanced around quickly, almost expecting to find her in the room with him, but she wasn't. His gaze was drawn to the open door. It was darker outside than the bottom of a well, and he couldn't see as he should, reminding him of Friday night.

"What? Dinner? Why no, I haven't had breakfast." He was having trouble paying attention to Jana.

The sensation of a presence grew stronger, powerful now, demanding his attention. David was both uneasy and excited, his heart pounding as though he were a teenager going out on his first big date. He took several deep breaths, but it didn't help. David licked his lips and wiped his sweaty palms on his pants. "That sounds great . . ."

Outside the front door, the mist suddenly appeared low, thickened, and then rose majestically skyward. The roiling tendrils moved toward the house, as they blotted out the entire front yard. He heard the gate quietly swing open. Liselle was here!

". . . But I have company." David managed to pull his gaze away from the window, but it kept wanting to continue searching for Liselle, flicking back and forth. "In fact they're just arriving. Could we try again?" His heart threatened to burst free, and he felt as though someone were grabbing his head, forcing him to look out the door. He fought it and said, "I'll call you tomorrow. Good. And, Jana, thanks for calling. It's nice to have you back in town. You, too. 'Bye."

As David hung up, he forgot about Jana and stared out the screen door. A darkness formed within the mists, then grew larger, taking on shape and color, and then transformed into a figure. Clad in a long, red dress with a sheer, black cape, Liselle strolled gracefully from the fog. Each movement was smooth with feline grace.

David saw her as though for the first time. Her long, curly mane was midnight black and glistening, wild and free, as though puffed by a wind where there was none. Her face was finely sculptured with a pert, upturned nose. Her almost almond-shaped eyes were dark and fathomless orbs. Blush slightly colored her angular cheekbones, and her features bespoke a European birth. It was impossible to describe her as anything less than ravishing; many men might say she was worth dying for.

David went to the front door and waited. With a perfect smile on her red lips, she stopped and put a hand on her hip, striking a pose. She was much shorter than he, shorter than David remembered. "Good evening again, David."

"Hello, I feel underdressed . . ." he began.

"Isn't dis a formal occasion?" she smiled.

David smiled and shook his head. "What makes you say so?"

"It is our first time together, really together."

He'd been wrong; it wasn't Liselle. She just reminded him of her. David was disappointed, but then, how good was a memory from a befuddled mind, especially since he'd only known Liselle for three nights, and had been intoxicated the entire time. "So true. And your name is?"

"I am Monique. I saw an interview wid you on television—'Tales of Texas' I believe it was—and just had to meet you. To be taped, seen on television, is fascinating, miraculous." Her gaze became suddenly direct and bold. "We are two of a kind, kin in a way, are we not?" She wetted her lips.

"We're related?" David was enthralled and confused. Just being with her was mind-numbing. It was hard to breathe calmly, and there was a hammering in his ears. Or was his head spinning? It was more than her beauty, but he couldn't define it beyond charisma—an aura about her.

"Blood relatives of a kind," she said coyly, slowly looking away, then glancing back.

"Would you like to come inside?" David asked, before he knew what he was doing. "Have something to drink?" David murmured. He needed time to sort this out. What did she want? Did he care?

"You are gracious. I am thirsty. It was a long trip from Narlins." David held the door open, and Monique stepped inside, turning off the light. Dim illumination still came from the kitchen. She looked about with a slightly amused expression. It was obviously not the opulence that normally surrounded her.

"Humble but home. No housemaid, and I'd rather write

than clean," David said. "Are you originally from New Orleans?"

"No, I am originally from Austria, New York, and then Chicago. My sister and I immigrated together." She was glowing the same as he, but not nearly as bright. Her complexion was creamy, and she wasn't dressed in white.

"Are you also stricken?"

Monique stretched, revealing and heightening all her curves and tightening her dress against her breasts. "I wouldn't call it stricken, but neither could I call it blessed. I have learned to live with *mein Geschick*—pardon me, my fate."

David was still confused, feeling as though he were running around in circles chasing his tail. "How long have you had it?"

Monique looked amused, and managed not to ungraciously laugh. "I've had it for about sixty-five years." She sat in a chair and crossed her legs, her dress sliding upward to expose shapely calves.

David was wondering if they'd be silky smooth to the touch, then realized what she'd said, "Sixty-five years!" He didn't understand and could only stammer stupidly, "You don't look a day over twenty-five."

"Twenty-seven, *danke*." She actually blushed. "Sixty-five is not long, though."

"I'm confused. No, I'm delirious." It's another attack, he thought. It had to be! David closed his eyes and put his head in his hands. This made absolutely no sense.

"Dere are others much older dan I, but some adapt to the endless parade of years better dan others. Some of us enjoy traveling. I do. It is a way to manage time. How old are you?"

"Forty. Yesterday." Although now he felt younger, brimming with lust.

"And you don't look a day over thirty. I see dat you are still adapting. Don't worry, you will mentally adjust as your body completes the final transformation. Yours is oddly late. Very much so, *ja.*"

"Final transformation?"

"It will all be clear soon," she smiled.

David didn't think so. How could anybody have such an effect on him and babble so, talk such . . . nonsense? "A drink?" David asked, as he headed into the kitchen. His mind was reeling, and he felt totally separated from reality, as though he had been drugged.

"Cognac?"

"Remy?" he asked.

"VSOP?"

"On the way." Relieved to be focused on something else—something simple—David opened the liquor cabinet and removed a bottle of 1800, then Remy. He did a hefty shot of the tequila, which left his eyes and throat burning. Now, why did he do that? Old, bad, weak habit, that's why. It would only make matters worse—if this was an attack of porphyria. He poured the golden cognac in a snifter and took it to her. "To your health."

"And yours. To endless health. Did it help?"

"Probably not. We'll see. Can I ask you some questions?"

"You may." She sipped her cognac, but her gaze never left David. It was almost as though she were peering into his soul, dipping into his being.

"You currently live in New Orleans?" he asked. Monique nodded. "Where were you born?"

"A small town in the Alps dat no longer exists. An avalanche destroyed it. I've lived in many places since, including Chicago, where I was . . . stricken." She smiled secretively. Again David's pulse rate jumped. "Can you believe I was once a tanz . . . a flapper. And I wanted to be on the silver screen, but dat is impossible. I don't know how you did it! Being seen on television! You must tell me! I must know!"

That almost threw David off track, but he forged forward.

125

He had to stay focused on his line of questioning. "When was the village destroyed?"

"Around World War Two."

"Um, Monique, that makes no . . . uh . . . I'm really uh . . . confused." David started to pace, and avoided looking at her so he could think straight. It didn't help much. "Are you telling me that porphyria increases our longevity, because we aren't exposed to the sun or something?"

"Porphyria? Ah, dat's a blood disease, is it not?" She rolled the cognac around in the snifter, then breathed deeply.

"You don't have porphyria?" he asked.

Monique shook her head no. "Shame the game you play. As soon as I viewed you on television, I saw dat our natures are one. Dere are telltale signs. But how were dey able to film you, is what truly astounds me. I can't be photographed or taped, and neither can the others I know," she sighed. "Intrigued, I came to visit, to find you and ask you questions. I love a good mystery. Dere are so few left."

Again, David was off balance. "How did you find me?"

"The book jacket of *Witch Hunt* said you lived in East Texas, so I drove this direction. After a time, I was able to sense you. We of similar natures are linked. Find and follow that link, and you will find what you seek, as I found you. The stronger the feeling, the closer the proximity. It is simple."

David remembered sensing the presence Friday. "Was that this Friday?" David asked. Monique nodded.

"David, what is your secret? Can you stand the sun's light?" Her voice was low and husky, her eyes fired by inner bellows.

"I don't have any secrets," David managed. Under her gaze he felt as though he were a flame twisting in a slow dance. He had to look away. "And no, I can't stand the sunlight. I begin to blister and grow nauseous. It's debilitating. And depressing."

"How strange."

David took a drink. "No, it's typical for people like me Monique, who are you?"

"An admirer. Someone who wants to get to know you. Be with you. Over the years, variety helps one enjoy the longevity." She licked a fingertip, then ran it along the rim of her glass. David didn't know what to say. "Do you want to live alone for eternity?"

"No. Eternity? I—"

"Even wid writing books, dat would be a lonely existence. We could travel together. Experience so much together, you and I."

Bold and beautiful, David thought. And he wanted to go with her, just drop everything and go. What kind of gorgeous nut was visiting him? David put his face in his hands. Was this some cruel joke? And why did she remind him of Liselle? Why?

"David, have you ever drunk human blood?" she asked sweetly, as though she were talking about a type of dessert.

"WHAT?" David exclaimed. He couldn't think of anything else to say, any other response. She was beautiful, but she was also a looney. Lord, he hoped she wasn't dangerous, caught up in some kind of weird fatal attraction. Not long ago, he'd been surprised to receive a huge packet of fan mail from the publisher. He hoped she wasn't kin to the deranged woman out of King's *Misery*.

David took a deep breath. He wanted her out of here, now! He'd moved toward her, then away. He also wanted her to stay, to take her in his arms, to taste her lips, and rip off . . . David fought with himself, but finally managed, "Would you please leave? I'm not feeling well."

"Odd, I usually have the opposite effect on men," she sounded insulted, then she chuckled throatily. "Dere is much for you to learn. Much you must learn, and wid my help, you will." Monique's stare grew intense, penetrating. As though lightly slapped, David felt it. "It is inevitable. I see you wish to contest me. Maybe it is because the transformation isn't complete, but it won't be long. Den you will be mine, and I will teach you, maybe unwillingly at first, then very willingly. I love strong-willed men, but you can't resist your true nature. You can't resist me." She smiled.

"What true nature?"

"You do not know?" She stared at him, dissecting him. "Ah, now I see. If someone had told me, I wouldn't have believed it. You really don't know. How amusing." David did not find it funny. "As you've guessed, I can read you, as you should be able to read me. Can you sense me?"

"Uh . . ." He didn't know how. Or why. "Yes. Now will you go?" David moved to the door.

"Don't you want me?" She stood, hands on hips, striking a pouting pose.

"Just go."

"I do love a challenge," she chuckled. "You don't know why you can sense me, do you?"

"Just go." David had his head in his hands. He needed a drink.

"Soon. When did you get sick?"

"A little over ten years ago. I was in Badgastein, Austria." He found he couldn't resist her questions. The words jumped out before he could stop them.

"What were you doing?"

"Traveling, drinking, and trying to forget."

"Tina?"

His attention snapped to her, his stare hot. "How did you know?"

"As I said. I can read you. Was dere anyone unusual in Badgastein?"

"Liselle."

"Of course," Monique smiled. "I remind you of her, no?"

"Yes." Suddenly, he wanted to run, but couldn't. He was morbidly enthralled. Only by thinking of Tina could he stay away. She was long dead, but their love was stronger than death. Sometimes he swore she was still in the house.

"You remember the delights?" Monique asked. David looked away. "Dat will be as nothing in comparison to us. Dis is going to be fun. I've never met anyone who didn't know dey were—about deir true nature. How marvelously challenging. Dis will be fun, indeed."

"Must I throw you out? I'd like to think I'm a gentleman and would prefer not to."

"You could not. Can't you feel it? The attraction between us? Don't you want me?" she asked again. Her gaze still called to him, demanding that he take her in his arms.

David could feel the attraction, almost an obsession. He twisted the words on his lips. "No," he lied. TINA! Lord help me! What is going on? Monique was so beautiful, she scared the hell out of him.

She laughed and said, "I don't want to cause too much undue trauma for my future lover." With two quick steps, she bridged the distance between them and kissed him.

David felt electrified, hot and chilled all at the same time. It was all he could do to stand rigid and not clutch her in his arms. But why not? Because of Tina! Tina. He felt her locket heavy upon his chest, next to his copper crucifix. The cross burned, but he barely felt it.

Monique's lips were succulent—a heady nectar—her tongue a darting snake. Drawn and yet disgusted at the same time, David could feel himself slipping away, giving into her demanding kiss. Finally and ever so slowly, she pulled away, and for a moment, David followed her. Then their lips parted. No other part of them had touched, and yet David was flushed and shaking, trembling with pent-up desire.

"See, dat wasn't so bad," Monique smiled devilishly. "And dere will be more. And it will be better. We shall do dings dat you've never dreamed of. *Auf Wiedersehen.*" She turned and left, disappearing in the fog the same way she'd arrived, dramatically and mysteriously.

David was still staring after she was long gone. Finally, he crumpled to the floor and cried, his bottled emotions pouring out freely.

Part Two:
The Hunt

One

Home Brew

Corey Stones sat on a fallen tree and stared through the gnarled mesquites at the MX Ranch. It was only an hour or so after daybreak, but Stones was in pursuit of a story—or the makings of one. He'd come to the spread just after daybreak, hoping Matthewson would be asleep.

In order to blend in with his surroundings, Stones was dressed in brown pants and an olive-colored shirt. As was often the case, he had slept in his now creased and wrinkled clothing. His eyelids periodically drooped, as did his chin, which slowly sank until he jerked awake. Adding to the unkempt look, his thin beard revealed that he hadn't shaved in a while.

The conversation in the barbershop had tweaked Stones's reporter's instinct, awakening it from a long slumber. He could tell by the boys' expressions and their voices that something unusual had happened here at the ranch, but they hadn't told the entire story. He intended to discover the truth. And even if it didn't supply what he needed, it might provide him with enough background to create a story.

A good news story didn't always just happen. Sometimes it needed the touch of a novelist—which Stones knew he could be, if he ever decided to go the purely fictional route—someone who could accentuate certain elements to create something special, magically crafting a best-seller through visualization, perspective, and imagination. The powerful ambiguity of the written word added to the mix. People wanted exciting stories, not just blasé news, which is why human interest stories were always back-page items.

Stones gulped coffee from a Thermos until his vision cleared; he felt his eyelids lighten, and his head buzz. He resisted the urge to smoke, afraid it might give him away. After all, he was covertly investigating the place. Stones pulled his binoculars, camera, and telephoto lens from his duffle bag, and assembled the equipment. He was ready. Now who'd believe that he had actually been a Boy Scout? At least until he'd sold a story to the newspaper about the den leader's promiscuity.

Stones removed his binoculars from their case and scanned the grounds. At first pass, the Matthewson Ranch appeared typical of all small family ranches, except it was too peaceful for the early hours, when hustle and bustle should be prevalent. The barn was shut tight, as was the house with its shutters drawn.

The barn's uneven, beige coloring stood starkly against the green pasture stretching toward the lake. Stones noted the small number of livestock in the pasture, mostly cattle. There were a few goats, and several horses ran wild. Near a large garden, numerous chickens wandered around hunting and pecking between the house and the barn. There were pigs in a muddy pen on the far side.

The house was nondescript and didn't like look much of a place for anything interesting to happen, but that's the way it was with real news. Unlike the plots of television shows and movies, interesting things happened in dull places, not always in zoos, amusement parks, theatres, or planetariums. The MX ranch appeared as dull as it could get, peaceful and isolated in the country, with its own pond and lakefront acreage. Not bad at all, Stones thought. Journalism should be so lucrative.

There was certainly nothing going on now, which didn't surprise him. It was what he wanted. Stones always preferred to scout a place during the daytime before returning at night, especially since Matthewson came out after dark, as if he were some kind of nocturnal beast. Stones laughed, deciding to wait a while and then poke around. With his binoculars he spotted the tractor and bushhog, recognizing them from the boys' story. Stones wondered if he would find footprints near there, and reminded himself to check the ditch where the stereo and projector had been set. Bubba Ross had been very helpful indeed. A little cash was a powerful salve for what ailed a poor deputy sheriff in training. A man had to eat, and Ross ate a lot. Whether a big city or a small town, some things were not all that different.

Stones's attention was still on the tractor, when he noticed something move in the woods behind it. The figure's movements appeared hesitant. Finally, the figure quickly stepped out of the shadows and crouched behind the tractor. Stones didn't get a good look at the man, but put down his binoculars and readied his camera. Showtime, he thought as he focused.

Stones waited and waited. Had the man fallen asleep? Or was he just waiting, too? Damn, the big lens got heavy. Stones used the fallen tree as a makeshift tripod.

Finally, the man stood, skirted along the edge of the woods, and made his way around to the rear of the barn. Stones didn't know who the tall boy might be, but he followed the pale stranger, taking pictures all the same. Maybe the kid would do some dirty work for Stones. He could ask him about it later. Money talked, the truth walked.

"So these three Polacks are out hunting," Kevin Grimm whispered to himself, as he snuck through the woods. He moved as though he were stalking, darting from tree to tree, waiting, then moving again without rhythm or pattern. Beyond two sets of trees, he saw the tractor and bushhog. "And they come across some tracks. First one kneels and looks at the tracks. 'Looks like bear tracks,' he says."

Grimm had parked his pickup farther down the road and off Matthewson's property, then he'd hiked in. Cautious, he had waited until the sun had been in the sky a good thirty minutes, figuring that the writer-dude would be in a dark place by then, not outside where Grimm would be roaming. There was no telling what he might find. "Maybe somethin' of use, Kevy."

"Yeah. So, the second one gets down on all fours and seriously eyeballs the tracks. 'Nope, gotta be deer tracks,' he says." Kevin paused behind the tractor and adjusted his fanny pack. It was black and read "Head," and contained the things he needed for breaking and entering. Grimm wanted inside the barn, figuring that Matthewson kept his liquor there.

Grimm waited impatiently and watched for any signs of life. Unlike Friday night, all the livestock and animals were out and about, and all the shutters on the house were closed. "Looks clear, Kevy."

Grimm sighed and continued, "And before the third one could say anything, a train hit them all." He chuckled and continued, "Two Aggies are out huntin'. They come across a pond, where a beautiful woman is skinny dippin'."

Grimm moved low, stalking through the tall grass and heading for the barn. "They look 'er up and down, then look at each other and smile real wide-like. The tall one says, 'Ma'am, are you game?' 'Hot to trot,' she says. The Aggies are confused, so she finally says, 'Yes, I'm game.' So the short Aggie shoots her!"

Grimm climbed over the fence and entered the barnyard on the far side, so that he was hidden from the house. "Mushroom enters a bar, sits down at the counter, and says, 'Bartender, I'll have a Colorado Bulldog,' " Kevin mumbled as he walked to the door. "Quiet!" he whispered to a pig that snorted at him, throwing up mud from the pen, then rolling over.

Satisfied, Grimm leaned against the door and listened. Good, it was quiet. If necessary, he could enter the barn through the pig's pen. Grimm reached into his boot and removed a switchblade, then put on gloves.

"Ready, Kevy." Grimm tried the door, found that it opened easily, then walked inside. Light filtered in through the dirty windows and highlighted the airborne dust and hay. The nearest side of the barn was used to store equipment: an ATV, a flatbed trailer, and an old rusted plow. Along the wall hung an axe, hoe, several rakes, ropes, and a scythe among other tools. Behind a low wall where salt blocks were stacked, were sacks of feed. Grimm quietly checked a set of cabinets full of bottles, cans, and other containers but didn't find any booze, so he kept hunting.

The other half of the barn held stables and shelves stocked with related equipment for riding, milking, and even shearing. There was hair and hay, as well as some droppings in the apparently empty stalls. "Smells great. Less filling."

Grimm eased his way along, peeking around posts and into stalls. He surprised one rooster searching for feed, then laughing, moved to the next. "Whoa!" he gasped, and yanked his head back as a chestnut stallion snapped at him. Grimm was going to slap it, when it bared its teeth. Thinking better of it, he said, "Eat shit and die, glue glands."

Grimm sighed, and continued his lifelong joke-a-thon. "Anyway, bartender says, 'I can't serve you, you're a mushroom.' " There had to be a liquor cabinet somewhere, and it wouldn't be in a stall. " 'But I'm a fungi,' the shroom retorted."

There! By the ladder to the hayloft, Grimm found a double-locked door. That had to be it! Nothing else had been locked, let alone twice. "Rope walks into the same bar and orders a drink."

Grimm reached inside his pack and pulled out a wire, then he began probing the lock. "Bartender says, 'I can't serve you, you're a rope.' " He'd hate to have to unscrew all the screws that held the locks, but that'd work. He had plenty of time.

"Dejected, the rope leaves and sits on the sidewalk. He has an idea and takes out his pocketknife and starts cutting the top of his head, then ties it, and continues to fray the end. Soon he walks back into the bar. Bartender says, 'You again, I told you I can't serve a rope.' The rope says, 'I'm a frayed knot.' " Grimm laughed at himself. "What's the difference between a kinky person and a pervert? The pervert uses the whole chicken, instead of just the feathers! Did ya hear how the Polish National Hockey Team drowned? Spring training."

"Finally," Grimm said as the lock clicked. He opened it, then suddenly shivered. He wasn't alone! He could feel it! What was that scraping noise!? Grimm waited, placing his back against the door. *Snikt!* His blade opened, ready to slash and jive.

For several minutes Grimm waited quietly, holding back the torrent of jokes and listening to his breathing and the slight wind, as it came through the barn. He didn't hear anything threatening, but felt something there, watching. More minutes passed and nothing stirred. It must be my imagination, Grimm concluded.

His patience finally exhausted, he wanted to know what was inside. Grimm pulled the door open. "The Price is Right!" In the dim light, he could see a refrigerator surrounded by cases of Jack Daniels, Wild Turkey, Tia Maria, and Jaegermeister. There was also some kind of medicine cabinet/first aid kit on the wall, above a few smaller, unlabeled boxes. Atop the stack was a very old-looking and faded, leather-bound book. The room was stuffy and had an unusual fragrance to it. Grimm pulled open the refrigerator. The light came on to reveal a compartment crammed full of squarish green bottles and fluted brown liters with big, rounded bases. None were labeled.

Grimm reached inside and pulled out a green bottle. The liquid inside was dark and viscous, reminding him of oil. He could read the raised letters on the side of the bottle. It was what hunters drank to stay warm! He opened the bottle and took a swig.

The liquid was thick and heavily spiced with an unusual flavor, almost a metallic tinge. Home brew! Grimm wiped his mouth with the back of his hand. "Ah." It wasn't what he expected, but it was tasty. He took another drink. It was revitalizing! Take home a six-pack today.

"Possession is nine-tenths of the law." Grimm grabbed another bottle and pulled a black plastic sack from his pack. He put two fresh bottles in the sack and then added three bottles of Jack. "What else?"

Grimm checked the boxes. There were all sorts of roots, flowers, and herbs, some dried and some fresh. He flipped through the book and found recipes—or something similar—which didn't interest him. "Pretty strange." Matthewson probably added stuff to the booze, which is why it didn't taste like regular Jag! Grimm started to leave, then took a fourth bottle of JD. He liked Jack. His grandaddy would drink nothing else—"Nothing but the best, and that's JD."

Smiling, Grimm closed the refrigerator and backed out of the storage closet. "Ahhhhh!" he screamed, as something landed atop him, then clawed its way down his back, ripping and tearing both clothing and flesh.

Panicked, Grimm whirled around, swinging. The claws dug deeper. But there was nothing there! It bit him and panic drove Grimm wild. It was still on his back!

Grimm slammed against the wall and crushed something. Claws dug deeper, and he screamed. Desperate, Grimm stepped forward and then hurled himself back against the wall even harder. Its grip weakened. Stepping away and whirling, Grimm sent the cat flying. There was a brief wail that ended with a snap as it struck the wall, then the black cat fell to the floor. "Holy shit!" he breathed. For good measure, he kicked the cat. It didn't move. It was as dead as a doornail.

Grimm relocked the closet door, grabbed the cat by its tail, and left the barn the way he had entered. He'd found what he'd come for, and it would keep him occupied for a while. He needed to give JJ and Jim Bob a call. Party time. He felt so good, that it was time to get real crazy.

Grimm stepped outside, then walked to the corner of the building. He dropped the cat, then tipped his hat to the writer-dude's place. The booze and killing of the cat almost paid the debt of scaring the crap out of him. But then, it might take one more visit to totally clear the bill.

Two

Porphyria

Corey Stones was trying to be patient, but it wasn't one of his virtues—if he had any. He hated the doctor's office for a variety of reasons, but primarily because he couldn't smoke. And he always did better interviews when he was relaxed. He was fidgety, sometimes sitting on the examining table and sometimes in the chair. Most of the time he was walking around reading the posters, articles, or diagrams posted on the walls, pertaining to health topics such as pregnancy, high blood pressure, safe sex, as well as charts on the back, the foot, and the intestines.

They had just been getting to know each other when Dr. Katyu was called away. That was over thirty minutes ago. Who did house calls anymore? Stones wasn't sick, just impatient. And not-smoking didn't help. All he wanted was information. Scheduling a physical was just the way to open the door and start a dialogue!

Stones couldn't help but wonder about the doctor's skills. The waiting room had been empty of bawling kids or wheezing geriatrics. There hadn't been any wait to see the doctor at all. That never happened in Houston, where you usually had to cool your heels at least a week to see your doctor, and a day to see an emergency room physician.

Could the lack of business be because Katyu was a nationalized American, a native of India? That didn't seem right. Everything he'd heard about the doctor from the town's people was good. Still, people often talked from both sides of their mouth; prejudice was a long way from dead, as he well knew.

Finally, the door opened, and Doctor Katyu entered. "I am sorry; it was a minor emergency." The reporter thought he saw a hint of a smile below a thin mustache. The doctor's dazzling white jacket contrasted with his dark complexion, and his glasses were on top of his head, as though he'd forgotten about them. "You know small towns. All the excitement and adventure."

"How right you are, Doc. In fact, a stress test is probably just what I need right now," Stones responded dryly. "In truth though, I need some medical information to do a story."

"On doing physicals, or the necessity and wisdom of having one done every so often?" The doctor might have been hiding amusement, Stones wasn't sure.

"No, I don't need a physical," Stones said, and Katyu's eyebrows jumped, but he said nothing, "and the story isn't about physicals."

"Are you sure you do not desire a full physical? The *Times* has good coverage. If you did a health article discussing the benefits of an annual checkup, I would give you one for free."

Stones smiled. "Naw, Doc. You'd just tell me the same thing as every other doctor: quit smoking."

"It is nice to know we agree on that diagnosis."

"What I need is information on a rare disease," Stones told him, then asked, "What's porphyria? I read up on it at the Athens Library, and didn't find much. All I know is that it's a blood disease."

"I am not surprised," the doctor said, pursing his lips. His expression was contemplative, as he asked, "Why are you interested in such an obscure disease?"

"As you can guess—because I can tell you're a sharp man, Doc—it pertains to David Matthewson. He's somewhat of a celebrity, and it's always interesting for the public to read a story about how someone overcame adversity to become successful," he lied with a smile. Practice made perfect. He reached into his coat pocket for his pack of cigarettes, then remembered that no smoking was allowed.

"The doctor-patient relationship is confidential. I cannot tell you anything about him without his consent. And since he is a very private man, I doubt he would give permission. Please come back when I can be of help with your health, not your welfare." Doctor Katyu moved toward the door as though to leave.

Stones rolled his eyes. He'd heard this song and dance before. Where there was a will, there was a way. If there wasn't a will, there was cash. But this time he'd need brainpower, not greenback power, besides, he couldn't afford to pay; doctors were expensive. "Surely you can tell me about porphyria in general though? I'd hate to write an article full of misinformation, and I will write an article. It's important news and good publicity. Not that much goes on around here that's newsworthy, but we do have a hometown, best-selling author."

Dr. Katyu stared at him, then finally said, "All right. I would hate for you to publish a hastily investigated story about the disease. That happens too often, and usually it just serves to needlessly scare people. I can give you some pages out of a medical journal."

"I'd rather get it straight from you—an expert."

"I am hardly such," Dr. Katyu sighed. "I will begin by telling you that it is rarely fatal, unless severe at childbirth. And it isn't contagious."

"Not communicable, huh? Great. Can we start from the top? I have several questions." Stones reached inside his jacket pocket and took out a minicassette recorder. Katyu's expression tightened. "Exactly, what is porphyria?"

"It is a disorder associated with an inherited or acquired disturbance in the heme biosynthesis. Porphyrins are tertrpyroole pigments that—"

"Uh, Doc, in layman's terms. Please. You sound like you're reading from a medical text."

Dr. Katyu's smile was one of infinite patience, tinged with amusement. "As I said, it is a disease that can be acquired or is congenital—" Stones's expression was pained. "Inborn," Dr. Katyu explained. "Such a person has problems with the biochemical machinery responsible for producing a particular iron-based protein called heme. Heme biosynthesis is essential to life. It can originate in the liver or bones, where red blood cells are produced. Heme is used most frequently in the production of hemoglobin, which is a blood component responsible for carrying oxygen as well as carbon dioxide to and from cells. So, porphyria is a breakdown, a malfunction, of the process which creates heme."

"Then it's a type of iron poisoning?"

"Certainly not. Heme is not iron, but a ferrous iron complex of protoporphyrin IX, and functions as a prosthetic group for hemoproteins such as hemoglobin."

"Doc!" Now Stones could tell that the small man was having fun with him. "So it's more than iron poisoning?"

"That is what I said. Iron is put into the heme afterwards. Low blood and low hemoglobin are the same, which is also anemia. Among other things, it can cause fatigue and dizziness, because the muscles fail to get enough oxygen. There are several steps in the development of heme, and whenever one of these breaks down, it creates a different type of porphyria. There are two basic types."

"What are the symptoms?"

"Both manifest very similarly. Clinical symptoms are neurological problems as well as cutaneous—or skin problems."

"And which type does David Matthewson have?" Stones asked. Dr. Katyu frowned. "Okay, okay. You said there were neurological problems?"

"Yes. Neurologic manifestations vary. They can manifest as abdominal pains, peripheral neuropathy, or mental disturbances. More often though, there is disorder of the motor action, hypesthesia and paresthesia—foot and hand drop."

"Then there could be mental imbalance?"

"It's remotely possible, though doubtful. Somebody with porphyria might be mentally disturbed or have an emotional outburst. There also might be restlessness, disorientation, or visual hallucinations."

"Can these people become violent?" Stones asked pointedly.

Dr. Katyu frowned again, obviously disliking the question. "Doubtful. It's unlikely, but given the fact that they may have mental disturbances, it is possible, though improbable. You'd have to speak with a specialist in Dallas to get a definitive response."

"But it is possible that they could see things—imagine things—or become upset and react violently?"

Dr. Katyu didn't look pleased at all and began to pace. "I will give you the number of an oncologist in Dallas, if you wish, or a hemetologist."

"Why?"

"They are specialists involved in blood type diseases, as well as cancer. Both involve the biomechanical breakdown of blood."

"Oh." Stones was momentarily confused. Dr. Katyu smiled patiently at the reporter. "Uh, you said porphyria could be obtained some other way?"

"You can acquire it. Lead poisoning or exposure to hydrocarbons might induce an attack. Barbiturates can precipitate porphyria, if the victim has a predisposition. This is also true of anticonvulsants."

"And what about alcohol?"

"Alcohol and barbiturates are very similar in their chemical metabolism through the body. Something other than drugs to precipitate porphyria would be tumors in the liver. Hormones can also lead to an attack of porphyria."

"So an addiction can lead to this?" Stones kept probing. He had the feeling the doctor was hiding something.

Dr. Katyu's frown deepened. "It could contribute to it, but the elements must already exist. The addiction, as you put it, would not cause porphyria, but exacerbate the condition. Symptoms such as disruptions of the skin, or hypertrichosis; red-tinted eyes, teeth, or bones would appear. The patient would be anemic, very pale—"

"They might look like albinos, sort of lab-ratish?"

"In some cases, yes. In other cases, no."

"And you said it causes skin problems. I thought I read something about it causing sunlight sensitivity?"

"Correct." Dr. Katyu began playing with his stethoscope. "Due to the breakdown, skin problems are caused by the inability of the body to repair damage. Open sores last longer than normal. Sometimes these sores occur without sunlight. Blisters occur and rupture just from an attack of porphyria. As far as the photosensitivity is concerned, sunlight is damaging to the skin. Every time we get sun, the skin needs to be repaired. Porphyria disrupts this process, so the skin can only repair itself with scar tissue. So these people can be disfigured with cutaneous lesions on the face, hands, and other exposed areas."

"So it's just sunlight. Not light in general?"

"Correct. Sunlight alone, as opposed to neon or fluorescent light. Forty nanometers is particularly destructive to skin, and that is usually found only in sunlight. Other manifestations might be hypercosis, which is increased hairiness in the face and forearms. In the past, sometimes it was foolishly linked with lycanthropy."

"Werewolves?" Stones asked in surprise. Katyu shrugged. "What's the treatment?"

"Avoidance. Each case would be treated individually, depending on study. Other treatments are to watch and limit iron intake, as well as other drugs that might create a reaction."

"There aren't any drugs available to help these people?"

"No. Besides avoidance, transfusions are sometimes recommended."

"So there isn't any definitive treatment or cure?" The doctor shook his head. "How long have you been treating David Matthewson?" No response. "You said earlier that this is a real uncommon affliction."

"Yes, very rare. Few physicians have ever seen or treated this type of disease."

"Does this usually manifest at an early age?"

"Depends on the enzyme problem and the severity of the that problem."

"But it could develop later in life, depending on alcohol or drugs?"

"You keep coming back to that."

"Sorry. What if the parents don't have it?"

"It has what they call variable expressivity. It can be transported through the genes, but the parents might not exhibit the disease. It isn't a dominant or recessive trait."

"You should be able to find it though, if the parents are tested?"

"Yes. Unless it was one of those brought on by a liver tumor, which creates those porphyrins in excess."

"So, if it's severe, it starts early. And if it's borderline, it takes some kind of event."

"Exactly. Now, if that is enough, I do have true patients to attend to and plenty of paperwork, as I'm sure you can understand." Dr. Katyu moved toward the door.

"Yeah, I can understand paperwork. Thanks, Doc, I'll be back."

"Do not hurry," the doctor said as he opened the door. "I prefer healthy patients to sick ones."

"Thanks, Doc."

"We do have stop-smoking programs."

" 'Bye, Doc."

"Good day, Mr. Stones. Just remember that the wheel of Karma travels a long way. And once a Karmic tie is created, it can't be forgotten, only resolved." Patiently, the doctor stood with the door open. "I will be eager to read your article and write a rebuttal to the editor, if necessary. I know your boss, Bill Bowers, very well. We spent some time together, when his daughter Carrie had a severe case of mono."

Without a word of reply to the implied threat, Stones left the office. He didn't care if the doctor and the owner of the Temprance *Times* were twins. It wouldn't stop him from printing a good story. And the way things were looking, he had a feeling that a great story was in the making. Nobody might like it, but everybody would read it and talk about it. That's the way it was with a good Corey Stones story.

Three

Just One Look

"I don't care, Jim Bob," Benny Joe drawled in response to his brother's question, as he leaned forward dejectedly. Under a truce, they'd come at dusk to an unfinished house along the south shore to talk. The moonlight reflected off the mirrored surface of the lake and onto the half-finished porch, where the two dispirited brothers sat. The house was still in the framing stage with lots of two-by-fours and no walls, ceilings, doors or windows—a skeleton of what it would be when finished. What would one day be the lawn was still dirt, full of scattered equipment, sawhorses, supplies, and several trash piles.

Elbows on his knees and chin in his hands, Benny Joe stared at the lake. The water was magically calm, the complete opposite of his churning thoughts and stormy feelings, but the peaceful surroundings had only a minimal soothing effect. His brother had let him down big-time, opening his eyes for the first time. Maybe what people said about Jimmy Bob was true.

Jim Bob snorted.

Benny Joe sighed and glanced at Jim Bob; he was playing with his hat. "Jim Bob, no matter how many times you try and explain it to me, you still ran off and left me with that . . . that whatever it was! High, dry, and thought I was gonna die! I'm your brother. I would've helped *you!*" His eyes were watering. He took off his glasses and put his head in his hands.

"Can you at least tell me what happened?"

"Ya know, Ma talks about it all the time."

"What?"

"Providence."

"Providence?"

"Yeah."

Jim Bob was dumbfounded and barely managed, "The Lord saved you?"

Benny Joe's smile was sad. "You know I never thought you'd desert me, but you did, and there I was, all alone and in pain facing . . . IT. Lord, Jim Bob, it couldn't have been a man. It was tall with blazing eyes and paler than a ghost! Even its teeth were red and sharp! You saw how it glowed! And its face was twisted. I saw hate—and hunger. I thought it was a—" Benny Joe was gripped by fear, as though they were still in those foggy woods.

"Its arms were long, reaching for me without the thing ever *moving!*" There was an edge of hysteria to Benny Joe's voice. "Its hands . . . its hands were twisted and bleedin'. And its fingers were more like claws!" Benny Joe let out a long breath, then his voice was flat. "Its claws were only inches away, when suddenly there was light all around us.

"It seemed surprised, stared at me for a second, then screamed, and ran away. I thanked God, then I prayed for forgiveness, but I can't find it in my heart to forgive you for runnin' away. No way."

Jim Bob appeared confused, but said, "I think I understand." He couldn't say that he had been scared, too, because it was the first time he'd ever been frightened, and if he admitted it, he would have to admit that he'd been wrong—wrong about his bravery. He reached out to touch his brother, to mumble an apology, when he saw something along the shore.

The moon was behind the silhouetted figure, so Jim Bob couldn't see any details, but he couldn't miss the shapely curves and long, bare legs. She was carrying a towel, and from what he could tell, was dressed in dark shorts and a light, oversized blouse. As though she noticed him, the stranger looked toward the house, stopped, then faced the moon-dappled water. Her towel dropped to her feet.

Jim Bob's breathing accelerated as his eyes traveled from the towel upward. He had to get closer! "Shhh, quiet Benjo," Jim Bob whispered, and lightly touched his brother. Annoyed, Benny Joe looked at his brother, and Jim Bob pointed to the shore. Benny Joe's mouth dropped open as his eyes widened. The woman was staring across the water, the soft wind pulling at her shirt, blowing through and billowing the fabric as she slowly unbuttoned it.

"Closer," Jim Bob whispered. The front yard was so cluttered that there was plenty of cover. In a crouch, Jim Bob moved forward, watching the ground carefully so he wouldn't alert the beauty. Quietly, he kneeled behind a stack of lumber some fifteen feet from the shoreline. Creeping, Benny Joe joined him.

Jim Bob peeked over the top of the stacks, his eyes widely rounded and his attention riveted, as the woman finally finished undoing the last of the buttons and slowly pulled off her shirt. Jim Bob swore he heard the whisper of silk and her sigh, as the breeze caressed her creamy skin. In the moonlight, she appeared flawless. Jim Bob grew hot and restless, readjusting his jeans.

Although she was still clad in a bra, it was the first time either of the brothers had seen a woman in such a state, such a mood. "Wow," Benny Joe whispered hoarsely, his mouth so dry his tongue almost stuck. His eyes were as large as saucers, and his nose was resting on the top piece of lumber. Slowly, his glasses fogged.

"Is that incredible or what?" Jim Bob said. "Thank you, Lord." He softly rubbed his sweaty palms on the front of his jeans. His tongue was thick, his mouth parched, and he licked his lips. He would love to get a hold of something like that.

"Venus," Benny Joe breathed, then caught his breath as she tilted her face skyward, letting the wind blow back her long, silken hair, as though it were the mane of a running mare. Then she unbuttoned her shorts, letting them slide down her legs. The descending clothes seemed to fall in slow motion. Barefoot, she stepped out of her shorts, revealing even more of her curves. She was lean and well-sculpted, with narrow hips and a flat stomach that disappeared into shadow.

Jim Bob wanted to yell "Go! Go! Go, baby!" to encourage her, but his mouth was a desert, and he didn't want to risk ruining the moment. He had straightened some from his crouch, and his head was easily sticking up beyond the stack of lumber. But he was safe. Her back was to them, and she couldn't see them, unless she had eyes in the back of her head.

Sliding her hands up along the inside of her legs, then across her belly to stop between her breasts, she unhooked her bra. "I . . . I . . ." Benny Joe mouthed. Both boys leaned over the lumber, drawn forward by the sight of the nearly naked woman.

She dropped the bra at her feet, then slid her hands across her breasts, caressing her nipples to hardness, before letting her fingers fall to her panties.

"Thank you. Thank you!" Jim Bob whispered.

She drew her panties off, bending over and slowly rolling them down her legs, as the moonlight gleamed off her buttocks. Before the boys could find another breath, she stepped out of her underwear and turned toward them. The boys could see her eyes gleaming in the dark, as though they caught the moonlight. Her gaze was direct and intense, touching them . . . boldly caressing them. She said something in a foreign language, maybe French, then spoke in English, so that they did understand her, despite her accent. "Attend me," she pointed to Jim Bob.

"Uh . . ." Jim Bob stammered and stood straight, taking off his hat. Although Jim Bob appeared to have heard her speak, Benny Joe heard nothing but the gentle breeze and the soft swelling of the water against the shore. The mademoiselle crooked a finger, which appeared to pull Jim Bob from behind the lumber, and without hesitation, he moved rapidly toward her.

Benny Joe looked at his brother. "What're you doin'?" His brother didn't answer. "Jim Bob! JIM BOB! W—" What was he going to say? Benny Joe wondered, as he looked from his brother to the gorgeous, naked woman. Wait? Why was she looking at him instead of Jim Bob? It made him feel uncomfortable. He swallowed. It was time to leave.

Jim Bob was with the naked woman. After a moment, he turned toward his brother and said, "You can go home. I'll see you at the house. Be careful riding home."

"But . . ." Benny Joe swallowed the rest of what he was going to say, as the woman turned her attention from him to his brother. Her eyes appeared to brighten as she looked Jim Bob over and smiled in a decidedly wicked manner.

I should stay, Benny Joe thought, Jim Bob doesn't even know her! She could be anybody! She might be . . . dangerous? Benny Joe blushed and turned away. His own brother had told him to go, so he could . . . do it. He wasn't deserting his brother, as Jim Bob had deserted him. He was told to go, and so he was gone. He walked to his bicycle, climbed on, and rode off, his headlight leaving darkness behind.

Back at the lake the woman ran her fingers through Jimmy Bob's hair, down the sides of his face, his neck, and then his chest, where she played with his nipples. "Mmmmm," she purred.

Every place she touched Jim Bob sparked fire, and he quivered at her touch. His eyes were afire, and his smile was ready to leap free from his face. He couldn't believe this! Sweet! "What's your name? You sound French, I guess."

"Oui," she responded and coquettishly batted her eyes.

Jim Bob looked confused and said, "I'm . . . I'm," he sounded similar to Patrick, "I'm Jimmy Bob Brookens. And you're incredible."

"I am Monique," she replied, her eyes holding his, cutting him to the core, and he became lost within the glowing whorls of her eyes, pulling him deeper and deeper. He would do whatever she wanted. "I like cowboys. They know how to ride."

"Yeah . . ." he began, then shivered as she pulled him close and wrapped her arms around him, kneading his back and grinding her hips against him, further stiffening him. Jim Bob thought he was going to rip free of his pants. Monique kissed him, parting his lips and silencing him. As her hands roamed wildly, her dancing tongue drew him in.

Jim Bob's breathing was heavy, his chest heaving as his fingers quested for the secret, sensitive places of her body. Monique slid her fingers between the buttons and ripped open his shirt. Her hands slid across his chest, as she pulled her lips from his, kissing him along his cheek and jaw, then down his neck. "Oh Lord," Jimmy Bob cried. "Do me!" He stroked her hair.

"I saw you at the Matthewson farm," she breathed.

"What?" he managed breathlessly. Her lips seared his flesh, and he couldn't think straight, aching for her touch. His attention was elsewhere anyway, caught up in passion as his fingers slipped across her belly.

"Send your last thoughts to your brother."

Monique gripped him tightly, locking down his arms and holding him easily, as though he were just a babe, then her teeth parted flesh, questing for his lifeblood.

Four

Communion

"Give me strength and wisdom, Lord, as I ask for forgiveness." David knelt at the prayer rail with the Reverend Page presiding over him. The pastor held a Bible in his right hand and a small tray in his left with a paper cup full of grape juice, symbolizing the blood of Christ, and several small pieces of bread, representing the body of Jesus.

Except for the two, the chapel was deserted, and other than the backlighting of the altar and the light in the foyer, only the flickering candles illuminated the hall. Still, David couldn't shake the feeling that they weren't alone. He felt watched; the sensation was not pleasant.

Regardless of what he imagined, David wouldn't let himself be distracted. It had been a long time since he'd unburdened himself, taken the sacrament, and renewed his dedication to the Word and the Will. He'd come to church in hopes of purging the taint of Monique—who he still often thought of as Liselle.

But despite his most fervent prayers, David couldn't keep her from his thoughts. He had hoped that by coming to the church, that he would be purged of Monique's corruptive influence, but he hadn't. Even as David uttered prayers, the memory of her burned through his thoughts, her movements whispering to him. Then he caught a strange, cloying aroma.

Now he could even smell her! He couldn't resist the urge, and breathed deeply. Her scent was all over him! How could that be! That hadn't been the case earlier, and he had showered since then, scrubbing himself shortly after she had touched him. Now David began to shake.

"Are you all right, my son?" Cooper asked him. David nodded.

"Nothing is right," Reverend Wright muttered, as he peered through the slightly open door to watch the two perform the holy ritual. The stern man wanted to halt the proceedings. He could barely contain the urge to storm forward and throw the heathen out.

A short while ago he had tried to prevent David from entering the church. David had said he was there by invitation of the Reverend Page. Regardless, Wright had told him to go away. But the Reverend had shown up and ushered David into the chapel; then Cooper had the audacity to ask his own assistant minister to leave them in peace! Didn't the Reverend understand that he was doing this to benefit David as well as the church?

"And this is the blood of Christ, spilled for us so that we could start anew," Cooper said, while he handed David the small cup. As soon as the grape juice touched David's lips, he stiffened. His head seemed to separate, then float away from the rest of his body. The world became a dizzying whirl, and David felt as though he were drifting . . . then departing . . . faster and faster.

Everything stopped abruptly, and David found himself along the shore of a lake. Despite the dancing moonlight upon the water, the night air was tense with an ominous weight. He noticed the occasional ripple across the water's glassy surface, but he felt nothing on his skin. He sniffed, but didn't smell the water; there was no sensation but sight! No sound, smell, or feel!

David glanced over his shoulder. He was in the front yard of a shoreline home that was under construction. The moon was low, casting a bluish illumination over the mounds of trash, stacks of brick, and piles of lumber and shingles spread throughout the yard. The silvery light cast a pall about everything, and the inanimate objects seemed poised, ready to burst into flight. Even the shadows seemed to be straining to break free, desiring to grow larger.

Suddenly David felt the gentle breeze and heard the soft caress of water along the shore. Now he could smell it, and he recognized it. He was at Cedar Creek Lake. How was that possible?

Unexpectedly David heard the sound of a noisy kiss to his right, then he tasted metal. He spat. As he began to turn, he felt a surge, a thrust of elation that nearly overwhelmed him. David became disoriented and dizzy, fighting to remain standing and blindly staggering toward the kissing sounds. Through the red haze in his mind, David thought he saw something crouched on the small, sandy beach. He shook his head and rubbed his eyes. The shape was dark, except for its smile. Suddenly, her flesh seemed to reflect the moonlight instead of absorbing it. "Lis—" he began, then whispered in hushed horror, "Monique!"

She held someone in her arms, his head dropped back and his neck exposed. It was stained, as though wounded and bleeding. Now David smelled blood! Tasted it! Dizzy, he wet his lips. Wait! He recognized the boy! He'd chased him last Friday night. "Monique, what's going on here?"

Letting Jim Bob drop as though he were a slab of meat, she stood tall and proud. "You mean you don't know?" Monique said with a smile, and a French accent that somehow combined sweet innocence with the lust that was in her eyes. "You can taste it, no? Feel the rich, warm, life-giving blood swell in your mouth, then slip down your throat, as though it were the nectar of God?" Her smile widened.

Good Lord, he could. David spat again, then said, "You are feeding on him! This is vampiric!" He couldn't believe he'd said it, let alone meant it.

"Exactly. We exist, no? Listen, you and I are linked together as though we're soul mates." She licked her lips, then smiled at the outrage, shock, and horror in his face and eyes. "Would you like to join me? Or would you prefer to take me?" Monique ran her hands down across her breasts, caressing the nipples until they were hard, then letting the palms sweep across her flat stomach before plunging between her thighs. "Feeding always excites me. Come! Join with me!" She threw her arms toward him, beseeching.

David felt both hunger and disgust swell together within him. How could he be in the church and here, too? This was insane! He was deliriously ill—a serious attack of porphyria. A nightmare couldn't be worse.

"Dis is not a dream or delusion. You will not stop it by waking, since you aren't asleep," her Austrian accent returned. "And you are not," she smiled, "sick at all. And you know what else? You can't stop it!" she laughed softly. "You will succumb to me or to yourself, sooner or later." Monique waved goodbye, and slowly she and her surroundings began to fade. "We shall dance again, no?" She stood up and spun on her tiptoes. "I promise it," her voice faded with her disappearance.

"NO!" David screamed, suddenly back in the church. He stood abruptly, knocking the Reverend Page backward and causing him to drop his tray.

The Reverend glanced at the mess, then stared at David. Matthewson was pallid, even whiter than normal, which Cooper wouldn't have thought possible. David's eyes were dilated and wide. His entire body shook. Was he having a seizure? Cooper wondered. He remembered Penny saying that David occasionally had neurotic reactions in conjunction with porphyria attacks. "Are you all right, my son?" Cooper asked, as he moved to David's side. The reverend knew David had been through a lot, and Friday probably hadn't helped. Earlier, Cooper had apologized for Patrick, but it hadn't made the reverend feel any better. David had just shrugged it off, saying it was nothing.

David stared blindly at the Reverend Page. The taste of blood had disappeared from his mouth, as had the surrounding vision. He could no longer smell or feel Monique. Was it real? Could Monique somehow reach out to taint him? Deep down, he felt tainted. David suddenly realized that the Reverend Page was staring at him with concern. "I'm all right, Father. I just need to sit for a while."

With the reverend's help, David made it to the front pew and sat. He was still shaking, and his hands didn't seem to obey him, trembling violently. "Did you have an attack?" Cooper asked.

"I don't know. I guess so. I was dizzy and started..." David stopped and took several deep breaths. It had to have been his imagination, or something caused by the elixir. There was a rational explanation; he wasn't crazy, just ill.

"Started to what?"

"Pass out," he said, hating to lie.

"Oh dear. Should we call Doc Katyu? Or call your mother or sister to come get you?"

"No, I don't think so. Let me rest. I think I'll be fine in a minute. It's the price I pay," he said bitterly, slipping into the belief that it was just another phase of alcoholism.

"The price you pay?"

"For being an alcoholic. Even when I'm not drinking, I

have problems. Just fewer and farther between. I'm still in the early stages of recovery."

"God grant you strength. I'd like to help any way I can."

"You are, Reverend, you are helping very much. Thank you. It's not easy for me to accept kindness or pity."

"I feel compassion, not pity," Cooper Page told him.

"I'm sorry," David said. "I haven't had to deal with people in a long time. I'm out of practice." David paused, then asked, "Reverend, why are some stricken with serious illnesses and others not? Could it be my punishment for falling from faith?" Cooper started to respond, but David continued, "Or could it be a test of mettle?"

Cooper smiled softly. "It isn't an overused phrase that the Lord works in mysterious ways. But I also feel that sometimes, if all is going well, when our world is bright and sunny, that sometimes we ignore the Will of the Lord. Often it is only in times of adversity that we seek guidance."

"That rings of truth," David replied.

"Is it possible that your illness has made you stronger?" Cooper asked. "Or brought you closer to the Lord? I know you believed you fell from grace after Tina's death. You'd already realized your mortality, but maybe there was—is—something else you must learn. Or something else you must do. The call of duty may come at any time and in any way. But it is up to each of us to decide whether or not to be of service. There is free will, not destiny. It is up to you how you respond to the challenge, and whether or not you accept the guidance of the Lord."

"You know, I haven't handled death very well. My brother and father at an early age. Later, Tina and Timmy. Now I fear something is wrong with my mother."

"No one handles death well, unless they have faith. Pray on it. Death does not always mean dying. It can also mean change. Without death, there is no rebirth." He smiled. "And don't worry about your mother. Last time I saw her, she looked fine. There is no use in worrying about things that haven't happened," he sighed. "I'm lecturing again. Patrick, my son, complains about it all the time." David smiled. "Would you like to finish communion or start over again?"

"Please, let's start again. I feel the need to be cleansed." David moved to the rail, still wondering whether his most recent encounter with Monique had been real, or a twisting of his vivid imagination.

Five

Addicted

Several times while en route to the farm, David nearly nodded off, exhausted. His arms were dead weight, and he could barely keep his eyes open. Whatever had happened to him at the church had drained him. He was relieved when he pulled safely into the driveway. David didn't remember running over anything while driving, but he wasn't sure. When he opened the gate, he searched the front bumper and looked under the car, thankful he found nothing amiss.

David parked behind his house and killed the headlights and engine. As he trudged toward the back door, he had little in mind but sleep. And yet there were chores to be done; ones he'd neglected. When David paused to unlock the door, he tried to ignore the call, but the elixir was summoning him to the refrigerator. Surely, he had the strength to resist. He'd just come from communion. Wouldn't that add to his strength of will?

David opened the door and, for a brief instant, he sensed something strange within. "Monique?" The odor was fleeting and oddly familiar, but he couldn't put his finger on it. He listened carefully, straining his senses outward. Was he imagining things? He heard nothing. The house was deserted. Soon he would be jumping at shadows.

Something rubbed against his leg. "Hello, Shady," David said, as he reached down to pick up his black cat. He stroked her, still feeling bad about kicking at her on Friday, when he had been obsessed with getting a drink of elixir. "Where's Midnight?" He hadn't seen his other cat since the night before. Oh well, cats were that way sometimes. She was probably presiding over a kill.

David slowly moved into the kitchen and set Shady on the table. "Want some milk?" he asked, as he went to the refrigerator. For a time, he stared at the chilled bottle of Jack Daniels and the unlabeled bottle, then grabbed the milk and closed the fridge. "None for me tonight, thanks. Doc Katyu says I'll never get better, if I don't stop drinking booze." He removed a saucer from the cabinet, then poured Shady some milk. She purred as she lapped.

David's attention returned to the refrigerator. He couldn't believe that he was contemplating a drink. It wasn't as though he didn't have reasons, but this terrible disease was alcohol-related. It seemed almost everything in his life was . . . except his writing.

Could that waking dream or hallucination be caused by alcohol? Monique a vampire. How absurd. She was strange, but not that strange! Madness. The D.T.'s. David tried to shake away the thoughts, but they wouldn't leave.

Monique was beautiful. And sexy. Lord, he needed a drink. It would help him sleep. If he didn't, he might dream about the terrible moments on the shoreline. It was almost as though he'd participated, aiding in the killing of the boy. But there wasn't any death! It was just a hallucination! David took a step toward the refrigerator.

He touched Tina's locket and wished she were there to strengthen him. He also felt his crucifix. NO! He must not! If he could avoid alcohol, there was some hope that the porphyria might go into remission long enough for him to spend some time in the sunlight. How long had it been? He pushed away that train of thought.

David shook his head, and suddenly found himself opening the refrigerator. Lord, I am so weak. Help me! He reached past the bottle of Jack and grabbed the square, green bottle of dark liquid. Twisting off the cap, he drank his home brew—the elixir which he swore was making him better. Shortly after he'd started consuming it, the lesions had disappeared, his skin began to repair itself at a normal rate, and he no longer got the shakes. An amazing home remedy, he thought.

With each mouthful, David felt better and better; miraculously, he was no longer tired. But, as if the bottle had been nearly empty when he started, David was amazed to find that it was suddenly drained dry. "What?" He turned the bottle over. It couldn't be dry! It had been full. He couldn't have consumed it all! He couldn't have! David immediately searched the refrigerator for another. There should have been several more. Where were they?

In a frantic search, he had soon emptied the refrigerator. No bottles of elixir. How could that be? He couldn't have drunk them all! Could he? He'd just restocked Friday night. He slumped to the floor. The empty refrigerator didn't lie. He was consuming the elixir at much too fast a rate, at such a pace that he couldn't remember drinking them.

That had been the problem Friday night. He'd been trying to fight off this addiction, go cold turkey, and had removed all the bottles from the house, storing them in the barn. For three nights he'd been okay, then Friday he'd awakened with a single-minded obsession, a thirst that nearly drove him mad. He'd been hot and clammy, unable to do anything but follow the undeniable urge. That was why his senses had failed him, and he hadn't noticed the pranksters. No. The truth was that his senses hadn't failed him; he had ignored them.

"Face it," David told himself. "You're addicted. I just won't make anymore. And I won't go to the barn. Lord, that's all I need is another problem. But I have to go to the barn to feed the animals and get supplies."

No more, David thought resolutely. He quickly stuffed everything back into the refrigerator, then closed it. Suddenly, he found himself outside, heading for the barn. Right now he didn't dare go there. "Right!" he breathed deep and stopped. David turned away from the barn and walked behind the house and into the chicken coop. As he entered, he gathered up a bucket and began searching the nests under the sleeping chickens. A few clucked drowsily, and one even pecked him sharply as he discovered her eggs.

Knowing things had to get done, he trudged to the barn. Suddenly, David smelled something foul, then all but stepped on a motionless cat sprawled in the dirt. Its eyes were wide and glazed. "Midnite!" David knelt, checking the broken body. His cat was dead. David began to weep. She had been more than a cat, she'd been of one his companions and confidantes. How had this happened? It appeared as though she'd fallen from a great height, but he knew cats better than that.

Wiping his cheeks dry, David walked into the barn to get a shovel. He needed a drink. Instead of heading for the wall of tools, he found himself in front of the closet. No, he wouldn't give in to another addiction. Angry with himself and distraught over his cat's death, he whirled around, grabbed the shovel, and went back outside. Behind the barn, David furiously dug a grave, crying silently and venting all his rage on the dirt. When he was finally through, David gently nestled Midnite in the hole and buried her.

Dejected, he walked back to the barn. David had intended to clean a stall and finish his repairs on the riding lawnmower, but he found himself standing in front of the storage closet. He began to reach for the key around his neck, and stopped. Sweating and shaking, he stood immobile. It took all his will to turn around and leave the barn. Maybe tomorrow would be better.

David hauled his tired body upstairs and trudged into his bedroom. He glanced at the windows to make sure the shades were drawn. Since he was drinking without remembering it, he wanted to be positive he didn't forget something important. They were closed. He didn't want to be awakened abruptly and painfully by a sunbeam.

Without taking off his clothes or reading the Bible as he'd promised himself, David collapsed onto the bed. He rolled around once or twice, then immediately fell fast asleep.

Six

Stories

"Ohhh," Grimm groaned and rolled over in bed, clamping the pillows to his ears. The ringing in his head wouldn't stop. "Too much Jack," he moaned. Free booze was dangerous. He started to laugh, then held back; any movement hurt. Maybe he would have been better off not finding the bottles of Black Jack and Jag in the writer-dude's barn. Naw. Finders keepers, losers weepers.

The ringing suddenly was louder, and Kevin realized that it wasn't in his head. He reached over and pounded on his clock radio, knocking it to the floor. Then he heard the front door open and his stepfather speaking to someone.

Kevin sat up, then wished he hadn't. The room spun, whirling around as though the Tasmanian devil was in charge. "I hate Tuesday mornings." He collapsed back onto the bed. At least his stomach wasn't lurching. It was made of cast iron, hardened from years of cafeteria food at "the Home."

Kevin heard voices more distinctly this time. Who was the mayor talking to this time? He doubted that it was the Avon lady. And besides, the voice was male. Who cared? It didn't concern him. "Doesn't it, Kevy? Listen up."

Kevin was having a hell of a time thinking straight, let alone listening. "Water," he breathed. His mouth was drier than west Texas. Somehow he managed to stand and stagger to the door. "What do you get when you mix a quart of whiskey and a thirsty man? Ronco's amazing vomitizer."

Kevin opened the door and started to blunder outside, when he realized that his stepfather was talking with the authority bag of wind himself, Sheriff Bricker. Oh, oh, trouble again, Grimm chuckled, then clutched his head. Blindly, he pulled back the door leaving it open a gap.

"Don't apologize again," Mayor Campbell said, long pauses separating words. "I know ya don't mean it."

Bricker laughed harshly, then spoke in his deep, rumbling voice. "It's such a pleasure being able to shoot straight with someone, Mayor Campbell."

"I hate beating around the bush," the mayor said. I love beating around the bush, Grimm thought. Just one of their many differences.

"It's about that incident Friday night at the Matthewson place," Bricker continued. Kevin silently groaned; an ill wind blew.

"You have more information?" the mayor asked. Grimm figured inquiring minds wanted to know.

"Yep. More than you want to hear. I spoke to Candel. He's talked to the Brookens' brothers, which was pretty worthless, as expected." Grimm's smile was sickly but pleased. He could pick them. Even now, he could see the hint of sneer in Jim Bob's expression, and the shine of innocence from Benny Joe's face. "But he also had a surprise visit from Judge Marshall."

"Really? What did the distinguished judge have to say?"

"He had a long talk with his son, Kenneth, aka Skeeter, and it was quite revealing." Grimm silently cursed. Seems he'd made a mistake in judgment. Always a first time. He slowly grew angrier, as Bricker recounted Skeeter's version of the evening. "Then I went and spoke to the Reverend Page."

Grimm groaned quietly. Lightning had struck twice. Hell's bells. "He also had quite a chat with his son, Patrick. Seems something had Patrick scared silly." Not hard, Grimm thought. "Since Skeeter was knocked out when he ran into a tree, Patrick's version had some added components—like gun fire."

"WHAT?" his stepfather shouted.

Bricker retold Patrick's tale, and with each passing sentence, Grimm moved farther from angry toward furious. Soon, he'd forgotten all about his hangover, as his rage boiled it away. TOTALLY BETRAYED! The little shits, they would both pay! First Becky and Lou, then Patrick and Skeeter. If they begged, he might show them some mercy. Might. On the other hand, they might never know exactly what happened, or why. That made him laugh. "What's brown and sounds like a doorbell?" he whispered to himself. "Dung. And I say you boys are in deep, deep shit."

What to do? There were so many choices. Should he give a warning first? Creativity was the key, if not originality. Maybe a dog's head in Lou's bed would hint that something was coming. The Godfather would appreciate the touch, and the suspense alone might almost be as good as the payback itself. Loosening the manifold donut would be a gas! Hey, how about some downers mixed with his beer? Or maybe Nair in his cowboy hat! Grimm started to laugh and felt much better. Besides revenge, laughter was the best medicine.

And what about the blabber twins? Cutting out their tongues would be too good for them. Grass spurs taped inside their shoes? Naw, no suspense, and it only hurt for a minute or two. A slow leak in that canoe they cherished so much? Sink and swim? Or how about an old-fashioned pounding by Jim Bob? That made Grimm shudder. Nobody deserved that. He still hurt from Friday night, and would for quite a while.

"Can you go easy on Kevin?" Mayor Campbell asked. "He's a troubled young man, but my wife loves him as though he were an angel. You know how mothers can be."

"Yeah, I've had to deal with Claire Brookens enough. But there's more trouble. Kevin started a fight outside a bar where he was spotted drinking. The complaint says he pulled a knife."

"So that's why he's so beaten up," Campbell replied. "There wasn't any motorcycle accident! Damn, I'd hoped he'd be doing better for his mother's sake." He sighed heavily. "Will you defer things if I have him see a counselor again? Treatment might help. He's only been out for six months."

Grimm's eyes bugged out. No way! He'd already been that route. The only good psychiatrist was a dead psychiatrist. "What do you get when you cross a Mexican and a psychiatrist?" he muttered under his breath. "A shrink that steals couches."

"Sure," Bricker replied magnanimously. "It was no big deal. Nobody was killed or badly hurt. Besides, everybody needs a favor now and then, a second chance. And we both know what a back-scratchin' place Temprance can be. Don't worry. At worst, he'll get a slap on the wrist, but I'm gonna nail the Brookens boys."

Nobody slaps me anywhere, Grimm thought.

"Thank you!" Campbell effused.

"Don't fret. We public-minded officials have to look out for each other, as well as the public," Bricker laughed. Kevin almost threw up. Logan, Bricker's deputy, might be a cop, but at least he wasn't a hypocrite.

"Nice to know great minds think alike," Mayor Campbell said. "See you at the office, Sheriff."

"I look forward to it, Mayor." The door closed and Bricker left.

"The things I do for my wife," Mayor Campbell muttered. Kevin could hear him moving in the kitchen. Probably searching for his keys, Kevin thought. He'd slept since yesterday and had probably forgotten where he'd put them. After a few minutes, the kitchen door shut, and Kevin heard the car start.

Good, he was alone. Paybacks should be carefully planned. Still cotton-mouthed, Kevin opened the door and headed for the bathroom.

After relieving himself, Kevin tried to freshen up, splashing water on his face and drinking several glassfuls. That made him feel a whole lot better—more like the walking dead instead of a corpse.

With his mind on what he'd do with Becky when he had her tied down, Grimm returned to his bedroom. The doorbell rang, stopping him in mid-stride. "Nobody home."

"Kevy, answer it. It could be opportunity knockin'."

"It just better not be Bricker," Kevin muttered, and trudged to the front door. He yanked it open.

The unkempt man did not appear surprised. Instead, he took a long drag off a cigarette. "Kevin Grimm, I presume?"

Grimm stared at him for a moment, taking in all the details; the sloppy dress, unshaven appearance, greasy hair, puffiness in the jowls and around the eyes. But his eyes, they were sharp. And there were bulges in the guy's coat pockets, as if he might be wired for sound or carrying a piece. "Who's asking?"

"Corey Stones. I'm a reporter for the *Temprance Times*."

"Well big shit," Kevin said as he started to shut the door. Reporters reminded him of doctors; they were always trying to trick you into saying something.

"Wait!" The reporter reached inside his jacket pocket, his quick reflexes belying his appearance, and shoved a photo inside the door along with his foot, just before Kevin got it closed. "I want to ask you about what happened on the Matthewson farm Friday night and yesterday morning. I also have some pictures that you might find interesting. Isn't this an amazing likeness of you?"

"I don't know what you're talking about." Kevin's voice was flat.

"See, the facial bruises even match." Kevin looked at it, as he leaned against the door, increasing the pressure on the reporter's foot. "Hey!" Stones yelled. Grimm only smiled.

"Amazing," Kevin said, "it does look like me. How can that be? I've been all but bedridden since Friday. Ask my mom. Guess you got a story on your hands, Mr. Stones. Somebody's impersonating me." Kevin cracked the door open, and Stones yanked his foot free.

"I can file a complaint," Stones said. He rubbed his arm and flexed his fingers.

"I can shoot ya and pull you inside, claim you was robbing the place," Kevin countered. He squinted. "Ya look like a thief. And remember, this is Texas."

Stones laughed. "I love it." He held up several more photos of Kevin moving toward the barn, then sneaking inside. The last one, the photo he held most prominently, showed Kevin carrying a couple of bags. "What'd you steal, boy?"

Grimm's smile was poisonous. "Get hit by a truck, Mr. Stones."

"I can take this to the sheriff. Or better yet, publish them."

"I'm the mayor's son," Kevin sneered. "Feel free. You'll never walk again in this town. Gotta question for you, Mr. Reporter. How do you break a reporter's finger?" Stones was momentarily speechless. "You smash him in the nose."

"Listen you little—"

Kevin slammed the door. "I wonder if that's somebody else I'm gonna have to take care of. Naw, it'll blow over. Besides, five is a bad number."

"Maybe ya can use him, Kevy. Give 'em the story he wants, just don't give him the truth. He really doesn't want anythin' on you. He wants dirt on Matthewson. Don't worry. We'll think of somethin'. Everythin' is comin' together. Reporters, just as doctors, have their uses, as will one of those bottles of Jack Daniels." The voice was laughing, and Grimm joined it.

* * *

Stones leaned against his tan Escort. "What a sonuvabitch," he muttered. Then, unable to resist, he flipped the house a bird. That made him feel somewhat better, except his arm still hurt.

Nobody got the best of Corey Maxwell Stones, he told himself. Nobody, and certainly not some snot-nosed kid that might have been recently exhumed from a grave. Stones shuddered. Just the look in the boy's eyes reminded him of someone who should be in a padded cell. Didn't anyone else see that?

Stones climbed into his car and started it. For a moment, he sat there pondering the last few days. There was something odd going on, he could feel it in the air. His reporter's instinct was wired, giving him a much-needed boost of life after months of lassitude. He was positive that Matthewson and Grimm were at the heart of it. A little bit of careful watching of both parties would reveal the truth. And the truth would set him free of Temprance.

Seven

Lost and Found

As he raced down the rough back roads, the wheels of Benny Joe's bicycle were spinning almost as fast as his worried mind. All day he'd been in turmoil. Where was Jim Bob? Benny Joe bit his lip. He hadn't seen his brother since last night . . . since he'd left him with that wild woman. Surely he would have returned home, unless something bad had happened.

"Where's your brother?" In his mind, Benny Joe could clearly hear his mother's voice at breakfast. The scene kept coming back to haunt him, interplaying with the disrobing of the shapely woman on the shore, and the casual way Jim Bob had approached, once beckoned. Then this morning, he'd discovered that Jim Bob's bed was untouched. He hadn't come home! Benny Joe had been trying to sneak out of the house when his mother saw him. At first, she thought he'd been trying to escape their punishment for Friday night, then she noticed that Jim Bob was missing.

"I dunno," Benny Joe responded, his eyes downcast. And that was the truth. Uncomfortably he adjusted his glasses.

"Well, when did you last see him? Y'all are supposed to help the Reverend Wright clean up the churchyard. You don't want to do it by yourself, do you? Especially with a broken wrist." Claire placed balled fists on hips. His mother always started the morning in a foul mood.

"No ma'am." He stared at his worn tennis shoes. One was undone and now fascinated him.

"Look at me, when I'm talking to ya." Benny Joe's head jerked up, and he met her gaze, trying not to squirm. "Well, when did you last see him?"

"Last night at Cedar Creek."

"Did he come home with you?"

"No ma'am." All hell was gonna break loose. He might even get switched, even though it was Jim Bob that was missing.

"Did y'all fight again?"

"No ma'am."

"Then where is he?"

"I dunno."

"What's gotten into y'all?"

"Nuthin'."

"Has Jim Bob run away?" His mother suddenly looked worried, sucking in her lips.

"He didn't say anything, except he wanted to be by himself." Benny Joe didn't like lying to his ma, and he hadn't lied, yet.

"That's odd. You both been acting pretty strange. Anythin' wrong?" she asked. Benny Joe shook his head. "You're not telling me the truth."

"I am, too," he said petulantly, then wished he'd used a different tone. Mother would be madder than a hornet, if she found out what had happened. But he couldn't shake the thought: What am I doing talking to Ma, when I should be out looking for Jim Bob? He should have started last night, but once he laid down to rest, he'd slept like the dead—fortunately for him, because he wasn't visited by nightmares.

"I don't like it, but I guess I need to talk with Sheriff Bricker and have him start looking for Jimmy Bob." She probably expected to get a rise out of Benny Joe, since he didn't care for the sheriff, but his reaction was only a shrug. That bothered her. "Come on," Claire said in an exasperated tone. "Eat some breakfast, then we gotta be off. The Reverend Wright will be waitin' on you, and I don't wanna be late."

Where'd the day go? Benny Joe thougt. The day had been long, and he'd been forced to do most of the work—as much as he could do one-handed—because Jim Bob hadn't been there. Benny Joe's hand hurt from raking, and his back from picking up trash. He'd had to wait until the 700 Club came on television before he could sneak out. It might already be too late. He glanced up at the sky as he rode. The sun was already setting. Benny Joe had wanted to get here earlier, but between the long day's work, his chores, and the watchful eye of his mother, it was impossible to get away. Soon it would be too dark to see anything, but he had to look. The house under construction was the last place he'd seen Jim Bob; and something was drawing him there.

"Damn you, Jim Bob, I hope you're all right. If not . . ." he shook his casted fist, then turned on his headlight. He came to a sign that read "Ranchos Verde" and turned right. He was getting close.

Benny Joe coasted up the gravel driveway, then hopped off his bicycle as it rolled into the high grass. He leaned his bicycle against a pile of bricks and looked around. As a breeze blew in from the lake, Benny Joe shivered. Suddenly, he wished he hadn't come. But then, how could he not? His brother was missing.

The sky was pink, and the clouds were highlighted in various shades of orange and red, but none of that cheery light touched the yard. Unlike last night, when all had seemed peaceful, the place was gloomy and foreboding, reminding

Benny Joe more of a demolition yard than a new housing development. There was a sense of decay, and the house struck him oddly, reminding him of the bony remains of some mammoth beast from ages long past. The piles and stacks of lumber could have been scattered body parts. The shadows within were much too dark for the time of day, as though concealing something, and the silence shouted its lifelessness. Where there should have been the noise of insects and small wildlife, there was nothing but the whispering of the wind, and the soft rhythmic sound of the waves lapping the shore.

"Get a grip," Benny Joe muttered. "You'd think you was wandering through a graveyard." He laughed at himself, but it sounded hollow and short. He couldn't shake the feeling of dread. Despite the wind, the air was heavy and oppressive. Was there really anything wrong, or was he imagining it? Between the recent nightmares he couldn't recall but could still feel, and Wright's angry outburst this morning at Jim Bob's no-show act, it was no wonder that Benny Joe felt as though something was wrong. Nothing had gone right since Friday night at the ranch.

But if something had happened to Jim Bob, it was his fault. He'd deserted his brother, just as Jim Bob had deserted him. Even though his brother had told him to leave, he should've known better.

Benny Joe looked for Jim Bob's bicycle. It wasn't where he had left it last night, leaning against the house by a concrete platform that had been laid for the placement of an air conditioner. Benny Joe peered inside the house, thinking Jim Bob might have stowed it there; or worse, somebody might have hidden it there. His eyes watered each time he stared within the maze of shadows. Benny Joe blinked, thinking he saw something move. There goes my imagination again, he thought. Still, Benny Joe couldn't convince himself to go inside.

Instead, Benny Joe walked around the house. As he neared

the garage, something shot from it, racing towards him. The small reptilian creature scurried low across the ground. Benny Joe's heart jammed into his throat, and he jumped at least a foot, then he realized that it was an armadillo. The animal was as blind as it was stupid. "Get outta here!" he yelled and stomped. It paused, then reversed direction.

As it disappeared into the shadows of the unfinished garage, Benny Joe began to chuckle. Scared by an armadillo. He was glad none of the others had been here to see it. Then he thought it would've been just fine if Jim Bob had been here to make fun of him. Benny Joe sighed and kept looking.

As he began to search around the piles of trash and supplies, hopelessness slowly replaced his feelings of dread. He wasn't going to find anything here. It was almost too dark to see. Deciding to head home before his mother noticed that he was gone, too, Benny Joe started toward his bicycle.

Then he smelled something rotten. "What died?" he gagged. The odor was so foul that his eyes began to water. He better get out of here before he puked. Jogging, he passed a trash pile and stumbled.

Without thinking, Benny Joe put down his injured hand to catch himself. "YEEOWWW!" He rolled onto his back and held the cast close to his body. Tears streamed down his cheeks. Anger mingled with pain, and Benny Joe sprang to his feet, ready to kick whatever had tripped him.

His eyes suddenly flew open and his jaw dropped. IT WAS AN ARM sticking out of the ground! The fingers were curled; the arm appeared to have shriveled up, dried from days in the sun. How come they had never seen it before? Who cared? He was out of here!

As he was about to run for his bicycle, Benny Joe noticed the watch on the wrist of the arm. It looked familiar. Unbelieving, he stopped his retreat and cautiously moved forward. That looked like Jim Bob's watch, the one that Father had given him on his tenth birthday. It was blue and gold and kept track of the movements of the moon.

It couldn't be Jim Bob's watch! Even if something terrible had happened to Jim Bob, Benny Joe shuddered at the thought, his brother wouldn't look like this. Holding his nose, Benny Joe leaned closer. His whole body tingled, and his mouth went dry, as he saw the chip in the crystal.

"Oh God, please no," Benny Joe pleaded. Unable to bring himself to use his hands, he found a long two-by-four and started to uncover the body. It only took a few moments of frantic digging to clear away the upper torso, which was bare and shriveled like the hand and arm. The corpse's skin was white, shrunken, and stretched taut against the bones, the ribs prominently displayed. The lower part of the body was clad in blue jeans.

Unable to keep his eyes away any longer, Benny Joe stared at its face. The flesh was pulled so tight that it resembled a grinning skull, with eyes bulging so much they looked like they had tried to jump free with surprise. Its lips were pulled taut, so that the grin actually reminded Benny Joe of a sneer. The hair was curly and white. And its neck! There were holes in it! It couldn't be Jim Bob, Benny Joe thought.

Then he did a double take. "Oh my God!" The hair was the right length and curly, but it was the sneer that made his hair stand on end. It reminded him of Jim Bob. Then he saw Jim Bob's black hat sticking out from under the corpse. This was his brother!

Horrified, Benny Joe turned and ran. He stumbled and staggered his way to his bicycle, grabbed it, and sprinted. Never looking back, he hopped onto his bicycle and pedaled as though the hounds of hell pursued him. Benny Joe was still standing on the pedals, running atop his bicycle, as he raced onto the pavement.

Jim Bob! His brother dead! How could it be? How could he be like that? Benny Joe shuddered. He wanted to vomit.

The wind tore at him, and his eyes teared so that he could barely see. His legs throbbed and quivered, but he continued to stand, following the small swath of light, hoping it would take him home.

He had to tell somebody! He had to get help! Oh God, his brother! Benny Joe started to cry.

The world was a dark blur, but even through his tearing eyes, Benny Joe saw something white in the distance. Standing along the road, it had a dull glow to it, as though illuminated by the moonlight. He wasn't stopping for anything.

The white thing grew closer and closer, losing its ambiguity and gaining shape. It was a person, a woman in a frilly white dress, and she was stepping onto the road. The night wind pulled at her long dress, and she seemed to stretch even farther into his path.

"Oh God no!" It was the same woman Jim Bob had been with last night. Fear paralyzed Benny Joe, and he stopped pedaling, but continued coasting along at a dizzying speed.

Then Benny Joe realized that he was going too fast to stop. Just before he closed his eyes, he could see her face. It was the same woman, except her expression was hard, not soft, as she smiled cruelly at him. He'd run her over!

Suddenly, coldness surrounded him, and there was mist whipping across his face. He opened his eyes as he blew through the fog patch. Benny Joe turned and glanced over his shoulder. Was that all it was? Relieved, he started to laugh. How could he think that was a woman? Now he was beginning to doubt both his eyes and his sanity.

Drained by the experience and starting to tire, Benny Joe sat on his bike seat. His pace slowed, but he was still in a hurry to get home. He had to tell his mother! He would probably have to tell her that he'd found Benny Joe's bicycle—or his hat—at the house where they often played. She would know what to do!

With renewed strength, Benny Joe began pedaling faster.

Then he saw another foggy patch on the road. It shifted as though the wind caught it, then gathered, pulling tendrils of mist together to form a shape. Benny Joe's fingers clenched, glued to the handlebars, and his knees froze. He tried to breathe, but couldn't. Once again, the strange, luminescent woman stood on the side of the road, waiting for him.

Eight

Words of Death

David was sitting at the bar getting thoroughly drunk. The only thing important was getting toasted and forgetting. If he passed out, Franz would find help and all but carry him upstairs to his room, where he would sleep in dreamless oblivion. It would be another night without Tina or Timmy.

In the spirit of the impromptu party going on around him—singing, backslapping, the pounding of hands on tables, and the clinking of mugs as well as lots of drinking—David threw back another shot of schnapps, to chase the lager he'd just downed. He wiped his watering eyes, then shivered. Where did that cold breeze come from?

The front door closed heavily, sounding as though a dull bell had been struck, and the lively place instantly became silent. Curious, David turned toward the door and was surprised to find the bar suddenly deserted, except for the cowled figure standing just inside the door carrying a tall scythe. Silently the dark stranger approached David. The temperature dropped even further, and his teeth began to chatter. He clutched himself with both arms. His legs were frozen to the stool. "Who?" David whispered.

The figure sat on the stool beside him, then set the scythe

against the copper bar. With long, brightly painted nails, she pulled back her cowl to reveal a timeless beauty. David caught his breath and forgot the cold. Liselle's skin was creamy and smooth, her cheeks colored from the cold. Her hair was long, wavy, and dark, falling to frame her lovely face and shoulders. Dark blue eyes, almost purple, were set between sharply pronounced cheekbones and dark brows disguised as blackbird pinions. She leaned forward to kiss him. The touch of her lips seared his, then their tongues cavorted, drawing them closer together. Finally, she slowly pulled away, then kissed his eyes. As though a burning butterfly fluttered along his face, she moved down his cheeks to his chin, then to his neck . . .

"Liselle!" David bolted upright in bed. His clothing was drenched. "Another nightmare. Lord, help me!"

And this time he dreamed about Liselle. Why was he suddenly thinking about her again? Over a decade ago he'd met her in an Austrian bar, when he'd been plastered and melancholy. David had been surprised, almost embarrassed that such an incredibly beautiful and classy woman would give him a second glance, but Liselle had done that and more. It had been a strange night, he recalled. The room had gone quiet when she entered, clad in a black cloak against the chill of the night.

Unbidden images flashed through his head, memories never clear, that he'd tried to both forget and remember at different times; the heat of Liselle's touch on his arm, as they walked under a full moon through the crisp and chilly alpine country; passion; their constant drinking; dancing until his feet were sore; and singing until he was hoarse.

And there was a dark place . . . Her trailer! That's right! She'd been a gypsy! Strange, he'd forgotten all about that.

But David hadn't forgotten—couldn't forget—the hungry look in her eyes or the sweltering passion brought by her kiss. He saw much the same in Monique, and that terrified him.

David shook his head clear; Liselle had been a mistake.

He'd been a weak man, even weaker than now. At rock bottom. A drowning man clinging to passion, when there had only been despair. Reaching out to flesh, when he should have been reaching out to spirit. And he was still paying for it with his illness; he'd been sick ever since.

Bad history, David thought with a heavy sigh, glancing at the clock. It read nine-thirty. Amazing. He'd slept the remainder of Tuesday and almost all of Wednesday. His mouth was dry, and he felt wrung out. He wandered into the bathroom and filled a glass from the tap. After a second glass, he looked at himself in the mirror. His eyes were clear and somewhat blue, losing most of their reddish hue, but his teeth hadn't changed from their ugly brownish red color. Doctor Katyu said they might not. He felt his face and neck, checking for lumps and bumps, and found none. With a smile, he ran a hand across his stubbled chin. And the hair certainly wasn't growing any faster.

Suddenly he doubled over, clutching his belly and the sink to keep from crumpling onto the floor. The stomach pain was agonizing, making his knees weak and his head spin. He reached into the medicine cabinet, twisted off the top of the pink antacid bottle, and drank from it. Stumbling, he moved over to the toilet, sat, and waited. After a time, the cramping lessened, and he was able to dress.

He made his way unsteadily downstairs and into the kitchen. He started brewing coffee; the cramps struck even more violently this time. The kitchen spun and he staggered forward, hands grasping for something to keep him from falling. A hand found the trash basket and pulled it atop him, as he crashed to the floor in a heap. He stared at an empty green bottle among the scattered trash. There was his problem; his pains were his need for the elixir. If he drank some of it, he would immediately feel better, but become more tightly bound to it. An assault of dry heaves put him in agony, and he blacked out.

Sometime later, David awoke, feeling cold and shaky. The pain was still in his stomach, but much duller now. David tried to stand, but couldn't. On his belly as though he were a snake, other times managing to get to his hands and knees, David crawled out through the kitchen door, down the steps, across the barnyard, and into the barn. Finally, after what seemed to be hours, David reached the storage cabinet. Clawing his way up the wall, he stood, leaning heavily against the door. He hadn't the energy to stand again if he fell.

David took off his necklace, pulling it over his head, inserted the key in the lock, and twisted. It clicked open. David unlocked the second, jerked the door aside, then rushed in to yank the refrigerator open and grab a bottle of elixir. Fumbling, David finally got the top off and the bottle to his mouth.

Several huge gulps later, he felt much better. Yes, the cramps were gone, as were the dizziness and weakness. He took another sip. David admitted he could only handle one problem at a time. First he would defeat his porphyria, then he would tackle his new addiction. Somehow it had replaced his drinking habit.

As he sipped, David stared into the refrigerator, then his eyes narrowed. Was he missing several bottles? He began to count them, then concluded that if he couldn't keep track of the few bottles he'd had in the house refrigerator, how could he keep a tally of all the bottles in the barn refrigerator? For all he knew, he'd taken several more bottles inside than he remembered.

David pulled two bottles from the refrigerator, then closed the door. As he began to leave, he noticed that one of the cases of Jack Daniels had been opened, and the old remedy book he'd received from the librarian, in exchange for signing several of his novels, had been moved. Pulling the cardboard flaps back, David checked the box. Several bottles were missing!

Had someone—the boys?—found the elixir! Taken some?!

David started to shake. He began to take another drink, then stopped. Not too much, he needed his head clear.

But the storage closet had been locked. He checked the door. There wasn't any sign of forced entry. "Another mystery," David bemoaned. Well, he would handle one at a time. Monique was first. He knew he must find her. There were questions to ask.

David looked at his clothing, which were filthy instead of white, but were still too light-colored. If he didn't want to stand out like a sore thumb, he would need to dress in something dark.

He walked back to the house, heading for his bedroom. As he passed his study, a blue glow emanated from the room. He stuck his head inside, and noticed his computer was on.

David didn't remember leaving it on. Was he going senile? First porphyria, now Alzheimer's disease. He walked over to the computer, sitting partially on the chair and intending to turn it off, when he was suddenly seized. He was paralyzed, unable to do anything but breathe, his eyes frozen to the blue screen. His hands began to tingle and quiver, then his fingers began to type without his will. White words from an unknown source appeared on the screen.

He is coming on his bicycle, the young man whose lifeforce burns brighter than a star in the darkness. His blood scent is richer than a fine wine. First was his brother—his tasty, arrogant, foolish brother—and now this one is mine, too. I can smell his fear, taste it in the air. It is delicious and intoxicating. Can you taste it?

David licked his lips.

I can see his face clearly, the windblown, white blond hair, the blue eyes open in surprise and fear, his jaw slack, and his mouth open. The reactions of those who see death coming are always so enlightening. HAHA-HAHAHAHA!

Softly now, I let myself drift as part of the night, as the mists expand and widen. One more time, ride through my body, I am enjoying the play. HAHAHAHA-HAHA!

David felt exhilaration.

There he goes, a bat out of hell, fading into the darkness. Maybe he'll be hit by a car, but I doubt it. He won't get far. The poor soul doesn't have that long to live.

Are you enjoying this, David? HAHAHAHA! I knew you wouldn't come with me, but I'm bringing you along anyway! For more than the ride, though. You will understand the true heritage that you have been denying!

David tried to move and still couldn't. He began to pray.

Stop that!

Slapped, David's head snapped sideways, then returned to stare at the screen, frozen once more. David tried to block out the sensations, but failed. They were overwhelming, his vision blurring as though a rock had been dropped in a placid pond, and he lost sight of his computer.

His body suddenly felt thinly dispersed, light, as though he were sick with a high fever, and his senses stretched wide, as if he were riding the night's air! He was the wind . . . or . . . or some kind of fog! He was hovering over a back road somewhere near the lake. The sky was clear, and the moon was high in the sky. He could hear the lapping of the waves in the distance, and smell the water.

David could also smell something else, a musty odor tinged with electricity—FEAR! Even as the boy rode away, David could smell Benny Joe Brookens, hear his heart pounding and his breathless rasp. The bicycle chain rattled as the wheels whirled.

Suddenly, David was pulled together, coalescing into something solid. He felt condensed, heavy, then once again he sensed a change coming. He was shrinking, suddenly smaller, and blind, but still able to "see"! Then he sprouted light, fan-shaped arms. With a flap of his pinions, he was airborne, truly riding the winds.

Below, David could sense Benny Joe, touching him all over and surrounding him. He could hone in not only on sounds that created pictures, but also the scent of Benny Joe's blood. It was calling sweetly to him!

David flew overhead and could see Benny Joe crane his neck to look upward.

Are you getting this, David? We are flying! We know no boundaries. NOW IT IS TIME TO FEAST!

David/Monique swooped low, swiping at Benny Joe's head. As their claws touched the boy, Benny Joe screamed and struck at them, but missed as they banked, then fluttered away.

Circling on the winds, David/Monique came back for another strike. David couldn't control himself. As one, they attacked again, this time snatching the back of Benny Joe's shirt. They extended, then flexed their claws, digging into flesh.

Screaming in pain, Benny Joe whirled, swinging at them. He missed. His bicycle wobbled, then went off the road. As the ten-speed slid sideways into the gravel along the shoulder, it flipped, carrying both boy and bicycle into the wire fence and weeds that lined the road. Stunned and caught as though he were a fly in a spider's web, Benny Joe just lay there, his face slack and his eyes closed.

They landed, then once again changed shape, filling out, becoming heavier, stouter, and larger. The wings and claws receded and disappeared. They walked toward the entangled boy and saw him differently. There was a reddish light emanating from Benny Joe, as well as a golden glow which seemed to suffuse from the middle of his chest.

They licked their lips. David tried to stop, but Monique pulled him along as if he were a reluctant puppy on a leash. They grabbed the Brookens boy, then shook him. His eyes fluttered open. "It is better when they are awake," Monique said, then sank their teeth into his bare, exposed throat.

David felt the flesh part underneath his lips, then blood rushed into his mouth. He tried to scream, but couldn't, as the viscous, iron-tasting fluid swelled within his mouth, then poured down his throat.

David vaguely sensed the Brookens boy struggling in his grasp. His pulse hammered within David's head, within his very soul, as though a blacksmith were working. Pound, pound, pound . . . then the pulse slowed, the thundering weakened, and Benny Joe's resistance grew even more feeble. David was expanding, growing larger than a giant, filling up the world. He could see all over Texas, feel the cycle of nature, and the movements of animals. David sensed he was more than an essential part of the world; he was an overlord, larger than life itself!

"NO!" David screamed, and pulled himself free of Monique's grasp. "No! No! NO!" David pounded on the keyboard. He could still taste the blood, still felt larger than life, as though this room could barely contain him.

"No!" David cried again, trying to regain control of himself, to push away the seductively alien feelings. He murmured a heartfelt prayer as he grasped his crucifix and the locket.

When he opened his eyes, the screen read:

Was it good for you too, David? MMMMMMMM . . .

Nine

Confrontation

"David? Is anyone home?" Jana called through the screen door. She could've sworn that she heard somebody talking, but nobody answered, and she'd rung the doorbell several times. Still, Jana was sure he was home. As she'd driven in, she'd seen a bluish light coming from a second-story window. The illumination had bestowed a ghostly appearance upon the front facade, giving the place an ethereal glow except where the shadows dwelled. The front door was very dark.

Jana was surprised to find that she had to muster courage to even approach the house, but then she was nervous already. She smoothed her dress; it was airy, a white, peasant-style outfit with a black belt, dark, puffy sleeves, and a sweetheart neckline that exposed her shoulders.

Since the party, she'd had an insistent desire to see him again . . . to get to know him once again. At the reunion—the last time she saw him—she'd been married. But she'd always been attracted to him.

"What?" David's white face suddenly appeared in the darkened doorway, his red eyes inflamed with anger. His expression spoke of ire and menace.

Frightened, Jana stepped back from the door. Her free hand went to her throat, as though to catch a scream.

"Oh hi, Jana," David said softly, composing himself. He opened the screen door, and she moved even farther away. "This is quite a surprise." He flipped on the light and stepped out onto the porch.

"H . . . hello, David." She was flushed as well as flustered. "You surprised me."

"I'm sorry. My appearance does that to people."

"No," she emphasized. "I'm sorry, it's . . . I had been ringing the doorbell and calling for a while, then suddenly you were here. I guess my mind was wandering. I didn't hear you coming." She wanted to ask if anything was wrong, but couldn't muster the courage.

"I listen to music while I write. I get few visitors, and the answering machine takes messages." David suddenly noticed that she was nicely dressed. Her visit was more than business; he could tell by the reaction on her face and the look in her eyes, which made having to leave that much more difficult. But he had to find Monique! He could feel her nearby, drawing him to her, as though he were the moth and she the flame.

David sighed, "Jana, I hate to be rude, but I'm on my way out. Are those papers for me?" He pointed to the stack under her arm.

"Yes. Late? For what?" Jana said in surprise. Was he already seeing somebody? "Well, I guess I could leave them," Jana said hesitantly, "but Michael really recommended that we go over them together, since there are several different offers. He would've come himself, but Lydia's sick. She caught what Billy had. Michael thinks he's probably next, and he doesn't want you to catch it." She sighed. "But he did say that they needed to be done immediately."

David managed a halfhearted laugh that put her at ease, when he said, "Agents are in a hurry when publishers are in a hurry. A day won't make any difference. It won't get my next book out any sooner, I guarantee that. We could do it by phone, but I'd prefer not." He wouldn't mind seeing her again. It would be a nice change after the events of the last few days. It was odd how a lot of his past was rushing forward to catch him. "How about tomorrow night?"

"That should be fine. I'll call first, just in case. Well, I'll see you then. Good night, David," Jana said with disappointment heavy in her voice. So much for fanciful expectations, Jana thought as she turned and headed down the walk. David was acting a little strange, but Michael had said David hadn't been interacting much with people. And despite the fact that she and David had once known each other, they were strangers now. Well, maybe she could make him a little less reclusive and skittish. Everybody needed a friend.

As he moved through the woods along the edge of the road, a figure watched as Jana climbed into her car and left. Why was she leaving already? That didn't seem right. He'd been hoping to get some good, juicy photos. The lady was a honey. Too bad. Oh well. Stones put down his binoculars and kneeled behind a tree, where he began to remove his camera from his duffel bag. He assembled it, adding the long lens to his Nikon, then looked through it at the house to check exposure and focus. Suddenly, he heard an engine start, then twin beams of light shone from behind the house to illuminate the thin veil of mist that was slowly rising around the farm.

"Shit!" Stones cried, as David's Blazer roared to life and shot from behind the house as though it were thrown from a catapult. Tires spewing gravel and leaving a cloud of exhaust, the Blazer raced up the driveway, around the curve, past the pond, and toward the front gate.

"Shit and double shit!" Stones shoved his camera into his bag. He spied the wide-open front door and hesitated. Maybe this was a good time to search David's place? But where was he going in such a hurry? Stones took off, running through the woods. It was hopeless, but he had to try and reach his car before David was long gone. Huffing and puffing he raced through the trees and into the moon-shadowed darkness.

David drove recklessly fast, the speedometer needle passing sixty, seventy, and continuing to climb. David prayed there wasn't a patrol car near, or worse, a cow loose on the road. Since he was outdriving his headlights, he would never see it in time. The twin beams were absorbed by the road, and it seemed to lengthen into an endless black trail. The tall grass and the fences alongside the road flashed by, blurring into a wall of muted color.

What were these nightmares? David wondered. If they were visions, they were terrible, ghastly, and reminded him more of flashbacks or tripping. And who was Monique? Why was she bothering him? And what transformation was she talking about?

David saw a flash of color out of the corner of his eye. He slammed on the brakes and screeched to a stop. As David backed up, he was struck by déjà vu. Benny Joe Brookens's ten-speed was tangled in the weeds. Benny Joe wasn't. Did Monique have him? This was crazy. Maybe he was still dreaming.

Burning rubber, David drove off. Moments later he felt a pull and turned right into a sparsely housed neighborhood. Shutting off the headlights, David drove past the houses to the end of the pavement, then continued on as gravel led to an unfinished house standing out against the silvery sparkling water. The place was as quiet as a funeral parlor; the denizens of the night were silent.

But Monique was here! Waiting for him!

He parked and jumped out of the Blazer. "Monique!" There was no response. All was silent, but he felt something hiding, either within the shadow-filled framework of the house or behind the scattered masses—piles and stacks of trash and supplies. Having been near death before, he sensed it as well as Monique's presence, unsure of where one started and the other ended. The air was heavy, thick with humidity but also smelling of something foul—the rotted flesh of roadkill baking too long in the sun.

David walked directly to the bodies. Benny Joe had been piled atop the mummified corpse of his brother in a heap of construction trash. Both had wounds in their necks, their throats darkly stained. David couldn't believe his eyes— didn't want to believe them. Candel must be informed . . . later.

David had to understand what was going on first. He had to find Monique! "Monique!" David called out again. There was no answer, but he pinpointed her presence; she was waiting for him inside the unfinished house.

David climbed the steps to the front porch, then stared into the bony beginnings of the house, all crisp lines, dark shadows, and patches of ivory moonlight. The black swaths were velvety, cut cloth instead of space. "I have questions!"

David heard soft, mocking laughter. He walked in where the front door would be, into a great room of tangled shadows and silver slivers of moonlight. They barely touched the stone fireplace to his left, where he saw the skirt of a long, frilly dress. It was pink and just the hint of it reminded him of Southern plantations.

"You are *un ubertoleln*," she laughed, stepping into the moonlight. The voice came from all around him, echoing oddly throughout the house. Monique was dressed as a Southern belle with her hair pulled back severely to highlight the fine bones of her face; her flushed cheeks and rose-hued lips matched her billowing dress. Including the gloves, she was virtually covered from neck to floor, except for an open diamond space above her breasts. She could have been a different woman. David tried to say something, ask a question, but couldn't. Calm down, he told himself, trying to slow his racing pulse and rapid breathing.

"Ah handsome fool, but still ah fool," her accent was now Southern, without the slightest hint of Austria.

"Monique, who are you?"

"Do ya mean *what* am I? What are *we?*" David was confused. "Ah'm just ah simple lady from Georgia," she drawled and smiled sweetly.

"Why are you doing this?"

"Am I bothering you? You don't like relatives to come visit?"

"We are not related."

"Oh yes, we are. We're connected. Haven't you felt the rapport?" she asked, and David nodded reluctantly. "We both belong to the night and shun the day."

"I don't shun the day."

"You will. Doesn't it make you sick?"

"Yes. So what's your point? Do you also suffer from porphyria? Does it drive you . . . mad? Does it lead you to kill?" Had she really killed the brothers? They were dead, but he hadn't seen it with his own two eyes. Or had he? But he'd been at church and on his computer. This seemed too real to be a hallucination.

"I don't suffer from porphyria and neither do you," she said, and David started to protest. "But it is a clever cover," she laughed. "David, how do you feel about living, while everybody else around you dies?" He said nothing. "I can see it in your eyes. You hate it. But," she chuckled, "you must learn to deal with it. It is your destiny. Your nature. As the years pass, everyone around you will grow old and die. You won't. You are immortal. Doomed to live alone, but I can change that. I can help you."

Her presence and words made it difficult for David to think clearly. "What are you talking about?!"

"You hate death, but you will see a lot more, whether you wish it or not. Let me help you with the transformation. It is glorious and exhilarating!"

"What transformation?"

"You don't understand, do you? It is truly amazing, another first." She paused. "David, you and I, we are . . . vampires."

David was sure he hadn't heard her correctly. "What?"

"You are a vampire. It is why you can no longer stand the sun. It is why you thirst for blood!"

"You're crazy. I don't thirst for blood!"

She laughed. "You can't lie to a vampire. I know about your elixir. It is a substitute. But it is not really what you need. Without fresh, human blood, you will be stuck in between mortality and immortality, neither a human nor a vampire."

"You are one crazy bitch!"

"Can't you feel it! Can't you feel the truth!" Her words struck him harder than any blow. She was compelling, even convincing, but she was wrong. David knew he wasn't a vampire. He'd been to church. He wore a cross. He believed in the Lord. David clutched his crucifix and locket.

"Come, David," she said smoothly, coyly moving closer. "Come feast with me. We will hunt with the night, then finish in ecstasy, your flesh intertwined with mine." She glided closer, overwhelming him and kissing him.

"No!" David leaned away, unable to get his feet to move.

"Yes, you want it. Through our link, you have already tasted the blood of the brothers. That is a powerful combination, but it was vicarious. Come experience the real thing," she chuckled, and moved to kiss him again.

David managed to free his crucifix and raised it. "Get away from me!" He was stunned when she jumped back as though burned.

"Amazing!" she said, flushing. "You have conquered the cross! No one has ever done so before! The others must be told!"

"What others?"

"More than you and I are vampires, my handsome friend. But none can do what you have just done."

"I'm *not* a vampire!" David cried. He suddenly found himself believing that she was one of the undead. Mere minutes ago, he would have thought that totally absurd. Now he didn't. He could read it in her eyes, feel it was the truth.

"Continue to deny it, and you will only grow sicker. You won't die, just suffer. Come feed with me. Simple, *ya?*" Her Austrian accent had returned.

"I'm not a vampire."

"Well," she turned to walk up the steps. "I will just continue to take you along with me, as I did tonight, whether you wish it or not. In time, you will come around. You won't be able to resist.

"NO!" David lunged and grabbed her. "This must stop!"

Snarling as she whirled, Monique easily lifted David off his feet and held him high. "Do not threaten me or touch me with violent intent. You are just a shade, not a true vampire as yet. I AM!"

David was having trouble breathing. Her strength was incredible! He tried to break her grip, but she only laughed. Then he struck her with his cross.

She dropped him and reeled backwards. "That was rude! I am intrigued by your uniqueness, how you have been photographed and how you have conquered the cross, but you must be taught a lesson!" A cold breeze suddenly whipped through the house, kicking up a tiny whirlwind of trash, wood chunks, and nails. They assaulted him, biting and stinging as though he were being attacked by killer bees. David covered his head, as her laughter mocked him once more. The wind lessened, then gusted again, pelting him with another torrent of debris as it suddenly grew much stronger.

"Don't even think it!" she shouted over the wind. "You are not strong enough to slay me. And besides, killing kin is a sin," she laughed. "It is our only sin. If you kill a vampire, the brethren will hunt you down."

The rain of trash continued hammering him, driving him to his knees, then prone on the floor. David wanted to cry out, to yell *stop,* wishing he had some control over it. "Are you afraid of me?" he called out. Suddenly, the night was calm, the trash noisily settling on the plywood floor.

"David. Sweet, innocent David. Just accept your nature. Besides," she said petulantly, "if you don't join me, I'll continue to take you with me to feast on young boys. Benny Joe and Jim Bob were about Timmy's age, if he were still alive that is. Youths are so tasty, so vibrant and full of energy," she laughed. "And after I run out of children, if you're not convinced, I shall start on your family. They are going to die sooner or later, no?"

David stood unsteadily to face her. How could such beauty and evil exist simultaneously?

"You will acquiesce," she continued. "I can see it in your eyes. You will deny yourself for a while, but even now I see doubt where dere was none before. You are discovering things about yourself, wonderfully seductive things dat you have never known. Don't you wonder what the intent to kill is doing to you?" Her laughter was loud and harsh. "It is growing, and as you think, so you are!

"Listen to me, David, and listen well. You intrigue me, but we cannot have rogue shades. They threaten all of our existences by clumsily revealing that vampires are not just legend, but real. I cannot let this happen. I will destroy you first. Think about it."

"But I just want to be left alone."

"That isn't a choice." Her voice was oddly chilling. "Think about it. For tonight, my unwilling playmate, I must bid you *auf Wiedersehen.* Just remember, my patience is short." Suddenly, she was gone, melding into the darkness, a drop of ink into a blot.

Dispirited, David left the house. The bodies appeared to stare at him, accusing him of bringing Monique into their lives—drawing the horror to Temprance. "It's not my fault," he whispered wearily, slumping, then dropping to his knees. What was he to do? They deserved a decent burial. Should he notify the sheriff? Then the terrible reality mixed with horrible unreality. Would the sheriff think *he* had done it? He'd have trouble answering questions as to why he was here. Talking about Monique would make him sound crazy, and they might say the murders were a result of his insanity. David uneasily remembered the story of the Jerome Carter lynching when he was young. The town might panic if they believed that their kids were in danger. And they were.

Sadly, David looked at the bodies again. He could imagine Mrs. Brookens's desperate reaction to her missing boys. David was sharply reminded of his own losses. Memories of seeing Timmy and Tina dead in the car flashed back to him. What was worse—seeing your loved ones dead and ravaged, or not finding them at all?

He had a shovel in the back of his Blazer. He could bury them. David shook his head. He couldn't believe what he was thinking! Hiding the bodies would be wrong. Let the builders find them. With regret and a promise to do something more after Monique was stopped, he wearily walked back to the Blazer.

Ten

Morning Walk

Soundlessly screaming, the Reverend Page shot from bed as though he'd been launched from a cannon. Gasping, he scrambled to the edge of his bed and looked around wildly. He was in his room. Thank heavens, it had just been a nightmare! It had seemed so real. The church or some other building had been burning, then it had collapsed upon itself. And he'd been inside! Just a dream, but his pulse was still racing, and his chest was heaving. Yes, it had seemed very real.

Cooper glanced at his wife; somehow she had managed to sleep through his titanic struggle and thrashing about. The covers and sheets were twisted much as a flag wind-wrapped around a pole. He was surprised that he hadn't been screaming out loud.

Cooper shivered, and knew he wouldn't be able to sleep anymore. Glancing out the window, he saw the sun was rising. He quickly changed from his pajamas into his work clothes, kissed his wife, and then murmured a prayer before heading outside for a walk. He needed to clear his head.

As Cooper descended the front steps, he glanced skyward. The horizon to the west was still a dark blue, while the east appeared to have been masterfully finger-painted by a child who loved oranges, pinks, and red with just a hint of purple. Another God-blessed day, Cooper thought as he smiled. With each dawn the world was allowed a fresh start—a grand reawakening. He glanced at the church, wondering if he should check to make sure all was safe and sound, then smiled at himself. The venerable Todd Hempton was the evening caretaker, and he was conscientious. Everything was all right. It had just been a nightmare.

Regardless of what he told himself, Cooper couldn't resist, and strolled across the lawn to check on the church. He did believe in visions, gifts sent by the Lord. Still, everything looked fine. Feeling a little better, he headed into town. Already Cooper felt the heat building; the nights never really cooled off during the summer, unless it rained. The relentless heat added to the tension that he was already feeling both inwardly and from others. He figured that was the reason for short tempers, harsh words, and confrontations like his a few days ago.

Cooper Page hated arguing—fighting with anyone—but that's what he'd done with Daniel Wright, and now they weren't speaking to each other. Daniel had confronted Cooper about David's communion. He'd been spying! Cooper couldn't believe it. Daniel claimed to have seen God's judgment of Matthewson's worthiness. As soon as the blood of Christ had touched his lips, David had gone into some type of spasm. Wasn't it obvious that the good Lord didn't want him taking communion, Daniel asked? Not only that, but David had struck a minister!

That wasn't how Cooper remembered it. It was this as well as the fact that he simply didn't agree with Daniel's point of view at all. He and Daniel had talked about David—his troubles, family, and writings. Daniel adamantly claimed that David was bad for the church; David wasn't penitent.

Cooper had told Daniel that he was being unduly hard on David. The best thing was to open a line of communication, allow the opportunity so changes could be made. Demanding something rarely changed people for long, while exposure to the Lord would open all the necessary doors and could create permanent change. Cooper believed that they needed to offer a helping hand, not an iron fist, to people asking for assistance and redemption. Seething, Daniel had stormed off, and Cooper had the feeling that stories about their meeting were spreading like wildfire. That's the way it was in a small community.

Absorbed in his thoughts, Cooper had absently entered the town square. He ambled past the Paperback Peddler, Henry Allbright's place for used books and Christian reading. As he stared in the window at the books on display, Cooper recalled Daniel's words. "There's something wrong in Temprance! Can't you feel it?! It started last weekend. Remember the commotion outside the church?"

Had he missed something? Cooper wondered. He didn't think so. The owners of these businesses along with other locals—his congregation—were mostly good people. He crossed a tributary street that fed into the square. Cooper knelt and patted the red-haired cocker spaniel lying in front of the entrance to the Main Street Cafe. "Good morning, Bart," he said to the dog. In a larger town, the dog catcher would've been called, but everyone knew Andrew's dog. Everyone was neighborly, or had been until recently.

Cooper continued on past a window with a big red and white sign advertising State Farm Insurance. He glanced across the street at the town's administrative building, and the clock on it read, six o'clock. His eyes fell to the statues of the town's founding fathers, distant relatives of Stephen F. Austin. They were men of good faith—good forefathers.

Yes, the town was full of good people, but everybody seemed on edge. Sunday morning there had nearly been two fights on the church steps. He remembered that it had been a beautiful day, everybody waiting outside to be called in to service. From what he'd heard, everything was fine until Claire and her boys had showed up. He sighed; that was not new. Only minutes later, Benny Joe and Jim Bob were arguing. The sheriff had stepped in, having overheard Benny Joe talking about Friday night. Supposedly, it wasn't the same story he'd given Candel.

Bricker had confronted them both, then taken them to Claire. She immediately accused the sheriff of mistreating her sons, and trying to trump up something on them. Her friends agreed. Suddenly, Claire and Don Bricker were face-to-face—nose to nose—yelling at each other on the church steps! Nobody was intervening, so he had. Finally, they all agreed to discuss things calmly after church, when they'd had time to think and pray.

Then he had called them all to service, asking them to direct their thoughts toward worship and the Lord. As he'd watched them file in, he noticed that everybody—not just Claire, the sheriff, and the boys—looked worn and weary, as though no one was sleeping well. He'd remembered his own nightmares, and wondered if Daniel might have noticed something that he hadn't. Was it possible that he too often saw only the good side?

The reverend sighed heavily and continued around the square, heading back toward the church. There was plenty of the Lord's work to be done today. Maybe by going around and visiting people, he could get a feel for what was wrong, bolster people's faith, and ease their fears. He promised himself he'd try to see Penny and David Matthewson this evening, maybe even Jana Martinez. They were all in need, experiencing troubled times. If nothing else, it would at least make him feel better, as though he were making a difference.

Eleven

Plea For Help

Logan had finally started his vacation four days ago, but was still feeling odd. He hadn't been to the office since Saturday, and that might be a record. He still had a week and a half left, if he survived it. His wife was keeping him plenty busy, but he'd gotten in some fishing, despite her honey-do chores.

As he climbed out of his squad car, Logan promised himself he'd go night fishing this evening. He'd only taken a few steps toward the brick building that housed the Temprance Sheriff's department, when he wiped sweat from his brow. He didn't need to slick back his hair today; it would do it on its own. The day was going to be a scorcher, something he should be used to by now. He'd only survived some forty-some Texas summers, including the record heat of nineteen eighty.

Logan stopped at the door to the sheriff's office and turned around to look at the square. It was deserted, not a soul in sight—all the smart people were indoors. At seven-thirty, the blacktop was already radiating heat, giving the buildings around the square a surreal appearance of wavering mirages. The leaves on the trees were perfectly still, and the flag hung from the pole as though it had wilted.

A heat wave was not what they needed, with the Summerfest coming up. Heat always made things worse, especially the drunks. They increased in numbers and severity. It was a good thing the sheriffs would be getting help from Palestine and Athens this year. Last year had been more than they could handle, even though Bricker hated to admit it.

As he pushed the door open, Logan noticed that the bench along the front of the building was empty. Where was Bob? The last time Logan had seen him was Friday. No matter what the weather, Bob was always there to greet him. Logan hoped something wasn't wrong, but his gut feeling was queasy.

Maybe it's the weird dreams, Logan thought. He hadn't slept well in several days. Edith complained she was having trouble, too, and almost nothing ever kept his wife from a heavy slumber.

Something grabbed his shoulder, and Logan spun around, his nervous hand reaching for his holster.

"Sheriff Candel! I need your help!" Claire cried, talking a mile a minute. Shaking and dishevelled, Claire was obviously distressed and a ghastly sight, still dressed in her pink robe and houseshoes. Her eyes and nose red, she'd been crying, causing her makeup to run down her face and around quivering lips. "Please, help me! My boys are missin'!"

For a moment, Logan was taken aback. He hadn't even heard Claire coming. He glanced beyond her and saw her Pinto near the curb, still idling with the driver's door open. He suspected she'd jumped out of the car and run to him, all without him hearing her. "Help you?" he asked calmly.

"Yes! YES! My boys are missin'. Yesterday it was Jim Bob! Today it's Benny Joe! Something's terrible wrong. I can feel it in my bones. Please, help me!" Her words ran together, and Logan was so surprised to hear her say please that he didn't say anything for a moment. Claire mistook it for indifference. "It's not a prank. I know it! Please, please, help me!"

The door opened, and Bricker peeked out. "Logan, what

in the hell is goin' on out here? Oh." He frowned. "I should have known it was Claire."

"Sheriff Bricker!" Claire exclaimed, thrilled at his arrival, then she did something that surprised them both. With outstretched arms pleading, she approached the portly sheriff and said, "Please, help me! Something's happened to my boys! They're missin'! Gone! Kidnapped!"

Bricker recovered from his surprise, his expression now critical and disdainful. "Is that all? I'm not surprised. They're probably hiding from doing clean-up duty. That's typical of boys and punishment. Not to worry, Claire, they'll be back when they're hungry."

"Please, Sheriff, I know we've had hard words in the past, but something bad's happened," she wrung her hands. "My boys wouldn't do this to me!"

"Why not?" he asked smugly. "They do it to everyone else." It was obvious to Logan that Bricker was enjoying himself, and the deputy sheriff didn't like it.

Claire looked ready to have a breakdown. She ignored Bricker's sarcasm and said, "Jim Bob didn't come home Monday night. I didn't notice then, but Benny Joe told me so Tuesday morning. Then Benny Joe didn't come home last night. I'm worried to death. I can't sleep! I keep having bad dreams. Something wants my boys! *Has* my boys!"

"I told you ya couldn't keep tabs on your boys." Bricker shook his head, convinced that Claire had finally gone over the edge.

"You mean they didn't disappear at the same time?" Logan asked. That didn't make sense. He felt even more uneasy.

Claire shook her head. "No sir. And Benny Joe was real worried. He even lied to me."

"Oh, he wouldn't do that, would he?" Bricker growled. He began to turn around to go back inside.

"Never before. Wait!" Claire pleaded. Bricker grimaced and turned around, his face reddened and tense. "To lie to me something must be mighty bad. Benny Joe was worried, I could tell."

"Claire," Bricker managed to contain himself and put his hands gently on her shoulders, though it appeared he would have preferred to shake some sense into her. "Just go on home. They'll show up soon."

"No," Claire said firmly. Logan expected her to demand help, claiming that she'd sit on his desk until Donald did something about her missing boys. Instead, she dropped to her knees and began to weep. "I'm not proud. I'm begging ya to help me. Find my boys, please, please . . ."

Wide-eyed and slack-jawed with surprise, Bricker glanced at Logan, who was also speechless. "Claire . . ."

"Please, Sheriff, if you help us, me and my boys will never be trouble again. If they are, I won't fight you to have them sent to juvenile!"

Logan couldn't believe his ears. Bricker was stunned, as though he'd been punched in the stomach. "Claire . . ."

"Sheriff, please," she lunged forward and wrapped her arms around his legs. Bricker tried to move back, but saw he was going to drag her with him. Claire's words blurred together, almost incomprehensibly, but they did hear, "I'm beggin' ya for the Lord's mercy. If not for my boys, how about for other kids who might be next!"

"Claire, please!" Bricker had trouble disengaging her desperate grip, and Logan had to help him.

When they pulled Claire away, she was limp. Logan had to hold her up; otherwise she'd have collapsed. "I should be embarrassed, but I'm desperate!"

"Here," Logan dug out his handkerchief and handed it to her. "Come in where it's cool, Claire. We'll help you. Of course we will. Won't we, Donald?"

"Um, uh," Bricker blustered, obviously not wanting to help Claire, even if she were drowning. That's not the way the job worked, Logan thought and glared at him. "We . . . we need to know more before we can help, Claire. Come inside," he managed weakly. He looked around to see if anyone had seen what had happened. Logan all but carried Claire inside and set her in a chair. "Lisa," Bricker called to his secretary, "bring this woman a glass of water and some Kleenex to stem the tide."

"I think we should call for Reverend Cooper," Logan suggested, looking at Claire but talking to Bricker. Logan couldn't believe that this proud and cantankerous woman had been reduced to this. She needed comforting they couldn't provide. At best, they could find her boys or give her an answer. Counselling had never been one of his strong points.

"What do you mean?" Bricker asked.

"Call Doc Katyu, then the church. See if one of the ministers will come over."

"Great idea," Bricker said with relief, obviously wishing he could wash his hands of the situation.

Their secretary, a thin, middle-aged woman with a concerned expression, brought a glass of water and a box of Kleenex. Lisa ran a nervous hand through her short, brown locks and bit her lip, then said. "Is there anything I can do?"

"Yes," Bricker said and repeated Logan's suggestion. Lisa moved off with quick steps, carrying an air of efficiency about her. "Claire, we've called for help. Doc Katyu and the Reverend Page should be here!"

"I don't want them! I WANT MY BOYS! OH LORD HELP ME!"

Logan sat next to her and took her hands in his. "Claire, we can't help you until you tell us some things. To help your boys, you need to be strong and calm for a while longer, okay?" She nodded, not looking sure but willing to try. Logan could tell another outburst was imminent. "Now, when did you last see Jim Bob and Benny Joe?"

She told what she knew of their disappearances. Logan tried to ask more questions, about the boys' favorite places to go—especially Cedar Creek—and their friends, but Claire was a wreck, incapable of answering. Finally, he gave up. "I think we should question all those concerned with Friday night, especially the kids."

"Agreed," Bricker said. He paced as he drank a cup of iced coffee with cream. Claire nodded and muttered something they couldn't understand.

"Maybe we should start asking for search volunteers," Logan said. His gut was twisted tighter; he had a bad feeling about all this.

"Not yet. It's too early. Let's first do some checkin' ourselves," Bricker suggested. "I don't want to panic the town, if this is just more shenanigans." That sent Claire to wailing that neither of the men could stop. Logan simply held her, letting her cry on his shoulder, and glared at Bricker. Shortly, the Reverend Cooper arrived and moved immediately to Claire's side.

Logan stared at Claire and had the feeling he wasn't on vacation any longer. It was going to be a long week.

Twelve

Kindred Souls

Speed thrills, speed kills, Grimm thought as he raced down the highway in his mother's gray Trans Am. The sides of the road were dark blurs, the only light was that of his high beams carving into the onrushing darkness. Road signs appeared quickly, grew rapidly larger, then were gone. Even with the windows down, it was still warm inside the car. The twilight air had yet to cool, and the humidity increased as he drove toward the spillway at Tool. He had the radio turned off, listening to the wind thrash though the interior.

"Thanks, Mom," Grimm said, then took a long drag on a Camel. His mother had wanted his pickup for some reason or the other, leaving him free to scorch the road in a real driving machine. This baby was twin-cammed and fuel-injected. A turbocharger would've been nice, too.

Driving fast helped him think, because he didn't think about it. When you drove slow, everything wasn't a blur and things caught your attention, interrupting your train of thought and blocking inspiration. The seductiveness of the dotted line merging into a solid one relaxed him, freed his mind from his body—freed his thoughts.

So what should he do about Lou and Becky? Skeeter and

PP? He owed them big time. Grimm was only now recovering from the thrashing Lou had given him. Grimm didn't want to just throw something together. He wanted to be creative. Revenge . . . paybacks . . . were a form of art. "That's right, Kevy. Just give it time. We'll come up with somethin' special, I promise." Grimm nodded. It would all work its way out in the end, like the constipated mathematician and his pencil.

Grimm snuffed his Camel butt into the ashtray and reached over to the cooler in the front seat. He removed the icy cold, dripping wet bottle of Jack Daniels. Next to it was a dark, squarish bottle of unlabeled Jaegermeister. "Thank you, Mister Matthewson," Grimm laughed. If he was supposed to be joy riding, then he needed all the pleasures at hand to truly enjoy.

He wished he had a good-looking honey in his front seat, instead of a cooler. It could be in the backseat . . . or they could be in the back seat. "I'd rather be hotter than cooler," he snickered. "Ah, why do women have two holes so close together?" This had been one of Jim Bob's favorites. "In case you miss, you don't miss out."

Grimm wouldn't have minded having Jim Bob for driving company. He could really hold his liquor and loved jokes, but it seemed that he had run off—or was missing, or something like that. Same with Benny Joe, but then it only made sense that he would follow his older brother.

Grimm briefly recalled his discussion with Bricker and shook his head. How was he supposed to know anything? He hadn't talked to them since Friday. Grimm smiled. It seems the Reapers had stirred up plenty of trouble . . . for at least a little while. But more trouble was coming; you can go down on a good man, but you can't keep a good man down.

Grimm drove through a cloud of bugs. Many splattered all over his windshield, inspiring a joke. "What's the last thing that goes through a bug's mind, when it hits a windshield at eighty miles per hour? Its asshole." Kevin laughed, picturing the event in slow motion, then changed the insect to Lou. Naw, too fast.

Well, since a beautiful babe wasn't going to just appear on the side of the road, he'd just have to see if JJ wanted to go for a cruise. He hadn't talked to the youngest Tubbs since Friday, but JJ also enjoyed racing along the road with a brew in hand, a buzz on, and the wind whipping through his hair.

Grimm briefly glimpsed a sign reading "Welcome to Tool," and reluctantly slowed to the speed limit. His stepfather didn't have any influence in the small, speed-trap town set across Highway 274. One had to be cool through Tool, the locals often said. Kevin knew he could be cool; it was another one of his abilities. The spillway bridge sitting high over Cedar Creek was coming up.

Suddenly the headlights were devoured by a large, billowing band of gray clouds. He sped into the flat, misty world of the fog, where he could barely see the flash of pavement just in front of the bumper. Grimm wasn't worried. There weren't any turns on the bridge.

Unexpectedly, there was a break in the gray mists. Grimm briefly glimpsed a slim, darkly tressed woman standing roadside with her thumb out, then the Trans Am was engulfed by the fog once more. Yeow! She had legs, and he hoped she knew how to use them. He started to hum some ZZ Top, as he braked and spun the wheel. The car did a squealing donut and left a curving black streak across the pavement, as Grimm swung it around to where the hitchhiker still waited.

He pulled next to her on the wrong side of the road and stared blatantly. The hitchhiker's stark beauty caused him to catch his breath, and for a moment Grimm was speechless. Clad in leather—a red halter top and short black pants that almost looked as if they might be chaps—and cowboy boots, the young woman radiated sex. Grimm could feel it, smell it. A slow smile crawled onto his face as his gaze slid up her lovely legs, past her well-rounded thighs and narrow waist.

His gaze slid over her flat stomach to rest upon the swell of her breasts, where the top button was undone. Eventually he looked at her face, and saw that her eyes reflected a starless night.

Grimm was held by the intensity of her stare. Finally, a smile begin to spread across her red lips, forming a wicked grin. For a moment Grimm thought she was going to eat him; he liked that idea. *I'd rather be in the back seat, in a heartbeat, than be beat.* Then, "Watch this one, Kevy, she's ah wild thang, a dark one."

"Ya going my way on the highway, beautiful?" he asked, and she nodded. "To Seven Points? Gunbarrel? Where?"

"I just want to ride, honey," she said softly.

"Well, you know the hitchhikers' payment plan: gas, grass, or ass." Without a word, she gracefully strutted around the front of his car and climbed inside. Grimm hastily placed the cooler in the backseat and then wiped his palms dry on his pants. "You'd better buckle up. I drive fast."

"I'm not afraid of dying," she said softly.

"Then, babe, you got in the right car."

"I'm sure I have," the woman said.

"Yeah, well, Teddy Kennedy taught Grace Kelly and me how to drive!" He put the car in gear, made a U-turn, and then stomped on the gas. The Trans Am's tires spun, screeching and smoking—*To hell with the Tool Patrol*—then they shot forward, jamming them into their seats.

"It'll be killer, man."

Grimm couldn't keep his eyes on the road, but what else was new? He was used to driving while blind—a red-eye driver at one with the Force. Despite her incredible legs and taut breasts, Grimm was having trouble leaving her ebony eyes. They drew his attention as though leashed. "My name's Grimm, Kevin Grimm."

"I am . . . Monique."

"Monique?" he asked, and she nodded. "All you have is one name?"

"It's all I need." Her eyes dominated Grimm, surrounding him in darkness. "You know, I believe we are two of a kind."

"Oh?" Grimm managed, his eyes flicking across her body, devouring it in a glance, then returning to her eyes. She slowly licked her lips. "Uh, do you know what's blue and sings alone?"

Monique looked at him for a moment, then said, "Dan Ackroyd."

Grimm laughed. "What kind of car does Renee Richards drive?"

Again a pause, her eyes never leaving his, then, "A convertible."

Grimm laughed again. This was great. He'd test her; he knew a million. "What do Loretta Swit and Richard Pryor have in common?"

"They've both had Major Burns on their face."

A babe after his own heart. "What's blue and comes in Brownies?"

"Cub Scouts."

"It's such a great night, I feel like celebrating. Would you like a drink?" Grimm reached into the back seat, opened the cooler and grabbed the bottle of Jack Daniels.

"No thank you." Then she spotted the second bottle. "What's dat?"

"A special brew."

"May I try it?"

"Of course! Help yourself." She did, pulling the dark green bottle from the ice chest, unscrewing the top, and putting it to her lips. She frowned, then smiled faintly.

"What's the sweat between Dolly Parton's breasts called?" His eyes moved to her cleavage.

"Mountain Dew," she replied without a smile, then undid another button on the halter top, leaving only two done.

"What do elephants use for condoms?"

"Goodyear blimps."

"What do a walrus and Tupperware have in common?"

"They both like a tight seal."

"I don't believe this! You're incredible!"

"Danka."

"Let's . . ." But his words were interrupted by the distant wail of a siren and the flashing of red and blue lights behind them. "Damn! Cops! I know to be cool through Tool. Shit!" He thought about outrunning them, then changed his mind. After braking, he was still doing seventy. Grimm stuffed his Jack in the cooler, then reached for hers.

"Don't worry," Monique said with a smile.

Grimm shrugged, pulled over to the side of the road, and stopped. Rolling down his window, he waited. Jail wasn't all that bad; he'd been there before. Dear ole stepdad would get him out; there was plenty of back-scratching between the small towns.

The black and white pulled behind them, its spinning lights flicking across the Trans Am and countryside. The siren was suddenly silent, then a tall, stiff-moving officer got out of the car and walked to the rear of the Trans Am. After checking the license plate, the thin-faced and hard-eyed officer came to the window. His badge identified him as Officer Preston. He peered inside and frowned, his thin mustache twitching as though it itched. "Driver's license, please." Grimm handed it to him. "Mr. Grimm, did you know you were doin' a hundred and five?"

"No." Grimm tried not to smile.

"Any reason you were going this fast?"

"Just having fun, Officer Preston," Monique said, leaning against Grimm's shoulder. Preston looked at her, began to say something, then stopped and stared. After a moment, his mouth worked as though he was muttering to himself, but he didn't speak aloud. "Don't you ever have fun, Officer

Preston?" The lean man nodded, his gaze still held steady. "And do you think people should be arrested for having fun?" She saw him pause, then sighed and said, "Why don't you give Kevin his license, let us go, and forget about this?"

With a glazed expression, the officer handed Grimm his license, said, "Have a good night and drive safe," then turned and walked back to his car.

"Whoa, lady, you have a way with men!"

"It's natural," she said, and stretched with feline grace. "I can be irresistible when I want. Or I can be a total bitch!"

Grimm could barely breathe during her languid movements. "I can imagine."

"Let's get going before he changes his mind."

"You don't have to ask me twice!"

In a minute they were cruising down the highway again, heading for Seven Points and Gunbarrel. Grimm was thinking he didn't have to worry about being ticketed anymore, when Monique asked, "Kevin, what do you get when you cross a pickle and a deer?"

Grimm thought for a moment. "A dildo."

"What's organic dental floss made from?"

Grimm smiled, beginning to perspire with excitement. He had to struggle not to readjust his crotch. "Pubic hair."

"Did you hear about the new designer condoms?"

"Uh," Grimm was having trouble thinking about jokes—that rarely happened. His lips were dry, and he licked them. Grimm pulled the package of Camels from his pocket and shook one free. "No."

"They're called Sergio Prevente."

Grimm shifted in his seat. He'd never met anyone like this bitch, and it was throwing him off guard. He lit the cigarette.

"You enjoy being wild," she said, "tasting the moment, and then racing forward and living without regret or looking backwards, don't you?"

He laughed. "Yes! For just meeting me, ya got me pegged."

"Why do women have two holes so close together?"

Grimm immediately felt himself go erect, cramping in his pants. He was having trouble breathing; his heart thundered in his chest. "I gotta find somewhere to park," Grimm mumbled, and slammed the pedal to the floor. The sign ahead read "Entering Seven Points. Population 450."

"Are you sure you wouldn't rather try it as we drive?"

"Uh . . ." Grimm's mind was frozen. All he could think of was getting someplace where he could use his hands. His friend, the voice, was laughing at him.

As Grimm looked for a side road, Monique ran her hands along his face, down his throat, across his chest, and into his crotch. Grimm saw a street sign and quickly pulled off the main road. He drove a short distance, then slowed to a crawl. To their right was the entrance to the Seven Points graveyard. "Mind cemeteries?"

Monique didn't smile. "No."

"Me either, but I'm not into necrophilia."

"No? And here I thought you were into everything. I bet I can change your mind and teach you some things." Monique leaned close to him, kissed his cheek, then moved to his ear. She stuck her tongue in it, then bit, drawing blood.

"Ow!" he yelped. Monique kissed her way down his body, along his neck, then along his chest, as she popped the buttons off his shirt. She lingered at his belly button, then unbuckled his belt, and peeled away his jeans. Grimm didn't wear any underwear. "Oh baby," he reached down next to the seat, moved a lever, and pushed the seat back.

Monique stared up at him, but continued to stroke him up and down. "Yes, we are kindred souls," she breathed heavily. "We enjoy the night, the darkness where we can do things that aren't accepted in the light. Night is when we slake our thirst."

"Yes," he moaned.

Her stroking grew faster and his breathing more rapid. "It

is also a time for revenge." Grimm's eyes, thin slits a moment ago, widened. "Nothing is important unless it pertains to us!"

"Yes! Yes!" Grimm moaned.

"Kevy, watch this bitch . . ."

"Go away," Grimm mumbled, reaching out to stroke her hair.

"I am an expert in matters of darkness," Monique continued, "while you are just beginning to learn." Monique began kissing her way up his body, while her hand continued in a slow, piston fashion. She suckled both nipples, then kissed upward, nipping and biting before reaching his neck.

"Crazy, babe. Let's do the bone dance!"

Monique began work on a hickey, then slid her tongue along his throat until she felt a pulse. She kissed, nipped, then bit him.

For long seconds, Grimm didn't even realize he'd been bit, then he felt the pain in his neck. "HEY!" It had stung, but the sharpness was subsiding. "What're ya doing?" he asked weakly. "That hurt. I'm not into that shit."

Monique pulled away, her lips bloody, her teeth brighter white than a full moon. "Just a sadist. Fine. I was bonding us. Making you mine." She moved to kiss his neck. Grimm was too weak to fight her off, and didn't know if he wanted to.

His head spun. "This is really wild," he mumbled.

Monique pulled away, wiping her hand on his pants. Grimm stared into her eyes and smiled. "As I said, we are kindred souls, but I would never make you one of us."

"What are you talking about?" He touched his neck and felt the tiny, twin holes. "You left wounds! You bitch!"

"You will live . . . and obey me. Dere is much we can do. Plenty of fun to be had in the darkness." She cocked her head, as though listening. "And we won't have long to wait," she said with a smile. "He is coming."

Thirteen

Defiled

"Now listen to me," Monique told Grimm. "You will do as I say, *ja?*" She stared at him as he zipped his pants and buttoned his shirt. He nodded. They were still sitting in the gray Trans Am, off the road in front of the Seven Points Cemetery.

"You will no longer bother David Matthewson," she told him. He started to ask why, found he couldn't, then didn't really care. He nodded. "Good. Now dere are some bodies I want you to dispose of." Monique told him where the Brookens' bodies were, and what to do with them.

"Kevy, now we know whut happened ta Jim Bob and Benjo. That could've been us." Kevin nodded once, curtly.

"Yes, you will do as I wish." Monique climbed out of the car, taking the bottle of home brew with her. She smiled, then looked down the road to where headlights appeared in the fog. "He is coming. Again, he would have been too late to save a child, but this time it does not matter." She sighed. "He has much to learn, he could have just flown," she chuckled, "but I will teach him. Kevin, go now!" She slammed the door.

Grimm nodded. "That's it, Kevy, let her think she's won. She can't see me! Let's get outta here!" Grimm started the car, turned on the lights, and had began to pull out as a Blazer screeched to a halt. "Hey, that's the writer-dude!"

"Monique!" David jumped out of the car. He was flushed and angry, carrying a Bible in one hand and a silver cross in the other. Just as Monique glowed—her skin luminescent as the dim face on a watch—so did David. Their eyes blazed red, fire-stoked, as though sheltered in deep caverns.

David glanced at the Trans Am. He was surprised to find Grimm still alive. He'd tasted the foulness of blood—felt Monique feeding—but unlike the last two times, he hadn't been immersed. Unfortunately, he was late again . . . or was he? He glanced at Monique, then back at Grimm.

"Join me for a drink?" Monique asked and held up the bottle, which immediately caught David's attention. David's face tightened as his lips compressed into a thin line. "Dis tastes terrible. Dis isn't it; you should try the real thing," she chuckled. "But now I understand how you do it."

Grimm was looking from one to the other, noticing similarities, when the voice said, "Looks like they're kissin'—blood-suckin'—cousins. Vampires, Kevy! This is bad, bad news. We gotta get out of here."

"Vampires. Sure. I gotta go bury some bodies," Grimm mumbled to himself.

"We'll see, Kevy. We'll see. I've some ideas. Some thangs are comin' ta mind. But let's go see the Brookens boys, pay our last respects. This oughtta be fun!" Grimm drove off.

"The real thing?" David said after a long silence.

"Human blood—blood from the living. Live! Up close and personal, not some distorted concoction."

David appeared to be totally confused. "You are truly mad. And maybe so am I." Warily, he approached her, cross poised and Bible ready.

"Only at you and your determined foolishness. I guess I will have to continue to educate you. To wear you down. The signs already show. The cross. I don't fear it. You are strong enough to wield it, yes, but you are not strong enough to use it!" Fog seemed to rise from her feet, curling upward to surround and protect her. Her shape wavered, then became hazy, as though she were fading away.

"What have you done to Grimm?"

"He is my thrall; I have tasted his blood, and he is in my power. He and I are so similar, I did not wish to kill him. But he is even more warped dan I. To turn him into one of us would threaten both races!" She laughed.

"This must stop!" David rushed forward, his cross held as a vanguard.

"Then come on! We shall dance again!"

Swinging the cross, David advanced into the fog. The crucifix passed through her as though Monique were already transformed into the very mists that surrounded him. David flailed about, trying to strike her, but all was fog and no form. Suddenly, he gasped, sucking down the mist and choking.

"Are you having trouble, my love? Have you ever wondered if I'm lying to you?" David felt her smile. "Maybe I'm your own personal hell, a vampire just come to torture you—a pious man—to twist and wring your soul by telling you dat you are a vampire, and den killing people just for the fun of it? That does sound marvelously wicked, doesn't it?

"Or maybe I was sent by Liselle, hmmm? Or maybe you are dreaming. Or lying on the floor, hallucinating because of another attack of . . ." she snorted, then laughed, ". . .porphyria. I see you, but then I see all about you, don't I? No such luck, David; we are as brother and sister. We are unified and created by the night. Face it. Understand it. We will be as one and equals, as soon as you drink human blood!"

"What do you know of Liselle?" David wheezed. His sight was blurred, his head swimming in circles. He staggered away, trying to escape, and crashed into the wall surrounding the cemetery. Pain rocketed up his legs, and David collapsed. She was real. And too strong! He'd been a fool to come. Now he was suddenly frightened of losing his soul! Could she force him to drink blood? Stop a passing motorist and make him feed? Madness! But it was happening to him! This was real! "Lord, help me!"

"God cannot and will not," he heard Monique say. Suddenly the mist whirled around him, as though a dust devil had sprung to life. The fog twisted upon itself, shrinking and growing darker, then changing shape and form, becoming Monique. "Ah, I love a humble man, one who kneels before a superior, but worry not," she said, staring at him for a time, watching him wheeze and gasp. "One day soon, you will be powerful. Each time we meet, touch minds, souls, and flesh, we become more akin. You cannot help but change. NOW STAND!" she commanded.

David stood unsteadily, then dove over the wall and into the graveyard. Monique laughed. "You will not find help dere!"

David rolled across the grass, trying to put distance between them. His breathing was ragged, but the stiffness was beginning to leave his body as he sprinted though a mine field of tombstones. He felt Monique enter the graveyard, and the night air came alive with an awful wheezing cough that shook the very earth below him. Staggering, David collided with a headstone, and stumbled on a few feet before falling to the ground. His legs were numb from a strange combination of fire and ice.

"You are in my playground now, David."

Spewing dirt, the earth erupted before his eyes. For a moment he stared at the fountain, then a bony hand shot from the hole, reaching for him. "I just want to hold your hand," she laughed, "and give you my kiss."

David rolled aside, and another hole exploded, a second skeletal hand snatching at him. He slapped it aside and lurched to his feet. To his right, he saw the wall in the distance, beyond row upon row of shadowed stones that were beginning to take root in an ever-growing fog. Belching from below the mists were more geysers of dirt, the entire yard filled with the sound of raining earth.

In agony and mouthing prayers, David ran for the far wall. With a wild glance over his shoulder, he saw a wave of darkness rolling after him, blotting out everything it touched, as though a devouring pit had been opened. She was coming! The ground continued to vomit dirt, creating small fountains of earth to surround him and clutch at him with undead hands. David danced and weaved, leaping over the grasping skeletal fingers of those forced to do darkness's bidding from the grave.

Almost there! David gasped, and leaped over a headstone. As he landed, the ground erupted and a hand caught his ankle, pulling him down. David hit hard, and was knocked breathless. A second set of skeletal fingers wrapped around his other leg. He tried to pull free to stand, but instead was jerked back as though tethered, and fell to the grass once more.

Monique was suddenly right behind him. "A merry chase. But why play hard to get, when you know you'll embrace what I have to offer?" In womanly form once more, she grabbed his shirt and pulled him to his feet with one hand, then let go. The skeletons didn't relinquish their grasp on his ankles. Their coldness had seeped from his ankles to freeze his knees and thighs. He couldn't move.

David stared at her with defiance. Her eyes transformed into obsidian orbs growing larger and larger, becoming all encompassing—the dark side of the moon. "Yes," she said, "You are strong, but it is futile. In the end, I will take your soul, but for now, I will just take your body. One step follows the next. Consider it part of your initiation. But remember, dere are many, many things that are worse dan what I will do for you. I think you will enjoy this."

With one finger on her lips, she looked him up and down. "Your body still desires me, although your mind rejects it.

And I am always lustful after blood. I am glad you came tonight." David tried to move, but couldn't tear his eyes away from hers. They, as much as the skeletal fingers, held him as though he were a frozen lake in the grasp of a long, cold winter.

Monique slowly unbuttoned another button on her halter top. David's mouth went dry. Why was she doing this to him! "If you play hard to get, you must pay the price when the debt comes due. At one time, long ago, before I learned to dance, I did this for a living. It allowed me to earn enough money for passage on a ship that brought my sister and me to the land of opportunity." She undid another button, then pulled the straps back. Her breasts, nipples erect, sprang free. With a smile on her face, she moved closer and closer, stopping inches away.

"And I was very good at what I did. It is amazing what a poor and hungry orphan will do to survive." Leaning forward so that her breasts were almost touching his chest, Monique said, "The cross around your neck protects some of you— protects your soul—but not all of you." She leaned a little closer, her lips barely brushing his.

"You can't resist me, David. And if you can't fight it, you might as well switch. Part of you already has, for you think of killing me. You have never thought of killing anything before. You have yet to recognize the marvelous transformation."

Monique knelt before him, her fingers undoing his pants, pulling down the zipper, and tugging on his Dockers. They fell, folding and crumpling around his ankles. Oh Lord, not this. David struggled against her will, tried to think of disgusting things, of cold water, the Brookens corpses, but he continued to respond to her touch. He felt the coolness and the heat of her flesh, and thought he would burst. "You will not regret this." Her head bowed, and he felt the wetness of her tongue and the tightness of her lips.

David wanted to cry out, but couldn't. How could he be so weak? David suddenly tried a different tack. He thought of the church, of the scriptures and of affirmations. He repeated them over and over, driving Monique from his mind. He became lost in the cadence of the mind-spoken words. He was somewhere else, his soul freed of her insidious torture. David was drifting along, gloriously happy at having escaped her.

Suddenly, he felt a sting across his face—once, twice, then a third time. His eyes now met hers. Monique wiped her lips, then sneered. "I guess you didn't enjoy it as much as I. You are strong-willed and make a mighty companion. One day I will forgive you for what you've done tonight.

"If I didn't have plans for you, if you weren't so fascinating, I would rip your soul from you, tear it out by the roots, and you couldn't stop me! The flesh, if you call what we have flesh, is one thing, but our souls are another. And I intend to win. You have no weapons left, even your faith is failing."

Monique whirled around, starting to leave. "But I still hunger, for Grimm only tantalized my real need. If you were to join me, we'd be gone from this place, and Temprance would be safe from my appetites. Oh well, *bon appétit!* Until tomorrow then, David. *Auf Wiedersehen.*" Laughing, she stepped into the shadow along the wall of the graveyard, melding with the darkness, and she was gone.

Weeping, David collapsed to his knees, praying for forgiveness and strength. What was he going to do? What? All he could think of was that he was going to have to give in. She was going to kill more young boys, more people, until he relented. But once a man lost his soul, what else was left?

Fourteen

Sanctuary

Something . . . a bumping or thumping . . . awakened Patrick from a restless sleep. His eyes barely open, he rolled over and looked out the window. It was dark outside, very dark, without any moon or street lights. That was strange. Could all the lights have burned out at once? Patrick's mouth went dry, as uneasiness oozed through him. Something was wrong.

As if on cue, the window slowly began to open. Patrick tried to rise, but couldn't, frozen by his fear and able only to stare at the ebony creature as it finished opening the window. Leering, it stared at him with red eyes full of fire, flung back the long dark hair which covered it like a shroud, and bared canine teeth that glowed as though the beast had been released from the deepest recesses of the earth. The smell of something sweet plus rotting meat filled Patrick's nostrils, and he wanted to vomit. He tried to scream, his lips moving soundlessly.

With the ease of a drifting shadow, the creature entered Patrick's bedroom. It slid over his desk, then slipped to the floor. Dark fingers stretched forward, reaching for Patrick

Suddenly he felt unchained from his fear, and bolted out of bed. The dark beast laughed and pursued, chasing Patrick out of the room. Patrick reached the end of the hall and slammed the door. Where was his father? He was making enough racket to wake the dead!

There was a sucking sound, and Patrick turned to find a black substance sliding beneath the door. As half of it slid free, it sprang upward and began to form a shadowy figure.

Screaming, Patrick ran through the house, from room to room, unable to find the front door. The beast was always just a step behind him, snatching and missing at the last second, as the boy slammed the door behind him, locking it. Each time, Patrick was frozen with fear as he was forced to watch in soundless terror as it once again slid under the door and then sprang upward to take shape.

As though timed for maximum terror and suspense, Patrick was free again, and this time, somehow, he found the back door, burst out of it and ran across the lawn toward the church. It wasn't far, but it seemed to take forever. Finally, he reached the door and found it locked. He fumbled for the key as the beast neared. His hair stood on end as hot breath touched the back of his neck. A presence . . . then . . .

As he shot upright in bed, Patrick snapped alert and awake, spraying sweat everywhere. He was perspiring profusely and shaking so badly that the bed shook, rubbing against the wall and squeaking along the floorboards. He tried to wipe his brow and almost poked his eye out. "I . . . I'm a w . . . wreck."

Tonight was no different than the last few. Night after night, ghastly creatures paraded through his head, threatening to break free and enter the real world. Sometimes they even came during the day. They mocked him, becoming more real—more tangible—with every visit. Soon they would show up, no longer a dream, but reality! Maybe even tonight.

Is that what he felt? A sense of impending doom? Knowing that something was coming, soon to arrive? Or was he just being childish, scared of the dark? Yes, that was probably it—a kid's imagination run wild. Puffing up, he declared he wouldn't let it scare him any longer.

Then Patrick made the mistake of looking around his bedroom. The usually comfortable and friendly confines did nothing to ease his gnawing fear. The place had an odd feel, as though it were full of watchful, expectant eyes. The light from the church knifed through his window, carving out islands of illumination among the fathomless shadows. In his amok imagination, they were pits leading to wicked places, homes for all sorts of nameless atrocities—demons, devils and hell's spawn of fire and brimstone. Wait! Did something slide along the edge of the bookshelves?

Swallowing a scream, Patrick laughed crazily instead and backed up against the wall. His hackles rising, he pulled his sheets close to protect himself and ward off the danger, as though there were still monsters under the bed. But it was too late already; there was no place to run. Like hounds from the Stygian pits, the shadows were crouched and ready to strike.

Patrick's eyes darted to and fro. Dark things were in his room with him! He could feel them breathing, their fetid breath poisoning the blackness. Then his gaze halted on the wicker chest in the corner. How did it get open? What if something—a constrictor-sized python—was waiting to wrap him in its coils and then swallow him? Or mind altering aliens? Or—

Stop! Get a grip, Patrick told himself as he fingered the cross around his neck. Be cool, just like the heroes on TV. Let the fear slide by. This sounded fine and dandy, but didn't work at all. Patrick thought about facing his fears, getting out of bed and checking the shadows, then he realized that he was too afraid. He reached for the light next to his bed and pulled the chain. There was a *click,* but nothing happened. He was terrified for a minute, then remembered that the lamp had burned out earlier today and he'd forgotten to replace the bulb. He wished it was morning, but the luminous clock face read twelve-thirty—a long way to go until dawn.

A breeze came through the open window, and Patrick shivered. It was chilling, far too cold for a summer's night. Something was wrong with the night all right. Patrick swore he heard it whispering, gibbering with unnatural sounds that usually tried to hide in the creak of the restless trees, the shifting of the house, and the rustling of leaves and bushes. The shadows by his desk under the window seemed to lengthen, reaching for him as though to silence him before he could call out to his father.

Well, he wouldn't! Patrick shook himself, then pinched himself hard enough to bring tears. He had to get out of here! It wasn't safe. The church! He'd go there! The nightmares couldn't get him in the Lord's house. Not like here, in his room where the shadows were alive and panting.

They wanted him. Caressing him, crawling over him as though he were covered with snakes. Stop it! STOP IT! He was driving himself crazy!

Patrick finally made a bold decision. The nightmares had come again, but this time, he somehow knew they were coming for real. They wouldn't be phantoms or delusions, but darkness personified.

Patrick threw the sheets aside and clambered out of bed, quickly pulling his jeans over his shorts and pulling on a shirt. As he hopped one-legged to the window, he put on his shoes, leaving the laces undone. If he was discovered leaving through the front door, his father would only chide him in a kindly way, and suggest he confront his fears and sleep in his own room. No way! Sometimes parents didn't understand, cut off from their feelings by practicality and logic.

Patrick opened the window and crawled outside, stepping into the night. Just across a long stretch of wet and gleaming grass dimly illuminated by the streetlight, the church waited for him—calling for him to come and be safe. The front door was lit, but the closest entrance, the side door, was draped heavily in shadow. Which way? Close or—Head for the light! Patrick ran carefully across the grass, already treacherous and slippery with dew. Churning with each of his steps, a fine mist slithered across the well-groomed grounds.

In the heat of the night there was another sudden, chilling breeze. It slipped through the gaps in his clothing, accosting and violating him. Patrick paused, a fox listening for sounds of the hunters. He didn't know how or why, but the darkness—IT—was getting closer. Slipping twice, Patrick sprinted for the front door of the church.

Monique was still hungry, her time with Grimm and David only stimulating her desires, not fulfilling them. Now it was time to teach another young one a lesson—a lesson about the darkness, where there was truly something to fear. The adults lied. Death did favor the night.

She swooped low, gliding between the trees and coasting on leathery wings. Ahead and in the gray stone house, she sensed Patrick. She had tagged his life scent—as she had tagged them all that Friday night at David's place.

The Page household was small, a one story building with white trim and a small porch atop several steps. The trees around the house were large and old, the bushes well tended, roses flourished on each side of the steps. A perfect setting for a funeral home. Monique smiled.

With a twisted thought, Monique sent the Reverend Page a nightmare—something to keep him riveted and prevent him from interfering—as preachers were wont to do. She hoped others would feel the resonance as they slept, instinctively fearing her, twisting and writhing in the turbulent winds of dreamland. Such was the power of a true vampire, something else she would teach David.

As Monique landed, fog spread from her feet, quickly moving outward to the houses on both sides of the street. Soon the entire area was clad in fog. She chuckled, loving the setting of the scene.

Monique willed herself to human form, clad in a clingy, but wispy black gown that covered everything but her face and hands. Dress for success, she chuckled. Why simply *feed*, when drama was one of the joys of life—or even unlife? The last minutes of the victim's life should be charged with emotion. Death, as much as life, was a state of existence to be explored. David would discover this.

Monique sensed other prey in the houses, but she was here to drive the dagger of darkness further into David's heart and soul. He must accept what he was, or be destroyed! She would put herself in rapport with him, then slowly stalk the minister's son.

Strange, Monique thought as she tried to connect with David—insert herself into his thoughts—he was already asleep. She tried to intrude, but failed. No matter, there would be other nights, and there were plenty of young boys in Temprance. Once she ran out of those involved in Friday's mischief, she would prey on others. She fed on more than just blood; the sensations of terror and fear were almost as heady as sexual ecstasy—almost. With each feeding, she felt more akin to an elemental force—a hurricane wind, a raging wave, a bolt of lightning.

Fear and flight! Monique sensed it. Suddenly her attention darted to the right, and she saw Patrick sprinting away from the house and across the lawn toward the church! That wouldn't do. With the speed of thought, she shifted into lupine form and pursued.

It was coming! Patrick put on a burst of speed fueled by his fear. He could feel the cold wind on his back, as though it were the breath of a hunting hound. He remembered his dream, and his skin crawled. Suddenly, he didn't think he was going to make it safely to the front door; it was too faraway. Well, any entrance would do. Patrick headed for the side door.

The shadowed entrance to sanctuary also seemed faraway—the distance across a ball field instead of just the lawn. For each two strides he took, he seemed to slip and slide, taking one step backwards. Forward and back in a tug-o-war, restrained by something trying to hold him back and another force pulling him toward the church!

Patrick glanced over his shoulder and saw something gray and formless chasing him, devouring ground with each stride. Patrick ran harder, stumbling several times. Closer. Colder. He glanced over his shoulder. The thing had grown larger, a wolfish face with fire for eyes, and spiked teeth that could carve an elephant! Just as in his nightmares, terror fully gripped him, trying to freeze him, and he tripped, spreading his arms for balance. It didn't work, and he fell, sliding across the slick lawn and soaking himself as water sprayed about. Desperate, he clawed his way to his feet.

It was getting closer! The fog was growing thicker, rising almost to his knees, as though trying to obscure his trail to sanctuary and slow him down. A wicked breeze whipped by, tearing at him, hurling dirt, trash, and leaves at him. Patrick could barely see, but kept running.

For long moments, Patrick kept sprinting blindly ahead, wondering if he was getting any closer, then he was there, jamming his toes into a concrete slab. Stumbling in pain and gasping for elusive breath, Patrick slammed into the side door. He started to slowly sink to the concrete, but grabbed the handle to stay upright. With his right hand he dug for the key. OH MY GOD! He couldn't find the key! Had it fallen out? Were these the wrong pants?

Patrick heard a low mocking laugh and dug deeper into his pants pocket. He touched metal and tried to pull his hand free. It stuck, so he jerked hard, ripping the pocket as he tore his hand out. The key slipped from his hand, spinning in the air. Patrick snatched at it and somehow caught it. Barely able to see the lock and shaking so much that the key danced around the hole, Patrick missed, the key scraping right. He tried again, the key scratching metal and sliding left. Praying, he poked about. The key caught, started to slide, but Patrick quivered just right, and the key slid home!

Coldness clutched at him, then enveloped him. The fog billowed upward to blot out the door. He heard a snarling laugh.

In one desperate motion, Patrick yanked the door open, threw himself around it and inside. The door smacked hard against the wall, then rebounded back toward the entrance.

Landing hard on the floor, Patrick almost blacked out. His head spinning, he rolled over to stare at the entrance, watching through stinging sweat and tears as the door slowly cut through the fog, moving as though it would close on its own; then it stopped short. The mist coiled around it, as though threatening to pull it open and enter, but didn't.

But Patrick feared it would. It was near, ready to jump into the church. Could it? Would it, if he left the door open?

Indecisive, Patrick chewed on his lip, then moved near the entrance. He must shut the door to be totally safe, and it was several inches from closing. A January breeze blew through the gap and cut him to the quick. He shivered and took a step back.

Somehow, he knew that if he didn't do something, It would enter and rip the life from him. Patrick snatched at the handle as though it were scalding hot, but his sweaty hands slipped off, as he tried to grab and pull in one motion. The door closed a few more inches, but still didn't shut all the way.

Patrick heard another low, throaty chuckle and almost scuttled down the hall away from the door. But he couldn't leave it open! The sanctuary was breached! Tentatively, Patrick edged toward the door. He started to reach, saw the fog coil upward, poised and waiting, and he stopped.

Seconds, then minutes, seemed to pass by with the strange sense of slow motion and timelessness.

Unable to wait any longer, Patrick grabbed for the handle and felt cool metal. Then an invisible force, like a frozen vise, seized his wrist. Patrick screamed, feeling his fingers go numb, the coldness racing up his arm. Slowly it began to pull him out the door. His sneakers slid, protesting as he tried to dig in and pull free. Patrick reared back with all his might and, lost his grip on the handle.

The door swung open, and he fell back, screaming as he watched the pale-faced woman-witch form in the door. Her crimson stare commanded his attention. Demanded it! Patrick sat up straight.

Hiding her pain, Monique stood haughtily in the door. This place hurt, but it was a challenge. "Come to me!"

Patrick stood shakily, then his knees buckled under the strain, and he collapsed. He tried to look away, but couldn't, feeling as though his attention was magnetized to the woman. She was tearing him apart, stripping him of his will and violating him.

"Crawl!"

Patrick desperately fought back. Pulling away and looking for some place safe, he curled into a ball.

"Look at me!" Patrick's head jerked around and he stared at her. Suddenly, his face went blank, and he curled up some more.

Monique futilely raged at Patrick for a minute, then laughed. What would they think when they found him catatonic and lying in the church? The worst, she hoped.

This was a different type of victory, if not quite as satisfying. It was just as well that David was not connected with her. Only blood would strengthen their bond and weaken his resistance to his true nature. Laughing, she turned away and disappeared into the night. There were other victims waiting.

Fifteen

Driven

What was he doing behind the wheel of a car, David wondered? And where was he going? He peered through a blurry windshield at the dark and rain. Hadn't he just been . . . Where had he been? Something about the car didn't look right. And he certainly didn't feel right. With ease, he could drift away, untethered from the world and distanced from his body.

David glanced in the rearview mirror. In the greenish glow of the dashboard's lights, he stared in openmouthed surprise at himself. He was young—much younger—and almost hollow-looking. David stared at his ghostly hands atop the wheel, then looked at the rest of his body. He was barely visible, translucent, as though he were just an image, not substance—not flesh.

David looked again at his hands, then noticed the steering wheel's design. Puzzled, he examined the dash. That was odd; he wasn't in the Blazer, but driving a Lincoln Continental, a huge, four-door machine—a family car.

A rumble of thunder interrupted his thoughts, then he became aware of other stormy sounds—the drumming on the roof, pattering on the windshield, and the hypnotizing, mechanical *swish-thump* of the wipers working in tandem.

Through the blurred windshield, the lines of the interstate were barely visible, the flat darkness interrupted by dashes of white and the wavering glints of oncoming headlights glistening off the wet road. The radio was low, only a murmur, the song unrecognizable. The heater blew, driving away the damp chill of winter.

Suddenly, David realized that somebody was in the car with him! Not her! Please not *her!* The intensity of David's dread immobilized him. Something terrible was going to happen! He didn't want to . . . but he had to look, his gaze inching to his right. David breathed a sigh of relief. Nobody there, thank God. He thought he was going to once more relive the tragedy that had shaped his life.

Then David remembered—the front seat *should* be empty. Tina was in the back with Timmy, who was sleeping peacefully in a child's safety seat. David whirled around to face Tina. With a dreamy and wistful smile on her face, his wife was staring at Timmy. Again, David was taken by her beauty. Tina was even more lovely than when they'd met in high school; and they'd been married seven years. Little in her appearance had changed, except that her shapely figure was fuller, more voluptuous than before. Her green eyes glowed in the dark like a cat's, and her golden hair flashed when touched by passing light. Her nose was pert, while her smile was fully from the heart. It made David ache, and he began to weep.

David knew where he was all right, and what was going to happen! Over and over, the events would be replayed, giving him a chance to succeed where he had failed his loved ones before.

"Stop! STOP THE CAR!" David yelled. Tina didn't even look up.

Then David realized his body hadn't turned with him. He was disembodied—a ghost! David leapt from his flesh and tried to grab his body by the shoulders, but his ghostly hand passed through it. "No, please." Fate was inevitable.

"No!" He wouldn't give up on this chance, dream or not. David jumped into his body and tried to take control of the wheel. Nothing happened; no matter how hard he tried, he couldn't make his hands so much as quiver. He tried to brake, but his feet refused to obey his will, the right continuing to rest on the gas pedal. He willed his body to stop, to pull over, to turn off the car. To do something! Anything! "Please, Lord!" David pleaded.

"Ah honey, I just love visiting your grandparents in Fort Worth," Tina said. "They are such wonderful people. They spoil us to death."

"Yeah, they do. They always have. It was Grandpa who gave me my first fishing pole." David heard himself saying.

"Stop!" David railed at his dream-self. He saw a blue sign flash by with symbols for gas and food, and knew that his time was running out. David put his ethereal hands to his temples and tried to send a message. "Stop for coffee."

"Can you see okay?" Tina asked.

"Yes."

"No, you can't!" David screamed.

"At least it's not freezing rain. Do you want to stop?"

"No, the road is nearly deserted," his dream-self responded.

"I think I ate too much," Tina confessed.

"I'm stuffed, too."

"Even Timmy ate too much," Tina said. The dream-David laughed.

The conversation was always the same, seared in his memory as though carved with a hot knife. The time was getting close, and they were just chatting away! Didn't they know what was going to happen? Couldn't they feel it? Futilely, David reached outside himself and tried to take the wheel in his ghostly hands, but they passed through it.

"I love you, Daddy Matthewson," he heard Tina say from

the backseat, while she caressed his neck. "I don't think anything would've kept us apart, kept us from meeting each other. It was fate . . . and now you're stuck with me, growing fatter with each Thanksgiving at your Grandparents," she laughed.

David didn't want to hear it anymore; he couldn't bear it! He jumped up from the seat, trying to propel himself out through the ceiling, and slammed into it, unable to escape—penned in. But he wasn't going to sit idly and watch this happen again! David slid across the front seat and tried to grab the door handle. His hand passed through as though he didn't exist. Maybe he was already dead! No, I'm alive!

Closing his eyes, David tried to will himself to the waking world, but he was held fast. David tried to imagine magical red shoes, clicking their heels together and taking himself home, but nothing happened. It was maddening. He was trapped, unable to change things and unable to leave, forced to watch. This was his living hell, a time he couldn't forget, accept, or rise above. His faith wasn't made of strong enough fiber.

David turned to Tina as he heard his dream-self say, "Nothing will ever separate us, dear. We will be together a long time, get old and crotchety together. You know, dueling rocking chairs."

"You're such a romantic." Her laugh was lilting. "See if you still feel that way after several more kids."

"Several!"

"Many, many. A farm full, maybe, like *One Hundred and One Dalmatians*," she laughed.

David didn't want to look, but couldn't help himself; he whirled to face the front windshield. "Look out!" his voice cracked. There were pinpoints of lights growing quickly larger. Headlights suddenly filled the inside of the Lincoln. Closer. Brighter. Blinding.

"Just a nightmare," David told himself. "Dead. All dead."

He closed his eyes and stuck his fingers in his ears, trying to hide from what was coming.

"Oh my God! They're on the wrong side!" Dream-David spun the wheel left. The car jerked, then slid, the rear end fishtailing as he headed toward the grassy median.

BAMKERRUNNCHH! The impact was jarring, the head-on avoided, but not the collision. The car thrashed, a mortally wounded fish thrown ashore. Dream-David slammed into the wheel, then jerked back, his nose bloody and a cheekbone broken. Glass exploded and metal squealed, peeling and shredding. Spinning out of control like an amuk top, the Continental careened across the grass median, tires spewing mud. The car bounced, went airborne, bottomed out with a whump, and . . .

BUMWHUMKERSCREEEeee . . . The impact was crushing as well as deafening. Huge lights blasted through the interior as the silvery grill of a semi—a grinning shark's giant teeth—struck them along the passenger side. More glass cracked, webbing or exploding. Deadly jagged shards whistled through the interior of the car, harmlessly passing through David, but tearing at the others.

The Continental skidded for a while, stuck on the front of the semi, a tiny antelope impaled on a giant rhino's horn. Then the truck finally stopped, and the car slid free, flipping over and over. It rolled as though it had been dropped atop a giant junkyard heap. Finally they stopped, still upside down. The Lincoln was bent in half, folded like an accordion that had been fallen upon. David turned to see Timmy in the contorted safety seat. His son was still secured, but bloody . . . dead. Slashed by thousands of cuts, Tina hung from the seat. Her eyes were open and vacant.

David looked quickly away and out the windshield. It was no longer webbed, and he was right side up, staring at the front gate of his ranch house. There was a car parked on the far side of the gate.

David groaned, feeling as though he'd just awakened. He was dizzy, and had no idea how he'd made it home. David turned off the lights and engine, then stumbled out of the Blazer. All he remembered was Monique . . . was Liselle . . . was Tina.

David closed the door and feebly staggered away from the Blazer, heading for his front gate. He vaguely saw the car parked ahead of him. "David!" he heard a familiar voice call, then David passed out.

Sixteen

Welcome Home

Jana had been waiting on the front porch, but the shadowy darkness unnerved her so much, she chose to pace back and forth by her sky blue Camaro. She had forgotten to call David and had just driven out, expecting to find him writing, but he wasn't. The place was locked up tight, all the doors and shutters closed, and no lights on. It wasn't far, but now she was disappointed, and felt as though she'd wasted a trip. She thought about checking the barn, then decided to walk around back.

Jana wondered where he was tonight. He was supposed to be a reclusive writer, not out gallivanting. But then this was his daytime, so if he was going to go some place, it would have to be now. That might be hard to adjust to, but her husband had sometimes worked the graveyard shift.

What was she thinking? She hardly knew David. Why was she having such thoughts about him? Why was she compelled to pursue him? He didn't appear to be interested. He might have changed; he might not be anything like the person she had known so long ago. He'd undergone a severe tragedy, and was combatting a rare disease that made him an outcast.

Jana rounded the corner and saw that his Blazer was gone.

It could be in the barn, but she doubted it. She wasn't going to check there; she would drive home and leave a message. Jana headed back to her Camaro.

She had always been drawn to David, often feeling a physical attraction, but thinking it could have been more. He'd been kind, sensitive, and fun-loving, as well as creative—many of the things her husband had not been. The main similarity was that they needed help in fighting their problems. She hadn't been able to help Hector. Could she help David? Could that be why she was drawn to him? She seemed to be interested only in men with some kind of difficulty—whether it be booze, drugs, or abusiveness. At least David's problems weren't self-inflicted.

As she reached her Chevy, she heard the sound of a car approaching—the raggedy grumble of the gravel and the hum of the engine. Someone was driving very fast, Jana thought. The headlights were weaving and appeared set too high for a car. Jana wondered if the driver was drunk. She hoped that David didn't drink to excess. Michael had never mentioned it, but then it would follow her fortune.

As it pulled behind Jana's car and lurched to a stop, she saw it was David's Blazer. The engine and lights died, then the door opened, and David stepped out. He stared at her vacantly for a moment, then collapsed.

"DAVID!" Jana cried, running to him. David didn't look good; he was paler than usual, if that were possible. Jana knelt and touched his throat. She found a pulse and sighed; it was steady. She debated a moment, then took the keys from his hands, and ran inside the house to call Dr. Katyu.

"There," Dr. Katyu said as he gave David a shot, "that should help." The doctor glanced at Jana, then stared at David, who was still unconscious. With a cold washcloth on his forehead, David was pale and trembling. He had been muttering warnings, talking about a pale woman and death. A moment ago he'd screamed, then lapsed into silence.

"I wouldn't be overly concerned, Jana. He can see things— imagine things—when he has a porphyria attack. Much like sleepwalking, I gather. It attacks his nervous system and is similar to drinking too much or taking barbiturates. He seems dehydrated and feverish, too, which are not symptoms, so he may have a bug as well. That could be a nasty combination. But, the injections should help." The doctor sighed. "And all was going so well. I guess I should call Penny, to see if she or Carol will come out and stay with him. I hate those late night calls," he murmured, "it always makes people think someone has died, and I think David will be all right."

"I'll stay with him," Jana volunteered. She was staring down at David, obvious worry on her face. She needed to be needed. And besides, being near David felt right. It always had. It had only taken seeing him in this helpless way to re-strike the chord. "I'll also call Michael."

Dr. Katyu nodded and adjusted his glasses. "As they say, he should get plenty of rest and drink plenty of fluids. I've left some Tylenol. Call me tomorrow."

"No," David croaked, suddenly awake, speaking through dried lips and a thick tongue, as though he hadn't spoken in ages. "Jana you shouldn't stay, something bad might happen." All he could remember was Monique. She loomed large in his mind. He felt ill, thoroughly violated. And she might be back tonight!

Jana looked at Dr. Katyu, who shrugged slightly. Neither was surprised that he was worried about something happening to someone close to him; it had happened often enough. "David, you need someone to stay with you, it's either Jana or I'll call Penny."

"Too late." He closed his eyes and slumped back into the pillow.

"David, what happened tonight?" Dr. Katyu asked.

David's face appeared strained, as though he was fighting to remember, then his expression finally twisted in frustration. He fought back bile. He knew, but couldn't say. "I don't remember. I was heading somewhere . . . Next thing I know, I had collapsed in a field." He lied. He wanted to shower, immediately, but knew that wouldn't help. He could still feel her on him. Her cool hands and searing lips . . .

Dr. Katyu sighed. "Have you been drinking?"

"No. Absolutely not." His tone was cold.

"I don't understand this," the doctor said. "You were doing so well. I guess we should just be thankful you made it home all right. I will come see you again, and take more blood samples."

"Okay." In the pit of David's stomach, a ball of acid churned; he was worried about Jana staying here. What if Monique attacked? Could he protect her? David doubted it.

"Tomorrow then," Dr. Katyu said, gathering up his bag. "I'll show myself out."

"I guess it's just you and me, David," Jana said with a small smile. "But you don't look as if you're in any condition to talk business."

"Very astute, Ms. Martinez. Smart, I always liked that about you. To tell you the truth, I could care less about a contract, movie, or book right now."

"Stand me up, then flatter me," she replied.

"I didn't intend to stand you up. This type of stuff happens to me," David said hoarsely, trying not to think about what had happened, but he could feel Monique on him. He wanted to claw himself, tear her memory away. But no, he had other concerns. Would Monique come to take advantage of his weakened state? She'd said something about wanting his soul. If she did come calling, he didn't want Jana around. "You can go, honestly. You have a day job." Thirsty, David reached for a glass of water and spilled it onto the floor.

"You can't even lift a glass of water," Jana snorted and

walked into the bathroom. "Masculine pride," she murmured. "I guess that's better than acting as though you're gonna die from a measly ole cold. Here," she returned, holding the water for him to drink. David downed it all, and she brought him a second one.

"Thanks, much better. I guess if I can't carry you out, you're gonna stay the night." David searched for Monique, but didn't find her presence. Maybe she'd settled down—or worse, gone somewhere else to feed! David started to rise, but didn't get an inch off the bed. There was no way. He prayed that tonight would pass peacefully in Temprance.

"Let's just say I'm watching out for my boss's interest. You're his golden goose now," she smiled. "If I let the goose die, he'd be very upset. Speaking of which, I'm gonna call him."

David glanced over at the clock. "Why bother him this late?"

Jana checked the time. "Yeah, with all the sick people in the Woods' household, they probably turned in early. I wonder if you caught this from Michael?"

"Could be," David lied, hating it, wanting to bite off the tip of his tongue. "So you're here to play the role of the beautiful young nurse," David said. His words sounded harsh to him, but her smile was gentle.

"I'm not so young, and neither are you."

"I do look as though I've been running around the block a few more times," David laughed harshly. "But you're . . ."

"Well preserved?" she smiled. "A survivor? A couple of months ago, I looked terrible and felt it. I'm glad you weren't there to see me. Divorces are nasty; people turn into demons, clawing and scratching, trying to rip each other apart."

"I'm sorry." He almost added that there were worse ways to be separated than by an angry, mutual agreement—at least it was by choice.

Maybe he did say it aloud, or Jana just read the look on his face, for she said, "I'm sorry I brought it up," and leaned over to kiss him on the forehead. David tensed. Her kiss was butterfly soft, delicate, and fleeting. The soft scent of her perfume enveloped him. Monique's memory faded, but didn't depart.

As Jana leaned back, David stared at her and caught his breath. Tina! Here! Her ghost looking over Jana's shoulder! Then she was gone, disappearing like fog exposed to summer sunshine. Was she real? An image? A flickering of guilt? David feebly felt for the locket. He hadn't been close to a woman, intimately, since Tina. All the others had been efforts to forget. Even Liselle.

"David, you okay? You look like you saw a ghost."

David shrugged. "Sometimes I think I do."

"Me, too, but I feel them more than see them," Jana said.

David smiled. Jana's kiss had truly touched him. He'd needed a bit of human kindness after that terrible Friday night, after Wright in the church, after the deaths, after . . . Monique. "I like your bedside manner better than Katyu's," he managed weakly.

"Ah, I believe that kindness and care, as well as pills and shots, can help make you better again. If you want to get better."

"That sounds good to me. I could have used this house call about a decade ago. Who knows, I might already be outside enjoying the sun." Not if you're a vampire, came the thought, and David slapped it away. The voice came in Monique's tone.

"It's not too late." Jana bit her lip, as though the words had slipped out. Her expression was hopeful, her eyes wide and luminous, dark pools reflecting what might be.

"I hope you're right." What were they talking about! He had a killer, a vampire following him, looming over him, slaying in his name, taking over his body, Violating him . . . and here he was trading innuendos about romance. How ludicrous . . . how weakly . . . human. Someone had once said, or he'd read, a good woman could work wonders on a man, even

246

bring him back from death's door. How about undead? No! He wasn't a vampire, no matter what that crazy woman thought. I'm just sick!

"Where have you been the last ten years . . . and what's a nice girl like you doing in a place like this?" David asked. Just her presence buoyed his spirits. They'd always affected each other like that, ever since they'd first met auditioning for the stage production of *Romeo and Juliet*. They had both ended up with minor supporting parts. He knew then that he didn't have a career in acting.

"That's a long, long story."

"I think I have some time." He touched her hand.

"I don't know. I'm not sure I want to keep you up too late," she smiled as David frowned.

"I'm usually up this time of night."

"Oh yes. Well, you look exhausted, but I guess I could give you the Reader's Digest version. You know about college and meeting Hector?"

David nodded. They'd discussed it at the reunion. "Yeah, and off you go to the big city to seek fame and fortune."

"As if one could make a decent living in Temprance."

"It has its good points."

Jana nodded and continued. Her abbreviated story took over an hour, and by the end David's eyelids were drooping, as he asked fewer questions. But they were holding hands. Jana told him about the thrill of working for Trammel Crow, and then later how the excitement wore off as the real estate market crumbled. And how her marriage, once rock solid, became a sinking ship full of too many holes to patch. Hector's drug addiction had been a strain, but his cheating on her had been the last straw. For the first time she gave up, just gave up and came home, years upon years down the drain.

"I guess I'm just trying to find some peace and quiet, a simple life with faith and a . . ." she saw that David was asleep, "good man." She sighed. "I sure have a way with them." She stood up and stretched. Maybe it's the lost puppy syndrome, she mused.

Jana grabbed one of his books and began to read. Several times he mumbled in his sleep, talking about ghosts, about Tina and Timmy, and about death. From those mumblings, Jana learned more than she wanted to know about the accident which had killed his family. When he spoke of the pale dark woman, he thrashed about, almost becoming violent. She moved to the bed and calmed him, gently stroking his forehead.

Finally, Jana went back to her book. She yawned, beginning to get sleepy. Her eyelids drooped several times—once her head dropped—then her stomach growled as though in response.

Eat or lie down? No contest. With the thought of a snack on her mind, Jana set down the book and stepped into the hallway. She looked back, staring at David and wondering if this was a new beginning for them. Maybe they had a second chance after squandering their first. Only time would tell, she told herself. What a hopeless romantic. With slow steps Jana walked down the hall toward the stairs.

Despite the pleasant ending to the evening, she couldn't shake a nagging feeling that something odd had happened to David tonight. His pants were torn and shredded around his ankles, and he had a faraway, almost lost look in his eyes. Would that have happened during an attack of porphyria? In truth she didn't know what could happen during an attack, but wanted to learn more. It was her nature to want to help; she couldn't turn away from David anymore than she could from a wounded sparrow. She had even stayed during Hector's problems, until he'd breached her trust.

Jana shivered, then looked around, wondering if the air-conditioning had come on without her realizing it. Jana investigated, but didn't see a vent, and then the frigid air was gone. The door creaked behind her, and her back crawled, her flesh goose-bumping, as though someone had poured icy water along her spine. Jana whirled about and saw Shady dart into David's bedroom and lithely hop onto the bed. The cat snuggled at his feet, then appeared to go to sleep, joining him in dreamland.

She'd been jumpy all night, from the first moment she set foot on the front walk. Rubbing her arms, Jana walked to the stairs and descended. Actually, she'd been a bit harried for the past few days. It all came from not sleeping very well. She'd never been an insomniac, but with the creepy dreams she'd been having, it was more pleasant to stay up watching the late movies.

Something thumped below. Probably his other cat, Midnite. Jana reached the first floor and turned left toward the living room. The only light was in the entry way, so she paused to fumble for a switch. There was another thump, sounding larger than a moving cat. She caught her breath, her fingers scrambling in search of the switch. Something rattled, metal against metal.

Her hands found the lightswitch and flicked it on. The hallway flashed, two of three bulbs exploding with a flash, then the area was dimly illuminated. Jana rubbed her eyes and turned, her back to the light, and looked into the living room. An end table and lamp were on the floor; probably knocked over by Midnite. Jana stepped into the dimly lit room, noticing how sparsely it was decorated. There were two pictures of Cedar Creek at sunrise. There was a couch, an end table, a coffee table, a lounger, and a TV stand with a television on it. But there weren't any knickknacks, nothing to personalize the place, as though David never spent time here.

Jana righted the table and placed the lamp on top of it, switching it on in the process. It was then that she noticed the stereo speakers; they hung from the ceiling and were swinging slightly, as though someone had bumped them. They seemed to sway with perfect timing, the movement mesmerizing, like a pair of silent metronomes.

Another cool breeze whipped about Jana. She turned as though to follow it into the entry way. The front door was still open. She was working herself into paranoia, she thought as she walked toward the front door.

Ever so slowly, the door began to swing shut of its own accord. Jana didn't feel a breeze, but suddenly the door slammed shut with a *whoosh* and *WHAM,* shaking the front hall and hurting her ears.

"And tonight on the Discovery Channel . . ."

Jana whirled about just in time to see the television set blink off, the blue light fading. She looked at the grandfather clock and saw that it was eleven-thirty.

Then Jana noticed the front door was once again open, the screen door still shut. Uneasy, she let it be and walked down the hallway. A cup of coffee or hot chocolate would settle her jangled nerves.

Suddenly the hallway closet door flew open, swinging into the corridor. Jana jumped back, the door barely missing her face, but scrunching her toes. "Damn!" Her welling fear was overwhelmed by pain. She hobbled backward and leaned against the wall, then slowly slumped to the floor. Rubbing her toes, she looked up at the door.

Without warning, the overhead light began to rapidly blink off and on. The flipping was so quick that each of Jana's movements appeared herky-jerky, split seconds of motion missing. The closet door slowly closed. There was no one else, nothing else, not even a cat in the hall; and yet, she felt a presence. "Oh God!"

As Jana scrambled to her feet, she saw something move at the opposite end of the hall, jerking in the flickering light. An entire section of blue carpet bulged, bowing, then rolling forward as if a giant rat ran underneath it. Like an uncoiling whip, the undulating carpet thrashed forward. Jana turned and ran. Just as she cleared the hall, the carpet leaped from the floor, tearing free. A snakish tongue snapped after her.

"David!" Jana tried to scream, it came out as a squeak. She ran for the steps. Suddenly, the bookshelf next to the clock began to shake and shudder. A book flew out, striking her shoulder, then a second hit her in the face as she ducked too late. A third, then more books followed as David's novels were fired from his bookshelf, leaping from right to left.

Hoarsely screaming David's name as she was pelted by dozens of books and wildly flailing her arms to knock away whatever she could, Jana fought her way toward the front door. The books whirled unnaturally, pounding her on the back as though trying to drive her out the front door.

Hyperventilating, Jana's breathing was harsh and abrupt; she was so scared she couldn't scream.

Jana tried to turn away from the front door, and tripped over a footstool that couldn't have been there moments ago. She hit the floor hard, bruising a knee. Crying, she crawled across the floor. The books continued to pelt her, falling, then rebounding to strike her again. There was a dragging as though the furniture was being hauled across the floor, coming to attack her!

"No! No more!" Jana hurled herself forward and desperately clutched at the screen door handle. It refused to open, stuck as though locked. Crying, she covered up, protecting herself until the books finally quit pummeling her.

Jana awakened with a start, straightening in the chair. It had been a dream! A DREAM! But what a nightmare! David's talk of ghosts must have registered all too well. She could have sworn it was real. That Tina's ghost was in the house.

Jana stretched, feeling a bit sore from sleeping awkwardly, and looked at David. He was sleeping peacefully. She thought about it for a second, then got up, moving toward the bed. She kicked the book she'd been reading, and it slid across the floor, stopping next to another book by the nightstand.

Weary and wanting to stretch out, Jana climbed atop the bed and laid next to David. She tried to push the dream away, fearful of it and the coming days. She had a bad feeling that things would get worse, before they got better. But it was easier if you had someone to help share the burden.

Seventeen

Town Meeting

Logan sat next to the mayor on the town hall's stage, his attention wandering over the crowd as he listened to the sheriff explain the situation from the podium. Usually the large, sterile chamber with its cold tile flooring, fluorescent, overhead lights, and faded wood paneling was as silent as a tomb. But today was different. The cavernous room buzzed with activity usually reserved for campaigns, community debates, or fundraisers.

Every chair was occupied, reminding him of a haphazardly packed can of sardines. Some folks leaned against the walls, while others waited outside. By word of mouth, news of the gathering had spread, catching the interest of almost everyone. Unfortunately, they hadn't expected this kind of turnout, so they hadn't bothered to hook up the PA system. Logan had heard plenty of grumbling, because coffee wasn't made and smoking wasn't permitted.

It seemed as if everybody who was anybody, and even some ranchers who rarely came to town, were present. The response was a good sign of Temprance's togetherness, especially since it was for the troublesome Brookens brothers, and it filled Logan with pride. There might be a few here for the spectacle, but not many. They didn't live in a big, violent city. Temprance was a good and peaceful place to live and raise children. Things had changed since the Carter incident long ago, and he was glad to be part of it.

Logan marveled at the wide diversity sitting next to each other. True, many looked tired and worn, but there certainly wasn't a typical-looking volunteer in the bunch. Several rows back sat Zane Harkness; the overweight barber was listening and absently plucking hairs from his white shirt. Next to him, Mr. Paul Pressley, the impeccably dressed and community-minded president of the First Interstate Bank of Temprance, appeared grim as he jotted notes in a leather-bound folio.

Bill Bowers, the owner and editor of the *Temprance Times*, and Corey Stones whispered to each other. Bowers was dressed in a white shirt and dark tie, while Stones was clad in one of his ten-worst-dressed-men-in-America suits. Even Ronnie, the vagabond, along with his sister Kathy, was present. It made Logan wonder once again about Bob. Where was he?

Those affected most by the meeting sat in the front row. Claire Brookens, looking exhausted and bedraggled, sat next to the Reverend Wright and was surrounded by her cronies Carrie Parker, Susan Acker, Betty Mathews, and Carol Peters. Not surprising, their husbands were absent. They were never with their wives, unless forced or shamed into it. The four women wore calculating expressions, as though any of the men in the room could be responsible for the boys' disappearance.

Still wearing their hats, the three Tubbs boys waited impatiently, chawing and spitting into cups. Hank and Buck were barrel-shaped and wore scowls. Buck was scarred, while Hank had a stained picket fence for front teeth. Both had recently been released from jail. The eldest brother, Rick, was tall and lean—a severe contrast to the others; he'd also never been to jail. He was the brains, while Buck and Hank were the brawn, wanting action, not words. Not surprisingly, they were cousins to Jeremy Tubbs, the ringleader that instigated the hanging in the Carter incident. The entire family was hot-blooded, amoral, and bigoted, Logan thought.

In a cluster behind them were Michael Woods, Penny Matthewson, her son-in-law Stan Hanson, and the Reverend Page, who appeared very concerned. His thoughts were obviously with his son, found catatonic last night in the church. Strange things were certainly afoot in Temprance.

Nearby, the postman Ernie Nathaniel seemed to alternate between being amused and dozing. Old Man Watson, wearing his Ranger's cap, kept poking him to pay attention. Logan guessed that they'd probably smuggled in a bottle. Usually Claire or Thelma Weaver, wherever she was, would be on them in an instant. It just showed how absorbed everyone was in the proceedings.

On a short stage and dwarfing the speaker's stand, Sheriff Bricker finished his well-phrased explanation with, "and that is the extent of our knowledge. Deputy Sheriff Ross is passing around Xerox copies of photographs of Jim Bob and Benny Joe supplied by Claire." Logan could almost read his boss's callous mind; he was probably thinking good riddance.

"Despite what his brothers have told us, we aren't sure when JJ Tubbs disappeared. It might have been as early as Friday night. We don't have any photographs as of yet, but all you have to do is look at his brothers. Stand up, boys." Rick, Hank, and Buck Tubbs got to their feet, then turned around for all to see. The brothers seemed to enjoy the attention, Buck even bowed a little.

We'd all be safer if they were still in jail, Logan thought. It was still one of his missions in life to put them away for good. With the current situation at hand, he was going to watch them very carefully. They needed little provocation to get out of hand.

"I want to thank you all for your support. I can't stress how important it is to have as many eyes as possible. Let's not leave any stone unturned. And pay particular attention to the areas around the lake and woodlands. If we act fast, we may have some success. Unfortunately, at this time, we don't have any leads—"

Bingo, it's showtime, Corey Stones thought as he stood and announced, "Oh yes, we do!" Everyone was stunned into a pall of silence so pervasive that a dropped pin could have easily been heard. With smug triumph and knowing all eyes were upon him, Stones walked to the stage. His clothing was frumpy and unmatched, giving pause to anyone who would credit his word. Even inside he wore sunglasses, and his unshaven appearance reminded Logan of a sleazy lawyer.

When he handed the sheriff several eight-by-ten photos, a low jabbering of speculation began. Stones smiled. A man in back stepped outside to pass on the latest turn of events. The tense crowd rippled with anticipation. Playing the crowd, Stones walked to the slack-jawed Tubbs boys and offered them a copy. There was an air about the reporter that brought out the worst in everybody. Before Stones continued, Hank gasped loudly, "That's JJ's bike!" The crowd was quiet no longer.

Buck nearly tore it from his grasp. "I'll be damned!"

"Where'd you get this?" Rick jumped to his feet, moving toward Stones.

"Stones, what is the meaning of this?" Sheriff Bricker demanded from the stage, waving the fistful of photos. He was red-faced and obviously angry.

"Sonuvabitch," Logan muttered. The mayor let out a long slow breath and shook his head. This was not what they needed. It made them look bad. Logan moved to Bricker's side, knowing that an explosion was imminent.

"You've heard it from his brothers! I have found JJ Tubbs's motorcycle!" Strutting and filled with his own sense of self-importance, Stones returned to his chair, reached under it, and pulled out a paper sack. With ostentatious flair he pulled out JJ's mangled black hat, held it high, and then tossed it to Buck. "As well as his hat!"

"I'll be goddamned! He's right!" Buck confirmed. All the Tubbs' expressions were the same, gaping and wide-eyed with quivering chins, as though a heavyweight boxer had stunned them with a lightning-fast haymaker.

The silence was destroyed by the astounding revelation, and a cacophony of voices erupted. Everyone asked questions at once. Many stood to get a better view, as some from outside crammed into the room.

The mood in the room had changed from uncertainty and anticipation to a combination of excitement and dread. Logan's sixth sense kicked in, the one that had kept him alive in the jungle and on the street. He suddenly became aware of and feared the mob mentality.

"Order! Order!" Bricker yelled, but no one listened to him. No one could hear. He pounded on the podium, but it was to no avail.

"Where'd ya find it?" Hank yelled, grabbing Stones. "You bastard, you've held out on us!" Hank's empty hand balled into a fist. Claire was moving closer, trying to hear.

"Near the road just outside the Matthewson farm," the reporter smiled. "Y'all can read about it in Friday's *Times*."

"Who's Matthewson?" Rick asked.

"That weird writer fella," Ernie offered.

"I want to know exactly where—NOW!" Buck grabbed him with both hairy paws and shook him. "Or I'll beat it out of you!"

Others moved toward the reporter, including his stunned boss, Bill Bowers. Having heard the name Matthewson mentioned, but not much else, Michael and Penny pushed several chairs aside and joined the throng around Stones.

Bricker jumped off the stage, causing some to step back,

and then he brusquely moved everyone away from Stones except for Hank Tubbs, who stayed. Logan was close behind.

"What in the hell do you think you're doing?" Bricker raged, then slapped Hank's hands away from the reporter. Resembling a baseball umpire in an argument with a team manager, Bricker confronted Stones nose to nose.

"My job," Stones said dryly, then gave him a slick smile that quickly weakened. He started to perspire. "I'm protected by the first amendment. Plus the right to assemble."

"Ain't Stones you should be questioning. It's that freak Matthewson," someone yelled from nearby.

"Yeah, he writes about devil worship stuff!" another joined.

Buck and Rick crowded close behind Hank, pressing in on Bricker and Stones. "We wanna talk to this Matthewson fella!"

"I just wanna kick Stones's ass," Buck yelled.

"String them both up by their balls!" Hank added.

Claire pushed her way to Stones. "What about my boys?" Her expression was hopeful, her eyes aglow.

"Nothing yet, honey," Stones said. "But I'll bet my bottom dollar David Matthewson knows something." Claire was crestfallen for a moment, then her face hardened, and her eyes grew wild.

Logan couldn't believe the way the emotions of the crowd had changed again. The gathering shuffled forward, wanting to hear something. A few were bumped a little hard, getting angry, and several chairs were knocked over. Temprance wasn't like this!

Michael Woods tried to say something, but Claire Brookens cut him off. She lunged past him and grabbed Penny's shirt. "What has your son done to my boys?"

The sudden act of aggression surprised the crowd and everyone stopped dead, staring.

Penny tried to pull away from Claire. "Get a hold of yourself, woman! He hasn't done anything!"

258

"Ladies, calm yourselves, please! Peace!" Cooper Page gently grabbed Claire. She struggled harder, almost getting free and striking Penny several times. "Help, please!" Logan and Wright came to her aid, and together they pulled her away from Penny. Angry and weeping, Claire shouted obscenities at Penny. The reverend as well as others were stunned. Profanity from Claire! What was going on?

"Damn, not again!" Logan muttered. Claire had gone totally off the deep end this time. "Mayor! Call Dr. Katyu! Claire needs help." It figures, Logan fumed, that the sleazy reporter would cause something like this, stirring them up just when everyone was already worried.

"I told you," Daniel Wright said to Cooper, "that David Matthewson was a problem. Everybody knows this. They can feel his evil, can't we?"

The Reverend Page started to respond, but was interrupted. "Yeah!" Somebody yelled. "Matthewson's trouble!"

"He looks like a demon," someone else said.

"He's got my boys!" Claire screamed, then slumped against Wright, who held her upright. David's name spread through the masses as though it were a revelation.

"People!" Logan began. Somebody bumped Michael hard, and he collided into Logan.

"See what you've done!" Bricker spat at Stones, who simply smiled.

Suddenly, the Reverend Page climbed onto a chair and waved his arms. Just the sight of him quieted the crowd. "This is not a time to drool and slaver like hunting dogs. We know nothing for sure and have no facts. Everyone is innocent unless proven guilty. And as we've all been taught, good people don't throw innocents to the lions." The crowd shifted guiltily. "People of faith shouldn't be making hasty judgments." His hands were raised, now he lowered them. "Let's be seated, so this can be handled in a civilized manner." There was some grumbling, but the spell was broken, the flashing heat of the moment passed. The people began to sit, milling around looking for chairs as though the music had just stopped.

"There will be an investigation, I promise," Bricker shouted. "After I talk with you," he promised Stones.

Logan looked over the crowd and his gaze met Page's, then Woods's. They all glanced at each other, and the same thought was obvious. Something strange was going on in Temprance, and it was rapidly tearing the town apart.

Eighteen

Revelations

"Hello, is anybody out there?" Grimm asked. He was virtually paralyzed; surrounded by a darkness, thick and heavy, with the consistency and texture of crude oil. Kevin tried to lift his arms, but they hung limply at his sides, not responding, as though someone else controlled them.

Grimm was cold—and alone. "Uh," he was barely able to think, but joking was an essential part of his nature, "anybody know why Polish and polish . . . are spelled the same?" He waited for a long time, but there was no answer. Kevin managed a weak laugh, "Because Webster didn't know shit from shinola."

From somewhere came a soft laugh, and Kevin felt the darkness ripple, a current radiating outward. Suddenly, he no longer felt alone. "Why can't you circumcise Iranians? Cause there's no end to those pricks!" His thoughts were clearer, the words coming easier this time. The darkness shifted, easing its grip. " 'Gain, Kevy." He was no longer alone!

"Did ya hear about the blonde who was found dead hanging in a cell at the women's penitentiary, with twelve bumps on her head?" Kevin asked.

"Tell me, Kevy."

"She tried to hang herself with a rubber band!" Suddenly, the darkness jumped back as though slapped. Kevin felt a sense of elation, but when the inky barrier moved away, it was suddenly replaced by a wall of spikes, as though he'd been encased in an iron maiden. Kevin didn't dare move, for even when he inhaled, the razor-sharp protrusions nicked him.

"Don't worry, Kevy, Ah'm comin'. Tell me another one!"

"Did you hear about the new brand of Jewish tires?" He felt the knives jab him in several places. "They're called Firestein. Not only do they stop on a dime, but they also pick it up."

"Good!"

Abruptly, Kevin felt a ripping sensation in his chest and back. He tried to look down, but the pain across his forehead discouraged him. Instead, he just rolled his eyes. A ghostly hand was emerging from his chest. It reached through the spikes and pressed against the dark wall that bound him. There was a sudden groaning, the protest of stubborn metal being forced, and the knives slowly parted. "Did you hear the one about the Aggie that couldn't spell?" Everything shook around him. "He spent the whole night in a warehouse!"

With a great metallic shrieking, the iron maiden burst apart to reveal a world of gray, hazy light. "We're gettin' there, Kevy."

Kevin looked down. Now two arms were protruding from his chest. Intense pain washed across the front of his body, as though he'd been slashed from crotch to throat, then doused with burning gasoline. Through blurring eyes, he watched as something—someone—stepped from his body. The wraith-like figure was tall and lean, his face shadowed by his cowboy hat. His friend was clad in a blue flannel shirt, worn jeans, and metal-tipped cowboy boots—shit-kicker specials.

He stretched. "That's much bett'ah! Now it's time fer ah good ole Texas exorcism. We gonna git rid of that purdy, undead bitch. There's only room fer the two of us. Three's a crowd." He pulled a rifle butt from his pants, then, amazingly enough, removed an entire shotgun, and pointed it at Kevin's ankles.

Grimm's eyes widened. There were chains with balls manacled to his ankles. KABLAM! BLAM—BLAM—BLAM! Kevin jumped at the deafening gunfire, and saw the buckshot tear through the chains. He was free! He wanted to dance, but still his arms felt leaden. Two more blasts lightened them.

Elated, Kevin took two steps, then couldn't move again, a sharp pressure clasping him at the ankles. Kevin screamed. This time there was a bleached skeleton hanging onto his legs.

"She's a stubborn bitch." The stranger put the gun away and reached for a pack of cigarettes in his breast pocket. "Tell me another one, Kevy."

Shaking, Kevin said, "Did you hear about the guy who had his vasectomy done at Sears? Every time he gets a hard-on, the garage door goes up!"

The stranger was laughing as he lit a cigarette, then he dropped the match at Kevin's feet. A flash fire erupted, scorching Kevin's legs. He started to dance . . . and could! Laughing, Kevin leaped away from the grasp of the charred skeleton, its fingers crumbling.

"She's still inside you!" His friend jammed a bottle of Wild Turkey 101 Proof in his face. "Kevy, down the hatch!"

Kevin grabbed the bottle and took two thirsty gulps, his throat catching fire and his stomach blossoming with a devouring warmth. Grimm handed it back to his companion, who did a shot. "To Texas," he said and passed it back. Kevin took another big swig. The bottle was passed back and forth. "Cannonball!" the stranger encouraged. As Kevin was drinking, his drinking partner grabbed the bottom of the bottle and tilted it upward, helping him to huge gulps. "Chugalug Texas tea!"

Kevin drained the bottle, then his stomach cramped, seizing his entire body. He started to shake, then crumpled to his knees. His stomach was a raging volcano; it erupted, and he began to vomit. With each retch, a black fluid spewed forth from his mouth in clumps and clusters. After minutes of wracking and heaving, a large puddle lay before him.

"Well, that oughtta do it," the stranger said. Kevin knew it had; he felt much, much better! Free and in control of himself! He wanted to say thanks, when the shadowy cowboy with the voice said, "How cain ah real man tell, if his girlfriend is havin' an orgasm?"

Kevin smiled. "Real men don't give a shit."

"Exactly."

Suddenly the pool of black started to bubble and boil, coming alive. Shortly, it began to grow, rising to form a small, thin pillar. "Persistent bitch." Black clay slowly formed a female.

"Well, since we ain't religious," the cowboy laughed, "there's only one thang ta do. Bring on the Texas sun! Move those clouds away. Pretend the fog is givin' way ta the rising sun!"

Kevin closed his eyes and pictured the blazing red orb of the sun majestically soaring above the horizon, searing away the fog. As though the lake were afire, the ripples flared orange and red. The mists were dispersed! Dark traces, the indigoes and purples, were burned from the sky, as were the stars. Bright colors raced across the clouds.

Grimm heard a piercing scream, then abruptly it died, as though a door had been slammed. He opened his eyes to find a wide, glistening smile on his friend's shadowy cheshire face. "She's gone, my friend. It's just you and me, Kevy boy!"

As though thrown from the dream, Kevin quickly sat up in bed. He was at home, in his own bed! How'd I get here, he wondered, his head feeling stuffed full of cotton.

Then he remembered the hitchhiker, Monique. She had bitten him. Was she some kind of vampire? Well, if so, her bark was worse than her bite. To make sure it was real, he touched his throat and found the indentations. "Don't worry, Kevy. You're free."

After leaving her with David Matthewson . . .

"Could be another vampire, Kevy."

. . . He didn't remember much. He was supposed to do something. An errand? Instead, weary and feeling as though he were catching the flu, he'd come home and collapsed.

Oh yeah! He was supposed to bury the Brookens boys. Yeah, that was it! Benny Joe and Jim Bob were dead.

Hate welled within him. Hate for Monique and what she had done to him. She'd tried to control him as surely as his father had, but instead of using fists, she used sex, and some unholy power that the taste of his blood gave her. But he was free! Free to avenge! She was another one to add to his list. It was getting long now: Becky, Lou, PP, Skeeter, Matthewson, and Monique—the bitch, the cowboy, the rat, the tattletale, the maybe vampire and the real vamp.

But why did she have to kill Benny Joe and Jim Bob? They were puppets, but they were also his friends, good dudes—guys who knew how to party. Kevin sighed heavily, almost shedding a few tears, but not wanting to give her the satisfaction. Whatever he did, he would get her back, and make sure that their deaths were not without meaning. He didn't know what he was going to do, but an idea was forming.

It was then that he noticed his parents talking, something about a town meeting today.

"So it was a full house?" his mother asked.

"Crammed to overflowing," his stepfather drawled.

"Did you convince everyone that a search party was needed to find the Brookens boys?"

They're deader than doornails, Mom, Grimm thought.

"No problem. They were raring to go. We're also looking for the Tubbs boy."

"He's missing?" his mother asked. Kevin wondered the same thing.

"Has been since Friday night. His mother's severely handicapped, staying over at the old folks place in Palestine. JJ visits her every Saturday and sometimes Sunday. He hasn't been there. The other brothers stopped by to talk to her, otherwise we might not have found out. Well, actually we would've, Corey Stones would have made sure."

"That reporter?"

"If you want to call him that. Stones has been prowling around on the Matthewson farm."

"Seems to be a lot of that lately. I thought we believed in privacy in Temprance."

"So did I, dear. Anyway, he found JJ's motorcycle hidden along the road just outside of the Matthewson ranch, and his hat in the woods on the property. There was almost a riot, I swear."

"How did he know whose it was?"

"The license plate. Now the Tubbses are in an uproar, as well as others. They want to go beat the truth—as they call it—out of David. And we almost had a cat fight during the meeting. Penny and Claire faced off, ready to go at it. I've never seen people so riled, and I blame most of it on Stones, maybe some on Reverend Wright. This could have been handled discreetly. Thank heavens the Reverend Page was there."

Stones is an asshole, Grimm agreed.

"So what's next?" his mother asked.

"The sheriffs are going to check out the motorcycle, then get a warrant, and search the Matthewson farm, see if they find anything. Lord help us, first the Brookens brothers and now JJ. If this keeps up, people will start jumping at shadows, if they aren't already. Everybody looked . . . bad, as though they've been staying up late and drinking."

Kevin didn't hear the rest of the conversation. His mind was awhirl, the creative juices flowing. He knew how to get at Monique and at David Matthewson! Yes, he knew how the Brookens brothers' deaths would have some value. They . . . or their bodies would anyway. Perception was more powerful than reality.

Nineteen

The Beguiling

"And his hat," Jana added worriedly, looking from Michael to David. Besides contract opportunities, his friends had come to tell David about the town meeting and the search for the missing boys. The three of them were sitting in the seldom-used living room around a large coffee table that Jana had dusted. Three glasses of iced tea were sweating on coasters, and the tabletop was covered with scattered files and papers.

David thought it was nice to see Jana again so soon, especially since her departure had been abrupt. After downing a bottle of elixir and feeling much better, he had met her downstairs upon returning to the house. She claimed he looked fine, and that she needed to get ready for work. He had wanted to tell her about his dream—a crimson string that linked him to Monique—but she was gone in the blink of an eye. And now she appeared worried, occasionally giving him a quick, tight smile. Michael looked merely perturbed—little worried him.

"They found it near the creekbed upstream from JJ's motorcycle," Michael told him.

"Is that confirmed?" David asked. His thoughts moved away from Jana, and he wondered if something could have happened to JJ Friday night during the chaos. Monique had been there... here! David remembered chasing the Brookens brothers, enjoying it as he was filled with hunger, the desire for revenge. The thrill of the hunt and the scent of blood had been strong. That had to have been Monique's doing, striking at him through their strange rapport.

"David, are you all right?" Jana asked. Her brow was furrowed with concern, her gaze searching his face.

"Oh, I'm sorry. I get a little light-headed sometimes. And I still tire easily. But thank you." He appreciated her concern, but he felt fine tonight, except for worrying when Monique might manifest again. He didn't want either of his friends to be harmed, and Monique harmed everything she came near. They had been lucky last night. David knew he couldn't have protected Jana, if Monique had showed up. "Now what did you say, Michael?" David asked. He tried not to think about Monique, but he couldn't let his friends stay long. They'd already been here long enough, thirty minutes past sunset, only indigo and stars in the sky now.

"It's confirmed. Earlier today I accompanied Logan and Sheriff Bricker, along with Stones, to the spot. As he said, the deserted motorcycle was there. The license plate identified it as being owned by the Tubbs family, and they say it's JJ's. Obviously it hadn't been there long. We haven't told anyone that cocaine was found in a Ziploc bag under the seat."

David shook his head; he wasn't surprised drugs were involved. He remembered Friday night with the feeling of being drugged. "And where was this, again?" David asked. Michael described the spot, and David recognized it right away. There was a vague memory...

"They're working on a warrant," Michael continued. "It might be ready tomorrow, so get ready for an official visit."

"Twice in a week," David groaned. "Just what I need, more visitors. I've had more people on my ranch in the last week than I've had in the past ten years!" Life had been peaceful until last Friday. "And you know I can't see them during the day. And I doubt they'll want to search the place at night."

"I know," Michael said, "be calm. I am your friend, agent, and lawyer, remember; I'll take care of you." He smiled. David didn't, so Michael smiled even more. "I discussed it with the sheriffs and suggested that under the circumstances, they bring the warrant to me first, and I'd act on your behalf. They had no problem with that. Do you?" David smiled weakly and shook his head. "They do understand. Logan is a good man, and Donald has his moments. I'll need keys to everything."

"Fine," David ran his hands through his hair. "I have nothing to hide."

"I know you don't. This will be painless. You can sleep through it. I'll make sure they don't damage anything. I'll probably be out of my office for an entire day, enjoying the sunshine." Michael smiled.

"It's not as if I'm hiding corpses in the haystacks." He hadn't—couldn't—forget about Jim Bob and Benny Joe. Both dead and buried in a trash pile.

"David!" Jana said, very surprised. Now she appeared worried, an unbecoming look settling on her beautiful features.

"Sorry, I'm guess I'm just a little upset. None of this is my fault! Absolutely none of it! I can't write! I can't think! I'm not sleeping well, either. I didn't ask for those kids to come on my property. They invaded my privacy! And it's obvious that this Stones is trespassing, too. What about *my* rights?"

"David. I know. I'm sorry," Michael said. "This isn't a normal circumstance. It's become an incident. Everybody in town—and I do mean everybody—knows about it. They're worried, ready to jump at shadows. And to tell you the truth, it's not the finding of the hat or the motorcycle that frightens me most. It's the way the crowd's moods swung from one extreme to the next. Mercurial is too mild a word. And the response to Stones's implied accusation was very persuasive, especially when the Reverend Wright made his feelings about you publicly known. It gave me chills." Michael sighed. "It seems history is repeating itself. Do you remember the troubles you had a long time ago?"

"I think troubles is a rather strong word," David responded. "Some people are just unnerved by my appearance. Jana reacted the same way the other night, when I surprised her."

"I did not!"

David laughed, so Jana smiled. If he could laugh while discussing these types of problems, then things couldn't be too serious. She felt he was a good man having to carry a burden too heavy for one.

"I believe there is some underlying current of negativity towards you, and it could be dangerous," Michael said.

"I think you're making a mountain out of a molehill. As long as I stay out of town, there's no problem," David said. He had forgotten about Monique entirely, until he felt a tickle, followed by a moment of disorientation.

He has changed, Jana thought.

"Listen to me, my friend," Michael's voice was tensely guarded. "I sensed a similar undercurrent toward me, when I went to college. It wasn't much, but the prejudice was there, usually from small-minded farm boys or sons of bigots, I guess. Most people accepted me as I am, especially once they got to know me. But some people don't care about knowing you. They think they know you by looking at you. In my case, and in your case, they worried about being infected . . . or simply sullied by our presence.

"I'm lucky, I've only had one serious encounter. I don't count simple animosity, verbal jabs, tricks, or caustic glances. I ignore them. I'm a bigger man. So listen to me, David, I don't imagine things. I'm sensitive, but not hyper about them. We are enlightened, right?" he said with a smile. "If you want, think of yourself as a minority. That's the way people react to you. You might as well be a modern-day leper."

"That's strong," David winced. Suddenly the sense of drifting, the disorientation, returned.

"Then why don't you go into town anymore?" Michael asked. "Have you been hiding? Hiding this from yourself?"

David didn't hear the question. He'd been pulled away from the ranch, his presence once again floating near the lake. There were dark houses all about, but a light shone at the gate. Skeeter, one of the boys from Friday, had stopped there. He'd been out riding his bicycle. David felt a breeze and could smell sweat. Skeeter's pulse began to beat rapidly within David's head. There was a red glow about the boy, and suddenly David felt as though he were right there next to him, no longer watching from the distant shadows.

After undoing the lock and chain, Skeeter pulled the gate open and rolled his bicycle inside. Shadows shifted near the closest house, a fleeting, furtive movement. David noticed it, then Skeeter's head turned toward the A-frame structure. Was it Monique?

Skeeter stopped. David could read the boy's expression . . . read his mind. Nobody was supposed to be at the Steele's house; it was a weekend getaway place. The lights were out, and there wasn't a car in the driveway. It was obvious by his growing fear and caution that he'd heard stories, and knew about the missing boys.

Was it Monique? David tried to reach for her. She had to be here, because he was here! And yet, he couldn't find her. And he couldn't move either. He appeared to be hanging around Skeeter, as if he were the boy's guardian angel. Could this be similar to his accident nightmares?

Skeeter peered into the darkness and swore that somebody was on the front porch, quietly watching him. Suddenly, David could feel it, too—eyes as sharp as knives dissecting him. She was here! RUN! David thought. Run for your life!

Skeeter stared a moment longer, shrugged, then went back to relocking the gate. Suddenly, a piercing wind cut Skeeter, and he jumped as though pinched, quickly rubbing his bare arms. The night was silent, when moments ago it had been typically noisy in a country sort of way. The wind was gone, but the coolness still remained, settling about him like a cold blanket.

Now David was thrown back to the ranch. Neither Jana or Michael said anything, thinking David didn't want to discuss Michael's question. David paused, then asked, "Have you ever had any trouble in this town, Michael?" He needed to get them to leave, but he couldn't be abrupt. If he feigned illness, Jana might want to stay, and he had to stop Monique! She was here because of him, drawn somehow by his disease, by the porphyria.

"No. You, Jana?"

"Only the type you get for being a long-legged female. It happens anywhere. I haven't had any trouble because of my Hispanic heritage, though."

"As I've said before, David," Michael continued, "you live deep in the heart of the Bible Belt. You'll find other men and women thinking along the same lines as Wright does, when they read your books with a puritanical point of view."

"That's a frightening thought," David said, momentarily thinking of something besides Monique. "You almost make it sound as though it's a conspiracy. Not that it matters since I won't stop writing simply because somebody doesn't like it."

Suddenly he was with Skeeter once more.

As though called by a siren's song, the redhead's attention was drawn to the figure at the house. Despite the deepening of the night and the distance across the yard, Skeeter could see the woman more clearly than before, as though she were basking in the brightness of day. At first, between her ivory-colored skin and stillness, Skeeter had the strange thought that she might be a statue. But her eyes were bright, a fiery bronze, which dispelled that image. Her features were distinct and fine, a pale but captivating vision with long, flowing hair the color of a mare's ebony mane.

Against her black outfit, her face appeared to glow—like the writer's did! David caught the thought, hesitating briefly before continuing his attempt to break free. He couldn't. All he could do was watch. Yelling at Skeeter was useless. David had to wake up. He had to be there in person to help Skeeter, not just in spirit through some kind of weird psychic link. But usually he was tied to Monique, not the victim. Why was tonight different?

Skeeter flashed back to Friday night and remembered. A strong sense of dread tried to suck him down into its quagmire, and he swallowed hard. He wanted to turn away, but his gaze was riveted to the pale woman. She stretched, her white arms reaching out toward him, imploring.

"No!" David screamed.

Skeeter took a stuttery step forward, then two quick ones backward, as though he'd been shoved. He bumped into the fence, and it shook, his bicycle falling against the back of his legs. "OUCH!" The pain caused him to whirl, and he stared down at his legs, finding long scratches where the bicycle had wounded him.

As Skeeter moved to pick up his bicycle, he suddenly drew a blank. He couldn't remember what had happened. He yanked his Schwinn upright. Did he fall off his bicycle? Maybe black out? Confused, Skeeter got on his bicycle and rode out of the gate. Where had he been going?

I need to wake up! David tried to think himself awake, willfully claw back to his ranch, to Michael and Jana. Suddenly, he was in his living room once more. "Uh folks, I'm feeling a bit off, tired I guess. You mind if we called it an evening?" Michael gave David a long look. "Michael, I'll think long and hard about what you've said. We'll talk about it some more after the search tomorrow, okay?" Michael nodded. David stood and said, "And then can we also take care of the contracts tomorrow night?"

"I guess so. All the negotiations are basically done."

"I trust you."

"Thanks, but I think you're too trusting. Just because you're not actively in the world, doesn't mean it isn't cruel and hard."

"I know," David said coldly.

Suddenly, Michael got a sheepish look on his face, "David, I'm sorry. I'm just worried."

"Michael, it's okay. I do believe you look out for me like family. We'll talk tomorrow. All of us," David said looking at Jana, "when we can laugh at this." If he could still laugh after tonight.

"That sounds good to me," Jana said. "Are you feeling all right?"

"Just a bit dizzy. And this is a lot to think about." David saw in her eyes that she wanted to share his thoughts. That would be all right, if they weren't about Monique. "Let me get those keys."

David did, giving them to Michael and noting that most were labeled—a habit of his mother's. David tried to shepherd them out quickly, but casually. Would Monique chase Skeeter down, as she had Benny Joe? Could he . . . would he feel Skeeter die, if he died right now?

David lingered over Jana's departure for as long as he felt he could, then waved goodbye to his friends. For a moment, he watched as they drove away, their red taillights rising over the hill and through a copse of trees before disappearing. It was nice to have friends; he had almost forgotten the feeling.

Suddenly he was sick with dread. What if Monique had killed JJ, and left him somewhere on the property? If he'd had a simple accident, that wouldn't be a concern—especially if there were traces of cocaine—but what if Monique had gotten him? What would he look like? Benny Joe and Jim Bob?

David wished he could tell Jana and Michael the truth, but

even they wouldn't believe he was being hounded by a vampiress who was convinced he was a vampire. What was he going to do first? Rescue Skeeter or search the ranch for JJ's corpse? No contest. Tracking down and destroying Monique was his first priority! Skeeter and many other kids were at risk, and more important than his image and reputation.

David turned to go inside to get his weapons and car keys, then sensed that he wasn't alone. There was a presence on his farm, an intruder watching him from a distance. Was it Monique or somebody else? She had mentioned brethren, whoever they were.

David stretched out his senses, listening and looking, trying to identify whoever was hiding at the fringe of the woods. It wasn't Monique, although he thought he could feel faint stirrings again. This aroma wasn't like Monique's evil stench, decay oddly mingling with the sweetness of budding flowers. No, the company he had was human—and alive. The Peeping Tom was a man, unwashed with stale sweat, stinking of cheap aftershave and cigarettes.

David walked down the steps, out the front gate, and headed for the woods where the interloper waited. He wouldn't be expecting David to walk directly to him. David thought he saw something move, then felt the man start, as though surprised. Now the intruder was running!

Suddenly David felt it, fought it, and lost. THE HUNT WAS ON! The bloodlust had returned. He forgot about Skeeter.

This man doesn't stand a chance, David thought and broke into a sprint. Besides knowing the woods well, he could see in the dark and hear the crashing movements as branches were pushed aside, leaves and sticks trampled, cracking. He could hear the man's clumsy footsteps, his harsh breathing, the rustle of his clothes, and even his heartbeat. David could smell his worry—soon to be fear. He could almost taste blood, the sensation just drifting beyond reach.

David easily jumped the fence and continued pursuit. The

intruder was less than thirty feet away, stumbling through the woods. His jacket was flapping, sometimes catching and tearing on bushes and branches. His heart was hammering so loudly, that David thought it should be echoing through the woods. The stink of fear reminded David of stale urine.

The man glanced over his shoulder, his glasses askew and wet hair plastered to his forehead. David didn't recognize him. "No! NO!" The man gasped.

David reached out, touching the man's flapping jacket; it slipped through his fingers. David tried again, this time snagging it, jerking the intruder off stride. Stones staggered and tried to slip free of his jacket.

Suddenly David staggered, struck by a mental blow as Monique intruded, ripping open his mind as though she wielded a sharp dagger. Suddenly he realized that Monique had been playing with him! As Stones slipped from his jacket and fled, David was once again overwhelmed and subjugated by the vampire.

"Hello there," Monique called to Skeeter, who had returned and was locking the gate. It was a soft call, almost a whisper, barely carried by the wind.

"Who?" Confused, Skeeter looked toward Monique, finding a shapely woman silhouetted by a window at the Steele's porch.

"Come here," her voice was soft but demanding. At first, Skeeter hesitated, struck by an odd sense of déjà vu, but then he shrugged and rolled his bicycle toward her, as though he were being reeled in. The world around him faded away, blurring to indistinction. All he could see was the pale woman with jet black hair, porcelain white skin, and radiant eyes. She was so beautiful. She smiled as he drew closer, and Skeeter smiled back.

David fought the desire; he had felt cravings even more desperate than this—his need for the elixir—but still it blinded him.

"Come in, you look thirsty." Monique reached out a hand. Skeeter's slowly rose to take hers. "And I am famished. Do come in. We shall get to know each other well. Won't we, David?"

David was suddenly back at the ranch. Dropping Stones's jacket and forgetting about the intruder, David raced back toward the house. He was surprised to find Jana climbing out of her car. She had come back! He didn't have time to waste with explanations. He thought about trying to sneak around the house, but she saw him and waved. "David!"

David stood still for a moment. Jana looked confused, then came toward him. The taste of blood welled in David's mouth.

"David! Is everything all right!" Despite the darkness, she could see him—see his expression. "You're not, are you? Can I help?"

"No," David suddenly made a decision. "I need time to think. I'm sorry, but I need time alone. Have a nice evening," he said and ran by her, having suddenly changed his mind about transportation. Skeeter and Monique were along the waterfront not far away. Cutting across the lake in a boat would be much quicker than driving there.

As David ran up the dirt road to the dock, he felt as though he were in two places, some of him here, but most of him with Monique and Skeeter. Time was running short.

David grabbed the lever on the post and yanked it down. The winch ground and whined, lowering the boat. Too slow. Damn, so slow! David could feel Monique toying with Skeeter. She wanted David to try to rescue the boy. She wanted David to know futility, so he would give in!

Released from restraints and floating, the boat drifted and bumped into the dock. David shook himself and jumped inside the old speedboat. It would be fastest, if it started. He hadn't used it in a long time. David turned the key and hoped. Amazingly, the Mercruiser turned over immediately, roaring loudly with a cough of black smoke.

Too late, he heard footsteps on the dock. Jana climbed into the boat. "David—"

No time. Without a word, David put the boat in gear, backing up and spinning around. "David? Please—" David jammed the throttle forward. Jana was thrown into a seat with a gasp of surprise. Her eyes widened as the boat leaped, then shot away from dock, leaving it shaking, as they raced across the lake and into the darkness.

Twenty

Burial Sightings

From his vantage point outside the run-down and deserted shack, Grimm saw a car pull out from David's driveway and head in the other direction. It didn't really matter whether David was home or not; he and his buddies wouldn't be getting anywhere near the house. Grimm laughed, he was headed for greener pastures.

As he returned to his pickup, Grimm pulled off his shirt. It was still hot as hell and muggy; the night felt like a steamy cotton blanket. And it was going to be hard work lugging the Brookens boys around . . . but what else was new? They'd always been deadweight.

Grimm reached into the cab and grabbed his fanny pack. It contained everything he needed for the exciting evening to come. Next, he snagged a spray can from the front seat, then drenched himself with Off. For good measure, he reached over the bed of the truck and covered the bodies with a mist of bug repellant. It soaked into the dark maroon sheets he'd wrapped around both corpses. He'd found the brothers in a pile of trash at a shoreline house under construction, right where Monique had told him. He'd come directly from there to here.

"Kevy, know who the meanest man in the world wuz?"

"You?" Grimm asked.

"Nope, the guy who raped the deaf and dumb girl, then cut her fingers off so she couldn't holl'ah fer help."

Grimm laughed and closed the cab door. There was plenty of moonlight to illuminate the woods for his journey. There wasn't a cloud in the sky, and the moon was past its quarter. It was gonna be a great night for grave digging and planting buds, he chuckled.

Pulling the tailgate down, Grimm reached in and dragged out the bodies. He hefted them onto his shoulder. "Let's go, boys, step lively." Grimm headed for the gap in the fence. He usually had good night vision, but tonight it was better than ever. Even the shadowed areas seemed to reveal what they once had concealed. Grimm didn't figure he'd have any trouble finding his way through the forest. He'd been here often enough.

"Happy landings," Grimm tossed the bodies over the fence, then climbed through the rusted wiring. Picking up the corpses, he headed into the woods. Bluish light filtered down through the trees, as though he were deep under crystal clear water, contrasting with a sea full of ebony islands of harboring shadows. There was only a slight breeze, so the only noises he heard was his own tread and the occasional shuffle of some nocturnal creature. In the distance an owl hooted.

"Hey, boys, what has six legs and goes 'Ho-de-do, Ho-de-do, Ho-de-do?' " He waited for an answer, then said, "Give up? Three niggers running for an elevator. Hey, did you hear about the new gay bar? It's called BOYS-R-US!"

"Ah, Jim Bob," he sighed, "it's just like old times. I'm cracking jokes and you're playing the straight man, or is it the stiff this time?! You always said you wanted to die with a hard-on, but I don't think this is what you meant!"

* * *

Corey Stones was thankful and cursing in the same breath. He didn't know what had made David Matthewson leave him alone, but he was mighty appreciative. He'd never seen anyone move that fast, especially in the dark. Sure there was a moon out, but Matthewson hadn't made a sound, as though he'd never stepped on anything! He, on the other hand, had been a raging bull in a china shop. His clothing was torn and flesh scratched, as a testament to his many run-ins with trees.

It was a good thing his camera was strapped over his shoulder and around his neck, or he would have lost it. The camera had taken some blows, but he didn't think it was broken. Unfortunately, he'd lost his binoculars. The loss of his jacket was no big deal. He hadn't even glanced back after giving David the slip by slipping out of the polyester.

Stones looked around. He was lost again. Why did this shit happen to him? Stones peered through the trees and thought that he saw a clearing ahead. He hoped it was the road. He'd parked in a different place this time, the pasture across the street. For extra cover, he had thrown a black tarp over his Escort.

As he moved toward the fence, he thought he heard someone talking. Who else would be out here? He tried to quietly move forward, crouching and hiding behind trees as he went.

"And after a long pause, a stout British gentleman jumps up and follows the Frenchman out the hatch. Long live the Queen, he yells." This was followed by chuckling.

What the hell is going on, Stones wondered? Who would be telling jokes out here in the middle of nowhere? There must be two people.

Stones knelt behind some brush and watched, seeing a lean man silhouetted with something large draped over his shoulder. He stepped from shadow to moonlight. The guy was barechested, his white skin gleaming as though wet. Stones had heard that Matthewson looked similar to this—cadaverous—but this couldn't be him.

Stones waited, then followed. He thought the voice sounded familiar, as it said, "There's a long pause, and then a big Texan stands up. On his way to the hatch he grabs a hapless Spic, then hurls him out the door yelling, 'Remember the Alamo!'"

I'm crazy, really crazy, Stones thought, but he knew he'd do anything for a story, and there had to be a doozy in this case. Damned if the guy wasn't alone, and it looked as if he were carrying a body! Stones waited until the joking man was well past him, then followed.

Grimm stopped and dumped his burden on the ground. He stretched, gasping, then pulled a half-pint of JD from his fanny pack. "Whoa-wee." He wiped the sweat from his brow with a forearm, then took another swig. "Here you go, my friends," and he poured a little onto the bundle. "You're gonna be famous."

Grimm smiled, pleasantly surprised. After feeling like shit all day, he was doing very well. And he was much stronger than he'd expected, having little trouble with Jim Bob's and Benny Jo's dead weight.

"Time to go, guys" Grimm said, and stuffed the bottle back into his pack. He wished he'd brought some of that special home brew David had stored in his refrigerator. Unfortunately, he'd finished the last of it. Hey, maybe he'd have to stop and get some more! It would be a great capper to the end of a perfect evening of revenge—payback numbers one and two.

Squatting, then throwing the corpses over his shoulder, Grimm continued on. He figured he was most of the way there. "Hey, Jim Bob, got another one for you. What's twelve inches long and white?" He waited, knowing an answer wouldn't come, but it was habit. Instead of silence, he heard a stick crack, and immediately stepped behind a tree and waited.

* * *

Oh God, did he hear me? And did I really hear him say Jim Bob? Stones wondered as he slowly and quietly moved from his knees to his stomach, lying prone on the ground. He tried to calm his breathing, his heart racing as though he'd just jumped off a cliff.

Thank heaven he was dressed in all black, dark slacks and a black shirt that clung to him as though it were made of glue. It was difficult to be quiet. He was shaking from the excitement of his forthcoming story.

How long was the guy going to wait?

Some ten minutes later, Grimm figured that everything was okay, but he didn't take it for granted. As he walked, he occasionally glanced back. Now he whispered his jokes to his friends on his shoulder.

"What's the perfect woman? She's deaf, dumb, blind, a nymphomaniac, and owns a liquor store." The running stream of jokes continued, Grimm chuckling to himself. "Of course, a perfect Cinderella is a woman who sucks and fucks all evening, then at midnight turns into a six-pack of beer and a pizza."

Seeing how the joking man had increased his vigilance, Stones followed parallel, far enough away that the only thing he could see was movement, and he certainly couldn't hear any more jokes. Thank God. Even with his own warped sense of humor, Stones found most of them trite and tasteless.

When Stones stepped on a loudly snapping stick a second time, he knew he was in trouble. He dropped to the ground, where a stick dug into his ribs.

This time Grimm knew he'd heard something! Lowering the bodies he reached into his boot and pulled out his switchblade. The *snikt* echoed after it snapped open. Grimm went hunting, knowing somebody was following him. He'd felt eyes watching him. Well, he knew what to do. He waved his knife. Cleave and heave.

Stones didn't know what to do. He saw the joking man advancing directly toward him. With his shirt off, Grimm was easy to see, his white skin gleaming in the moonlight.

Suddenly there was an odd sound in the night, as though several doors had been slammed. Stones tried not to move. Grimm stared in the direction of the barn, then resumed his search.

The unfortunate Stones thought he was going to sneeze. Desperate, he found a small stick and threw it away from him. It crashed through some underbrush, bounced along for a while, then stopped.

Grimm turned. Yes, somebody was here all right, and they were scared. He could feel it. It made him smile. "Benny Joe, why do women like hunters? Three reasons: they go deep into the bush, they always shoot twice, and they always eat what they shoot."

Grimm continued advancing, until something scuttled across the ground. In the moonlight he saw white gray fur and pink eyes. Damn, just a possum. Grimm gathered his burden and continued walking toward the pasture.

Breathing a quiet sigh of relief and thankful that the sneeze had never arrived, Stones did something he'd never thought he'd do. He removed his shoes, then continued following the joking man, sticks and stones digging into his feet.

Stones spotted a clearing ahead, the moonlight casting an ethereal, almost smoky glow across a field. He watched as the man stopped, then tossed his bundle up and over something. Stones squinted and saw a fence. Quietly, he huddled and waited, watching as the joking man backtracked along his trail.

Stones waited as long as he could stand it. He just had to

see what the bundle contained. Just as he started to move forward, the sound of a shotgun ripped the night.

He tripped. Staggering forward with his arms flailing, he managed to squelch an outcry. Something grabbed his ankles and he gasped. Twisting and losing all balance, he stepped on the side of his foot. Somehow he managed to swallow a scream as he felt a snap. Pain burrowed through his foot.

Tears welling in his eyes, he gingerly felt the ankle. Either he'd broken or badly sprained it. Damn his luck!

After a few minutes, the pain hadn't lessened, but he'd gotten used to it. He checked the ankle again; it was swollen larger than a softball. He pulled out a pack of gum and stuffed all the sticks into his mouth, wishing he had a rubber bullet.

Should he stay here and wait to see if the joking man returned? Or should he check the bundle? Stones crawled slowly to a tree and began to claw his way up to stand. He was totally soaked in sweat and hurting badly. The night was silent, the air oppressive and stifling. He was ready to trade in his upcoming Pulitzer Prize for a cool breeze, a cold beer, and an ambulance.

But there was a story to discover. Stones had a feeling he wouldn't have to make anything up this time. He heard a voice and knew that the joking man was returning. Stones quietly slid down the tree to hide. It was just too bad he'd lost his binoculars during his earlier flight. He couldn't run the risk of a camera shot, even though he was sorely tempted.

"We're almost there. Brothers together, thick and thin, all that stuff," Grimm rambled on. When he reached the barbed wire fence he tossed the bundled corpses to the other side, then he found a tree and climbed over.

"Hey, know what the only thing used sanitary napkins are good for?" He picked up the shovel, pulling it from the wrappings, then stared down at the bodies. "Vampire tea bags. I figured you guys would appreciate that one."

Grimm began digging. "Not too, too deep, Kevy boy. Ya want someone ta find it."

"Yeah, I know; it has to look good, but not too good."

"Exactly. Hey, know whut soybeans and dildos have in common?"

"No."

"They're both meat substitutes!"

Laughing, Grimm started digging again. He tried to pile the dirt carefully next to the hole, so he wouldn't have much trouble just shoving it back in.

Grimm stopped periodically to rest and swig some Jack, but he was amazed at how well he was feeling. Revenge was sweet, sweet, sweet. He just wished he could be a fly on the wall when Matthewson saw the unearthed bodies surrounded by sheriffs. It was about time Bricker was good for something.

Finally, after about an hour and a half, the hole was deep enough. Grimm unwrapped the bodies, then dragged them into the pit. As he stared at them, he felt melancholy. "Okay, one more joke. You'll need to know this where you're going. Why was Jesus Christ crucified on the cross, instead of being stoned?" He waited. "Because it's easier to cross yourself than hit yourself all over."

Feeling better, he reached down and ripped a section of Benny Joe's shirt. He stuffed it in his pocket, then proceeded to shovel dirt into the pit.

After he was finished, he arranged the sod, then stood back to look at his handiwork. "Not bad, Kevy. Time ta celebrate."

"Soon," Grimm replied. He moved to the wire fence, removed the shred of cloth from his pocket, and made sure it stuck on a barb.

He inspected things one more time, wiped away his footprints, and picked up the shovel. "Damn!" he gasped.

"What, Kevy?"

"I forgot to tell them the one about the Jew, the Wop, and the Greek that went to heaven."

"They've probably already heard it."

"Yeah, you're right," Grimm replied. "Home brew, here I come." He crumpled the sheets, then stuffed them under his armpit. Grimm covered his hands with a bandana, got out the empty bottle of Jack Daniels, then dropped it. Swinging his shovel onto his shoulder as though he were a lumberjack with an axe, Grimm headed along the fence toward the barn.

A stunned Stones watched him go. What a story! What should he do? Should he call the cops, or just wait to see what unfolded? Well, for one, he'd wait until the joking man was long gone, then take pictures. Then he'd have to hobble back to the car. That might take the rest of the night. Thinking about it, maybe he should wait until morning.

Switchblade in hand and shovel leaning against the wall, Grimm waited outside the barn door. He tried the handle and found it wasn't locked. At least the cat wouldn't bother him, he chuckled. Grimm opened the door, then quickly slipped inside.

The barn was dark, but some light came in through a few gaps in the boards and the windows facing the house. Grimm wrinkled his nose. Seemingly heightened by the heat and lack of draft, the place held a heavy stench as though dusty grain, fertilizer, dirt, and manure were being sautéed.

Grimm heard noises outside—smashing, crashing, and a gunshot. Moving to the window, he peered outside and saw the Tubbs boys involved in one of his favorite activities: vandalism and simple destruction. Have at it, Grimm thought.

He walked to the closet, pulled out his pick, and began work on the lock. It didn't take long.

Taking off the lock and pulling the door open, he stepped

into the lightless maw disguised as a closet. "Do this fast, Kevy. We don't want the light on for long."

"Gotcha." He pulled the door behind them, turned, and found the refrigerator. Grasping the handle, he snatched open the door and closed his eyes to blinding light. As he pulled out four bottles, he suddenly had an idea.

He kneed the door shut, letting his eyes readjust to darkness, then backed out of the closet. Smiling, he crept over to the shelves that contained chemicals and fertilizers and started examining labels. He grabbed several boxes and carried them toward the window, where the light was better. "What would Princess Grace be doing, if she were alive today?" Grimm held up a box triumphantly. "Clawing at the insides of her coffin."

Grimm returned the other boxes to the shelf, then poured the contents of one into his palm. "A little rat poison will put hair on your chest." He unscrewed the tops of the bottles then carefully poured the powdered poison into them. He shook them, then wiped them clean.

Grimm reentered the closet and swapped bottles. Then he hid the maroon sheets under a bag of feed, leaving just enough visible to be easily seen.

He slipped back outside, a huge smile on his face. Now, if there was only some way to get Lou and Becky involved, it would be nice and neat—a perfect payback! Oh well, maybe a vampire would get them.

That's it! Grimm thought as he picked up the shovel and gathered up the square bottles.

"How sweet it is," he whispered, wanting to shout as he headed into the woods.

Twenty-one

Burning Down the House

David experienced a strange double vision, as well as simultaneously sensing sounds, smells, and feelings. On one hand, David was outside with the wind rushing by him, his eyes tearing as the boat raced along, water slapping against the fiberglass. The humming of the engine was a mesmerizing drone, adding to the static of the waking nightmare. But most of him was inside the silent house with Skeeter and Monique, her hunger and thirst so pronounced that it twisted his gut into knots.

Still, David was vaguely aware of Jana asking him questions. She gently held onto his arm. "David? Where are we going?"

"Don't worry. I'm trying to help somebody." Even his own voice sounded odd. "It's hard to explain . . ."

"You don't look . . . yourself. And what about lights? It's dark, and you might run into something."

"I . . ." He suddenly became lost in what was happening to Skeeter. Hands neatly folded and feet flat on the floor, Skeeter stared at Monique. He was seated in a chair by the breakfast table adjacent to the yellow, flower-papered kitchen.

The overhead light was on, but two of the bulbs were burnt out. The third gave off a dim amber light.

David looked around. The kitchen and small breakfast area stood atop the steps on a balconied area. All about, hanging baskets were empty, giving the place a barren feel. The air was musty, the aroma full of dust and disuse. Below, the great room was dim and shadowy, the weak light barely reaching the far drapes. Behind them were windows and sliding doors leading to the lake.

With a pleased smile, Monique leaned against the counter. Skeeter shifted uneasily under her gaze. Monique smiled slightly, first at Skeeter, then at David.

Her red-painted lips looked garish against her bright white teeth, and her creamy skin glowed in the dim light as though she were a creature of the deep. Her dark locks glistened in the light, framing her fine, delicate features that were somehow impossibly attractive and repulsive at the same time.

"Now, be a good boy," Monique said. "You're going to be too late, David."

David could feel Skeeter struggling, his body refusing to obey himself. He was panicking, his heartbeat racing as though he were a trapped rabbit, but his breathing was calm and peaceful, as though he were meditating. Monique laughed loudly, the mocking sound was chilling and heightened the fear that never showed on Skeeter's face.

David could feel Skeeter's emotions seize him. With nowhere to go, nowhere to run, Skeeter's fear fed upon itself, growing and festering . . . summoning all sorts of terrible fates.

"David!" Jana had slapped him and was now shaking him. "Look out! The dock!" David saw it and quickly jerked the wheel hard to port, missing the dock by only a few feet. A wall of water buried it as the boat headed swiftly away from shore.

"Drive!" David yelled over the wind and the roar, then

stood and gently guided Jana into the driver's seat. He placed her hands of the wheel, then he pointed to the shoreline, where a house with lights on stood out among several dark structures. "Over there!"

"Where?" Jana asked. She'd never driven a boat before! It was exciting. "David, please . . ." She was no longer frightened of him, just frightened for him.

Gone again, David hung onto the windshield and stared ahead, his face contorting with fear, then curiosity.

"Hello, is anybody home?" came a voice. Skeeter tried to look toward the door, but failed. Annoyed, Monique glanced at the entrance, then stared icily at Skeeter. David felt pierced.

It was Skeeter's grandfather! For a moment, David rejoiced. Then he realized that she would kill him—kill them both! Skeeter realized it, too. Panicked thoughts whirled a million miles a minute through Skeeter's mind. I've got to do something!

"Hello," Monique responded coldly, moving toward the door. "Who is it?" she asked, knowing before speaking. Skeeter's eyes followed her, as though attached by an invisible string.

"Name's Oliver Marshall. I came to check on the gate and saw the light and my grandson's bicycle. Well, there he is!" Without an offer to come in, Judge Marshall entered.

"He's telling me about the area. Dis is my first time here," Monique said coolly. She read what she needed from his eyes, and continued, "I'm Bernie's niece, Monique Steele." She held out a hand as though she expected the Judge to kiss it.

Instead, the Judge shook it. "Well, this is a pleasure." His gaze flicked over to Skeeter. "I must be getting old. I didn't hear a car. Heck, I didn't even see one in the driveway." Monique's face tightened, her lips forming a thin line. "I almost went home and called the police, until I saw Kenneth's bicycle. You okay, son?"

Monique glanced his way, and Skeeter was compelled to

say, "Sure, Grandfather, just a little tired." David knew he wanted to scream, *I'm scared to death. RUN FOR YOUR LIFE!* Intense fear for his grandfather wracked them both, and Skeeter prayed it was oozing out of him, and that his grandfather would notice.

"Then I guess you better get on home, I'll help Mrs. Steele with whatever she needs."

"Can I stay for just a while longer?" Skeeter's voice took on am unusual, whining quality. His heart continued to hammer piston-fast.

Judge Marshall let out a long sigh. "I don't think so." He stared at Skeeter a long time, his frown becoming one of worry. "You don't look well."

"Enough of dis posturing," Monique said coldly, and stepped behind Judge Marshall. With one hand, she grabbed Skeeter's grandfather and spun him around.

"Hey, what's—" Judge Marshall almost fell.

"You will do as I say, *ja?*" She stared at the judge, her eyes appearing to grow larger and larger, opening up into a starless night's sky. David knew all too well what was happening.

"I . . ." started Judge Marshall in surprise, then the briefly defiant expression disappeared, replaced by a calm look and a compliant stance, where he'd just been tense. "Indeed, I will, madam." His eyes were dull and flat, absent of his usual fire.

"Skeeter," Monique said. "Watch. Dis is your future. David, this is your . . . life." She waved his grandfather toward a chair on the opposite side of the table. "Sit." The judge did.

"Now watch. Maybe, just maybe—I will spare you, if I drink my fill." Monique walked around behind Judge Marshall, who sat as still as a church mouse with a cat nearby. She placed one hand on the old man's forehead, tilting his head to the side, as though she were a barber with a razor. Then she placed her other hand on his shoulder.

NO! STOP! NOoooooo . . . David and Skeeter struggled. David tried to aid Skeeter, to encourage and bolster him.

Skeeter vibrated, feeling as though he were going to explode into a thousand pieces, his emotions boiling, but capped. His eyes widened minutely, and his lips quivered. Again he tried, but he couldn't take his eyes away.

"You should be honored, old man," Monique whispered, then she bit him, diving into his flesh.

Horrified and inwardly flinching, Skeeter watched as a brief spurt of blood spattered her cheek. His grandfather's eyes went wide, and he began to shake, as though trying to break free . . . or break down.

David gagged as he tasted the blood, felt it swell in his mouth, then gush down his throat. As its vitality filled him, David fought against the sensation, railed against the pleasure, and focused on the nausea. Still, the taste was a mixture of poison and nectar. David swam in a sea of opposing sensations, swinging from one extreme to the next. He was heartened and invigorated; he was disgusted and sick. He rejoiced, and he was outraged.

Skeeter's trapped emotions erupted, hauling David along and madly carrying them both in a hundred different ways. The teenager wanted to jump up, to scream, to flee, to die, to strike Monique, and much more, but his body continued to betray him. He berated it, and cursed it, but nothing moved it. Tears rolled down his face. Oh Lord, God Almighty, please help my grandfather. He is a great man. PLEASE!

David tried to pull free of Skeeter, but couldn't. He briefly wondered about Jana. They hadn't turned, and he felt the night's wind.

Shocked, Skeeter watched helplessly, his vision blurring. His mind became empty of everything but the clawing terror that ripped away at his sanity. Suddenly, he couldn't breathe.

Judge Marshall's eyes drooped slowly and his shoulders sagged. His hands trembled, until, with a final shudder, his head collapsed onto his chest. As Monique stepped back, Skeeter's grandfather crumpled, then fell to the floor.

"Now it is your turn," Monique told him.

Skeeter screamed silently, as blind panic and terror overtook him.

"No!" Somehow David threw himself free and returned to the boat. Before him the water might have been a plane of polished onyx, while behind him it gleamed brightly with wavering gold highlights, touched by the rising moon's light. Ahead in the distance, a light called to him, a beacon saying Skeeter is here! Docks loomed, resembling spectral arms across the water, rapidly growing closer and closer.

"David?"

"Let me have the wheel, please, we're docking," David told Jana, then gently touched her arm. She stared at him, then stood.

David took the wheel and headed ashore without slowing. He killed the motor and pressed the tilt lever. The engine died and rose. "Brace yourself." He grabbed the windshield. With a soft but jarring thud, the boat bounded onto shore, carving into the grassy beach. Cattails and weeds parted along each side, and the sand hissed.

"Now, please stay here. Please! I . . . I can't explain." David vaulted over the side and landed in the shallow waters, then splashed ashore. As he climbed the seawall of railroad ties, David felt Monique grab Skeeter. David sprinted for the house, trampling through the garden and leaping up the back steps to plunge through the sliding glass door.

It shattered, slashing and ripping him as he plowed into the drapes, then pulled them with him to the floor. He rolled free of the clinging cloth and through the jabbing debris, only to bounce off something, then spring to his feet to face Monique. "STOP!"

"Ah, the pale knight cometh," she chuckled, straightening from Skeeter. "The shred of faith you find at times is both annoying and amazing."

He was in time! But what was he going to do? All he had was his will and his crucifix. He reached for it.

"Why do you bother to come to rescue dis pathetic boy?" Monique asked from the top of the steps. "Does he mean something to you?" As her gaze seized his, Monique began to glide down the steps. David tried to pull away, but found it impossible. Already she had him paralyzed, a puppet to dance on her strings. She stopped just a foot away from him. Eyes forged from a furnace, she stood beautiful before him. A huge smile was on her face, then she licked her lips, a panther ready to dine.

"I'm going to enjoy teaching you who is master, showing you the true power of a vampire, Shade." Her eyes widened and her stare intensified, sucking him in as though he'd fallen into a bottomless pit.

Skeeter felt some of the pressure ease . . . some of the string slacken. For a brief second, relief overwhelmed him, then he thought of his grandfather. It was his fault that his grandfather—his best friend—was dead.

That cold dagger pierced his heart, killing all emotion. A seething hate began to slowly grow. Skeeter had already been scared to death, now even death didn't matter. He wouldn't be frightened anymore. Something had to be done! There wasn't time to be frightened. He was going to avenge Judge Grandpa.

David felt himself losing to Monique, barely keeping his head. He remembered what happened last time she had controlled him and became desperate. What would happen if he lost? What would happen to Skeeter? And the others? Would Monique continue to terrorize the town? Could she turn him against those he loved? What about Jana and Michael? Could he be forced to hurt those he cared for most? Would they die just as Timmy and Tina had? How come all he loved died? Wasn't love stronger than hate? HELP ME, LORD!

With a tremendous effort, David raised a trembling right

hand and slapped Monique. The blow rocked the vampire, snapping her head back and staggering her.

"*Verdammt!* You'll regret that!" Monique raged and struck back. David's head whiplashed. He saw stars and barely managed to remain standing. His left hand groped for the cross around his neck.

"*Stoppen!*" Monique cried and grabbed his arm. They wrestled.

Suddenly, Skeeter found a door out of his cage. He yanked it open and ran out, jumping to his feet. He was so surprised that he staggered across the kitchen and collapsed against the counter, where his legs refused to hold up his body. Hanging on, he glanced into the main room, and saw David and Monique locked in a hand-to-hand struggle. Skeeter yanked open the nearest door, hoping to find a knife. Instead, he found a junk drawer filled with notepads and old mail. Nothing he could use. Then he saw the silver letter opener. It looked very sharp and shone silver in the light. In fairy tales silver as well as iron was the bane of monsters. Praying, Skeeter turned and hurled it as if it were a dagger. It spun awkwardly, butt over tip.

I'm losing it, David moaned to himself. His senses were fading, the darkness closing in.

The letter opener struck Monique in the back, the point burying deeply. Monique screamed and whirled. "Dat hurt you little bastard! *Hervorkommen! Verdammt!* Come here!" Skeeter felt as though someone had grabbed him, and he staggered forward. He danced down the steps, then she struck him with all her might, sending him airborne.

Suddenly freed, David jerked on the cross, breaking the chain. He looped it around Monique's throat, using it as a garrote, and yanked savagely.

"NO! *Araugh!*" The cross cut into her throat, scorching flesh as it burrowed ever deeper. Monique clawed at the sizzling object, the heat and pain unbearable.

"Die! Lord help me, please!" David hung on as she thrashed about. Monique's throat began to bubble and hiss. An acrid, terrible smell filled the air. Her fingers began to smolder, then they caught fire, bursting into flames as if they were dry kindling instead of flesh. Monique screamed as the flames spread, dancing up her arms. Then her throat erupted, the fire climbing up her neck and engulfing her head. Her hair caught next. Desperate, she threw herself against David.

He staggered backward, twisting her around and throwing her to her knees. Her flailing hands grazed the couch. The dustcover caught fire. With a life of its own, the fire leapt to a nearby table. The flames spread, cavorting and adding new dancing partners.

I'm burning, David thought. His hands were so hot that he could barely hang on, his skin began to melt. The chain had bitten into the flesh of his hand, and was buried so deep he wasn't sure he could let go even if he tried.

"We can both die," Monique gasped.

"Fine!"

Monique lashed out and grabbed his leg. Caught off guard, David was floored, but didn't let go, pulling Monique on top of him. Now they were both human torches.

Blurring before David's eyes, Monique tried to change shapes. She began to grow indistinct, and he yanked even harder. She solidified. She tried something else, and for a moment, she began to shrink. David stuck a knee in her back and tried to pull her head off. The chain ground against bone.

Gagging, Monique lurched to her feet, jerking David with her. He screamed out in pain and staggered forward, then started to fall. Resolute, he pulled her down with him. She dove forward, twisting, then bounced off a wall. They crashed atop a chair, setting it afire.

Through the heat and pain, David could feel her weakening. Now all of her was on fire, and she was no longer beautiful, but revealed as she truly was . . . death alive. Her burning flesh was melting, taffy-soft but scorched. Her teeth were jagged and broken. Empty eye sockets stared at him.

The seconds became timeless. David couldn't feel his hands, but his arms screamed as though a thousand needles were driven into them. He knew he was going to die, and that was going to be okay. He would go doing something right with his life.

"David!" He heard Jana screaming. "Get out of there! Please! The whole place is burning!" She was on the patio.

There was a large cracking sound, as though timber had been split. Dully, David glanced at the ceiling. The entire house was on fire. Black smoke roiled along the ceiling, resembling a mighty indoor thunderstorm. Burning wallpaper slowly unraveled, dropping to the floor and leaving a fiery heritage behind. All the furniture had become massive braziers, and the carpet smoldered and smoked. No longer hanging, a flaming pot fell close to David, exploding and spewing fire. The room grew darker and more choked with smoke. The ravenous roar of the fire was deafening, threatening to consume everything.

David was having trouble breathing, choking and rasping, and he could barely see Monique. She hung slack, no longer struggling. Was she dead? Could she die? There was another thunderous cracking, and something else fell from the ceiling.

David let go of one end of the chain, freeing himself of Monique, and staggered to his feet. He couldn't see anything. Which way was out?

"David!" Jana screamed from somewhere ahead, her voice barely loud enough to be heard over the devouring flames.

Crawling on his elbows, David headed for Jana's voice. Each movement was agonizing, driving spikes of pain through his shoulders. David bumped into something on fire, a blazing chair, and backed up. Trying again, he crawled around the chair. He made it a few feet, then slammed into something else. The leg of the table collapsed, the top landing on the backs of his legs. David screamed, rolled over, and tried to kick his legs free. They were held fast.

There was a large rumbling, then another part of the ceiling fell.

Twenty-two

Fear Flight

"David!" Jana stood at the jagged opening in the glass door, where foul smoke billowed out, swirling about her. Between the charcoal plumes and the darkness, Jana couldn't see anything at all, but she thought she'd heard something—someone moving among the billowing flames.

Desperate, she looked around, finding flames dancing on the roof and devouring the shingles. Jana didn't think this place was going to last long.

Suddenly, the entire glass wall erupted, flames belching outward as though a bomb had been detonated inside. Jana reacted instinctively, jumping back and staggering, only to fall and land atop something soft, but uncomfortable. As though a strange hail had fallen, glass covered the back porch. The opening was huge and fiery, smoke pouring from it like the mouth of a fire-breathing hydra.

What about David? Then she noticed that she'd fallen on a hose attached to a nearby faucet! Praying that the water was on, she turned the spigot. The sound of rushing water was music to her ears, as the hose swelled. Hauling the hose to the doorway, Jana began spraying inside the house.

The stream of water cleared away a section of the churning

darkness, allowing her a glimpse inside. The place was an inferno, a massive funeral pyre for whoever was within! David, please be all right. Please! He couldn't be dead, not after they'd rediscovered each other.

Jana suddenly thought that she saw something moving and turned the hose on it. Not ten feet away, David struggled with a burning oak table that had fallen across his legs.

Knowing she was crazy, Jana turned the hose on herself until she was dripping wet, then took a deep breath, and darted inside the conflagration. The water cut a narrow path for her, but the smoke still engulfed her; then the heat suddenly struck her with the force of a blacksmith's hammer, and she staggered back a step. Recovering, she turned the hose on herself, then doused David.

"I can't move my legs!" David cried.

Jana dropped the hose on David and moved to his feet. With a desperate strength, she lifted the tabletop from David's legs, then grabbed an arm, and threw it over her shoulder. David could barely help her. Jana hauled him along, and together they staggered outside. All but blind, they fell down the steps, where they lay gasping and coughing.

David had never felt such pain. All he wanted to do was lie there and die. His only wish was to plunge into a cold lake or dive into a snowdrift—anything to silence the screaming of his burning body.

Jana couldn't believe she'd actually braved the inferno to save David. She hurt all over, but something told her they were too close to the house to rest. "David," Jana started, rubbing her eyes and face, "come, we must move farther away. The whole place is going up!" She took a good look at David and gasped.

David was blackened and burned, his clothing scorched and devoured. What little rags were left were still smoking. His face was puffy and swollen, burned red and charcoal black. His arms were a charred mess, the clothing stuck to them. His hands were twisted, the flesh molded thinly against the bones, as though some had melted away.

"That bad?" David managed through gritting teeth. She nodded, her eyes unable to hide her pain. "You'll have to help me. Then go call the fire department."

Jana helped David to his feet. David felt a sharp pain, a new jabbing attack, then spat blood. "Think I broke some ribs, too."

They had only moved a few feet, when there was a crumbling noise. Jana turned and watched as the upper walls began to buckle inward, and the roof, awash in flame, sagged. In slow motion, the top of the house seemed to implode, then fire geysered upward, mocking a giant fireworks fountain on the Fourth.

Suddenly, there was a wailing scream, then a fiery projectile exploded out the back of the house, skipped off the back porch, and bounced several times.

David couldn't believe his eyes. It was Monique ... or what was left of her. No longer white and creamy, she was charred and still burning. Now she didn't even look remotely human. How could she be alive? Her clothing was gone, revealing that she was more bone than flesh.

Monique rolled over to face them. Her face appeared to be melting wax, the skin around her eyes drooping, her nose sagging, and her lower lip stuck to her chin. Her teeth seemed huge, resembling a wolf's more than a human's. Her hair was frizzled and matted, as though glued together. "I'll kill you both!" Then she began to move.

"The boat!" David yelled hoarsely. He moved, but Jana didn't. "Jana! Come on! She kills!" Jana's mouth dropped open, her eyes somehow widening even more. David tugged, and she moved without thinking. They leaned together, holding each other up as they stumbled across the lush yard. When they reached the edge, Jana glanced over her shoulder.

Despite his pain, David could feel Monique coming. "You

start! I'll push!" They jumped to the shore and lurched for the boat, barely reaching it. "Get in!" Somehow David found the strength to help her into the boat. Jana moved despite her shock, slipping across the seat and crawling under the windshield. She pulled herself into the seat and turned the key. The engine roared to life, as white water churned up mud.

David pushed against the bow, but nothing happened; the boat was beached solidly, stuck fast. He tried again, channeling his anger and pain, wanting to scream. He kept at it, pushing so hard that he felt his muscles would tear and the veins in his head explode. The boat moved ever so slightly. His legs began to straighten and slide. He saw red, feeling dizzy. "Reverse!" he yelled, and glanced over his shoulder.

Still smoldering and cast in shadow, Monique stood shakily at the top of the tiered wall of railroad ties. Her cold eyes sought his. David ignored her and continued to shove the boat.

Jana yanked on the throttle. It didn't move. She didn't know how this worked! She felt something under the grip and depressed it. Something clicked loudly, and she pulled on the throttle, surprised to find it unlocked. The boat began to move away from shore. David desperately grabbed at the bow as he fell into the water, pulled along by the retreating craft.

"There is nowhere to run!" David heard Monique flop onto the shore, then slide toward him.

Gasping and choking, David tried to get into the boat, but was too weak to pull himself in. Monique screamed in rage.

Jana suddenly appeared above David, and helped haul him into the boat. Together they fell inside, slipping off the cushion and onto the floor. Unpiloted, the boat continued to chug backwards into Cedar Creek.

For a minute they both laid there trembling, then David said, "Jana, are you all right?"

"I don't know. Are we safe?"

"I don't know." If the fire hadn't killed her, what would? A stake? David hauled himself into the driver's gray bucket seat.

"What is it?" Jana asked, as she climbed into the other bucket seat. "Oh my God!" Jana looked back at the shore.

The house was no longer a house, but a giant bonfire signaling death and destruction. Smoke roiled from it, blocking out the stars and blotting the heavens with a massive stain. Most of the structure had crumpled into a pile, but some still remained, a glowing red husk. Several nearby trees had caught fire, dropping flaming branches as though they were trying to shed the fire. A small one rocked unsteadily, ready to collapse onto the nearest house. The inferno's radiance ignited the entire area, casting the burning light of a false dawn across the yard, other houses, and the shore.

David saw the shifting shadowy thing on the shore where Monique had been. She had changed into something winged. Leaving a trail of smoke behind, it launched itself toward them.

David jammed the gearshift fully forward. His hands ached, and he grimaced as he spun the wheel around and headed into open water. Besides the pain, all he could think of was flight. There was no way to fight Monique. Maybe they could outrun her. The speedometer passed fifty, and the tachometer reached into the red as they raced across the glittering lake, cutting across the placid waters toward the moon.

"Are you wearing a crucifix?" David yelled over the wind. He'd seen the chain around Jana's neck. Unable to speak, she nodded. "Get it out, you'll need it." David coughed and spat blood over the side. "I'm sorry you came along!"

Jana was sorry, too, but then if she hadn't, David might not be alive now.

David glanced over his shoulder. Against the burning backdrop, he could see the vampire quickly closing. "You steer," David told Jana and left the seat.

"Where're we going?"

"Away from that," David pointed toward the oncoming bat shape, "and toward the middle of the lake."

"O . . . okay. David, I wish you could tell me about—"

"No time." David moved to the rear of the boat, lifted up the bench seat, and removed an oar. He wished he'd been a better baseball player, because his batting skills were going to be very important. He stood in the back of the boat with his legs spread for balance, and the oar ready. He didn't think he'd last long. Already his legs shook and his injured ribs protested, feeling cut in half.

Monique was almost upon him. Through the darkness, David could see her twisted form, a mockery of a bat. Her wings were too long and warped. Her eyes matched the dancing color of the conflagration they'd left behind, and her mouth worked, teeth silently gnashing. He thought that this time she'd be willing to kill him instead of subjugating him.

The bat was upon him, diving and screeching. David swung the oar and missed, but drove Monique away. She circled, then returned for another attack. As though defying nature, the bat creature seemed to dance about him as he struck frantically and futilely, just slicing the air. It didn't take long for his arms to tire and his blows to weaken. Quickly, his vision began to blur. His legs wobbled, and he almost fell.

Jana glanced over her shoulder, ducking and staying hunkered down, nose against the windshield and chest almost against the wheel. What was she supposed to do? Dodge?

Monique darted in close, avoided a weak blow, and bit into his shoulder. David barely felt it but lashed out, striking her. The impact jarred him, and he almost dropped the oar.

For a moment, Monique was stunned and spun through the air, limbs sprayed and askew. But she recovered quickly, spreading her leathery wings and curving back toward him.

She soared low over the water, nearly blending in with the ebony surface. She raced across the bow, and darted over the windshield past Jana toward David.

David swung but had to alter his blow to keep from hitting Jana. He struck the top of the windshield, and the oar shattered, leaving him with only the long handle.

With supernatural strength, Monique rammed David in the chest and bowled him over. Arms flailing, David fell across the back bench, his head snapping against the padded sun platform. He almost blacked out, tasting his own blood. David tried to move, but his body failed to respond. Monique was astride his chest.

With odd detachment, David watched as she changed shape into something vaguely human, a monstrous form made of lumpy black clay haphazardly thrown together. Her hands were massive, long fingernails transforming into talons. With her burning eyes locked on his, she smiled, unveiling her incisors.

Jana couldn't believe it, so she just pretended that she was caught in a nightmarish movie. Be crazier! She yanked the wheel to the right, and David slid across the seat to the left, slamming into the padded wall. Screaming, Monique fell off him, ripping what little was left of his shirt.

Jana pulled the gearshift almost into neutral, killing the speed and nearly stopping the boat, then she gave it gas again. It bolted forward, the bow jumping into the air.

Monique slammed into the back of the passenger's seat, then reached out to grab Jana's leg.

Jana screamed as the claw bit into her calf, then Monique pulled her from the seat. Jana's hands slipped from the wheel, leaving the boat turning on its own. Jana tried to jerk free, and her head slammed into a fire extinguisher under the dashboard.

David leaped atop Monique, hammering her with all his might. Monique laughed, spat, and then hurled him backward, as though he were feather-light. "Dere are worse dings dan dying, David!" She pounced upon him.

"I will suck your soul from dis decaying form," she hissed, then laughed. She sat, charred legs spread, trapping him. Her hands rested on his shoulders, her fingers curling and digging into flesh, as her eyes sought his.

David tried to avoid her gaze, but could not.

"Dis shall be slow and agonizing." Monique's hands began to glow brighter and brighter.

David felt something strange and painful happening, but it wasn't the pain of the flesh. He felt as though someone had grabbed his insides by the roots, and was trying to pull them free. White sparks cavorted before his eyes, tearing through his vision. Monique was now glowing all over.

Oh my God! MY SOUL! Suddenly, David felt something rip, and screamed.

Dizzy, Jana grabbed for the fire extinguisher. It was probably hopeless, but she had to try something. She wouldn't die easily! She turned toward Monique and pulled the trigger. White powder burst from the nozzle, the wind whipping it into a cloud, but the brunt of it struck Monique's face.

Choking and screaming with rage, she whirled on Jana. Her slap stunned Jana, knocking her backward and to the floor.

For a moment, David thought he saw himself doubled, a ghostly image like a jiggling mirror danced before him. He quivered like a snapped rubber band, so dizzy he almost blacked out again, but then Monique returned to capture his attention by torturing him once more.

Monique reached out with a claw, and David could see her pull at something translucent—a mist encircling his body. Each time she plucked it, he screamed in agony, feeling as though his entire body was being twisted and bent. "I'm enjoying this, David. Since we can't be partners, I shall absorb you."

The wind blowing under the windshield and through the aisle to the bow revived Jana. Groaning, she rolled over, then climbed onto her hands and knees. She didn't know what kept her going, but David was calling to her. He needed help! Her hand bumped the shattered oar.

David's tortuous scream was so terrible that it caused Jana to grab the oar and launch herself at Monique.

The wooden spear made a sickening sound as it pierced Monique's back. Screaming in rage and pain, she whirled on Jana. David slumped back to the floor, no longer tight as a harp string.

"You die now, mortal!" Monique rose, staggering some, thrown off balance by the huge wooden stake that still hung limply in her shoulder. It poked out above her right breast, having missed the heart.

I'm dead, Jana thought. How could this thing still be alive?

Monique gathered herself and smiled. Slowly and with claws outstretched, clicking and scratching, it approached Jana.

Monique laughed, then the boat stopped dead, striking a sandbar. Jana was slammed backward, her head striking the windshield and knocking her unconscious.

Surprised, Monique was thrown forward, as though launched from a springboard. She sailed over the windshield, clawed for it, but missed. She landed in the water and began screaming.

David had been thrown into the back of one of the padded bucket seats, and was still conscious. He heard Monique's screaming, and his gaze found her flailing about in the water. Smoke surrounded her, as though she were burning once more. Monique tried to fly, but the spear prevented her escape. Twisting around, she tried to grab it. Because of the thickening mist, David could see little else. He cursed, too weak to finish her.

David struggled into the driver's seat, briefly looking at

Jana—a truly incredible woman. The night began to tilt. He grasped the lever. Then he couldn't feel anything—not himself, Jana, or Monique. Escape was his last fleeting thought as David yanked on the gearshift, then slumped against the dashboard.

Twenty-three

Dawn Race

Slumped against the steering wheel, David awakened staring at the dashboard. As it slowly came into focus, he found he could easily read the gauges; then he realized that the lights weren't on. In the flat gray light, David could see all of the dashboard. Morning! Dawn was coming! He'd been out a long time. David sat up too quickly, and dizziness assailed him.

He grabbed the wheel and closed his eyes to slow the spinning. He could hear the motor chugging away, and sensed that they were slowly heading backwards across Cedar Creek. What had happened to Monique? And what about—David quickly looked around for Jana. She was crumpled in the aisle under the windshield.

David knelt next to her. Jana's chest rose and fell steadily, and now that he listened, he could hear her heart's rhythmic cadence. Thank heaven she was just unconscious.

She would be all right, but he might not. David looked skyward and found it pink, full of orange, red, and indigo clouds that resembled fields of cotton candy. Soon they would become fiery with the sun's rising.

David stood, stretched, and looked around to try to identify their position. They had slowly moved northward, a long way from home. The sun would catch him before they made it back to the ranch. A few months ago, he knew what would've happened. He would blister, then the wounds would fester, and the lesions would swell. Now? There was no telling what the effects might be, since he'd been drinking plenty of elixir. He might be fine. On the other hand, he might die—or wish he had.

David shifted into forward, then high gear. The bow of the boat reared as it leapt ahead, then planed to slice across the water. The wind with its early morning coolness whipped about him, and he noticed that Jana was snugly and safely held by the aisle walls. David hoped she was okay.

There had already been too many casualties in his insane conflict with Monique. His curse was more deadly to others than himself. Sometimes he thought he harbored a spectre, waiting to reach out and deal death to anyone nearby. But now wasn't the time for self-pity, only survival.

With the boat up to speed, David steered with one hand and touched Jana. "Jana! Are you all right? Please wake up!"

She groaned. At first, Jana hurt too badly to move. All she wanted to do was lie there and enjoy the cool wind. Then she remembered that she was on a boat and recalled the terrible flaming thing from last night.

Screaming, Jana abruptly sat up.

David lightly shook her, appalled by her facial bruises. "Jana! It's me—David! She's gone! Gone, Jana! You're all right!"

Dazed, Jana stared at David, who looked disheveled, but no longer scorched as she remembered. "David? You look okay. Wasn't there a fire? Weren't you burned? I don't understand." Neither did David. "I can see you." Then she realized, "Is the sun rising?"

"Yes. Can you steer, while I put up the top?"

She nodded. Both worried and woozy, she asked, "What'll sunlight do to you?" As she remembered more, she became even more confused, not understanding why he looked almost unscathed.

"I don't know." David glanced at himself. His hands were healed! He was unblemished, as though never burned. The same wasn't true for his clothes; they were fire-ravaged. "Depends on how much sun," David said, as he pulled the rolled canvas and poles from underneath the sun platform. "Just keep going straight."

"I think I can do that." Jana was confused, thirsty, and drained. She noticed her hands. They were smudged charcoal black, and her clothing was burned. Her eyes widened. It had happened! She wasn't crazy! The dent in the metal atop the windshield confirmed it. Wooden splinters—part of the oar—were on the floor along with a clinging white powder. The discharged fire extinguisher peeked out from under the seat.

"Jana, I need your help for a minute." Jana didn't move. "Jana, are you okay?" Dropping the top, David moved to her side. She was staring, her eyes wide and faraway. David glanced skyward. He didn't have much time. "Jana, I know a lot of terrible things happened last night. So many that you'd like to just shut down and try to forget, but I need your help. I really do! The sun might kill me! And I have to get home, indoors. Please."

Slowly, Jana turned to stare at him. Her mouth worked several times, before she said, "I'll try." David laughed softly and hugged Jana. It felt good.

"Go ahead," Jana said. "I'll be okay. Have faith." She stared across the bow, trying to gather herself. She would break down later, when it was convenient. The expanse of water stretching forward before her was hypnotizing in its calmness.

It was a bit awkward, but David managed to set the poles, tighten them, and then stretch the canvas by himself. Lastly, he snapped the top into place. He didn't think it was going to be enough protection. Crawling under the windshield, David made his way to the front sun deck and lifted the seat cushion on the right. He pulled out several towels, then wrapped himself in them, becoming a terry cloth mummy. In the glove box he found an old faded baseball cap and sunglasses. He put them on. He looked for a tube of zinc oxide, found it, and smeared it on.

Jana continued to stare straight ahead, silent and unquestioning. David checked to make sure she was still conscious. Her eyes were open. David didn't know what to say—how to explain—so he said nothing. All there was to do was wait for the sun, and it wasn't long in coming.

When the first rays of sunlight touched his back, he started to sweat, despite the chills riffling across his flesh. "Jana?"

Jana didn't see the expanse of water ahead; over and over again, all she kept seeing was the burning bird of prey bursting out of the inferno, then chasing them. Catching them. It was pale, deathly so, with hate-fueled eyes and teeth larger than a Doberman's.

David reached out and pressed the horn button. Jana jumped and turned to look at him, bewilderment in her eyes. When she saw him, all she could think of was that some kind of brightly clad California/Arab/Indian had come aboard. "Hang in there. Just another twenty minutes, then we can both collapse." David said. She nodded, not noticing that he was sweating.

"Just take us to the dock left of the dam. Do you see the dam? The dock has a huge windsock hanging on it. The sock is shaped like a fish, bright red, yellow, and blue. Do—" David started to shake. The chills had grown more pronounced, an invisible someone sticking icicles into his shoulders and neck. As though he were poisoned, nausea welled, then swelled.

"A bright fish?"

David nodded. Poor Jana, she didn't deserve this, but then neither did any of the boys. David shifted, then collapsed, nearly blacking out. The pain was getting worse. Even when

314

he'd been on fire, he hadn't felt this bad. Despite the chills, he felt as though he were a melting popsicle.

Soon, it hurt so bad he couldn't speak. He slumped, his head landing atop the glove box, and prayed. If he didn't stop Monique, who would? She was alive somewhere; he had a vague sense of her being out there, also in pain. Her rage would be terrible and devastating. David began to drift, then rambled, mumbling about Monique's first visit, her being a vampire, and all the killing. Why was she mistakenly pursuing him? Why?

Jana half-listened to him, trying to put together his ramblings with the recent events. They seemed to match in a horrid manner. A vampire? Jana almost laughed hysterically. The sun was driving her crazy, as it was David. Better not to think about what he was saying.

"I see it!" She steered toward the dock with the fish sock. "David?" All he did was groan. Were they going to be too late? Jana tried to push the gearshift forward, but it wouldn't go any farther. She tried to will the boat faster.

Ever so slowly, the dock grew closer, the limp, bright fish larger. A soft breeze caused it to sway. The sun had cleared the horizon and appeared to sit proudly atop the waters, an overseer of all creation.

They were almost there when the motor coughed. Jana cringed, then looked at the gas gauge. It was on *E*. She eased back on the throttle. They cruised on for a few more seconds, several hundred feet away from the dock. Again the motor coughed, shuddered, then kept on running.

Jana steered directly for the nearby shore instead of the dock. Less than fifty feet away, the motor shuddered and died. The boat slowed abruptly, water sloshing over the back and pushing them forward. They drifted toward shore, wallowing a bit, but still making progress. Ever so slowly, they neared shore. Twenty feet. Ten.

Finally, they softly bumped into land. "David! We made

it!" Jana flopped over the side and pushed the boat ashore. After making sure it was secure, she climbed into the back of the boat. "David!" She shook him. He groaned and muttered something unintelligible. Jana was afraid he was dying right before her eyes. She saw David's Blazer and began laughing and crying at the same time. She pulled the keys from the boat's ignition and jumped out, running to the Chevy. She got inside and started it, thrilled that it fired up immediately.

Jana threw it in gear, pulling as close as possible to the boat, then parked. She left it idling and went to David. He was slumped, bent double with his head between his knees. "Don't be dead," Jana whispered as she opened the windshield door. Nothing. "Damn you, don't give up!" Jana began to cry. Angrily, she wiped away the tears and grabbed David, shaking him vigorously.

"Didn't know you were the violent type," David groaned and tried to smile.

Jana returned it weakly. "Come on. The car's close by." Grunting, she managed to maneuver David into the front of the bow. He wasn't much help, and the effort was exhausting.

"Roll me out." She did, and he fell into the water with a splash. Jana jumped from the boat and grabbed David. His eyes fluttered; they were dull and distant. He moved feebly, as though attempting to stand, and she had to help him.

Dripping, they managed to stagger to the Blazer, where Jana opened the door and guided him inside. As soon as David hit the seat, he collapsed into oblivion. Jana kept pushing, feeling she was shoving a mule. Finally, she rearranged David's dead weight so she could close the door, ran around to the other side, and climbed in. She drove toward the barn, bouncing down the hill at an alarming speed.

At the doors, Jana hopped out and opened them, then drove inside. Exhausted, she pulled the doors close. She spotted a water jug sitting on a shelf. Grabbing it, Jana found it full and filled a plastic cup, then carried it to David. "Here," Jana said, her voice anxious as she poured water into David's mouth. She rubbed some on his face. Jana couldn't believe that he was so cold to the touch; he was sweating like a frosty glass sitting in the sun. It was so stifling and warm in the barn that Jana was having trouble breathing, each intake was similar to inhaling from a steaming pot.

Groaning, David opened his eyes. He still had to squint, but the pain was mild, nowhere near the nerve-ripping agony he had experienced before passing out. "Thanks." David rubbed his face, feeling the bumps. "That's twice you've saved my life in less than a day." He suddenly wanted to hug and kiss her, hold her close and pretend things were going to be fine.

Jana was too exhausted to react. She still wasn't thinking straight; she didn't understand all of this. All she could think to say was, "You need a doctor. I'll call Dr. Katyu."

David shook his head. "No time. She is still out there! I have to stop her before it's too late. I know I'm asking a lot, but would you get some things for me from the house?" David's eyes pleaded for him. He looked terrible, drawn and exhausted, with his hair going every which way, as though he'd stuck a finger in an electrical socket.

"Why? I don't understand." Jana was so tired and confused, she felt on the verge of a nervous breakdown; all she wanted to do was collapse and rest for a few days. Then the thought struck her hard, and although she couldn't believe she entertained it, she found herself saying, "Monique is still out there, you mean? The vampire?"

"You . . . you *know?*" His face was crestfallen.

Jana couldn't believe they were talking about this as though it were real. "I thought you were feverish, delirious. Are . . . are those boys really dead?" David nodded sadly, understanding her disbelief. "And it . . . *she* is still alive?" David nodded again. "How do you know?" She bit her lip.

"I don't know how I know. I just do. We seem to be linked

in some sort of strange psychic way; I can feel her." David couldn't think of another way to describe it.

"She'll come for you?"

"She'll kill you," David said, "and others. Probably me, too. I must destroy her, while it's still daylight." He weakly clenched a fist. "If I wait until tonight, she might recover. I can . . . feel that she's badly injured, and recuperating in the darkness somewhere not far away."

"You can find her?" Jana asked. This was surrealistic, she finally decided, another one of those nightmares.

"I can and will, even if destroying her kills me."

Jana couldn't continue to deceive herself. David believed this wholeheartedly, and she knew him as kind and trustworthy. But what if he were mad? Then she thought back to last night. "And what will you do?"

"Track her down. Drag her out into the sun. Cover her in crosses. Drive a stake through her heart! Whatever it takes!" He spoke harshly, sounding insane.

Jana winced. "You'll drive?"

David nodded. "I'll need to protect myself. Wear clothes and bandages, as well as this stuff." He looked around. "I have what I need here to block the windows. But I need some stuff from the house. Will you get it?"

"Only if you let me drive," she said wearily.

"Absolutely not."

"You won't make it. You need me! The sun in your face will make you wilt. This way you can . . . you can concentrate on finding her. IT." Jana couldn't believe she was doing this. David hesitated. "And if you don't, I won't get the clothing you need from the house," she said stubbornly. Jana was tired, but resolute. If she'd been crazy enough to pull him from a burning house, then she surely could help him solve this madness—and not by sacrificing himself.

"But—"

"I'd be crazy to let you drive about delirious in the daytime!

318

You might kill someone, even yourself. I won't let you commit suicide! Not like—" Her anger melted away her exhaustion. "So what's it going to be? Do I drive you?" Jana hated being demanding, but she'd been forced into it.

David looked at her for a long time, and wished it was another time and place. She was attractive despite her dishevelment, the bruises Monique had caused, and the fatigue she wore. He hated it, but he knew Jana was right. He felt fine now, but what would happen if light reflected off the hood and into his face? He was willing to die trying, but if he died before destroying Monique, there would be hell to pay—literally. He just hoped he wouldn't be sacrificing Jana. David prayed for forgiveness . . . for what he was about to do. "Okay. You drive," he said heavily. "But you have to do exactly what I say."

"Okay. What do you need?"

David told her, had Jana repeat the list and where to find everything, then let her go. He'd forgotten that her sister had once tried to commit suicide. He wasn't surprised to find that Jana had a steel foundation under a soft and attractive exterior. Again, he wished it was another time and place, but Monique had to be destroyed. Deaths were on his hands, because she thought he was a vampire!

David looked at the car clock. It was after seven. What time would the sheriff come with the warrant? It seemed likely that he might not be here, instead he'd be trying to destroy Monique. Oh well, he'd explain his absence if he lived.

He'd never be able to destroy Monique feeling this weak. And he didn't have time to just sit around and recuperate. He was sure that Monique would come for him with a vengeance once it was dark. His eyes fell on the storage closet. The elixir might help him recover more quickly.

David felt so weak he wasn't sure he could stand, let alone make it to a closet all of ten feet away. He climbed out of the truck, using his shaking arms for support. When he put his weight on his right leg, it buckled. His arms failing to hold him, he fell to the dirt.

Crawl then. It wasn't too bad. David felt a little dizzy, and sometimes he had to drag his legs, but he made it to the door, managing to haul himself unsteadily to his feet. Shuffling to the side, he slipped the key into one lock, then the next. Yanking the door open, David staggered inside and fell against the refrigerator, hugging it like a long-lost friend.

It was nice and dark in the storage closet. Swaying, he pulled the refrigerator open; its coolness drifted over him. Almost mesmerized, David just stared at the bottles. After a minute he began to wobble and fell forward. Almost too late, he grabbed the top of the refrigerator and steadied himself.

David opened a bottle and drank. The elixir tasted so good, sweet as honey, but with a bitter aftertaste. He was enjoying it so much, that he didn't realize he'd finished it until he'd held the empty bottle to his mouth for some time. Then he noticed that he felt better, revitalized, as though he'd just taken a refreshing shower and had a nap. He drank a second bottle and felt even better. David was just starting on his third, when he heard, "David? David!"

"I'm in here, Jana." David closed the refrigerator door and left the closet.

"Your house has been vandalized!" Jana was holding a stack of newspapers, an umbrella, an overcoat, a sheet, a roll of tape, and some other things. "What are you drinking?"

"A folk remedy."

Jana stared at the bottle "It looks like Jaegermeister."

"It's not alcohol. I just use the bottle. This is a blend of herbs, roots, and vegetable juices. It's supposed to help combat certain blood diseases. I grow most of it in the garden out back."

"Oh." She looked skeptical.

"Don't I look better?" he asked, and she nodded. "What were you saying about the house?"

"It's been shot up and broken into, shutters forced open, and windows smashed. They've spray-painted graffiti all over the place, calling you a murderer and child molester."

David was quiet for a long time, then said, "Come on, let's tape all the car windows but the front. With the side mirrors, you really don't need to see out the back."

"But what about your house?"

"I'll call the sheriff when we get back." If was almost what he said. Jana just shrugged with resignation. They spent about twenty minutes taping newspaper to the inside of the windows, then rigged a curtain between the front and back seats, which they'd reclined into a flat bed. David finished a third bottle during the work, and was feeling much better.

"How are you going to find . . . It?" Jana asked as she watched David put on the long trench coat, wrap his neck in a bandana, and don a wide-brimmed hat. Sweating as though she'd been working out in a steam room, Jana didn't understand how David could stand it.

"I just can." David finished resmearing zinc oxide on his face, then put on thin gloves. He tossed the umbrella in the front. David put on his sunglasses and gave Jana a weak smile. He placed his Bible and a large silver cross in the back, then walked to the shelves and grabbed a rubber mallet. He found several wooden gardening stakes and tossed them inside. "Thank you for helping me," David kissed her on the forehead. "Let's end this nightmare."

Jana stared at him a long time, as though burning his face into her memory, then watched as he climbed into the back of the Blazer and pulled the curtains closed before lying down. She knew this was absolutely insane, but she couldn't help herself. Jana opened the barn doors, and they drove out into the daylight.

Twenty-four

Deadly Sun

As soon as the Blazer left the shade, David could feel the sun clawing at the metal and glass to get at him. "Turn on the air conditioner, please," David asked. Jana did, and the curtain between them billowed. David reached up, slightly parting the makeshift drapes and allowing the cool air to reach him. Already he was beginning to ache, as if he'd come down with a serious virus. Never before had he felt this horrendous, but he would endure. Monique was an abomination, and must be destroyed! Earlier, a dream had shown him a red thread that connected him and Monique. Now he would follow it! Find her before she found them tonight!

The sound of the blower filled the silence between the two as Jana drove toward the front gate. At the road, David said, "Turn right." His disembodied voice carried through the curtain, hoarse and strained.

Driving in a daze, Jana did as she was told. She didn't even try to think about anything except keeping the car on the road. As though it had a mind of its own, it seemed to drift sometimes. She alternately watched the speedometer and stared intently at the road, the scenery passing by unnoticed. Everything else was insane . . . but real. A house afire. Her crazy rescue. The chase. The attack. The accident. And David's house vandalized. Why was she doing this? For David? As though compelled, Jana seemed helpless to do anything but what he told her to do.

David now knew that he never would've been able to drive far. It was plenty dark in the backseat area, and the air-conditioner was running on high, yet he was still nauseous and feverish, alternately freezing, then burning up. David pushed the painful sensations aside, trying to ignore it all and focus on the red thread that would lead him to Monique.

How long they drove, David wasn't sure. He was lost to pain and time, following the string wherever he could and catching up with it when he couldn't. Several times Jana shifted into four-wheel and steered them across a field. Suddenly the crimson string became more distinct as Monique's presence grew stronger, but the thread was oddly frazzled and worn. "We're getting close." His voice cracked. The threadbare string went around a thick copse of trees, then bent quickly to the right and across a yard.

Now David was starting to shake and shiver, his skin crawling, as though it were trying to slide from his bones. He ignored the growing agony. "Stop! Is there a house near?" As though he were drunk, his head swam in circles. David wondered if he was going to make it, and decided it was do or die.

"Yes, on the right. It's run-down," Jana replied.

The abandoned house wasn't much, a boarded, one-story dwelling with a partly shingled roof and battered aluminum siding that was no longer white. The place was overgrown with cracks in the concrete drive and sidewalk. Weedy grass and wild bushes had taken over, threatening to overrun the place. The derelict house was secluded, the closest residence was a trailer several hundred feet away.

Could IT really be here? Jana wondered. And how did David know? Was he psychic or something? It was too much to think about, piling atop her as though she'd opened a closet of skeletons stuffed too full.

"Jana, are you okay?"

"Y . . . yes." She was idling in the middle of the country road. "There's a garage, separate and on the right."

David concentrated. Monique was not there. "That won't do. Just find some shade near a window." Jana drove across the lawn, parking along the left side of the house and in the shadow of several trees.

Knowing he couldn't last much longer, David climbed from behind the curtain and opened the passenger door. He had the silver cross and mallet in hand; the Bible and stakes were stuffed in his jacket pockets. As soon as David was outside, his face twisted in agony, and his legs gave way. As David began to collapse, he grabbed the luggage rack and managed to hang on.

"David!" Jana ran around to help. Trembling, David took the umbrella from Jana. While he leaned on her, David opened it, holding it above them. Instantly, he felt better. "David," Jana began, "I don't think you should do this. You're almost dead on your feet. Let me take you to Dr. Katyu."

"Later. This might be our only chance to destroy her." David gestured to the nearby window. Jana hesitated, started to say something, but didn't, then she reluctantly guided him toward the window. David had to lean heavily on her arm. He staggered and almost fell, nearly dragging them both down. By the time they reached the house, she was almost carrying him. They stopped before a shaded window. David leaned wearily against the faded aluminum siding. "She's resting somewhere inside. I'm . . . I'm not sure where."

"You can barely keep your eyes open."

"I'll be all right once I'm inside." David took the mallet and struck the glass, shattering it. Suddenly, something crashed against the window, shaking it. Scratching and clawing noises filled the air, and then the shade began to shred. After a few seconds, it stopped.

"Guard . . . dogs," David said with exasperation. "Jana, there's a gun in the glove box." She returned shortly with the .45, handing it to David by the barrel. She no longer resembled the Jana David knew. Her stare was hard, her lips tight. Surrounded by swelling and bruises, her once-beautiful eyes were now haunted.

David wet his lips, then said, "Stand back." With a shaking hand he smashed the rest of the glass. Again something large and dark pounded against the window, and this time the wall. The shade was suddenly ripped away by canine fangs. Insane eyes tried to hold its prey. David fired once, twice, three times. The Doberman jerked, then crumpled soundlessly.

"David . . . you . . . It didn't bark, yelp, or snarl," Jana said with horror and wonder. Both hands were on her ears. Her stare lost its focus, then she came back to him.

David touched her shoulder, afraid he was going to lose her to madness. He wanted to comfort her, but now was not the time or place. "Maybe it's not an ordinary dog." What did he know about vampire guardians? David didn't care if Monique heard him coming. If she could feel anything besides the pain, she would sense him nearby, as he did her.

Taking off his sunglasses, David peered inside. The animal was still twitching. "I think it's dead." Pistol first, David entered through the broken window. Pausing part way, he was careful not to be surprised if the dog rose from the dead and attacked. David entered the house, turned, and said, "You wait out there." He leaned against the wall, the gun hanging limply from his grasp.

"You can barely stand!"

David put the mallet in his pocket and held the cross. "Please. Just stay there."

"I . . ." Jana began. David turned from the window and unsteadily crossed the room. Jana fumed and began to follow him in. How come people who deserved help and needed it, were the least likely to accept it? "I'm coming with you."

David looked at her, and with just a glance realized he couldn't stop her. He hoped he wouldn't have to watch someone else he cared for die, but the stakes were high. Hesitantly he nodded, then paused at the door, and listened. David didn't hear anything, but could feel Monique even nearer.

Cross in one hand, pistol in the other, he was ready. With any luck, he'd find her resting place without meeting any more guardians, set the cross on her to paralyze her, then drive a stake into her heart. Just as legend would have it. David prayed it would be so easy.

Steeled for an attack, he opened the door. Nothing. David looked left and found three closed doors. No sunlight slid under any of them. Apparently all the windows had been masked or blocked. To the right, he found that it opened into a larger room, probably the living room.

Which way to go? David had thought he'd be able to tell once he got into the house—closer to Monique and out of the sun—but he couldn't. She was all over. David decided to head in the direction of the bedrooms. There would be less windows to cover. He glanced at Jana, who was chewing on her lip, and then entered the hallway.

Moving quietly through the dimness, the only light angling in from behind him, David stopped at the first door on his right. He took a deep breath, then in one motion he grabbed the knob, turned it, and entered with his cross ready.

The room was tattered, as was everything else he'd seen in the place, the carpet rotting and threadbare. The wallpaper sagged, as would a little old man bereft of his cane. An old chest of drawers sat in the corner with all the drawers pulled out onto the floor, as though the place had been looted. The window was broken and boarded up from the outside. She didn't appear to be in here, but . . .

David stepped further into the room and saw that the closet

was closed. The second of the two doors was off its track. Holding his cross before him, David moved to the closet and yanked the door open. It slid with surprising ease and slammed against the wall. The compartment was empty except for dust and trash. David breathed a sigh of relief, turned, and left the room.

"Nothing." He moved past Jana to the next door. David listened, then yanked it open, peering into a bathroom. It was pitted and ravaged, the tile floor broken and cracked. Even the commode had been shattered. Surely she wasn't in here, sleeping in the bathtub. He quickly moved on to the next door.

Just as David touched the knob, he hesitated. There was another room unchecked, but he had a feeling this was the one. Taking a deep breath and saying a prayer, he grabbed the knob and threw open the door. The darkness was deeper and alive, more reminiscent of an underground cavern than a room. David smelled dirt and . . .

Something powerful and black slammed David, driving him staggering and stumbling back into a wall. Silently snarling, six German shepherds overwhelmed David. The devil-dogs' eyes shone as though touched by rabidness. The only sound was the snapping of jaws as three missed, and the ripping of fabric as one got his shoulder, another his leg, and the last his left arm. His heavy coat protected him a little.

"Jana! Run!" David fired wildly, two of his slugs hitting home, but the dogs kept coming. He dropped the gun and struck one with the cross. The beast staggered back whimpering, but not cringing. The other devil-dogs tore at him. David screamed.

"David!" Jana was paralyzed with fear. One creature quit attacking, stared at her for a moment—long enough to lock gazes,—then bounded toward her. Jana fled.

David wielded the mallet in one hand and the cross in another, as he hammered away at them. One dog went down, but a trio swarmed about him, their bites pulling at him as they tore into him. One of David's blows broke a dog's jaw, but another retaliated, snapping his right wrist. Screaming, he dropped the mallet.

Before she knew what she was doing, Jana was running down the hall, pushing through the doorway and into the sunlit room. She sprinted for the window. The devil-dog pursued, sliding into the door frame in its haste, but nipping at her heels as she threw herself out the window. The beast didn't follow her outside, but peeked out the door, staring at her for a long moment. Then the devil-dog winced, whimpered, and went back inside.

Jana staggered to the Blazer and climbed inside, collapsing against the wheel. She was safe! But David!

David could no longer feel his right arm. Four of the devil-dogs were down, stunned by his blows, but one was left. The cross had been more effective than either the gun or mallet. David held the fifth off with the silver crucifix, as he backed down the hall. He could feel the dim sunlight streaming into the dark hall through the open door.

David darted into the room and collided with the slavering beast as it returned from the window. The devil-dog's bite caught him high on the shoulder, knocking him to the ground. The second beast piled atop, snapping and ripping. David screamed.

Jana heard him. He was dying! She had to do something but if she returned to help, they'd kill her. But then she—IT—would kill Jana tonight anyway. And running never solved anything. Then Jana remembered that the dog hadn't followed her outside; that rekindled a memory from a movie. She laughed madly, shifted into reverse, backed up, and then shifted into drive. Stomping the gas pedal to the floor, she steered for the window, intending to ram it.

The wall exploded as though struck by a grenade, caving inward and erupting, throwing debris everywhere. Frame and drywall rode on the hood of the Blazer for a moment, then flew across the room. A heavy cloud of dust and debris hung in the sunshine, as the bright light poured into the room. The devil-dogs suddenly shivered, halting their attacks, and began to whimper as they backed off, leaving David alone. Suddenly they turned and fled the light.

Exposed to the sun, David felt paralyzed, unsure of which hurt more. He was dying, too weak to move. He hadn't even gotten close to Monique before being defeated. She would kill more innocents. Slowly, he slipped away into oblivion.

Jana threw the Blazer in reverse and pulled out of the house, causing more of the wall and some of the ceiling to collapse, letting in even more light. She waited for the dust to clear, then saw David lying alone, ravaged and bleeding. With a desperate strength, Jana dragged him into the Blazer, and drove like a mad woman to the ranch.

Part Three: Prey

One

House Call

Through cold, dark waters, David swam stiffly toward the surface of wakefulness. With each stroke he not only grew closer to the hazy, faded light, but became more aware of himself. It seemed that he had been swimming for a long, long time, trying to reach whatever he knew was bright and shiny waiting in the air above. And yet, his lungs didn't burn as did his throat, flaring as if he'd swallowed something foul.

In the distance, David heard someone say, "This is not good. Has he been exposed to sunshine?" The accent was clipped.

"Yes, we went boating last night and ran aground on a sandbar." This voice was feminine and sounded tired. "We got stuck, forcing us to get home about an hour after sunrise. I tried to protect him however I could, but . . ."

"I can tell. I shudder to think what would have happened if you had not." David thought he recognized the voices, but couldn't place them. He blamed it on the cotton stuffed in his head. David continued swimming, the color of the water fading from inky-black to gray, as he grew closer to the light. "Look at these blisters." Something touched David's face, and he felt a wash of pain. The sensation drew him closer to the surface, now within his reach.

Sore, raw, and chilled, David awakened, his eyes fluttering open. Doc Katyu leaned closer, staring at him. "What's up, Doc?" David croaked. He was dizzy—still swimming—and nauseous.

"Ah, David, it is good to see you awake and communicating," Doc Katyu told him. Behind the doctor, Jana looked battered, worn, and very worried. Somehow she still managed a wan smile.

Just seeing her smile made David feel a little better. Jana had stuck with him and saved his life more than once. In many ways, her loyalty, determinedness, and caring reminded him of his beloved Tina. David felt terrible about involving Jana, particularly for the beating she'd taken at the hands of Monique.

"David?" Doc Katyu prodded. "How do you feel?"

"Terrible," David rasped. "Stomach. Head. Sort of a bad case of the flu." David vaguely remembered last night . . . and this morning.

He'd failed; Monique was still alive, able to kill again. Damn those guard dogs! David feebly felt for their bites, and was surprised to find none. Had they healed? Or was he delirious? It was getting hard for David to tell these days. The fact that he felt sick—more violently ill than torn up—wasn't what he expected. What had happened to his wounds? The bites and burns seemed to have healed, but not the sun damage. Maybe this was all just a bad dream; he'd just passed out at home, and Jana had found him.

David wasn't dressed as he remembered, his clothing was no longer ripped and torn. He was clad in sweatpants and was bare-chested. David noticed that even Jana had changed, dressed in faded jeans and an orange UT T-shirt—some of Tina's old clothes. "What happened, Doc?"

"You can't tell me?" Doc Katyu asked. David shook his

head. "Jana said you were boating and ran aground, causing you to get home after sunrise. You've been severely overexposed to the sun, evident by these strange burns. You are badly blistered and will probably scar." Doc Katyu scratched his chin, "And your body temperature is too low. I am very concerned."

Doc Katyu sighed. "I don't know what to prescribe besides bed rest, consuming plenty of fluids, and staying indoors. Keep the shutters closed except at night. No more testing your tolerance for a while. And you will need someone to care for you for a few days. If I don't see improvement soon, we will have to send you to Dallas. While you slept, I took another blood sample. Your last one was very, very odd. I want to compare the two."

"That's why my arm hurts," David said, and Doc Katyu nodded. "How were the heme and porphyrin levels?"

"Better, much better in fact, although still not normal. I want to recheck your blood. There must have been some kind of mistake. We'll talk more after the next test."

"Speaking of tests, Doc," David began, "what were the results of my mother's?"

"She hasn't told you?" The doctor sounded surprised, his eyebrows peeking above his glasses.

"No." David was immediately more alert and concerned.

Doc Katyu took a deep breath. "The tests reveal that your mother has an advanced case of liver cancer. It is terminal, unless treatment begins immediately, and she has refused chemotherapy. Penny said she didn't want to waste away, especially since the chances for remission are slim. At best, the treatments might extend her life for a short time."

"How long do you think she has?" David asked.

"At most? Six months." Doc Katyu sighed. "I called her earlier, she should be on her way over. You two should talk."

The silence that stretched over the room was as heavy as though the death shroud were already being laid out. Jana moved to his side, and took his hand. David just stared at the ceiling, wondering why he kept going. Everything was going wrong—again. The curse's grip was tenacious. He was outliving more of his family. David recalled what Monique had said, about living forever and watching all those around you die. He knew that his mother would die one day; she was older, but now it seemed so sudden. Tears welled in his eyes. Jana sat on the bed and hugged him. She started to say something, then didn't.

"David," Doc Katyu said. "I will check on you tomorrow. I suggest you call the sheriff about this vandalism, but please, get plenty of rest." As the doctor packed, he said, "And, Jana, try the poultices and salves I suggested as well as ice. Such a lovely face should be treated with extra care." Doc Katyu nodded and left without another word.

"David—" Jana began.

"Don't say anything, please. Let me say thank you. I know this has been . . . horrible." David almost choked. "But you must go! Monique will be coming!"

"Maybe. Maybe not. You don't know for sure, you said so yourself. Besides, I'm too tired to leave, too tired to run. I'll sleep here and help you recover." David didn't know what to say, so he just held Jana. He thought he heard a voice and looked up. There was a fleeting shadow and the wisp of a hauntingly familiar scent; then there was nothing at all.

Two

Warnings

"See ya, sheriffs," Hank Tubbs chortled as he sat down in the abused plaid recliner. He popped the top off a beer, spat tobacco juice into a plastic cup, and then took a swig. Attracted to the trash, dirty dishes, and scattered food, there was an abundance of bugs. Buck, Hank's brother, was on the worn couch, and waved at Logan and Bricker as they turned to leave. The two officers looked at each other, silently saying that there was nothing else they could do—despite their wishes. They'd wasted hours searching the place for contraband or anything related to the vandalism at the Matthewson Ranch. Unfortunately, the Tubbs boys had plenty of experience in hiding things.

"Sorry ya had such a boring afternoon," Hank spat again. "Good luck finding something at Matthewson's." Rick opened the ragged screen door. Stone-faced, the third brother ushered Logan and Bricker outside.

"Come back for a beer sometime, when you feel like partying with real men," Buck said, then scratched his scar. "And bring Judge Marshall along with you! He'll already be toasted!" The two stout brothers hooted, slapping each other.

Coldly, Logan turned back. It had been a long day, and he wasn't going to accept disrespect for his friend.

Bricker could read Logan's mind, so with meaty paws he grabbed his partner, slowly pulling Logan aside and placing himself in the doorway between the opposing parties. "Listen up, boys. Except for Rick, you're two-time losers. My bet's that you're on the verge of being three-timers. We'll be watching the Matthewson farm. See you there." He started to turn away, then said, "I'd warn ya to stay away, but I know it won't do no good. Besides, throwin' you boys in jail always bolsters the town's confidence in the department." Then he smiled widely, a cat eyeing cornered mice. "And it feels good, too."

"Don't worry," Hank stammered, his eyes darting about, "we ain't going . . . going there."

Rick just shrugged and said, "I don't like ranches. There's shit all over the place."

Bricker looked around at the pervasive squalor. Chuckling, he guided his fuming partner down the steps to their car. Seething, Logan got inside the black and white Mustang. "They've already been there!" He was mad enough to spit bullets. "We both know they've vandalized the Matthewson place!"

"We just can't prove it, yet," Bricker drawled. "But we will. And if they're involved in the Siete Hombres fire, we'll nail their asses. I promise it. Just be patient. We're still waiting on the investigative report. It'll tell us what started the fire—accidental or not. 'Til then, we can't do anything," Bricker said, for once being the cool one.

Logan nodded. The judge had been a great man—and a good friend. Logan remembered stopping the car just outside the gate to Siete Hombres. Had that really been just this morning? It seemed like days when he thought about his fatigue, but just minutes ago in memory, where the recent past kept intruding on the present.

Responding to a 911 call, Logan pulled to a stop before the entrance to the peninsula neighborhood where the judge lived. Even from a distance, the fire was obvious. Up close, Logan stared through the glowing windshield, awestricken by the raging power of the inferno. The area looked as though it had been bombarded with napalm. Flecks of ashes and burning debris floated about like inflamed confetti. Already the houses were burning, massive bonfires with guttering trees gathered around, looking like an unruly mob. The roadway was a flaming channel, the lawns smoking, and the overhanging trees creating a fiery archway. One glance at the closed and locked front gate told him they hadn't left by car.

Logan drove in reverse to the nearest house, where a man clad in pajamas was hosing down everything he could. At their mom's direction, the three younger kids were stuffing things into their station wagon and van. "You seen the Marshalls?"

The stout, round-faced man glanced at Logan, his expression one of forced alertness and fear. "No! Where the hell's the fire department!?"

"They'll be here soon. Besides the Marshalls, is anybody else living there?"

"Nope. All the others are vacation homes."

"Can I borrow a boat?"

The man looked at him as though he were crazy, then said, "Canoe's the best bet. It's sitting on the dock. Good luck, Sheriff."

Logan sprinted to the dock, set the craft in the water, and took off paddling along the lakeshore. The water's surface flickered with a variety of ethereal shapes and fiery colors. Like huge, snapping flags, wavering fire billowed from the trees and across the finger of land. The roar of the conflagration was thunderous, as though a massive stampede was in progress.

Several hundred feet away he could see the Marshall house, blazing as though the sun had set on it. In between the smoky gusts and across the peninsula, he could see their boat winched under the beveled roof. It appeared he was too late.

Then Logan thought he saw movement out of the corner of his eye, and scrutinized the area near an A-frame house being totally devoured by fire. Serpentine flames rippled across the land, slithering and undulating through the underbrush. Suddenly, something rose from the ground, staggered forward, then fell face first. Yes, he had seen someone trying to make it to shore. The survivor was now crawling feebly.

As though possessed, Logan rowed to the shore. He jumped into the water and ran into Hell on earth. Cinder, ash, and bits of flaming trash fluttered about, imitating incandescent moths. Singeing his hair and clothes, fiery, evanescent hands grasped at him as he ran toward the downed survivor. He had quit crawling, either dead or exhausted.

Logan knelt by the boy. He was badly burned. Could this be Skeeter? Was there anybody else alive? A powerful blast of heat nearly overwhelmed Logan, and made his decision for him. He scooped up the boy and carried him to the canoe.

"She's not dead," Skeeter moaned. He looked almost dead himself. He'd lost all of his hair; his skin was raw. Some of his burns had already started to ooze.

"Who's not dead? Is your grandmother around here? What about the Judge?"

"She's not dead," was all Skeeter would say. Logan put him in the canoe. He looked hopelessly back at the house, then paddled back to the nearby dock.

"But who is *she?*" Logan asked aloud, his thoughts unable to leave the fiery scene. He glanced outside and noticed that they were nearing town.

"She who?" Bricker asked.

"The 'she' Skeeter was referring to. It wasn't Mrs. Marshall. She was found dead on the couch, probably died in her sleep."

"The boy was probably just delirious," Bricker said.

Logan remembered watching as the volunteer fire fighters picked through the smoldering ruins of the seven homes of the Siete Hombres peninsula. They hadn't been able to extinguish the inferno, but had contained it to just the Siete Hombres neighborhood. The houses were charred husks with smoking piles of embers atop scorched concrete slabs. The trees reminded him of huge, burned matchsticks that had been stuck into the ground as a warning not to play with fire. Even the grass was blackened, so the land appeared to be formally clad for a wake.

Unlike earlier, when the area had an urgent carnival atmosphere, the peninsula had become quiet, except for the bony clatter of charred branches rubbing against each other in the rising breeze. There had been quite a crowd, both volunteers and gawkers. How people loved to watch tragedy unfold! And Logan had the feeling Temprance was a tragedy unfolding.

"Logan, you doing all right?" Bricker drawled.

"I'll be fine."

"Not much of a vacation. I'm sorry," Bricker said. "I'll make it up to you, when this is all over."

"Not much of a retirement for the Judge. Where is he? Was that his body found at the house near where I found Skeeter? Nobody was supposed to be there."

"Maybe he was doing some caretaker work for the Steeles. I left a message on their machine. But, Logan, it's over for us, for now anyway. Go home. Rest. The warrant for the Matthewson Ranch may be available tomorrow, and I'll need your help." He paused, then asked, "Say, did you notice that Hank appeared unnerved, almost frightened, when I mentioned the Matthewson Ranch?"

Logan nodded, thought for a moment, and then said, "You're right. I wonder why? Nothing much would scare those bastards." For a brief moment, Logan recalled walking inside David's house to search for him. Sensations of disquiet and danger had been prevalent.

A rumbling of nearby thunder diverted his attention, and Logan looked skyward. It was full of churning, purple black clouds, angry thunderheads just waiting to unload in a forty-days-and-nights deluge. "Storm's coming," Bricker said.

"And it's going to be a nasty one."

Bricker appeared worried. "Hunch?" Bricker asked. Logan nodded. "Really?" Logan nodded again. "You and your hunches," Bricker drawled. "We don't need to go from bone dry to flooding."

"You been sleeping all right?" Logan asked, attempting to sound casual.

"Yeah. Like a rock. Uh, been meaning to mention this. I've been seeing Delores, so falling asleep after a while isn't a problem. Best I've slept in ages."

"Really? Seeing Delores?" Logan was surprised.

"Yeah, I finally figured that mourning Patti for two years was long enough. She'd want me to get along with my life." Finally, Bricker said, "Why? Bad dreams keeping you awake?"

Again, Logan was surprised. It seemed that Bricker had been changing, coming out of the unsympathetic shell which had surrounded him since Patti had succumbed to cancer. Logan had been too preoccupied recently to notice the metamorphosis. Logan told himself to shape up, because if he didn't notice Bricker's transformation, what else might he be missing?

"Logan, are you sure you're all right?"

"Just thinking, Donald, that's all. Yeah, I've been having odd . . . very vivid dreams. Sometimes I think I'm tuned into 'Tales From The Crypt.' "

"Funny, Delores said the same thing. Didn't know you watched that crap," Bricker said.

"I don't. My wife does."

"Anyway, Delores has been having nightmares, too. Sometimes she thrashes about so much, I have to hold her down until she wakes up. Says friends of hers are experiencing the same thing. It's quite the talk of the town. Carrie Parker claims she's going to write a book about it!" Bricker laughed.

Logan wondered why he hadn't heard the same. He had noticed the sleepless expressions on the volunteers at the meeting the other day. Could that be why the crowd was so volatile? Look at him, losing his temper just minutes ago. That never should have happened, but sleep deprivation had serious consequences, or so the military had said.

"I also heard it at Sam's this morning during breakfast," Bricker continued. "There were four topics of conversation, not necessarily in this order: the nightmares; the fire out at Siete Hombres—now the favorite; the search for the missing boys—becoming old news fast—and by the way, there's a volunteers' meeting tomorrow at the church."

"Wonderful. What was the last topic of conversation?"

"David Matthewson and his books. Hotly debated, I hear. Some think he's a bad influence. They don't like somebody in their neighborhood writing about weird stuff and violence."

Logan snorted. "You know, I don't know what's happening to this town. I realize we're somewhat simple, not big-town sophisticated, which is fine by me, but there seems to be more gossiping and bad-mouthing than I've ever heard before."

"Things have been odd for about a week. Since that Friday incident at Matthewson's place."

"Now, Donald, don't you get started, too." Logan remembered that evening vividly, David drunk and crying into his bleeding hands, as though a broken man. Blood splattered all over the ravaged door. Not a trace of anger had been visible, only sadness and anguish over his privacy being destroyed, possibly caused by his success and publicity—a terrible twist of good fortune leading to bad.

"Don't worry, I'm not jumping to any conclusions. I try and stay objective. Patti used to tell me all the time, don't get huffy, get objective. I think David Matthewson's a bit strange, but I don't think he's a murderer. Still, we have to follow leads, and it will do the town some good if we check out the ranch and find nothing."

"Warrants, searches, and volunteers looking for lost boys," Logan sighed. "What's Temprance coming too?"

"Hell," Bricker chuckled, "it's not coming, it's going, if you believe what the Reverend Wright claims. Maybe the times have just caught up with us. Small towns certainly aren't immune to kidnappings, violence, drugs, or AIDS just because they're small. Still," Bricker smiled, "I say good riddance to JJ Tubbs. I wish the other brothers would follow suit and disappear, although I'd rather arrest their asses. And I find it hard to shed a tear for the Brookenses; you reap what you sow."

Now this was the Donald Bricker he knew, Logan thought. "I wonder about that group of boys. Tubbs and the Brookens brothers are missing. Skeeter is found nearly burned to death, and Patrick Page is catatonic. Somehow this is all connected. Maybe we should talk with David again. And Kevin Grimm. He's the only healthy survivor of Grimm's Reapers." Before Bricker could reply, Logan suddenly wondered aloud, "Did anything else odd happen on that Friday? I don't think I've read all the reports. Friday's are usually pretty active."

"Don't bother," Bricker said casually, still staring at the road. "I've already checked. Did I tell you I talked to the mayor and Kevin about that Friday night incident? Kevin will undergo counselling—again."

"Good. He's a strange bird." Logan sighed, then said, "That Friday. You know, I have that nagging feeling again. Sort of an itch needing to be scratched."

Bricker shifted uncomfortably. "Maybe some rest will

help." They entered the town, passing the sign reading "Temprance City Limits—Population 1,728," just as the clouds burst, and the deluge began.

Three

First Offer

Jana left David's room quietly so she wouldn't disturb his sleep. All she wanted to do was collapse and rest for a week, but she knew Monique would be coming to exact revenge. Jana shivered, hugging herself. As she left, she checked the cross nailed to the door, then glanced back for the umpteenth time to make sure David's crucifix was resting visibly on his chest. Jana fingered the one around her neck, then moved toward the spare bedroom where she was staying temporarily. She found herself whimsically wishing it were a permanent arrangement.

Suddenly the silence was interrupted, and Jana heard a hissing, as though David's cat was getting ready to fight; the sound stopped just as abruptly. A strange, cool breeze appeared from nowhere, and Jana shivered violently. The chilling draft was a stark contrast to the usual temperatures, biting instead of muggy. Drawn, Jana followed the current to the top of the stairs and looked down. The foyer was dim, as though the light she'd left on in the living room had burned out, leaving only the one in the kitchen to give a pale yellowish ambiance.

Jana found herself compelled to walk down the stairs. She hesitated, fighting it, but failed miserably, as though her body belonged to someone else. As she descended, the light disappeared, swallowed by the darkness. The coldness enveloped her, caressing her goose-bumped flesh, as blackness whirled around her like a wind-whipped cloak. Abruptly the air grew calm, and a white face appeared before her. Jana stopped, surprised and scared, her hand going to her throat. Jana simply stared, mesmerized. Monique?

Hers was not a pleasant facade, although it had been earlier. Unmoving and truncated, the vampire's face could have been a floating mask. Monique's lips were overly full, mocking, and a little crooked. Her nose was wider than it was before, as though recently broken, and her cheekbones were gaunt, almost sunken. Monique's eyes were uneven, crazily so, but they weren't empty, but rather smoldering in the fashion of firing kilns. Her hair was still lustrous, but her once proud brows were gone.

Jana's mind reeled, and she realized she was caught between sleep and waking with one foot in each world. Clutching her crucifix, she fought her way through the mind-numbing haze and thrust the cross forward, trying to drive away Monique as she'd seen in the movies.

"Come on. Wake up, my pretty bitch," Monique snarled, baring her teeth. "Dat would do you little good, having been used too late, *If* I was going harm you as you have tried to harm me. Not dat I do not have cause!" The power and anger in Monique word's made Jana tremble. One minute asleep, Jana thought, the next dead.

With the grace of a master sculptor molding clay, Monique's face was transformed, changing back into her former beauty. Except for a crimson scarf around her neck, the vampire was dressed completely in black and sitting in a chair directly across from Jana's bed. Everything but Monique's face was covered, giving it a disembodied appearance as she sat in the light coming in from the streetlights.

"But it is not solely up to me whether you live or die!"

Monique continued. "Dere are . . . it matters not, I ramble. Besides," Monique smiled sweetly, "I still wish to know how David was filmed. I dream of becoming—" She coughed. *"Ja,* wake up, I wish to talk. I have an offer to make you."

Still holding the crucifix in a defensive posture, Jana realized she was in her own house—her own bed—and Monique was here! Jana glanced around; the windows were closed. She heard the soft cadence of rain and the distant rumble of thunder. Seconds later, lightning flickered, whitening the room and causing Monique to stand out, a black hole in the light.

"Not a pleasant night for man or beast," Monique said, "but what I have to say to you is worth braving dis foul weather." She coughed several times, grimaced as she touched her throat, and then continued, "I know you want David. I know it more truly dan you do. The reasons why I will leave for you to decide for yourself." Jana started to say something, and Monique waved her to silence. "Don't you realize dat he is as I? He is vampire, although just a fledgling shade, but still a vampire—a prince of the night!"

"Get out of my house!" Jana suddenly cried, filled with an irrational anger fueled by fear. She was going to die! Jana started to pray and tried not to cry as she shoved the crucifix at Monique.

"Stop dat!" Monique hissed. "I promise I will not hurt you, tonight anyway. You must understand dat to join David, to be with him in nightly love, you must become what he is! A vampire! Yes, you must!" Expanding outward as a cavernous maw—a growing pit with its sides caving in—Monique's eyes filled the room. Jana cringed, the cross wavering, but not her faith.

"I offer you the chance to join him! To live forever with your man! You could travel the world many times over. See it all! Explore ancient secrets, and learn so many things. You would have fun, and most importantly, be in command of your existence—your future—and not fall prey to some whimsical fate, as you have before."

"N . . . no! That's not right. I don't want that. Really!"

"Oh, yes, you do. I see it," Monique smiled, then began coughing again.

Jana raised her cross. "No! It's definitely not what I want! And David's not a vampire, he's just sick! Now leave!" Jana thrust the cross toward Monique, and feeling brave, she began to slowly rise hoping to force the vampire to leave.

"Do not trouble yourself," Monique hacked several times, the coughing fit strengthening. "I will be going. As I told you, I came only to make you an offer. If David doesn't accept his fate, wid or widout your assistance, he will be destroyed. It must be so. He is too dangerous, a threat to all who live the night. David either learns, understands, and accepts . . . or he will be tossed to oblivion like a bone to a dog." Monique rose, then moved unsteadily away from Jana and into the shadows. The vampire melded with them, disappearing as if she'd stepped into a secret passage.

It was gone, but for several long minutes, Jana continued to clutch the crucifix tightly. Finally, she relaxed, but her mind ran wild with the impossibilities and possibilities. Could Monique be right? Surely not! Jana thought, as she mentally slapped away the ridiculous idea.

Four

Grounds Search

Figures, Ross thought, that it would rain on the day they had a search warrant for the Matthewson Ranch. Water poured from the bent brim of his hat. It had started yesterday afternoon and hadn't stopped. It was amazing how cold summer showers could be. Why, after over three weeks of Sahara weather, had it decided to imitate monsoon season? He hated soggy weekends, and it was just his luck to get assigned to search the woods along with several others on loan from Seven Points, Tool, and Malakoff.

As Ross continued his search, the downpour intensified, nearly blinding him. Ross actually felt the pelting impacts against his slicker, and the noise off his hat, along with the slapping sound of the driving rain, almost deafened him. Reminding Ross more of a swamp than a ranch, the ground was saturated and muddy. The air smelled of damp woods, earth mingling with decay and mold. The sky was a turbulent sea of gray and black thunderheads. Adding to the torrent had been sporadic, albeit brief, hail, plenty of thunder, and jagged forks of lightning.

Ross wasn't glad to be back, and it was more than just the weather that bothered him; the ranch gave him the creeps. He still had nightmares about finding Matthewson slumped against the barn door. In his dreams, the bloody author would rise up to grab him or grasp his ankle, as if he were some sort of crypt thing. Ross shuddered.

He didn't expect to find anything and felt that Bricker didn't expect him to either. Nobody had found anything so far, and probably wouldn't. The house search had revealed nothing, and now Bricker was searching the barn, while Logan was investigating the pasture. There was plenty of land to hide something, but there were only ten of them looking.

Ross heard the rushing of a overflowing stream, where not long ago there had been a meandering creek. In some places it had spilled over its banks and taken a more direct route. All sorts of forest debris—leaves, sticks, and branches—were carried along in the current. Ross knew he was near where they'd found the motorcycle with the cocaine.

A flash of lightning ignited the woods, the world bleached starkly white except for the midnight-hued shadows. Ross had to blink his eyes several times before he could see again. Then the thunder struck, nearly driving him to his knees; the air quivered, while the forest trembled. Ross wondered if hail was next. He hoped not. There would be time for searching later, he was heading for cover!

Again the lightning flashed. Just ahead, motion caught his eyes. A tree was listing, slowly tipping over the stream as the wall of a ravine collapsed into the ravaging current below. Bobbing and just barely visible, something strange stuck out of the muddy water. Ross blinked and took a couple steps forward. Could that be an arm?

Damned if he wasn't going to make a huge discovery! This was probably one of the boys! This might mean a raise, or at least some respect. Either would do, although he now had a second—inconsistent—source of income.

Ross moved closer and pulled out his Instamatic, taking several photos. If needed, he'd buy a new camera! Ross couldn't make out a head, but he was sure those were arms. The corpse must have been washed downstream, or been unearthed by erosion.

Ross carefully climbed into the small ravine. The corpse was almost underneath the tree in an eddying mud pool; he'd have to wade. Ross took a step, gasped at the chill, then kept going. He didn't want his ticket to becoming a full-fledged deputy to wash away. Each of his steps sank more deeply than he expected, once reaching above his knee. When he finally managed to extricate his leg, his boot stayed behind.

With soggy boot in hand, Ross neared the body. He got out his flashlight and turned it on, training the beam on the corpse. From the back, the body was very stout, but baggy and somewhat shriveled. Wondering if his camera was still working, Ross took several pictures. Reaching out with the flashlight, he prodded the corpse, then tried to roll it over, but failed. It was stuck fast. Ross tossed his boot on land, put his camera and flashlight away, then moved closer, and grabbed the body, wrenching it free and turning it over. It slipped out of his grasp, twisting toward him. Ross screamed.

Logan didn't mind the rain. It was refreshing and cleansing, if also more than a little abundant today. What a great way to spend a Saturday afternoon, let alone his canceled vacation. But now was no time to be enjoying leisure activities or catching up on chores. Logan walked along the fence, eyeing the pasture and nearby woods for anything out of place. The field was virtually deserted; the cows in the barn. They probably didn't like the lightning either. The last flash had nearly blinded Logan, and the thunder had deafened him for a moment. At least the winds hadn't been too bad. The dam and the concave lay of the land helped protect them.

He'd almost come to the end of his route, heading northward along the fence. It joined an eastward section heading toward the lake. Government property—the dam—was ahead and beyond the wire barrier. There was a massive mud puddle ahead, as though there'd been a slide. Next to it was a bottle. Logan approached, then knelt to pick up the empty bottle of Jack Daniels. Why, he began to wonder, but didn't finish his thought.

Ross's scream carried through the pattering of rain and between grumbling thunder. Logan thought it came from the woods south of him. He hopped the fence, pulling his gun as he rushed into the woods.

With Michael Woods behind him, Sheriff Bricker stared into the closet that held the refrigerator. The overhead lights were on in the barn, since only flat, gray light came in through the windows. "My, my! There's a lifetime supply of booze in here! Jack Daniels, Jaegermeister, Tia Maria," Bricker read the cartons, "and Wild Turkey. But no tequila," he chuckled. "Man's got quite a drinking problem." His words were almost drowned out by the crescendo of rain against the tin roof. Lightning flashed outside, then thunder rattled the barn.

"Had," Michael told him. He sneezed, then rezipped his raincoat. It was cool as well as damp in the barn, but this was better than a hot day; then the search would seemed to have taken two forevers instead of one. The things he did for his best buddy, Michael mused. He'd rather be in his office working, even on Saturday.

The Sheriff continued to claim that this was mostly for show—to show the town they were doing their part to find the boys. It would also clear David's name. Bricker was digging around in the closet and came across bags, jars, and shoe boxes full of herbs. "What this stuff?" He proceeded to open things, sniffing and tasting. He even took a few samples. "Smells like ginger root," he mumbled. "Don't know what type of root this is, but here's some ginseng, I think, garlic and even some oregano."

"Anything else?"

"Nope." Bricker pulled open the refrigerator door.

"Looking for frozen heads? We're not in Milwaukee."

Bricker proceeded to move the bottles around. Satisfied, he closed the door. "Looking good," Bricker smiled. "What's a book doing in here?" he asked, as he pulled it from behind one of the boxes where it had fallen. Its once-dark leather was now flat and worn, the title on the front and side unreadable. Bricker flipped it open. "A book of remedies." He put down the book, shrugged, and left the closet. Michael relocked it. Bricker moved across the room and had just begun to rummage through some shelves full of chemicals, feed, and fertilizers, when he faintly heard Ross's scream.

"Come on!" Michael said, reaching the door first and pulling it open.

Logan reached Ross first, finding him almost waist deep in muddy water. Gasping and clutching his chest, the deputy in training was lying against the slippery wall of the ravine. Ross appeared uninjured, if one didn't include his paper-white complexion.

"Ross, what is it?" Logan asked. Ross didn't answer. He just continued to stare at the corpse in the water. Floating face up, the emaciated skull stared skyward. The skin appeared to have shrunk as though it were a size or two too small, the bones shrink-wrapped. Its eye sockets were empty, but its teeth were revealed, the neck and jaw muscles locked in a hideous smile.

"Well, Ross, you look all right," Bricker said as he and Michael approached the edge of the flooded stream. Several other officers were right behind them, fanning out in a semicircle to see what was going on.

"Nice scream, son. Good comportment," Bricker chuckled. So did several of the other men. Bricker was carrying a soggy jacket in hand. "Look what I found on my way here. I guess we know where Stones has been. What have you boys found?"

"It's a body," Logan stated the obvious, "but it looks long dead. I wonder whose?"

"L . . . look closer. The neck," Ross stammered, pointing his flashlight at the emaciated corpse. His beam wavered, but stayed mostly on its neck, where there were two neat wounds. The rain suddenly grew colder, and Logan shuddered.

Five

Payback

The sun finally sank behind the trees, heading toward the western horizon. Grimm was leaning against a tree and had been sitting in its shade, melding with the shadow, for quite awhile. He glanced skyward, removed his sunglasses, and massaged his face. *About fucking time you set.* The sun had been unbearable. Grimm had always been a little sensitive, but today was the worst ever. He felt like death warmed over. Grimm pulled a cigarette from his pocket and lit it. *The wait was almost over,* he thought, as he scrutinized the now quiet neighborhood. He was glad the brats had quit playing a stupid game of wiffle ball.

The subdivision was relatively new, but already neglected. Young trees were prevalent, while backyards still composed of only dirt were common. In some yards, the patchwork of sod, some green and some brown, looked like a grass quilt. Blocky shadows from the westward homes were stretched long across the street, muting the houses' colors—several of which clashed, and none of which matched. The homes were simple, mostly one-story. It was rare to see costly brick or stone; most were constructed of wood. More often than not, the lawns were neglected, weeds instead of grass. Several yards had kids' stuff littering them, but one in particular had adult junk—a refrigerator, three cars, and a couch. It was a nice, peaceful, small town neighborhood, where nothing nasty ever happened. Until now, Grimm smiled.

"An artist's work is never done." Grimm reached in his backpack for the bottle of Jack Daniels, then changed his mind. Instead, he grabbed the bottle of David's special home brew. Shit! It was already empty. Well, it was hot, and he had been thirsty. For several hours, he'd been sitting across the street from Becky's house, waiting for the perfect moment: a time after twilight when peace had descended and everybody was relaxed.

And now might be that time. Earlier, the street had been busy with romping children, but it was now deserted. Soft country music was coming from Becky's place. The house was a small one-story structure with blue aluminum siding and white trim—an architect's one-hour special and a builder's prefab assemblage. Becky had added some personal touches, though. In immaculate beds lined with rock, short bushes and colorful flowers thrived, surrounding the front porch and house. Several young trees had been recently planted and were thriving. A bird feeder hung from a fledgling willow. What a nice little homemaker.

Grimm wondered if Becky were being hospitable. Lou's red tricked-out Jeep Comanche was in the driveway, parked next to her garish yellow Geo Storm. Lou had arrived ten minutes after Becky had returned home, and that was just fine with Grimm. Lou was an essential ingredient in his payback recipe.

Thank you, Monique. You're a bitch, but thanks for the idea—the gift of the perfect payback, or how I could hose everybody at once and walk away squeaky clean. Grimm chuckled. You might have been worth the trouble after all. Maybe. Grimm rubbed his neck. The punctures were healing, but the skin was still rough, the area tender. He hadn't felt well since he'd been bitten, even though he had purged Monique's influence from his mind, body, and soul.

What he really wanted to do was celebrate, to get stinking drunk, but he hadn't felt like it. He had thought that getting rid of Monique's taint would instantly return him to his normal health and vitality, but that didn't seem to be the case. This morning was worse than any hangover he'd ever had, and he'd had some doozies. Had he really purged all of her? Grimm was afraid he might have been infected or something.

Oftentimes Grimm doubted that Monique was what she claimed—a vampire. She was probably just a twisted bitch— just a life-support system for a pussy. Oh, how he looked forward to telling her that!

Yes, payback time was here; Grimm could feel it; nervous little spiders crawled restlessly along his body. He glanced at his watch. Time should be up, if he'd guessed correctly.

"Why don't bunnies make noises when they screw?" As usual, Grimm waited, then said, "Because they have cotton balls." He laughed, then snorted. He stared at the door once more, wishing he had X-ray vision. They should have eaten and drunk by now, so they should be thoroughly drugged and totally out of it.

His plan had been a stroke of genius, of understanding his prey and putting it to use. It had started yesterday. With his shades on, he had sat outside the front entrance of the TU Electric administrative offices and waited for five o'clock, when the doors became a blur of motion as workers headed home. Minutes passed, and he grew impatient. Feeling terrible didn't help. Many people had left, and for a time he'd thought maybe she'd left early. Finally at five-ten, Becky left the safe confines of her workplace and walked to her lemon-colored Storm. She was so lovely, she could have been an advertisement for summer fun in a blue jean skirt with a flimsy, flower top. She exuded something special that called to him. It had been hard, very hard to resist driving over, jumping out of the car, and pulling her inside. Becky looked good enough to eat, and he wanted a taste, but that would have ruined everything.

Grimm intended on following her home, and he did, along with stops at the grocery and liquor stores. Despite the thunderstorm, it had been impossible to lose the brightly colored car in what little traffic there had been. He had checked the address, then driven around to make sure he knew the area better than the back of his hand. She lived south of town toward Malakoff, in a neighborhood called Sun Chase. The houses were close together, and the lots weren't very large.

This morning Grimm had hauled himself out of bed, grumbling about the greasy waves in his gut, rippling throughout his body. After selling Buicks and hugging the porcelain god, Grimm had felt a little better. His stepfather, the Mighty Mayor of Temprance, and mother were long gone, when he snuck into their bedroom and dug through their medicine cabinet. The Valiums were easy to find, but hard to grind into dust, but he'd managed it with a hammer and a Ziploc bag.

The morning drive to Becky's had been sheer agony. The sun had been low in the sky, and shone through the front windshield like a thousand probing searchlights. Luckily, he had passed her driving to work just a block away from her house. He'd parked a decent distance away, walked to Becky's place through the undeveloped woods, and then had darted across the street, quickly cutting between her house and another. With an easy leap, he had cleared the fence. Somehow he had just known that no one had spotted him. Maybe he was invisible! The sliding glass door on her porch had been locked, but a bathroom window wasn't.

He'd almost become distracted, detouring into her bedroom when he'd spotted clothing scattered all over her bed, but he'd resisted and had headed to the kitchen. There everything had gone just perfect. There were two bottles of open wine in the fridge, a chablis and a white zinfandel. He'd added valium powder to both, as well as an open, two-liter Coca Cola and a container of orange juice. Sleepytime down south. The array of food, including marinating steaks, had revealed there were definite dinner plans in the making.

On his bicycle, he'd returned around dinner time. His mother thought he was locked in his room, brooding. While the music played, he'd snuck out the window.

"Awl's goin' perfect, Kevy. I think it's time."

"Yep. Hey, where's an elephant's sex organ?" Grimm waited, then said, "Its feet. 'Cause if he steps on you, you're fucked!" He closed his backpack and stood, throwing it over his shoulder. Before he left the shadows, he checked to make sure all his knives were in place. This time he'd added a piece, carrying a Saturday Night Special he'd found in his stepfather's nightstand. He'd take no shit-kicking this time.

Moving like the wind, Grimm quickly guided his bicycle across the street toward Becky's house. He dropped it in her front yard near Lou's pickup, then suddenly turned, and walked between the houses. Just like this morning, Grimm moved quickly and confidently, hopping the fence in one fluid motion. Waiting, he remained crouched at the base of the fence, where he blended with the darkness, clad in black pants and a navy T-shirt. The sliding glass door was open; the screen door closed, and the curtains drawn. A light was on in the living room, and C&W drifted across the backyard.

"Kevy, got a good one for you. The Pope is working on a crossword puzzle one Sunday afternoon. He stops for a moment, scratches his head, then asks the Cardinal, what's a four letter word for 'woman' that ends in u-n-t? Aunt, the Cardinal replies. Got an eraser? the Pope asks." They both chuckled.

With the author-dude setup with the buried bodies, it was time to take care of Lou and Becky and compound "Dick" Matthewson's problems. Grimm watched the curtains. No shadows and no sounds besides music—no groaning, laughing, or voices.

Grimm moved to the back door, passing a still-warm grill,

and stood pressed against the wall, listening to every little sound. He moved next to the screen door and laid his ear against it. Noise reached him. Grimm pulled on his gloves. He didn't know why, but he sensed that they were just on the other side of the curtain.

Taking a deep breath, Grimm pulled open the screen door and stepped inside. He pushed aside the curtain, and there they were, passed out and only partly clothed, just as he'd imagined. Looking beautiful and wanton, Becky was on her back with her short skirt hiked, legs spread, and blouse open. His jeans pulled down around the tops of his boots, Lou was atop her.

Grimm placed the pistol next to Lou's head. "Don't move." No response. He jammed the snout into the back of Lou's neck. He still didn't move. Smiling, Grimm pulled Lou off Becky. For a moment Grimm eyed her lustily, then sighed, and continued on with his masterpiece. He redressed the unconscious cowboy, and tied his boots together at the ankles with fishing line. Next he pulled a small towel and roll of masking tape out of his pack, and wrapped several revolutions around Lou's wrists.

Grimm stared at Becky again, taking in her long legs and their silent invitation. He sighed, deciding on business before pleasure. He walked into the kitchen and surveyed the dining table. It looked as if they'd gone directly from dinner to fucking. There was still food on the plates and in the serving dishes. A glass of wine and a Coke with all the ice melted were still half-full. He saw a bottle of Bacardi on the counter.

Grimm poured the white zinfandel down the sink. The other bottle was already empty and in the trash. Grimm rinsed them both, then put them in the wastebasket. He did the same with the two liter Coca Cola, as well as emptying the orange juice.

Removing two towels from the kitchen, he walked back to Becky. He wrapped one around her wrists, then taped them together. "Hey, heard the one about the special apple discovery? There was great excitement in the laboratory, when a famous scientist announced a new discovery. That is, until they heard it was an apple. That's nothin' new, his colleagues said, the apple has been around for a long time. Yes, the scientist said, but this apple is special. It tastes like pussy. Skeptical, one of his colleagues tries it, then quickly spits it out. Hey, this tastes like shit. Turn it around, the scientist said." Smiling, Grimm gagged Becky, then began to play with her, moving her about, turning her over, and doing what he'd wanted to do since he first saw her.

When he was sweaty, satisfied, and spent, Grimm dressed her, then bound her ankles as he had her wrists. "Sorry you missed it, honey, but it was good for me. You are one tight bitch. Nice ass, too. Like to do it again, but time is running short."

Grimm spent the next few minutes preparing a picnic dinner and a cooler full of drinks. He threw the bottle of Bacardi in the basket along with cheese, crackers, chips, some fruit, and one of the empty wine bottles. He found a tablecloth in the pantry and grabbed a roll of paper towels. He also cleaned the dishes, putting them in the dishwasher; once the kitchen was done, he turned on the dishwasher for good measure. The phone rang once, but he ignored it.

"Just good clean livin', Kevy."

Grimm found Lou's keys and hat on a counter. He put on the hat, then grabbed a blanket from atop the couch, and walked out to Lou's Comanche. Everything was going just fine. The truck bed even had a cover. Grimm unsnapped one side of it, then rolled back the cover. He grabbed his bicycle, put it in the bed, and then went back inside. Again Grimm was surprised at his own strength. Lou looked as though he might weigh at least one-eighty, but Grimm carried him easily.

As Grimm started to step outside, he heard, "And don't forget the butter this time." Damn, Grimm thought, roving eyes. He all but pulled the door close and waited impatiently, chewing on his lip. Finally, the car started, then pulled away. Eager but cautious, Grimm continued to wait in the doorway. Finally, the next-door neighbor's front door shut.

Grimm closed his eyes, sensing all was clear for the moment. He moved quickly, depositing Lou in the bed of the truck, then he did the same with Becky and snapped down the cover. The picnic basket and cooler went on the front seat next to him on the floor.

On his last tour through the house, he closed and locked the back door. He grabbed Becky's purse and keys, then closed and locked the front door. The neighborhood was still quiet as bedtime neared.

The Comanche started right up, the digital clock reading about nine-thirty-five. It had all taken a little over an hour. Putting the truck in reverse, Grimm backed out of the driveway and headed toward the Cedar Creek Dam.

Grimm drove extra carefully, making sure to stop at all signs and intersections, and kept just under the speed limits. Still, the drive only took about twenty minutes.

When he arrived at the gate, the moon, just past its quarter, was already above the lake to the west. After two days of storms the sky was clear, and the stars were dimmed near the lunar light, but brighter above, some just starting to show in the west. The humidity was slightly stifling, but a soft breeze blew, easing the oppression. "A great night for a picnic," Grimm said as he began to pick the gate lock.

He was finished in less than a minute. Opening it just enough to walk through, he returned to the Comanche. Grimm undid the snaps, then grabbed Lou—still dead to the world and soon to be dead period—and threw him over his shoulder.

"Killed by a vampire, right, Kevy?"

"Absolutely." Grimm grabbed the blanket and headed through the gate. It was about a hundred yards to the shoreline. There, he dumped Lou on the ground and laid out the blanket. Grimm threw Lou on top, then pulled an ice pick from his fanny pack. "Hey, bud, know why Puerto Ricans don't like blow jobs? It interferes with their unemployment checks!" With medical precision, Grimm delicately poked two holes in Lou's jugular and left him there to bleed to death. He got Becky and repeated the procedure with her, then set up the picnic scenario as the life drained from them.

Grimm opened the basket and set out some of the contents. He cut the cheese and left the knife next to it. He removed a chip from a bag of chips. He crumbled a cracker or two, then opened a couple of beers, and poured them in the lake. He threw the cans next to the blanket. Grimm did everything he and his friend could think of to make it look as though Lou and Becky had been having a picnic. Lastly, Grimm cut their bindings and put her towels in the basket.

Stepping back, he examined the entire scene. It looked pretty convincing. Just a loving couple having a picnic, when attacked by a vampire—one named David Matthewson, maybe? There would be no doubt, once they found Jim Bob's and Benny Joe's bodies. Already the town was buzzing about the mummified corpse Ross had found on the ranch earlier today. Somehow a picture had appeared in the afternoon edition of the paper.

Satisfied, Grimm returned to the Comanche, locking the gate on the way out. Somebody ought to find them in the next day or so, especially with all the volunteers searching for Jim Bob and Benny Joe.

Grimm pulled his old bicycle from the bed of the truck, adjusted his leather gloves, and then rode toward Temprance and the mayor's mansion. Soon, the shit would hit the fan, and everything would be just fine.

Six

Visitations

David felt as though he were slowly being lowered, extremities first, into a pool of ice. Sharp pains suddenly heralded a bone-chilling cold, and soon numbness reigned in another part of his body. Winter's malevolent touch continued to spread quickly, moving through his legs and arms. Freezing fingertips crawled up his stomach.

Was his exposure to the sun going to kill him? The chill-grip seized his throat, sealing it, then clutched at his chest. Despite his efforts, David couldn't cry out. He was going to be dead by the time somebody came back to check on him. On his way to heaven and not hell, David hoped, when Doc Katyu came to pronounce him deceased.

If it weren't for Monique's existence, David wouldn't have been distressed about dying, because he was so very tired of living. So much tragedy had dogged him over the last decade, and now he might outlive another family member, his mother this time, leaving only his sister. But then he might not; he was very, very sick—never before had he felt this bad.

Monique. Dead, but not dead. Able to think and act, although her body was dead. Almost as he was now. His body was lifeless, but David could still think. Dead, but not dead. How terrible, a curse even worse than his own.

David was suddenly very disoriented and found himself standing outside a derelict house—the abandoned place where he'd tried to destroy Monique—a faded and decaying structure in a lawn jungle of weeds. In the dark he was reminded of an evening long past, when as a youth he'd walked and whistled his way through a graveyard—a place alive, yet empty at the same time. In the air outside the house fluttered red weavings, alive but cold. One strand appeared sickly with unraveling threads.

Everything felt strange, but David didn't believe he was dreaming. More likely he was entranced, connected with Monique through some kind of horrible psychic bond. The world seemed real enough, but had a very odd texture, painted with emotions at a premium, sometimes extreme and short-lived. And David felt, in a truly strange way . . . craftier.

"You do not look well," he heard someone say with an accent. It sounded as if it was Monique. "I will be fine." It was Monique, except that she felt wrong, twisted and decaying. He had injured her badly! Thank God! Otherwise she would be after them right now. Suddenly, David started to feel ill, slight nausea and fever along with listlessness. Then he clutched at his throat, where a new pain was born, he felt as though he'd been branded.

"I think not. I will take care of him." David was confused. It sounded as though two spoke.

"He is strong in dat wretched faith. It lets him cling to de shade of his life and makes him dangerous. I believe you need my help once more." Were there two vampires here? And yet, David only felt Monique, her condition overwhelming and weakening him. "Dat accomplished little but to satisfy your tastes and harden his heart, fortify his strength. I was . . . am making progress. He can be very powerful among us, and maybe even show us how we may be filmed!"

"Filmed! And you have said dat *I* was conceited and self-centered. He may well destroy us. Listen, if things do not change quickly, it will be out of your hands, and maybe out of our hands." There were two, but then why he didn't sense the other? "You know as well as I do dat if he cannot be reasoned with, den he must be destroyed. He is either wid us, or against us. It is dat simple."

David heard his door swing open, the hinges squeaking, followed by a few footsteps. He was disoriented again, awake yet not awake. "He appears to be sleeping soundly," his mother said. David lost all contact with Monique.

"You know, I try not to, but I always feel sad for him, having to sleep during the day, and missing out on another glorious day," Carol said. "I try to pass on to the kids how wonderful it is playing outside in the sun, instead of staying inside and playing video games!"

Mom! Carol! Call Doc Katyu, David tried to scream, but nothing moved, the words were frozen solid in his thoughts and unable to take form. DEAD! Dead. Couldn't they see?

His mother touched his forehead, felt shakily for a pulse at his throat, and sighed, "He is sleeping. I can't believe I've been shopping and delivering for him for nine years.

"Ever since he refused to do his own shopping, because of what happened at the grocery store. I wish I'd been there. I would have shamed some neighbors, I imagine."

David started to drift away. He remembered people he knew staring at him. Kids pointing and whispering, while mothers clutched them close. He had been confused, hurt, and angry all at once. They said he looked like a freak. He still looked like a freak—was a freak—but not a vampire. Being dead would be all right, except that Monique still walked the earth! She was his personal curse. If he could destroy her, then he might rest in peace!

"The time he's been reclusive has only made matters worse," his mother said sadly. "I told him so, but he doesn't always listen to me anymore. Stories have already reached me, probably intentionally. People who haven't even seen him say he looks like a cadaver."

"In the grocery today," his sister continued, "I heard Jenny Burns telling Tom Henke about yesterday's volunteer meeting at the church, and she said she was sure David was involved, because he wrote about evil things. Where else, she said, would someone get such ideas, unless they were sick and wanted to act on them. Last night, Stan heard something similar at the hardware store. They were wondering what tools he'd used on the kids!"

"I used to hear whispers in the church, not from many, but some. It disgusts me. And these people call themselves Christians." His mother's voice rose, anger welling. "Oh, I'm getting angry and loud," his mother said. "We better go before I wake him." They turned to leave.

NO! Don't leave me alone! David tried to yell. But they were gone, the room empty again. As he drifted away, David could feel them go downstairs . . . feel their heat depart.

Sometime later, David was thrown alert by his rebelling stomach. He ran to the bathroom and began vomiting. Overwhelming heat ravaged him, as he emptied himself abruptly and brutally. Exhausted, he slumped on the commode; he was burning up, yet freezing at the same time. He needed some elixir!

David managed to stand, wash his face, and change his shirt. Walking made him dizzy, and the stairs were an ordeal. He tried to call out to his mother and sister in the kitchen, but his voice was still failing him. David stumbled to the front door, surprised that his family hadn't heard his clumsy journey. He thought about going to them, but how would he explain?

Managing to get outside where the night seemed oddly cool, David staggered to the barn. Surprisingly, no voices called out to him, so he made it to the barn unseen. David felt stronger as he opened the locks, then rushed to the refrigerator. The next few minutes were lost to him, sitting in the darkness finishing the first bottle. It brought him to vigorous alertness, nearly a rush of a high. He opened a second and drank. The second took away the burning and chills, then the shakes disappeared, too. David waited, and finally even his stomach felt a little better, although still somewhat queasy.

Now that he wasn't feeling so bad—and obviously not dead—David couldn't help but wonder which symptoms were his own, and which were Monique's. She had felt sick, her crimson string frazzled and twisted. If he could get better quickly, he could destroy her before she was too strong. But was someone else with her? Or was he just crazy?

David looked at the bottle of elixir in his hand. It seemed to have strange and wondrous powers. His sister had told him that herbal remedies could be miraculous. The dusty and damaged book the old librarian had given him was thick with remedies for virtually everything, including Witlessness. Inside the front cover, there was a handwritten note in ink, a gift from one friend to another. Several early pages, including the title page, were missing.

David loaded several bottles under his arm and walked back to the house. On the way up the front steps, he began to get light-headed and chilled. David grabbed the handrail with one hand, holding the bottles with the other. A shadow seemed to cross him, and he looked up. For a moment, he thought he saw Tina, but she was gone before he could do anything but think her name. David rushed up the steps, wheezing, "Tina," his voice still hoarse. Gone. David stood shakily, wondering if he'd been hallucinating. How was he to know, he wondered with frustration as he touched her locket. Tired once more, he wandered through the front door and trudged up the stairs. David put the bottles in the small cabinet under the nightstand, then collapsed on the bed.

* * *

Jana jumped out of her car and raced to David's front door, where she forced herself to pause and collect herself before calmly knocking. When Penny Matthewson opened the door, Jana was glad she'd swallowed her panic. The elderly woman's face was shaped by worry, but still Penny smiled. "Jana! Come in! What a pleasant surprise." Penny opened the door wider to invite her in.

"Thank you. Is David all right?" Jana blurted, then swallowed hard, holding down the insanity of what she had to tell David. She . . . It had been in her room with her!

"Now don't worry, Jana, we Matthewsons are pretty stubborn." Mrs. Matthewson gently took Jana's hand and guided her up the stairs. "When last we looked, David was sleeping soundly. That was a while ago. Let's go see. I know he'd want to see you." They reached the second floor. "When he was awake once, we talked about how you saved his life. I do want to thank you so." She gave Jana a motherly kiss on the cheek. "David needs all the friends he can get right now. Things are . . . but here I'm rambling, and you're here to see David. Go on in."

Jana paused at the door. "Mrs. Matthewson, David told me about your health. I'm sorry."

Penny shrugged. "Bodies break down over time, and I'm not young anymore. From what they tell me, the cure is worse than the curse. No thank you. I'm going to see David well, and then Carol and I are going traveling. The kids and I need to see Disney World." Without any sign of illness and only little signs of age, Penny descended the steps. Jana thought she was a marvelous woman.

Quietly opening the door, Jana stepped inside David's bedroom. Her anticipation and urgency gave birth to fear, when she saw him lying so still on the bed. He was thin and drawn, seemingly wasting away. But he did look better, his blisters almost gone, the skin now just blotchy and uneven. "David?

David, please wake up!" She moved to his side and sat on the bed. Hesitantly she took his hand in hers.

"David, you're looking better, and I don't understand why, just as with those dog bites and burns. But then there's a lot I don't understand. Am I going mad? Oh, David," Jana blurted out, almost weeping, "that wo—It came to see me last night. She was looking . . . better, but not well. It was hard to tell, her face changed, and . . . She says you're a . . . a vampire and wants me to join you. Has offered to help me join you in . . . in . . . not being dead. Being immortal. Oh, God," Jana began to cry. "I know that sounds crazy, and I wish you were awake, 'cause I know you'd understand. I'm at my wits' end. What if she comes back tonight?

"David, is she really a vampire? Can she do what she says?" Jana softly caressed his forehead, then kissed him. "David, please wake up, so you can tell me what to do." She wanted to know, but wouldn't shake him to awaken him "Maybe I should talk with Michael, but he'd think I was a lunatic." Suddenly, David shook his head. "David?"

His voice had finally returned, and David said hoarsely, "No Michael. Nobody else dies. I don't want you to die either. I . . . care a lot about you, and we've only just began to get reacquainted. I heard what you said about Monique, but I couldn't speak. I'm weak, but I am getting better, I think, just not well enough yet." David squeezed her hand, trying to reassure her. "Although I am weak, maybe we could protect each other. Would . . . would you care to stay until this is over?"

"Yes, I don't want to face her alone again. Thank you," Jana hugged him. "I am so glad you're getting better." Jana thought he was healing before her eyes, then assumed she was imagining it.

"We can't hunt Monique; we must wait for her to come here. Maybe prepare a trap. But, Jana, you need to help me think of a reason to send my mother away! Please! I don't want to, but I have to. Monique will come here, maybe tonight!"

"David, calm down. Monique . . . It doesn't commit random slaughter," Jana told him.

David stared at her for a long time, then finally said, "You're right."

"I still think we should talk with Michael."

"No," David sighed. "No more deaths, too many deaths. My mother is dying; the teenagers are being murdered; Tina and Timmy are dead; and my father and sister are long gone. I don't want to lose anyone else! Not you . . . not anyone! I can't handle it! And that's the whole problem! I feel as if I should have been able to do something to save them, but I couldn't. I even brought this terrible sickness on myself! And there is nothing, absolutely nothing worse than not seeing the sun . . ."

"You will pull through. Your mother says the Matthewsons are stubborn."

"Pigheaded."

"Yes!" Jana replied, then smiled. "Your mother and I spoke. I don't think getting her to leave will be a problem. She said once you're getting better, she and Carol are taking the kids to Disney World."

"Then if I convince her I'm capable of taking care of myself, you think she'll go?"

"Only if I stay and help."

"Only if you stay and help?"

"Uh-huh. Your mother likes me being here, I can tell."

"Oh. Good." David was silent for a minute. "I hate to have her go, there's still so much to say, and if . . ." David wrung his hands. Jana took them once more. "But it's for her own good. We'll set a trap and catch Monique!" David vowed. "Then everybody will be safe, and we can sort things out."

Seven

Grisly Discovery

By the light of a peach sunrise, Logan drove along the oil-dirt farm roads, while his mind wandered. To escape having to be alert and watchful, he had driven away from Temprance. North of town and toward the lake, it was deserted and peaceful, even quieter on Sunday mornings when both weekenders and ranchers were resting. No stop signs, dogs, kids, or anything else. All he wanted to do was drive. It helped him think, and it was good practice to go patrolling. Many times Logan had discovered things on both his mental and physical rounds through the countryside.

Tonight Logan hadn't been able to sleep, and he couldn't blame it on a nightmare. He just couldn't turn off his mind. Bricker was right; there was something very wrong in Temprance. Now that he gave it careful thought, Logan had sensed something off-key ever since the Friday he'd gone out to see David because of Claire's phone call. So much had happened since then. Three of the six juveniles were missing. A fourth was catatonic, and another terribly burned. At least one kid was involved in drugs. A house had been burned, killing at least two people and damaging lots of property. And they'd found a mummified body on David Matthewson's ranch!

How could it be one of the missing boys? It looked very old. Actually, now that Logan thought about it, the corpse hadn't really looked old, as much as dehydrated—shriveled as a prune.

All this crap had the town in an emotional uproar, beating the bushes to no avail, and getting impatient. Some were getting scared. Rumors and guesses, sometimes even outright lies flooded Temprance. The townspeople were demanding that the sheriff's department do something—anything—to settle things. Logan couldn't blame them; they were worried about what was going to happen next. And so was he.

Neighbor was suspicious of neighbor. Usually they were only wary of strangers. Everybody had thought they knew everybody else, but now they weren't quite so sure. The town was on edge, and the Reverend Wright wasn't helping any. Word around was he'd advised the Reverend Page not to let David return to the church.

Logan could almost feel the explosion coming. And while it might not be David's fault, somehow the storm whirled about him like a Biblical plague.

Logan looked ahead and saw the entrance to the MX ranch. Surprisingly, the gate was open. Logan would've expected it to be closed.

It was too bad that David was very ill once again. Despite the tragedies he'd endured, David was a fine man and an excellent writer. Despite his distress, he'd actually been looking better than ever the last time Logan had seen him. How quickly things could turn in life, good and bad.

As Logan drove on, the thought of the open gate bothered him. Could the Tubbs boys be visiting again? Something beyond vandalism and graffiti? They were capable of it. Logan was surprised David hadn't filed a complaint. Of course, if he were sick, he had more pressing concerns. Speaking of files though, Logan still needed to do some research on the

Friday night incident at David's ranch. There was so much to do, he sighed heavily.

The thought of the Tubbs boys coming to the farm continued to nag Logan. Just as he'd decided to turn around and check on David, Logan spotted a red pickup parked next to the gate on the service road to the dam. It was a tricked-up Comanche, with all the bells and whistles, looking very, very sharp—the urban cowboy look. The passenger door was open, and the bed cover was hanging over the side of the truck.

Logan stopped the Mustang, then got out, and searched all about the truck. There didn't appear to be anything wrong or out of the ordinary, besides the door being left open. He glanced at the gate. It was easy to climb, and this wouldn't be the first time someone had done so. It was one of the more popular off-limits spots.

Logan walked back to his Mustang and got his ticket pad. Trespassing would be the charge, a minor violation and a fine. He filled out the ticket slowly, hoping that somebody would return or he'd see movement. As he put the ticket under the windshield wiper, Logan noticed that the cab light was out. With the door standing open, it should be on. Was it burnt out? Or had the door been open for a long time? If so, they would need a jump. Logan got into the car and tried the lights. Nothing. He had a bad feeling about this. As Logan climbed out of the Comanche, he unsnapped his holster.

Before he climbed the fence, Logan used the radio to awaken Bricker. Logan informed him of the situation. Bricker gave him thirty minutes to call back, then he was coming out.

The sturdy gate was an easy climb. At the top, the barbed wire had been bent and rearranged so many times, that a permanent gap remained. Logan squeezed through it, climbed down, and walked along the dirt road toward the lake. It was too quiet, almost preternaturally so.

Logan soon spotted the owners of the pickup. The two people were asleep on a blanket, entangled as lovers. At least they're dressed, Logan thought. The last ones he'd interrupted hadn't been. Logan noted the basket and ice chest and figured it was a picnic—some kind of sunrise breakfast. Food, chips, and beer cans were scattered about. Then Logan saw the blood on the guy's shirt and stopped cold, his face flinching before becoming stony. There was plenty of blood, all over.

Logan jogged to the bodies. They were set in such a fashion that he couldn't tell who was bleeding. Their shirts, his pants, and her skirt were saturated. His eyes widened as he searched the man for a throat pulse and found wounds in his neck. Logan checked on the woman and found an identical situation. They were both stone dead.

Logan immediately began searching for the murder weapon. He started with the picnic basket and spiralled outward. Nothing. He couldn't put his finger on it, but there was something odd about this, besides the way they'd died.

It was after he'd walked back to the car, climbed the fence, and called Bricker, that Logan identified the missing element. There wasn't any sign of a struggle. He wondered if the autopsy would find any bruises. Well, Doc Katyu might be able to tell them something before they sent the bodies to the county coroner.

Stones was in a limping hurry. He left his car, tossed his cane over the fence, and began to climb. He'd hurriedly parked his car across the street in a field, on the other side of the rise, north of the gate to the dam, and out of sight of the sheriff's car.

Stones slipped several times during his climb, because he couldn't put his full weight on his bad ankle, but he wasn't going to let a bum wheel stop him. Stones got caught in the barbed wire several times as it grabbed his shirtsleeve, camera bag, and pants. Finally he made it over to the other side and grabbed his cane; crutches were too bulky. He would just have to gut it out. Possibly the biggest story in his life, and he was a gimp!

Murder was always big news. Always. Out here it was even bigger. Things just seemed to be getting more and more interesting, and Stones was loving it. Soon, he'd have something he could send out to the big papers. Stones remembered thinking that Temprance was a sleepy, boring news town. That had thankfully changed.

Grimacing, Stones worked his way toward the dam. He leaned heavily on the cane and cursed often. He tried to stay in the shadows and behind trees, stopping often to rest and wheeze, then hobbling determinedly onward. Already he was drenched in sweat. The humid air was thick enough to slice with a knife.

Stones knew he was near when he heard the sheriffs' voices. He waited until they grew quieter, then moved toward the lake shore. Through the trees and about forty yards away, he saw the gathering. Stones quickly found a concealed spot and prepared his camera and minitripod.

With a telephoto and multiplier he began snapping pictures. Great stuff! This might get him back to the big city, all right. Two dead, slaughtered at a picnic. He would get the details from Ross later. How many missing? How many dead? Stones couldn't wait to see the edition of the Tuesday afternoon *Times*. He was going to set this town on fire!

Eight

Restless

Absentmindedly fondling her crucifix, Jana stood before the dresser mirror in the guest room. The cross caught the light, and she wondered if it truly had the power to stop Mon— to stop It. Fire had not; Jana prayed the sign of the Lord would. She thought she heard a swish of cloth behind her and glanced up at the mirror. Nothing. She was just jumpy, that's all. No one was in the house but David.

It had been surprisingly easy to convince Mrs. Matthewson to go home with Carol. Once she saw that David was fine, or looked fine, she had slipped away so that she no longer intruded on them. She was a sweet woman and a dear soul. Once alone, David had immediately begun to prepare the house for Monique's visit, putting up crosses everywhere.

Jana looked carefully at herself in the mirror. Even though she was almost forty, she had looked youthful until two days ago. Now her eyes were dark-circled and hollow, with just a hint of confusion tainting them; she didn't understand what was going on with David—or with her and David. Jana touched her face. Her cheekbones were gaunt and bruised, while the flesh around her lips was pinched. And was that a gray hair?!

"You're so vain, but aren't all beautiful women?" came a heavily accented voice from behind her. Jana's eyes flashed to look behind herself in the mirror. Nothing. "I believe I can see why David cares for you."

Jana whirled around, angry. One look at Monique quelled that fire, and fear clutched her. Under Monique's stare, Jana was held fast, as though gripped in a bear hug. She was having trouble breathing. "I . . . I . . ." she struggled to raise her crucifix.

"Don't bother," Monique said disdainfully. She coughed once, then continued. "I will not stay long. Ah, I see you have told him. I am not surprised. Listen to me, my little lovebird, your time is running out. And David's time is running out. You both need to make a decision, to live a different existence, or to be destroyed. Look into my eyes, drink of the visions, then ponder your fate, for you have little time to decide."

Jana tried once more to look away, but failed. She could see David in Monique's eyes. He looked very healthy, if a little pale, and so was she. Jana's natural tan was absent, but she was smiling, holding David's arm. They were traveling, she believed she was in London. Yes, there was Big Ben. And then they were in Venice, a nighttime serenade under the full moon, while lazing in a gondola. Then Rome and the ruins under the lights. The shadows and walls were speaking to her, and she could understand them! David was with her, laughing and smiling.

They were in Tokyo among all the bright lights, the hustle and bustle. There were people everywhere, crowding and on the go—living, having it all. She began to grow hot, then her travels continued to Paris, Milan, and Zurich. Off the Greek shore, they sailed the Caribbean. In Monte Carlo they gambled, then traveled by snowmobile under the moonlight in the Alps. She loved the mountains. Jana had always wanted to see them and other places she'd dreamed of while watching those travel shows—places faraway from Dallas.

They continued traveling, seeing and doing, but mostly there was David. He was writing about their adventures, selling them as fiction. He was rich and successful, writing under several different names, even David Matthewson, Jr.! And yet, there was no child. No family. Just the two of them. Oddly enough, it felt a little lonely, empty and sad. It wasn't what she'd expected.

"You would have all the time in the world," Monique told her. "And there are many ways to fill it. You could learn to play the flute." Jana gasped. It knew! "Sharpen your neglected painting skills and much more. Think of it! You and David would be together forever. Soon, we will both get what we want from David, whether he's dead or alive," Monique chuckled, then left, stepping into a shadow gate and disappearing. Released, Jana crumpled to the floor and began weeping.

David was tired, and despite his promises to forge ahead and finish his preparations, he sat down on the bed and drank a glass of water. He wanted to collapse, but knew he couldn't afford it. Monique might arrive at any time, and he wasn't ready for her yet!

Suddenly his skin crawled, and David felt a chill. Swirling about him was the odor of perfume overlaying a slight scent of rotting. Monique was here! Close by! In his house! David jumped to his feet, and grabbed his silver cross and Bible off the nightstand.

He rushed for the doorway, but Monique reached it first, leaning against it and striking a seductive pose. Appearing healthy, the vampire was clad in a gauzy black dress that hid nothing but revealed little. Her lustrous hair was pulled back, held by a red ribbon which matched the color of her crimson lips. She ran a red gloved hand invitingly down her shapely body. Her legs were clad in black as well, but her pumps were red. Spinning away, then stepping back into the doorway, she struck another pose and smiled for him.

David thrust his cross at her, and Monique winced. "Surprised to see me, *Liebling?*" Monique licked her lips. "You do not look well, sit down and rest." She waved at the bed.

"Get out of my house . . . Jana! Jana! . . ." David rushed forward.

Monique held out both hands as though to stop him. "She is fine, fine, just resting. I haven't touched her—yet. I may let you do de honors," she laughed. "You know, David, I was serious. You don't look well, but the transformation always makes one look sickly. You'll look better when you're fully dead. I know I do."

David advanced with his cross, but Monique just stood there. "I came to tell you dat your time is short. My offer for . . . training," she smiled, "is only of limited duration. You must either consent to accept your true nature . . . or," she adjusted a glove, "you won't have to worry any longer about outliving anyone, even your mother. Simply, become one of the brethren or die; and dat would be so sad, when there is so much we could teach each other. You about the cross and television—"

"The only reason I live now is to destroy you!" David began reading from the Bible with his cross held as a vanguard.

Monique grudgingly backed away. "I doubt your words. Remember, I know you. Can read you. You are tired of being alone. You care about Jana and desire to spend time with her; but the only way she can, and surely you know this deep down, is to have her join you in the world of the undead. You have more than one foot already there, my shade. And what about your writings? Don't you live for them, live through them?!"

"By all that is holy . . ." David continued reading. Monique coughed, then appeared to have a fit. In exasperation, she flailed about, no longer paying any attention to David. Seeing his chance, he rushed toward her with his cross, ready to strike. Monique suddenly whirled, slashing his face with her fingernails, then she sailed down the stairs as though borne by the wind. David reeled, clutching his face, then blindly tried to follow her down the stairs. Pulling away, Monique raced out the front door and into the night.

Enough of her; Monique was long gone. Jana! David rushed back upstairs. He found her in the guest room, sitting on the floor and weeping. "Jana, are you all right?" David sat next to her and took her in his arms. She continued to cry, but nodded. David touched her neck and found only smooth skin. "Thank heaven." He drew her in close and hugged her as she continued to cry. David tried to say that everything would be all right, but couldn't manage the words.

Outside he heard a car pull up, stop, and then a door slammed. "Who now?" David said, quickly standing and rushing to the window. David quickly undid the blinds and opened the windows and shutters. He knew the stout figure with the gentle walk and air of calmness. "Jana," David went back to her. She was watching him, the tears having stopped for the moment. "It's the Reverend Page. If you'll be okay, I'm going to send him away. I'll be back. Will you be all right? I don't feel Monique's presence." Jana nodded. David briefly hugged her, then grabbed a towel, and staunched his facial wounds. The reverend would probably think it was just another one of his many problems. David ran downstairs and opened the door just as the Reverend Page was preparing to knock. "Hello, Reverend."

"Ah, good evening, David. I am glad to see you up and about. Oh my! Your face! Are you all right?" the reverend asked, obviously aghast at David's appearance. David simply nodded, trying to look nonchalant. Disconcerted, the reverend looked about the house at the graffiti and vandalism. "Um... have you been attacked... the place?"

"Thank you for caring," David said honestly as he dabbed at his face. "The sheriff's department is taking care of it."

"Good, I mean . . . well," the Reverend Page was obviously thrown by what he'd seen. Pausing for a breath and straightening his shirt, he asked, "Is Penny with you?"

"No, she just left." David checked again for Monique and couldn't detect her presence; the house was safe for now. It was just as well; he wasn't in any shape to fight her, let alone pursue her. Still, she might return at any time, so he needed to get the reverend to leave. No one else must be at risk.

"Well, this would be a good chance for us to chat. May I come in?"

"I'm sorry to be rude," David said, "but I'm still not feeling well. Doc Katyu said I'm having a porphyria attack, as well as some kind of flu or viral infection along with it. He said I might still be contagious. I'd hate for you to catch what I have."

"Oh my, trouble comes in bushels sometimes." Page looked momentarily dejected. "Well, Doc Katyu is a good man, he and the Lord will return you to health." He paused, then said cryptically, "If you also want good health, that is. How are you bearing the burdens, my son?"

"I am very tired, and to tell the truth, not well."

"Would you like to talk about it?"

"Another time, Reverend, tonight is not the night. I don't believe it's in anyone's best interest to be around me tonight."

"I see. Well, just remember, there may or may not be much time to talk things out. Your mother called me earlier today, and asked if I'd come out. I was distressed when I heard the news about her illness and your relapse. I will stop and see her. Is she at the Hansons?" the reverend asked.

David nodded, then said, "Please don't worry her. She thinks I'm doing better. I promise to tell her soon."

"I will be diplomatic, I promise. Good night, David." The reverend started to turn, then paused, to offer one last word of consolation and advice. "Death is so sad, but it's part of the natural course of God. Come talk with me soon, or call me, David. We haven't talked since Monday, and I still want to see you more at church. Ignore Daniel Wright and come directly to see me. I know you have a phobia about death, but denial and avoidance are not good ways to handle it. Just remember, miracles have not been forgotten. Don't lose hope. Good night and God bless."

"Good night, Reverend. I'll call when this is over."

"We have been praying for you at the church." Cooper waved, then climbed into his white Camry.

As David watched him drive away, he wondered about that—and much else the reverend had said. He had been able to see in the reverend's eyes that there were problems in the church. His congregation was split over the issue of David, as well as other things. His mother had also said as much. Pushing it all aside, David rushed upstairs to check on Jana. As he went, David vowed to let no more harm come to her, even if it cost him his life.

Nine

Rebellion

Staring down over the edge of the shuddering spillway, Grimm stood alone in the mist-shrouded darkness. It was a long way down, the gray wall disappearing and melding into the fog where the rushing of the river—usually a bubbling creek—could clearly be heard. The trembling underfoot—as tons of water were released—and the fog, gave the roadway the ambiance of otherworldliness. Instead of the cool winds usually found atop a mountainous pinnacle, it was hot and muggy. Grimm smiled as he stood high above and apart from the world.

Back at the scene of the crime, Grimm thought, to where Monique tried to turn him into her undead servant. He spat over the edge, then smiled. He was ready and waiting to finish it—finish her. He would enjoy putting a wrap on the last of the paybacks, first Lou and Becky, now Monique, and soon, he supposed, the writer-dude, "Dicky" Matthewson. Kevy always got the last laugh, and it didn't matter to him that PP and Skeeter had already gotten theirs without his participation.

Somehow Monique had summoned him to this spot, sending an urgent message with images of the spillway to him. Well, Grimm thought, she was expecting a simple lamb hurrying to slaughter, but what she would find was a bull ready to batter and butt. Grimm nervously ran one hand through his slicked-back hair, then caressed the walking stick he carried. It was specially made for the occasion. At the end he had carved three niches, and inset a trio of crosses he'd taken from his mother's jewelry box. He also placed a smaller one in the butt. Grimm had tried to wear one on a chain, but had become sick, then disgusted with the idea. He couldn't wear what he didn't believe. Where was this savior when he'd needed him years ago? Grimm spat again.

"Why did Jesus fail to get into college?" Grimm said, then paused before answering himself. "Because he got hung up on his boards."

Grimm chuckled. He didn't need that kind of protection; with the help of his friend, their combined will was stronger than Monique's. She wouldn't enthrall, let alone touch him, ever again. This would be her final performance—a death scene. No, a scene of self-destruction. She had created the monster.

"That's right, Kevy, we gonna give that undead bitch a taste of 'er own medicine."

"Hey, my man, what do eating pussy and the Mafia have in common?" Grimm asked. He could feel his friend shrug. "One slip of the tongue, and you're in deep shit!" Grimm abruptly stopped laughing and looked around, tensing as though ready for flight or a fight.

Twisting and swirling like a genie being freed from a magic lamp, the fog began to whirl all about him. Well, Grimm smiled, readying himself, he only wanted one wish. Alert, he held tightly to his walking staff, as the air grew ever colder, a biting chill snapping at him. "A cold bitch, Kevy. Be cagey."

The summer night became winter, and soon the pale-faced bitch stood before Grimm. He took on a simple and obedient expression, hating it, but hiding his emotions. Grimm kept his eyes lowered, knowing she could read his eyes and know his thoughts. He didn't want to spoil the surprise.

"Ah, thrall. How nice it is to have someone obey my whim, unlike—" Monique bit off David's name. Her anger swelled and she flushed, her nostrils flaring and her lips tightening. As Monique silently fought to control herself, she clenched and unclenched her hands.

After a glance, Grimm noticed that Monique didn't look quite right. Her pale skin lacked its usual sheen, and her dark eyes hinted at weariness. Even her hair had lost some of its lustre, and the ever-present arrogance was now gone from her beautiful features. Instead of being clad in something seductive, Monique was dressed in a long, black robe with a hood. A red scarf was softly wrapped about her throat, so that virtually no flesh was visible. Grimm wondered what was wrong, then pushed away the thought, trying to be empty of mind.

"It matters not," Monique finally recovered and continued grandly. "I am weary and famished, to tell the truth, but I cannot afford to leave any more bodies to be discovered. There is already too much suspicion, too many whispers about our kind. We cannot let it grow into more. Fear is only effective when people do not know what dey fight, but den you know this, because we are two of a kind. Now, come here! I wish to kill something!" Monique screamed, then calmed a little. "But tonight I will make do with a simple feasting. Do not worry, you will not die . . . tonight. I still have plans for you."

But you will die tonight, Grimm thought as he did as he was told. Trying to relax, he plodded toward her. Obedience was not something that came easy. Grimm didn't crack a smile as he thought, *she's gonna look like a mashed potato covered with catsup in a minute.*

Smiling confidently, Monique glided closer. She took his head in her hands—strange how she could seem taller—then bent forward, ready to kiss his neck. She coughed once, and then Grimm struck with all his might, slamming the end of his modified walking stick into the soft flesh underneath her jaw. Monique's head snapped back, her teeth clacking together. Flesh sizzled at the brutal touch of the holy sign, and Monique staggered backwards toward the guardrail at the edge of the spillway.

Laughing and yelling, "Take this, you undead bitch!" Grimm drove the butt of the staff into her stomach.

Monique doubled over and groaned. She couldn't understand what was happening. He was hers!

"Yes, I have broken your hold! I am stronger than you now! Much Stronger!" Grimm chopped, then hammered at her exposed back, pounding her repeatedly, until she was driven gasping and screaming to her knees. Grimm paused for a moment, and she lifted her head. Smiling, Grimm rammed the walking stick into the side of her face. Screaming as the crosses scorched flesh, Monique collapsed onto her side, writhing and grasping at her face.

"You know, I have half a mind to show you what a real stick can do!" Grimm laughed. "But as I said before, I'm not into necrophilia. And you're just too dangerous, so I'll beat you to death, kind of like stoning in the old days. But we'll call it sticking it to ya!" With all his might, he struck her again and again. Monique tried to cover up and protect herself, but soon her arms were blistered and smoking.

Grimm stuck the stick between her legs. Monique screamed, bolted upright, and struck the staff in the middle, snapping it in two. "What the hell?" Monique swept a foot outward and knocked Grimm's legs from under him.

He fell hard, his head striking the concrete. As with being kicked in the head by a horse and Lou's blows, Kevin saw a flash of white, but this time there was the roaring of jets in his ears. Still, he struggled to his knees, ready to use the broken staff.

Too weak to continue combat, Monique rolled to the edge

of the dam and slid under the guardrail. With another roll, she slipped over the side and disappeared into the mists below.

Sometime later, Monique pushed open the front door of her sanctum and collapsed onto the floor. A shadow touched her as someone stood over her. *"Mien Gott,* Monique! You do not look well, *schwester.* It appears you cannot even handle my thrall, can you?" The shapely woman lording over Monique suddenly broke into a haughty laugh, then her red lips twisted into a sneer. She was dark-haired and starkly beautiful, in the same way as Monique had been. Monique's companion also dressed with shock in mind, her black outfit leaving little to the imagination. "Den certainly you can't cope with David. I do believe it is time to give you more unwanted help."

"Marlena, you are such a bitch," Monique said, as she tried to sit up but failed. "I will recover, *lieb schwester,*" Monique finished, sounding exhausted.

"You do look battered and famished. Do you need a meal brought to you, as if you are an infant?" the pale woman with fathomless eyes asked. "Yes, I see you do. Poor baby, you have lost all your strength. After what you've done to me, *lieb schwester,*" Marlena said bitterly, "I should just let you die, but it is not my decision alone to make."

Marlena moved to leave, but turned at the door. "Don't worry, we shall set things straight tomorrow, putting an end to David's resistance and Grimm's rebellion. I know how to handle them both. This will be fun, maybe even more than the first time." Chuckling, Marlena departed, leaving Monique on the floor, weak and cursing.

Ten

A Body of Evidence

Ross jumped out of his car and ambled to a pay phone. He'd just left Doc Katyu's office and a meeting with Candel, Bricker, and the mayor. Logan and Bricker had said they were going to the office, and the mayor had said he had a headache and was going home to rest. Along with a phone call, Ross had some money to make. He was almost bursting with the news.

Ross squeezed inside the phone booth and pulled the door partly closed, then changed his mind. He would cook if he shut the door. His pimply brow was already damp. Twisting, he faced the phone and stuck in a quarter, then dialed the *Times'* number.

A woman answered, *"Temprance Times."*

"Corey Stones, please." As Ross waited, his head swiveled around, nervously watching for people watching him. What if someone discovered he was leaking sheriff's business?

"Stones here. Who's this?"

"It's Ross."

"Ah, Bubba! Hey, big guy, got any juicy news?"

"Do I ever, but it's worth at least double the usual."

Stones paused, then said, "Let me be the judge of that."

"We were called to Dr. Katyu's office early this morning. He'd finished the autopsy on the mummified body I found on the Matthewson Ranch."

"Who's we?"

"Mayor Campbell, Sheriff Bricker, Deputy Candel, and myself."

"And?"

"The dental records on the body match those of JJ Tubbs."

"JJ Tubbs! Honestly? How can that be? The pictures you gave me make it look like that body has been dead longer than Jimmy Hoffa."

"I know, I know. It gets weirder," Ross still drawled, despite his racing words. He was no longer perspiring from the heat, but sweating from the excitement. This might even be worth triple! "The autopsy, Doc Katyu said, revealed several things he can't explain yet. Anyway, something caused accelerated decomposition."

"It's obvious he didn't die of natural causes," Stones said sarcastically. Ross could hear him drag on his cigarette.

"Yeah, well get this. The autopsy also revealed a lack of blood. JJ was totally drained."

"Bled to death."

"The doc thinks that might be why the body was found in the shape it was." Stones started to speak, but Ross continued, "The problem with the theory on bleeding to death were the wounds. Katyu also found tiny bite marks on JJ's neck, on the jugular he said. They were very neat, not like any type of animal bite, no ripping or tearing."

"Are you telling me some kind of vampire killed JJ?"

"I'm telling you what Doc Katyu said the autopsy revealed. He knows he bled to death, but not how he was wounded. There's no sign of a struggle, and the clothing wasn't stained."

"You're bullshitting me!"

"I am not! They don't know what killed JJ. When the mayor

mentioned a vampire, the others looked at him like he was crazy. You should have seen Bricker's face, he was outraged."

"What about Candel?"

"He didn't say much. Just seemed kind of thoughtful."

"Hmmm."

"Doc Katyu said he'd continue his investigation, but that there was no reason to continue searching for JJ. We've found him. I expect they'll release the news in a couple of days."

"What about the bodies found at the dam? They weren't decomposed or shriveled up," Stones interrupted. "What do they know about them?"

"Doc Katyu said he hadn't finished, but he should be done in a day or two. He has to send test results to Dallas, then the bodies off to the county coroner."

"Does he think there's any similarity?"

"He didn't say, but there were similar marks on their necks. I saw them. Two holes in the jugular vein."

"Okay, okay, keep me posted. I have a story to write. And, Bubba, this is definitely worth double. Same goes for the information on the picnickers. See ya, big boy, you got a big dinner coming as a bonus." Ross was beaming as Stones hung up.

Leaning back in his chair, Stones also wore a huge smile. A vampire had killed JJ. Sure. And probably the picnickers. Right! He wondered about the Brookens boys. Did it get them, too? It didn't matter. In fact, it didn't really matter, if it was a vampire or not. The truth was not important. In today's world, perception was much more powerful than reality. The people would *think* it was a vampire, and that's all that counted. He had a helluva story!

Stones turned on his computer. This type of story was self-generating; once it found momentum, it would make its own news. This was going to sell a lot of papers, and get him back to the big time!

Eleven

Stirring the Pot

Weary from being a cane-carrying cripple, but excited about the state of his story, Corey Stones left the central square and walked a few feet to the First Street Club. The combination bar, grill, and pool hall had been around for over fifty years. It was old and well worn, but not run-down by any means. Over the years, it had taken over the entire brick building, expanding from its original space to occupy a shop on the left and an office on the right. Those spaces now held pool tables. Stones knew that plastered along the paneled walls were pictures of America's Team, the Mavericks, and the Rangers. The Cowboy cheerleaders had one wall to themselves.

Most of the facade was tinted storefront windows surrounded by wood, not aluminum. Neon beer signs were proudly displayed in the windows. Another sign, not made of neon, read RANGERS VS A'S BIG SCREEN. If nothing else, the First Street Club was adaptable; it was now converted into a sports bar. If one wanted to drink, membership was required by county law.

Stones certainly didn't come here for the forgettable company, the inexpensive drinks, or the not particularly memorable food. He came to the First Street Club because it was close to work, and most importantly, a local favorite, thereby a hotbed for gossip and news. No other grapevine compared to it for current events, not even the church's bingo games.

Nimbly but not gracefully, Stones stumbled through the front door. Despite having been here many times, he paused, as was his way upon entering a room. When you wrote for the paper, and were good at it, you made enemies. They knew your face, but you didn't know theirs.

The First Street Club was a little less than half-full, but active. The background noise reminded Stones of a citified night in the country, the hum of crickets and frogs replaced by the mingling of conversations and television sets on low. The bluish haze might have been late night mists in a ravine.

With a long glance, Stones looked for faces he recognized. Off to the right at the four pool tables, Stones didn't see anybody he knew. Stones never knew if that was good or bad. The more people he knew in town, the more he knew what to expect.

Ahead and to the left was the original bar and central hub of the club. It was all made of fine but well-worn oak. The brass-railed bar stretched almost the entire length of the room, ending at the left wing where balls clacked together on more pool tables. At the far end of the bar, trouble was brewing in the form of the right to assemble and freedom of speech.

The Tubbs boys—Rick, Hank, and Buck—were throwing beers back and talking with Ernie Nathaniel, Zane Harkness, Jack Huntington and several others he recognized as henpecked hubbies who talked big when they were out with the boys. The two stout brothers looked as though they were bookends for the tall drink of water and quiet ringleader, Rick. From the look of things, they'd all been here for a while. The group wasn't rowdy yet, just a bit glassy-eyed and extremely animated; lots of gesticulating, pointing, and waving were going on. A few regulars—Kenny Mays the plumber, and Bart who worked at the hardware store, as well as the guys from

Gus's Garage who were still in greasy overalls—had been playing pool, but were now gravitating toward the discussion at the end of the bar.

Stones hobbled closer. There was a place open at the bar just a couple seats down from the crowd. He dragged himself to the spot and sat down. Rich Stiff, the bartender, saw him right away and did as he was tipped very well to do. Silently and without show, he brought Stones a soda with lime. Stones put his elbows on the bar and stared at the bar top, concentrating on hearing the discussion at the end of the bar.

"I heard it was a mummy they found," somebody said. "Well, not exactly. It wasn't actually wrapped up, but shriveled up like a raisin." Stones thought it was Jack Huntington, a retired Army man who was rumored to have once been an officer in the Alabama KKK. Somebody else laughed. A crude comment was made about California Raisins, then California in general.

"A body's a body," Ernie slurred. "Ain't never found one on my farm." He sounded dejected.

"Just alien molting skins," came a laughing reply from one of Gus's guys.

"But they didn't find anything else in the search," Zane told them. "It hasn't been proven that David has done anything wrong. He hasn't even been charged."

"So he's tricky, look at the books he writes," one of the Tubbs boys rumbled, slightly slurring his words. "He's gotta be clever." Stones glanced up. The scar on his face meant he was Buck. Hank, who had terrible teeth, was sitting closest to him and was chewing tobacco. They were both wearing their cowboy hats. Rick didn't, wearing instead the look of someone thinking too hard about something.

"And what about Becky Sue Handley and Lou Callahan? They were murdered near his property!" Stones recognized the gravely voice of Old Man Watson.

"They were found dead at the dam. That's the state's property, and not the same," Zane defended David.

"Bullshit," Kelly Mane offered. Besides working at Gus's, he worked as a fishing guide on Cedar Creek. He was a ruthless character, doing whatever needed for money.

"It's close enough," Hank squawked. "He could easily walk there. Heck, the way I hear it, about twenty years ago it was the Matthewson property before the government took it and made Cedar Creek Lake." They were getting louder, Stones thought. He'd arrived just in time.

"I heard they bled to death," Billy Bob Barker said, fondling a pool cue. He was tall, freckled, and redheaded. Stones wondered if he were twenty-one.

"I heard they were bit in the neck by a vampire," Ernie slurred.

Dick Grissom, Gus's barrel-chested mechanic, gently slapped Ernie on the shoulder, and said, "Did the aliens who landed in your backyard tell you this?" Several people hooted and laughed. Everyone knew Ernie well, and even laughed when Zane started to defend him, but Ernie spoke up for himself.

"Hell no! They don't know nothing about earth vampires," the postmaster sounded exasperated, as though everyone should know that. "I heard it from Betty Martin, she works as a part-time clerk at the sheriff's office." That brought abrupt silence. Ernie had said something credible! "They had two neat holes in their necks just like a vampire had bitten them. Betty says she reads a lot about vampires. You gotta know about a lot of things when you work for the government."

Just about everybody knew about the picnickers, but the wounds weren't common knowledge, yet. It would be coming out in tomorrow's edition of the *Times*. Well, he still knew some things that they didn't. If the Tubbs boys knew it was JJ's body found in the creek, they would roar out to the Matthewson Ranch in a heartbeat. Hey, that gave him an idea!

There were still those bodies buried in that field by the joking man. He couldn't investigate it by himself. Maybe . . .

"So you think Matthewson's a vampire," said some guy in a Cubs cap, as he waved a pool cue at Ernie.

"Well, he ain't never seen during the day," Ernie continued. "And the *Times* article said he's allergic to the sunlight. Same's true with vampires."

"He's just sick," Patti, the blond waitress, said as she went by without slowing.

"I heard," Jack began, "that David wanted to come back to the church, but Reverend Wright wouldn't allow it. He and the Reverend Cooper argued over it, some say . They haven't been getting along all that well for a while. I expect a new assistant minister sometime soon. Too bad, Wright knows the flock needs to be kept pure."

"See! There is something funny about that writer guy!" Buck shouted. "I knew it! They won't let him into church!"

"Hear they won't let you in either," Zane mumbled.

"Hey, you guys, keep it down!" Rich yelled in their direction.

"Up yours!" Hank yelled back, slurring the words.

"Hank, don't," Rick warned, putting a hand on his brother's shoulder.

"Nobody tells me to shut up," Hank said angrily.

"Aw shit, I'm clearing out!" Ernie stumbled away. Jack and Zane quickly followed. The others moved back toward the pool tables, cues ready, just in case. Fights rarely broke out at the First Street Club, but with the Tubbs boys, you never knew.

"I didn't say shut up. I asked you to pipe down. You can holler and whoop all you want during the games, but this is a little too early." Rich looked at Hank for a moment, then said, "Maybe I should cut you boys off. You've been here for quite a while."

"You wouldn't . . ." Buck stood up. Hank did the same.

Rick grabbed them both by the arms. Buck shook it off, so Rick grabbed him again, getting a better grip, his fingers turning white as they dug into flesh.

"We were just going, weren't we, boys? Thank the man."

"Hey, aww . . . okay, we're going," Buck said. Then with a hard stare, he said, "Thanks, we'll come back . . ." His voice grew softer before trailing off. Hank just spat into a cup.

Rick guided them toward the front door. It was all he could do to keep them walking in a straight line. Still, the trio made it outside without falling down or knocking anyone over. Only one drink was spilled, and none of the Tubbs wore it. Hank glared over his shoulder as they departed. Stones downed his soda and followed. He didn't want them to get away; he had a proposition for them. Outside, they'd be away from inquisitive ears.

Stones stumbled out the door and hobbled quickly down the sidewalk, following the boys away from the main square. "Hey, gentlemen, may I speak with you for a moment? It might pertain to your missing brother."

"Well, if it ain't the reporter, Corey Stones," Hank spat. "He always seems to know something about JJ that we don't."

"And we ain't gentle with nuthin'," Buck added. "Especially guys that hold out on us!"

Rick just stared at him.

"I couldn't help but overhear what you said," Stones said. He suddenly realized that he was in trouble; they were still mad about how'd he'd presented his information on JJ's motorcycle. He spoke quickly. "I don't know if Matthewson is a vampire," he tried to chuckle, but only smiled lamely as he changed to a quieter, more conspiratorial tone, "but I do know that there's more than one body buried on his ranch. In fact, there are at least two the sheriffs haven't found!"

"What?" They said in unison. Their glazed and angry expressions were replaced by confusion and curiosity.

Stones briefly explained about the joking man burying two

bodies, but he never bothered to describe him. He didn't say anything about the names he heard mentioned. "And since I'm hampered," Stones finished, pointing to his walking cast, "I haven't had a chance to check it out. I thought the sheriffs would find them."

"Aw . . . they're just covering up!" Buck exclaimed.

"Anyway," Stones finished. "I would like to investigate, see if the bodies are still there. You boys interested in helping?"

"What's in it for us?" Rick asked.

"One of the bodies might be JJ's, or lead you to JJ."

"And what's in it for you?"

"News. A scoop," Stones replied. "I am a reporter at heart, first and foremost."

"And you haven't told the sheriffs?" Hank asked.

Stones shook his head. "It wouldn't be a scoop if I had, would it?"

Buck smacked Hank. "Hey, I'm for it. I'm getting tired of sitting around anyway!"

"Yeah!" Hank added.

Rick thought for a second, then said. "I guess we just need to pick up some shovels."

"Great. When?" Stones asked. It was a couple of hours until sunset.

"Let's go! Right now!" Hank said, belching, then spitting. "I drive!"

Rick shook his head. "I drive. Always."

"I'll follow you to your place in my Escort," Stones said. "What are you in?"

"That old black pickup," Rick said and pointed. Just at that time, a few doors down from the derelict-looking truck, an attractive woman with lustrous black hair, a rich tan, and an eye-stopping figure wrapped in a white dress, caught the brothers' attention. Stones didn't notice, he just nodded and headed for his car.

The brothers walked on, heading both toward their pickup and Jana, who was unlocking her car. "Hey, look! It's that sexy spic that's been seein' Matthewson. I bet they got somethin' goin'."

"I know I would," Buck added. "Hey, let's get somethin' goin'," he slurred and leered.

"She probably knows somethin' about JJ," Hank added. They quickly moved toward Jana.

"Just questions," Rick said. "Remember, no touching."

Stones had just started his car, when he noticed what was happening in broad daylight, and downtown no less. He couldn't believe they'd be that stupid; or at least he hoped they wouldn't be. As Stones put the car into gear, the trio quickly surrounded Jana, who was loading something into the trunk of her car. She was surprised and taken aback by their appearance and demeanor.

"Hey, babe, wanna tell us some secrets 'bout your squeeze, David Matthewson?" Hank said.

"Or would you prefer to be squeezed?" Buck asked.

"Leave me alone. I have nothing to say about David to the likes of y'all. He is a kind man. Now *vamanos!*"

"The likes of—" Hank reached out.

"RAPE!" She dug into a her purse, but Buck moved quickly—his bulk belying his speed—and slapped her. Jana's head lashed back, and her eyes rolled. She collapsed, striking her head against the car as she fell to the pavement.

"Maybe she knows somethin' about JJ. Do ya?" Buck grabbed Jana by the hair and hauled her to her feet. She didn't move; her eyes never opened. "Hey, I think she's gone to sleep on us. Let's wake her up." Buck carried her to the open car door and began arranging her legs.

Stones was about to yell when he heard, "RAPE! Stop this!" Michael Woods came running out of his office. "I've called the sheriff!"

"Shit, let's split!" Buck said.

"Should we take her with us?" Hank asked.

"Hell no, you idiot!" Rick yelled as he fled. The two brothers followed the first, running for the pickup. Climbing inside and firing it up, they burned rubber and sped away.

Hunched down in the seat of his Escort, Stones followed. This might ruin everything. Now the cops would be looking for the brothers. He had to move fast, or all was ruined.

Michael watched the cars go, memorizing every detail, then he rushed to Jana's side. She was bleeding from the nose and mouth. Was she dead? He searched for a pulse. Where was the sheriff? Jana needed help, fast!

Twelve

Ultimatum

David paused in his painting to look around, again searching for hints of Monique's coming. Steamy and foggy, the night mocked a tropical jungle glade, the air filled with the thrumming of insects and the furtive shuffling of animals. David sensed life in the underbrush, grass, and trees—literally everywhere—as it should be; the ranch and barnyard felt right. David breathed deeply, and it smelled as it should, rich with lively aromas and an earthly fragrance. All were good signs that Monique was not nearby; otherwise, the night would become deathly still—all life having fled her wretched path. David wished he could do the same, but he had to face her, trap her, and destroy her. There was no other choice.

Where was Jana? David wondered. This had been their joint plan. He prayed she was all right; the sun had set over an hour ago, and she was long overdue to arrive. Afraid something might have happened to her, David's worry continued to grow until he was almost ill with it.

Upon awakening and finding himself alone, David had called both Michael's office and Jana's place trying to find her, but had only reached answering machines. David had wanted to go searching for Jana, but felt too dizzy and weak to drive. And besides, unlike Monique, David wasn't linked to Jana; he wouldn't be able to divine her location and drive right to her.

And yet, if Jana were simply delayed, safe somewhere else when Monique appeared, that would be just fine with David. He constantly feared that Jana would die, and for that reason alone he'd rather face Monique by himself. David didn't think he could stand to be accountable for another death, especially hers.

Thankful that Monique had come neither in flesh nor dream, David quickly finished painting Biblical verses in clear lacquer on the outside of his shutters, then stepped back to examine it. Nobody would notice the religious script among all the profane graffiti. The inside renderings were finished and drying, hidden behind shades, unnoticeable by all but vampires. With any luck, they would work as some kind of Christian pentagram, if he could manage to get all the shutters closed once Monique had entered.

The mounted crosses hadn't been enough to prevent Monique's visit. He hoped the verses would weaken the vampire, so he might be able to attack and drive a stake through her heart. Now prepared, the house might be the only place where that was possible. David didn't think she'd invade a church to get to him, but then who knew what havoc she might wreak while she waited for him to leave such a sanctuary. Besides, the people didn't want him at their church.

David took down the ladder and headed for the barn. After all the work, he needed a bottle of elixir to revive him. His feet dragged, and his muscles felt like soft lead. The elixir wasn't curing him, it simply kept him going, his health improving little by little with every bottle.

Unfortunately, it wasn't working as well or as fast as at first. Could he have built up a tolerance? Maybe he should drink more. The only thing it didn't seem to cure was the gut-wrenching nausea. Still, he was weak, but not bedridden;

and he'd healed dramatically in a short period of time from terrible wounds. When he had time, he was going to review the remedy once more.

David set the ladder against the barn, then returned to gather the paint can and brush. He pushed the door open and put things away, sealing the can and wrapping the brush in plastic. Then he walked to the closet. Despite shaky hands, David had little trouble putting the keys in the lock. The storage room seemed stuffy, until opening the refrigerator breathed new life into it.

As David removed several bottles and set them atop the fridge, he began to wonder if Monique would come at all. He thought she'd already be here by now. Maybe she was too ill to attack or seduce him, and would only come to taunt, cajole, or bully. David wondered if there had ever been such a female spawn of wickedness before. And why he was cursed to cross this one's path?

As David began to drink, he felt a strong, overwhelming presence—both suffocating and sickening, its sweet aroma hiding something far too old. Monique was here!

David whirled to face the doorway. Monique felt more powerful than ever, renewed and wanton. David walked out of the closet and saw her standing in the open barn door.

Dressed as though celebrating Mardi Gras, Monique was adorned in an outrageous outfit. The entire ensemble was gold and crimson, from her feathered hat, along her revealingly cut dress complete with frills at the shoulders and arms, to her spiked pumps. Monique's face was painted in gold and red swaths, with some strips of pale flesh left untouched. A cold, cruel smile touched her lips, but did not reach her eyes; they were flat and studious as though examining an insect. *"Auf Wiedersehen,* lover-soon-to-be. Or maybe just dead man."

If Monique died with him, it would be a fair trade, David concluded. He was afraid this might happen, but he couldn't just hide inside all the time. David hoped he might be able to draw her into the house. He set down the bottle and reached for the cross in his back pocket. She had caught him outside the trap, but he wasn't totally unprepared. He raised his crucifix and waited.

"Dere is no need for such an annoying display, David," Monique told him. "I have come to talk one last time. And dese words must lead to action. Dey must."

Maybe if he walked toward the house, Monique would follow him inside. Maybe? He certainly didn't trust his luck. History taught him that much. "Speak." David continued to hold his crucifix between them.

Monique laughed, but stayed in the doorway instead of coming to walk around him and touch him as she usually did. "You are not a priest. And you simply don't believe strongly enough anymore. You are beginning to understand what Monique says is true. Yes? You are vampire. And if you do not embrace your nature—your destiny—den you will have to be destroyed. It is dat simple, *ja?*"

David started to say something, but was stung by a bout of dizziness.

"And I see you do not feel well. The pain—chills, fever and nausea, confusion and weakness. Don't be concerned, it is as you've been told before, part of de transformation from de living to de undead. It doesn't last long, a few days maybe, once a catalyst has stimulated the process." She sighed, "If you want to ease your pain, you can speed up de process by drinking human blood. Your denial is what has delayed your evolution.

"But I have not come to give advice, just an ultimatum! At dis time tomorrow, you will either join me in feasting on a human, or you will be dead. It is your choice! But I am generous, I will even bring de victim!" She chuckled. "No more games, you see," her voice became brittle. "We must be gone from here, and quickly. You have," she laughed softly, "until tomorrow night to decide."

"What about Jana?" David asked, but had the feeling that Monique had not bothered his friend this time.

"I care nothing for Jana. She was already given her ultimatum."

David heard a car driving the gravel road. Monique briefly glanced over her shoulder, and said, "You have another visitor. It is so nice to be a popular author, *ja?* Until tomorrow, David." Monique stepped into the barn, then moved lithely into a shadow, gone as though she had never been.

Squeaking brakes focused David's attention outside, where Michael's Forerunner was stopping. His lawyer hurried out of the car and rushed toward the front gate. "Michael, I'm over here!" David yelled. Michael stopped, turned, then began walking rapidly toward David who moved to meet him. "What's up?" David saw urgency in Michael's expression and dress. Usually when in a suit, he was impeccably dressed, but now his tie was loose, his collar crooked, and his jacket rumpled.

"David? You . . . I thought you were sick and in bed."

"I'm getting better," David lied. Suddenly, his knees felt very weak, his stomach stormy, and his face flushed. What if Monique was right about it being some type of transformation? Nonsense! But her expression said she truly believed it. David pushed the thoughts away and said, "You look upset. What's wrong now?" Oh no, David suddenly thought, not Jana!

"Are you sure you're all right, you look—"

"I'm fine. Now what—"

"There's been trouble. Jana's been accosted by the Tubbs' boys!"

"What?" David felt the reach of his curse. He grew even dizzier, and his knees buckled slightly.

Michael caught his elbow. "Come inside and sit. She's going to be okay. She was just frightened and scratched up a little. She's at the hospital overnight, recovering."

"Let's go!" David said, starting to guide his friend toward his Forerunner. "I want to see her."

Michael stopped, dragging his feet, and said, "David, I don't think that's a good idea!" David kept pulling, weakly. "David, listen to me. It wouldn't be wise for you to go see her just now. The Tubbs boys attacked her because they thought she was your woman."

David stopped, his expression formed by amazement. "Sh—She was attacked because she's been out here to see me? Me?"

"Yes! Some of the town's gone crazy. With the missing boys, the mummified body, and the dead picnickers, people's attitudes have really degenerated. Fear and paranoia are running rampant. Let's go inside, and I'll tell you everything." Michael took a deep breath. "I've called the sheriff about providing protection for you."

"What?!" David exclaimed. That was the last thing he needed—more cannon fodder for Monique.

"Come on," Michael dragged David through the gate. "We can call Jana. I know she'd like to talk with you."

"Okay." David reluctantly let his friend lead him inside. Could things get any worse? He wanted to see Jana, but he certainly wasn't up for a visit. Hopefully, she was well, safe in the hospital for the present time. Maybe it was for the best. Jana wouldn't be here when Monique arrived. It worked to his advantage that Monique had given him a twenty-four-hour ultimatum. At least he knew when she would show. He would be ready, and then it would be over one way or another.

Thirteen

Findings

Tired from another long day and depressed about the sad state of affairs in Temprance, Logan walked through the empty outer office of Doc Katyu. Logan hoped this after-hours meeting would shed some light on things. It was as though there were dark clouds hanging over Temprance. In less than a week, three were dead, two had been critically injured—one in mind and the other in body—and two were missing—three if he counted Bob, the town derelict. There had also been vandalism at Matthewson's ranch, and now the Tubbs brothers had accosted Jana Martinez. At least she was going to be all right.

Despite Bricker's opinion, Logan didn't feel everything could be attributed to the Tubbs boys; there was something else going on. And Corey Stones's articles certainly didn't help matters any. All they did were scare people or make them angry! How was he getting his information? And what would go wrong next? Logan hated to even contemplate it, because he just knew it was going to be bad.

When Logan pushed open the door to the examination rooms, he heard voices drifting down the short hallway. He headed toward them, his boots rapping a steady cadence on the tile. Logan walked past the walls decorated with baby pictures, some over thirty years old, from all the infants Dr. Katyu had delivered during his tenure in Temprance. Ahead, it sounded as though the mayor and Donald Bricker had already arrived. Logan wondered if Ross would be there. Logan had not wanted to discuss things with him there, but they were going to have to. Who else could be leaking information?

Logan entered the doctor's private office and found Katyu pacing back and forth behind his small mahogany desk. The place was cluttered; papers, books, charts, and files were scattered all over his desk, the counter behind him, as well as some of the bookshelves that graced the walls. Logan found the mess odd; the few times he had been here the office had always been neat and tidy, typical of the Indian doctor.

Sipping coffee and looking worn, Mayor Campbell was sitting in a plush chair in front of the doctor's desk. Sitting next to him, Bricker was still wearing his hat, although it was casually tilted back. Ross, still far from impeccably dressed, was relaxing in the corner and eating a bag of chocolate chip cookies. Bricker turned as he heard Logan enter, and said, "Hello, Logan. You look awful. Been a long day, hasn't it? Jana okay?" Logan nodded. "Finally some news." Bricker handed him a sheet of paper, and said, "Here's a copy of Doc's findings."

"Thanks. I hope this tells us something. I'm frustrated."

"Who isn't, with all that's been going on?" the mayor drawled. His eyes were bloodshot, and his jowls appeared to be sagging more than usual.

"Gentlemen," Doc Katyu said curtly, "if we can proceed, please. I have had a long day, and expect a busy one tomorrow." The doctor's worry was plainly obvious by his furrowed brows, glasses set high on his nose instead of absently slipping, and his tightly compressed lips. The elderly doctor exuded an air of impatience and displeasure, which surprised Logan. Normally Doc was cordial no matter what the hour or the problem. In fact, his patience was legendary. Some said it was because he operated at a different pace, the unhurried one of Southern Asia.

"Aw right, Doc. Lay it on us," Bricker said gruffly.

"I have completed cursory autopsies on the bodies of Becky Sue Handley and Lou Callahan, the two picnickers found dead at the dam Sunday morning. As I suspected, there was little similarity between this duo and the mummified body of JJ Tubbs. It's true that all three died from blood loss, but JJ died much more quickly, as demonstrated by the strange decomposition of his body. Handley and Callahan definitely bled to death, in a normal fashion, from the wounds in their neck. To be honest, I am still unsure how JJ bled to death or what bit him, if anything. There was no blood residue in his clothing, while the other two corpses were soaked."

There was a moment of silence as he paced, glanced out the window, and then continued in a monotone. "Not surprisingly, I found traces of alcohol in Handley and Callahan's blood stream, but there were also traces of a depressant."

"Doing drugs," Bricker moaned. "Damn! It's getting worse, I tell ya, all the time."

"It was not a recreational drug per se, just Valium," Doc Kate pointed out.

"Not exactly something you take on an evening picnic," Logan said, and scratched his stubbled chin. "I'd expect some kind of amphetamine instead."

"Who knows these days," Bricker complained. "Doesn't matter what it is, as long as it alters their minds."

"My conclusion so far, gentleman," Doc Katyu continued, running over the Sheriff's grumblings, "is that the murders are not related, since the deaths were only vaguely similar. But more tests certainly need to be conducted since I cannot hazard a guess as to whether JJ was murdered or not; I am not even sure how he died!" His tone dripped with exasperation. "But Handley and Callahan were certainly murdered. I also found abrasions around Callahan's mouth, but don't know what to make of them as of yet."

"Any strange bruises or lacerations?" Bricker asked.

"They were not struck or cut in any other way. If I were a guessing man, and I am certainly not, I would say someone wishes the deaths to appear similar in nature."

"Why would somebody do that?" Logan asked, as he began to scan the report.

"I am just a doctor, but I will put in my two cents worth, as people say." Katyu took a breath, started to speak, changed his mind, then finally said, "I, as many, do not like what has been happening to this town. This is my adopted home. But unlike some, I believe there is a simple murderer loose in Temprance, not some dark monster as I have heard bandied about in talk and rumor. This conclusion is obvious from my findings. There is a monster in town, but he is human, of flesh and blood, not some spectral creature of legend or unearthed from the dark pits of our paranoid imagination."

Doc Katyu took another breath. "Gentlemen, I think it is a terrible travesty that people are connecting any of this with David Matthewson. He is a fine man. Only his illness makes him different, so people fear him. That isn't right. As you might suspect, I have faced similar situations, because I am just a naturalized American, not a native born."

The mayor began to speak, but Doc Katyu waved him quiet. "I believe this information, along with your search, should clear his name. You should do so publicly," he stressed the last word, staring first at the sheriff, then the mayor. "Without some word from our elected officials, the townspeople assume you agree with them; and in a sense, we condone their acts unless we speak out. I believe I have given you the necessary facts to shed some light on the subject. Now, I believe it is up to you all to stop the fear of the unknown, stop the prejudice, and make what we know public! Who knows, maybe somebody will come forward with information about suspicious characters, or leads, or something." Logan thought Katyu looked more distressed than tired; he also had the odd sense that the doctor wasn't telling him everything, but what else was there to say?

Then Logan noticed something odd on the report. Doc Katyu had found undigested steak, peas, corn, and potatoes in both stomachs. That didn't match the picnic scene at all.

"But what about the Tubbs boy?" Bricker asked.

"I don't know, but I will continue to test. For more expertise, I've sent samples to Dallas, so it will be a few days. I am working as quickly as I can, for I must send the body to the county coroner soon."

"Wait as long as you can, Doc," Bricker said.

"Certainly," the mayor agreed. "We need to keep a lid on this, with the Summerfest coming up. We don't want to drive away customers during the most profitable week of the year. Now, if only Bill Bowers would collar Stones . . ."

"I agree with Doc," Logan told everybody. "Money is not the issue. If we don't say something, things will get worse than they already are. People are already jumping at their own shadows, and using the fear as a rationale for doing things. It's an acceptable excuse."

"Like the Tubbs brothers this evening," Bricker pointed out.

"They don't need a rationale," Logan said in an angry tone. "And I don't believe it's been accepted, at least I hope not. If it has been, then Temprance has degenerated further than I suspected, and it's time to burn down the place and start all over!"

"It has not," the mayor said testily. "And it's not that bad, Logan. You are tired indeed, my friend. Donald, I believe it's time you had a chat with Bill Bowers. Maybe we can get something in tomorrow's paper that will cool things off. Lord knows we need it." He dabbed at his face with a handkerchief.

"So we say that the two sets of deaths are unrelated, and

that Becky Sue Handley and Lou Callahan were murdered?" Bricker questioned Campbell who nodded. "And that David Matthewson is not a suspect? He has an alibi for Saturday night, his mother and sister were staying with him, because he was sick in bed. Can you think of anything else?"

Logan was going to express his observation when Doc Katyu interjected. "I have a question. Might their deaths be related to the bar fight they were involved in two weekends ago?"

"Bar fight?" Logan asked. He and Ross both looked confused. Neither Bricker nor Campbell said anything. Logan looked at his boss, then back to the doctor. "What bar fight?"

"It was two Fridays past, the fifth I believe. I work in the emergency room in Athens on every other Friday night. I was there that night when Lou Callahan brought in Becky Sue Handley. Said he'd been in a fight at some bar, I don't remember which. Becky had been knocked unconscious, her face is still slightly bruised, and he'd been cut." Logan vaguely remembered the facial bruises. "Lou needed a few stitches, but it was nothing really serious. The report I dictated was filed, I called and checked. I supposed he had pressed charges. He was mad enough to do so."

Logan's surprise was total; and he was speechless for a time, staring at Bricker, who didn't look at him. Finally, Logan managed, "Donald, I thought you said nothing else interesting happened the night I went to the Matthewson ranch! Would you like to explain?"

"Definitely, before you bust a gut." Bricker still wasn't looking at Logan. "I followed up on the complaint, in fact, went out there that night and spoke to the bartender, a woman named Peg and the owner Pat Borders. Peg had called us for Lou Callahan. Lou and Becky were already driving to ER when I arrived. I was with . . . well, you know. Anyway, I spoke with Peg. She got a good look at the guy who walked out with Becky and supposedly fought with Lou. In fact, all three agree on the description of the assailant."

"And?" Logan was still in shock.

"The suspect was tall, thin, and dark-haired, with skin so white, Peg said, it reminded her of ivory. I thought it might have been David Matthewson. I showed her David's picture on the back jacket of a book, but she said it wasn't him. We don't have any other suspects or clues."

"And you've posted the description on the network?" Logan asked. Bricker nodded, but their eyes still didn't meet. Logan had that intuitive itch again. "Did you talk with Handley and Callahan?"

"Yes, the next day," Bricker nodded. "They didn't add anything that helped. I showed them the same picture. They said he was younger than that, and clean-shaven."

Of course, it wasn't David Matthewson, Logan thought. He and Ross had seen him at the farm, bloodied and leaning against the barn. Suddenly Logan couldn't believe what he was thinking. If a light bulb had exploded inside of his head, the enlightenment couldn't have been more obvious. He started to say something, choked on it, and then began to see red. Logan fought to regain control, and held his voice tightly in check as he asked, "You said the boy was dark-haired, very pale, tall, and thin?" Bricker nodded. "Young, early twenties?" Bricker nodded again. "Clean-shaven? Did he smoke?" Bricker nodded. "It was Kevin Grimm, and you know it even more surely than we know that the Tubbses vandalized the Matthewson ranch," Logan said tightly.

Neither the mayor nor the sheriff reacted immediately, which told Logan what he needed to know. "Kevin left the Matthewson ranch, then drove to the bar, right? It was your stepson, wasn't it, Mayor?" Logan asked acidly.

Campbell didn't say anything, but Bricker nodded. "That's true," he drawled. "When I told Lou how bad Kevin looked— the guy had really beat him to a pulp—he agreed to drop the charges, Kevin agreed to stay away from Becky Sue. Handley was pretty upset, but she finally agreed to drop the charges on those conditions. Remember, the mayor agreed to more counselling for Kevin. I didn't consider it significant after that."

"You didn't—I—Donald—" Logan sputtered. He'd already received the impression that the mayor was involved. Worse, there sounded as though there was coercion. Was Temprance rotting from within, as well as without? "I don't believe this!" Logan finally exploded. "No matter how you justify it to yourself, you lied to me! We're peace officers, not judge and jury. This is wrong! Dead wrong! Grimm is a prime suspect, and you're not doing anything about it! I want to talk with him, right now!"

"I questioned him," Bricker admitted impassively, "but it wasn't all that necessary. He has an alibi for Saturday. He was at home that night in his room."

"He told you this?"

"Yes, and the mayor was there all night. Kevin never left his room, except to go to the bathroom, and later for a late snack. Uh, things haven't been going well at home and—"

"Might he have snuck out or something?" Logan suggested, now coldly furious instead of outraged.

Campbell finally glared back at him. "My wife had his pickup. He didn't have any transportation. The other cars never left the house. I would have heard."

"I still want to talk with him. Right now! Where is he?" Logan was afraid he was going to lose control. The mayor and sheriff looked so smug, so self-assured, that Logan wanted to strangle them. Under the circumstance, it would be justified manslaughter. Logan thought he might be jumping to conclusions, but his gut feeling—his instincts—told him otherwise. This cover-up only solidified those feelings.

"Logan, don't be this way—" Donald began.

"This is the only way I can be! This is how I am, and you

know it! That's why you did this! I want to speak with Kevin. Now! Where is he? We can do this quietly, or I can request assistance."

Mayor Campbell's face was flushed. Downcast, he wrung his hands, then managed a faint, "I don't know. We can't find him. His pickup's still at home, but he's gone. We don't know where he is."

"When was the last time you saw him?"

"Early yesterday evening, I believe."

Logan growled. "He could be long gone. I'm putting out an APB."

"But . . ." the mayor began, "My wife. Oh God," his face was overwrought with despair, "Stones and other reporters. I'm gonna be ruined!"

Logan didn't care about that; he only cared about doing what was right. Stiffly, he headed for the door, then turned and said coldly, "I'll put out the APB. Donald, you talk with Bill Bowers as you agreed. Tell him the truth; everything but that we think it was Kevin Grimm. He's just a suspect at this time. No reason to blow it out of proportion. But David's good name must be cleared. It's the right thing to do. I'd hate to see another Carter Incident; you remember that, don't you? A Tubbs was involved then, too!" Campbell nodded, while Bricker just stared straight ahead.

"And Ross!" Logan began, snapping Bubba to alertness. "If I hear or read anything about this meeting, I'm holding you personally responsible. Understand?!"

Ross dropped his bag, the cookies spilling all over the floor. "Uh . . . What . . ."

"You heard me. I mean it!"

"Logan," Bricker began.

"Donald, history has a nasty habit of repeating itself; but I don't intend on letting that happen. I'll call David and Michael, too. They should know. Then I'll drop in on the Tubbs boys. Maybe even look in on Jack Huntington, and see if he's causing any new trouble."

"I'm ruined!" The mayor moaned.

"You reap what you sow," Logan countered. "This could have been dealt with quickly and quietly, if it had been done up front . . . and honestly. Now it will probably be messy. I have one of those feelings. I just hope we can find Grimm before somebody else dies."

Fourteen

The Exhumation

Stones pulled his Escort off Cedar Dam Road and parked along the Matthewson ranch's barbed wire fence. He shut off the lights, then turned, and scowled at Rick Tubbs. "Sure you boys are up for this?" Stones wasn't happy about the incident in town or his current situation. The reporter didn't like relying on these three; but he'd dealt his own hand, and now he had to play it. The truth be known, he'd kept worse company. Besides, the Tubbses were going to investigate with him or without him, and he didn't want to miss out on an exclusive scoop—especially this one. It would blow the town wide open.

But, just in case things got out of hand, while they'd been stopped at the Tubbs' shack, Stones had pulled his gun from the glove box and stuffed it in his waistband, where it dug uncomfortably into his hip and back. Still, he had a feeling the story was going to be worth the hardship.

"I reckon," Rick finally replied, then took a long, slow drag from his cigarette. The thin brother was sitting in the front seat, while his stout brothers were in the back. Stones had convinced them not to bring along a six-pack. They had plenty to carry as it was—and more if they decided to haul out the bodies. "How about it, Hank?" Rick seemed unconcerned that the sheriffs were looking for them.

"You bet your ass!" Hank spat into a cup.

"Buck, you ready to do some grave robbing?"

"What he said!"

"Then let's get cracking," Rick said and opened his door. Raring to go, Hank and Buck all but leaped out of the car. Stones moved a bit more slowly, still having trouble with his ankle—and adjusting to the gun he'd concealed.

"Stones, you're too slow with that damn cane," Rick said. "Leave it here. Buck and Hank will carry you, while I handle the shovels and picks." Rick held out his palm for the keys to the trunk.

Stones gave them to him, a little concerned about leaving his cane and putting himself in a compromising position; but he was a reporter—much too important to kill. Stones placed his camera strap around his neck and a pocket recorder inside his jacket. He'd also stowed away a penlight.

Rick walked around to the back and opened the trunk, getting out a couple of shovels and a pick. He set them on his shoulder and said, "Let's do it." Buck and Hank moved to help Stones. They easily lifted Stones to his feet; he put his arms over their shoulders, shifting to make sure they didn't feel his gun. Between the two of them, Stones hardly had to put any weight on his walking cast. Rick looked at Stones and turned on his flashlight. Hank followed suit. "Which way?"

Stones guided them to a place in the fence near the stream, where it was easy to climb through the wiring, even for him. "That way," Stones pointed to his left and into a cluster of deeply shadowed trees. Knifing rays of moonlight occasionally cut slashes through the opaque sea of ebony that choked the woods. A soft breeze ruffled everything with a slow, wavy motion reminiscent of the tropics. The forest was full of silent noise, the humming of its dark denizens.

As they trudged along, Buck asked, "I wonder who that 'joking guy' was?"

Stones shrugged. He had an idea, but wasn't going to tell anyone just yet; although he'd left notes just in case.

"Aw, that Matthewson guy is plenty twisted. It was probably just him. Maybe he's writin' a dirty joke book!" Hank spat onto the ground.

"You doing all right?" Rick asked over his shoulder. He was at the forefront, his beam dissecting the darkness and illuminating an easy route as he led the trailing trio into the woods.

"Fine," Stones said, "it's easier on the pits than crutches. How about you boys?"

"We'll survive," Hank replied, then spat to the side. Buck nodded.

Moving as silently as a shadow, Grimm followed the quartet at a good distance. Their lights made trailing them very easy. Grimm moved carefully, gliding around the trees, quietly stepping over roots and bushes, and circumventing the patches of moonlight. His grace and light-footedness resembled that of a native stalking game.

Grimm didn't know why they were headed toward the Brookens boys' bodies, but he intended to find out. Since reading Stones's articles on the picnickers in Sunday's paper, Grimm had been shadowing him. Because of the tone of said stories, Grimm and his friend felt Stones might know more than he was telling. And now it appeared they were right, since Stones was leading the Tubbses to the unmarked graves in the pasture—the graves that the sheriffs had somehow missed!

When Grimm thought about it, it didn't matter who found the bodies, as long as their deaths were blamed on Matthewson. Actually, this might be better than the sheriffs finding the bodies. With the Tubbs boys involved, there might be an old-fashioned hangin' in the near future. Perfect. In fact, it was more than he'd even dreamed.

Grimm stopped next to a tree and watched the foursome's progress. He chuckled, then whispered, "What's the dumbest part of a man?" Grimm could hear Buck and Hank jawing away. "His prick. Its got no brains, its best friends are two nuts, and it lives next door to an asshole. The four stooges," Grimm waved at the group.

Yes, he was feeling much better. Laughter and revenge, especially when combined with the darkness, were absolutely the best medicine. Whatever had happened to him—probably that bitch Monique's fault—made him extrasensitive to the light, much in the same way as Matthewson. "But nobody thinks you're a vampire, Kevy!" his secret friend said.

Grimm smiled. "That's right." Thanks to the rumor mill, many townspeople wondered about David Matthewson's true reason for hiding from the day. Grimm almost began to laugh with glee, then shushed himself.

The Tubbses and Stones were nearing the fence surrounding the pasture. Grimm saw Stones point, and the Tubbs brothers led him to a tree which he leaned against. Then the three brothers pitched the tools over the fence and began climbing. As Grimm moved closer for a better view, Hank and Buck located the spot and started digging. The *schuck* of the blades biting earth, followed by the scattering of clods, was just a little out of time.

"Good ole Texas gumbo, just sticks to the shovel. This is easy!" Grimm heard Hank say, right before he spit.

"Good thing it rained," Rick told them, "usually this would be rock hard, and you'd be pickin' at it and cussin'." He wiped sweat from his brow and flicked it away.

"Still hot though. Nuthin' like the steam bath of a warm summer night in Texas!" Hank joked.

Grimm stopped not twenty feet from Stones. Suddenly, Grimm wondered if that had been the reporter in the woods the night he'd buried the boys and had kept hearing things. If so, the reporter would have to die, but Grimm didn't really think it would be wise to kill anyone right now; there'd been enough . . . for the time being. Besides, more deaths might just ruin his carefully laid plans.

Stones suddenly noticed that outside of the sound of shoveling and the boys's chatter, the woods had become very quiet. The crickets and other insects had grown silent, as though wary and watchful. Was that because the boys were getting close? The bodies hadn't been buried very deeply. A cool breeze wafted by him, and he shivered, finding it strange considering all the waves of heat. Weather around lakes could be funny sometimes.

"Hey, look!" Rick exclaimed softly. Hank and Buck stopped digging, as their brother focused his beam on what looked to be a foot. "Be careful."

"Why? It's dead," Buck said.

"It might be JJ," Hank said.

"Aw, all right," Buck agreed. He carefully removed the dirt from around the body, only to find another next to the first. "Hell, there's two!"

"Hey," Rick exclaimed. "I'll bet its them Brookens brothers, Jim Bob and Benny Joe. Take a closer look, Hank. Remember the pictures? Speakin' of which," he pulled a piece of paper from his pocket, "match 'em with this."

I'll bet you're right, Stones thought.

Brilliant, Grimm had to stifle a snicker.

Hank took the photocopy and rolled a body face up. "Yuck. Look at them. And the smell!" Hank quickly sprang away. The corpses resembled rotting prunes. He held his nose, then spat. "It couldn't be the boys, they've only been missin' a week!"

"Looks like they been dead for months. What could have happened?" Buck asked.

"Same thing as whatever happened to that body the sheriffs

found near here. I wonder why they didn't find these two?" Rick asked.

"A good question," Stones replied.

Yeah, good question, shit-for-brains, Grimm thought. Though it didn't really matter. The bodies had been found on the Matthewson farm, and soon all hell would break loose!

"Probably a cover-up!" Buck said.

"Well, do they look like the Brookens boys?" Stones asked.

Hank got close, but not too close, as Buck shone a light on the paper and Rick on the boys' shriveled faces. "Ya know, I think it's them. I really do. Goddamned, godawful, but it's them!" Hank shuddered, then spat. "They looked used, ya know, sucked dry."

"I think we should go kill him right now," Buck began. He hefted his shovel. "Nobody does this in our town!"

"Who?" Hank spat.

"David Matthewson."

"Sounds fine to me," Hank said, and grabbed the pick from Rick. "He won't do to us what he did to them! And he'll tell us what he did with JJ! I swear on Pop's grave."

Go! Go! Grimm wanted to shout.

"Hey, boys, I got an idea," Stones said. The trio stopped in their tracks and looked at him as though he were spoiling their fun. "You mentioned wanting to change your reputations. Want to be heroes for once? Laugh at the sheriff?"

"Heroes?" Hank spat, then wiped his chin.

"Hey, laugh at the sheriffs," Buck replied.

"Yeah, heroes," Stones continued. "Don't you think the town should have a chance to share in the revenge, to purge itself? They'll thank you, maybe even give you a reward—a key to the city . . ."

"Free drinks at the First Street Club!" Hank cried.

". . . And I'll make you look real good in the paper," Stones continued unabated. "You'll be the toast of the upcoming festival. Probably free booze and food."

"Hey now," Rick said. "Pictures in the paper?"

"You bet," Stones said. "At least in two issues."

"Naw, I'd rather do it now," Buck said. "I hate waiting."

"But what if he's a vampire, like the rumors," Hank began, then pointed, "and this here, says?"

"You'd believe in the Boogey Man," Buck laughed.

"If he is a vampire—and we aren't sure he isn't—then you should get help," Stones said. "Lots of it."

No! No! Grimm wanted to scream, but managed to stand impassively.

"I don't want no help from the sheriffs." Hank reached into his back pocket for more chew.

"Just tell your friends—you know a couple of guys in the bar—and see what happens. I'll bet there's men willing to help you, just to protect their families. Don't you see? The town's scared, and they got good right to be. You can help them free themselves of their fears. They'll love you for it."

"I think he's right," Rick said slowly, as though measuring each word.

"Naw, I want to find out about JJ tonight!" Hank said. "Ma's worried herself sick. We'll find out, then he'll disappear in the lake or something, just like—"

"Hank, be quiet!" Rick shouted.

Suddenly, Grimm felt her! Or thought he did; Monique's presence was more powerful than he remembered. It made him take a step back, unsure whether he wanted to mess with her. And yet, if Monique interfered, she might ruin everything.

Mists appeared, thickening, as though a fog bank had blown in from the lake, sharply cutting visibility. "Hey, this is weird," Rick said, looking around at the fog. He moved his light around, "Hey, do you smell something?"

"Should we grab the bodies?" Buck wanted to know.

"I . . ." Stones began, then shivered as a chilling wind cut him to the quick. His teeth chattered, and then he felt a raw fear, so powerful it set off all his survival instincts.

"Naw, we'll cover them back up and bring the folks—" Rick didn't have a chance to finish his sentence. It was cut short, ending with a gurgle as something grabbed his neck and squeezed. Easily lifted off his feet, Rick was kicking and swinging futilely.

"What the hell!" Hank rushed forward with his shovel poised and ready.

Magically, a strange facade of gold, crimson, and ghostly white appeared next to Rick's choking and sputtering blue face. Hank stopped short, his eyes bugging. Buck's mouth gaped, as though it had come unhinged.

Stones pushed through his shock and let the fear carry him away. Despite the agony, he crashed through the dark woods, moving on his walking cast as though it were only a minor inconvenience.

"W . . . what is that?" Buck managed.

"I don't know, but it got's Rick!" Hank raised his shovel and finally mustered enough courage to attack. He swung all around Rick, trying to hit something and free his brother, but only found the swirling and twisting mists. The masked face laughed at him, mocking him. Hank attacked it again to no avail, and screamed in frustration. Its smile grew larger, taunting; then its face turned, and Monique bit Rick, blood spurting all over his brothers. Screaming, Hank and Buck hopped the fence and ran, gaining quickly on Stones. Grimm also fled.

Behind, the vampire fed, letting the others go. It didn't matter. Soon it would be over, and she would be gone. Let them fear her, tell their children of her in choked whispers. The chattel deserved to die, as perhaps did one of her own.

Fifteen

Under Siege

"It's just totally unbelievable," Michael told David, incredulously. The two were in the living room. "But the Tubbs boys openly attacking Jana isn't the only strange thing going on in town. People in Temprance are short-tempered and scared."

"But they attacked her because of me!" David stood and wrung his hands, pacing back and forth. His anger suddenly flared, and he kicked over the coffee table.

"David! Please! Get a grip, my friend. She's fine, really, just a little bruised and disoriented. She's a real trooper. Listen, we'll get the brothers; the sheriffs are already looking for them, I swear. The APB's out. Don't worry. She's safe, but you may not be. I came to warn you about them. They think you're the cause of JJ's disappearance. When I spoke with Logan, he even offered protection."

"No . . . no thank you. I can protect myself. This is a homestead state after all." He had a Smith and Wesson upstairs and a twelve-gauge shotgun in the downstairs closet. Thoughts of using them on the Tubbs boys warmed him; David felt only a little guilty about such thoughts. "I . . . I just can't believe she's been hurt because of me!" But at least not dead, like so many others, David thought.

"Hey, knowing the Tubbs family, they might have attacked her anyway. She's a very attractive lady, and Buck and Hank have a history of such actions, as well as a rap sheet. But as I said, that's not our only trouble. Rumors are rampant that you're connected to several deaths, including the picnickers found at the dam. If it's bad, people are blaming you for it! Word is that the Times is going to validate your link to the deaths in Tuesday's paper. I spoke with Bill Bowers, and he claims he knows nothing about said story. But he hasn't been able to reach Stones, who I feel has perpetrated a lot of this. I'd love to wring his sleazy little neck!"

It took a moment, but Michael retained his cool. "Listen to me, David, paranoia is history and fear reigns, rearing its ugly head in the form of hostility, and soon, maybe even violence. And Stones's articles aren't helping! There have been several confrontations, and a couple of fights. One of your buddies punched out a customer at Walmart."

David groaned. "Must have been Matt." Michael nodded. David burped slightly, then touched his stomach. Waves of nausea suddenly spread from his stomach, overwhelming him. He quickly sat in a nearby chair. His head swam, then felt as though it were going to drift away.

"Are you all right?" Michael was concerned and touched David on the arm.

"Just indigestion." David burped again, then felt a spasm. It was growing worse.

"Is there something you'd like to tell me?"

"What do you mean by that?" David rubbed his stomach. It was a churning ball of fire, growing and expanding. He felt perspiration appear on his forehead.

"I was with Jana, and she was mumbling something about wanting you to tell me something . . . something terrible."

"Oh," David said, then suddenly grabbed his stomach and doubled over. The pain . . .

* * *

David abruptly awoke from his reverie of yesterday's conversation with Michael and staggered to the bathroom, where he vomited; his stomach continued to heave long after it was empty. He flushed the toilet, then slumped to the cool tile floor.

Sometime later, David realized he must have dozed, and that his head was ringing. After several moments, he recognized that it was the doorbell, not his head. David washed his face and rinsed his mouth before staggering back into his room and clumsily pulling on a shirt. Barely able to stand, David headed downstairs.

The ringing didn't stop, the cadence moving closer to desperation. "Stop it!" David yelled weakly. It didn't, but he did, trying to gather his strength on the stairs. The ringing continued, assaulting his hypersensitive ears.

David stumbled down a few more stairs. Lord, he'd never felt this bad, except maybe the time when he'd had salmonella. Tina had nursed him back to health, suffering with him through the gut-wrenching food poisoning. For a moment, he thought he saw her again at the bottom of the stairs, as though in a faded dream, but he knew better; it was just delirium.

Ring. RING. RINGRING. "Stop it!" David yelled again as he reached the door. His visitor must have heard, for the ringing finally stopped. He looked through the peephole and saw Michael . . . and Jana! She was all right! David immediately felt a little better.

He unbolted the door and swept it back, pretending that he felt much better than he did—almost human instead of half-dead on his feet. "My friends, come in." David didn't have to force a smile when Jana smiled.

Despite the facial bruises and a matching shiner, she was still a lovely sight to behold. Jana stepped forward, and they hugged as though longtime lovers. David saw that Michael was a bit surprised, but he also appeared to be pleased.

"I am so glad to see you," David said. "Especially after what happened yesterday. Enough people have—" David began, then he spasmed and started to collapse.

Jana grabbed David, holding him up. "Michael, help!" Michael quickly rushed forward, and together they carried David to the couch and laid him there.

"He's so cold!" Jana said, worry crafting her face.

"But he's sweating," Michael said. David's shirt was soaked, and he was sweating like he'd just stepped out of a steam bath. "David! David, talk to me!"

"David, please!" Jana took his hand and squeezed.

"Call Doc Katyu," Michael said. Jana grabbed the phone and began dialing.

"Michael, got to tell you . . ." David whispered.

"What? David?" Michael leaned forward.

"He's awake!" Jana put down the phone.

"Jana, call Doc Katyu!" Michael repeated. She hesitated, then reached for the phone again. "What, David? Tell me *what?*"

"Jana's right, should have told you, already."

"About what?"

"Monique."

"Who's Monique?"

"A creature of the dark. A myth come to life. A real life vampire."

Michael looked at David, then at Jana, who was still dialing. "Jana, he's delirious and ranting. He said something about a dark creature—a vampire!" Jana stopped dialing and stared at him. "David, it's going to be all right."

"Listen to me, my friend," David said and feebly reached up to grab Michael's shirt for emphasis. "Monique really is one of the undead. She thinks I am, too; for some reason the porphyria confuses her. Says I'm caught partway through the transformation, not human, but not yet a full-blown vampire either. She calls me a shade." Michael's expression was one of utter disbelief. "She wants to help me with the transition by showing me how to be a vampire—by teaching me to kill and how to survive by drinking blood."

"David . . ." Michael didn't know where to begin, what to say.

"Michael, he's telling the truth, I've seen It! Her! IT is horrible. It burned down a lakehouse and almost killed David, when he was trying to save someone," Jana said breathlessly. She looked at Michael, then the phone, started dialing again, and said, "He really is telling the truth. I'd swear on the Bible."

"She killed Skeeter—"

"Skeeter's not dead, just critically burned."

"Ah, good news at last, though still terrible news. He probably wishes he were dead. He'll never look . . . never be . . . normal."

"You're right. Now about this vampire . . . uh, remember, you've . . . uh, well, you've mentioned seeing Tina's ghost before," Michael reminded him, as if to point out that hallucinations were not totally out of the ordinary for him.

David nodded. "Monique's not a ghost. And she's not a delusion. She's really a demon—a temptress—a true spawn of evil." David choked and coughed. "She tortured me, killed JJ and the Brookens brothers because they are the age that Timmy would be right now, if he were alive. I guess she thinks the threat strikes close enough home that it will convert me."

"Did she try to kill Patrick Page?" Michael asked. David shrugged that he didn't know. "You know I don't . . . can't . . . believe this."

"She's killed Bob and some others, I think." David didn't tell his friend that he'd experienced many of the deaths vicariously—sometimes firsthand.

"Lou Callahan and Becky Handley, I thought . . . hey, I spoke with Logan. He said that you've been cleared of any connection with their deaths, and they're going to do it publicly. In fact, it should be in tonight's paper. Logan thinks Kevin Grimm, the mayor's stepson, might have killed them. He's missing."

"Grimm! Oh, God, no! He's one of hers!"

"What?"

"He's under her thrall—he's a puppet! A slave."

"David, I'm sorry, this is too wild, and it simply doesn't make any sense." And yet Michael continued to listen, because they were his friends. Still, he didn't believe it—couldn't; it was absolutely too farfetched. "David, why are you telling me this now?"

"Michael, the phone's dead," Jana said.

"I think I'm dying," David said.

"No!" Jana dropped the phone and rushed to his side.

There was the rumbling of several cars coming down the driveway, the rocks pinging, then crunching as the cars slid to a stop. Several doors slammed, and there were many voices. "Jana, stay with David. I'll see who it is!" Michael went to the open front door and looked outside.

It was no longer dark but well lit from the headlights of a half-dozen or more cars parked out front. At least a score of men had climbed out, leaving the lights on, but shutting off the engines. The night was far from quiet, as angry voices clashed. Michael grew more worried as he studied the group.

Michael pulled the open door to, then closed it when he saw that Hank Tubbs was in front, with Buck right behind him, each carried a shotgun. Behind them were other rowdies, the crew from Gus's garage, Kelly Mane, and Jack Huntington—serious troublemakers. He was surprised at some of the others, henpecked husbands of cronies, Jake Parker and Adam Mathews among others. Each appeared to be carrying some kind of weapon; some had rifles, while others wielded axes and clubs. Michael quickly locked and dead-bolted the door. "Jana, we need to carry David upstairs."

"Who is it?"

"Trouble." Michael didn't want her panicking. "Come on, help me carry him." Together, they hefted David onto his feet, so he could throw his arms over their shoulders. David was so weak, they virtually carried him to the stairs.

"What's going on?" David asked weakly. He was having trouble staying awake, drifting away to someplace quiet and painless—someplace where the sun shone, and everybody wasn't always dying.

"Some of the town has come lynching!" Michael growled, as they made it halfway up the stairs. When they reached the top, he noticed the crosses and smelled garlic.

"Oh Lord, no!" David moaned. "They're coming for me!"

Hiding in the distance behind a tree, Grimm watched the scene and smiled. His plan was coming to wonderful fruition. *The Art of The Payback,* a best-selling novel by Kevin Grimm. Well, this should even his score with Matthewson. Yep, paybacks were hell! And revenge was sweet! He licked his lips.

"Hey, Kevy, how do they say fuck you in LA?"

"Trust me! Hey, bud, how many Mexicans does it take to grease a car?" he asked his friend. "Just one if you hit him right; this time I hope they hit her right. Hey, hey, what do you call a black millionaire physicist . . . or a lawyer for that matter?

"A nigger, Kevy."

"Right you are. I hope they thrash all three, the spic-babe, the nigger-shyster, and the vampire-dude!"

Standing back, away from the other cars and next to his Escort, Stones watched his story develop. He had his tripod and video camera all set and running. This was going to be an incredible story! Screw journalism, he thought as dollars danced in his head. He could sell the movie rights, with him—Corey Stones—playing a starring role. The twists and turns alone would be enough for a miniseries. But that would all come when he spread the news. He'd start with the *Dallas Morning News,* and then go from there. This was rich. He'd be rich! Screw you, Houston. "Hardcopy" and "A Current Affair," here I come!

Down below, the pounding began as someone shouted incoherent demands.

Turning on a hall light as they went, Jana and Michael set David on a bed in the front guest bedroom. "Stay with him, I'm going to talk with this rabble," Michael began, "and see if I can talk some sense into them."

"You're not going down there, are you?" Jana heard several men yelling David's name, along with a torrent of curses and profanity.

"No," Michael replied, as he moved to the window and pulled on the shade. It snapped open, and he unlocked the window, lifted it open, and pushed back the shutters. He felt something tacky and noticed the paint. He didn't know they'd painted graffiti inside, too. What was David up to in his delirium? Vampires, crosses, and garlic. What was next?

But more importantly, what was he—Michael, a man who made his living making convincing arguments—going to do about this crowd? You couldn't reason with a mob, but he still had to try. The lives of everyone depended on it. Michael hoped he would be more compelling than ever before.

Michael heard them mumbling and grumbling below, then someone bellowed, "Come out, Matthewson, and speak to us, or we're going to huff and puff and burn your place down!" It sounded like Hank Tubbs, then a shotgun blast rocked the night. Several men cheered. "You got a lot to answer for! Come out Matthewson, and face us like a real man!"

"I owe you for JJ! And Rick, too!" Buck yelled.

Michael crawled out the window, then walked across the short, flat porch roof. He knelt at the edge, then leaned out, and said, "Can I help you, gentlemen?"

"Oh God!" Ernie screamed, grabbing his chest in fright.

"It's that thing that got Rick!" Buck screamed.

Jack Huntington whipped around, pointing his flashlight at the voice. The beam of light flashed across Michael's face as Buck whirled, his shotgun ready. Somebody near the front gate had lit a firebrand, and pointed with it. "Hey, somebody's on the roof!"

Buck fired wildly, "It's that thing again!" The blast blew apart several shingles. Michael screamed and collapsed onto the roof, clutching himself.

"MICHAEL!" Jana screamed, rushing to the window and leaning out. He wasn't moving. She looked at David; by now he was barely conscious.

"Jana, get one of those bottles, you know, the green ones, from my nightstand. Please?"

"Why?"

"Gotta do something. Try something. It will help me stand, I think. You've seen it work." Jana nodded, hesitated, glanced out the window and then at David. Biting her lip, she left the room. David tried to get up, but couldn't move. Again, he was going to just lie there while those he loved died around him. David began to curse, then prayed instead. He'd do anything to save his friends! Anything!

"Stop! Stop! I'm Michael Woods!" Michael yelled hoarsely, "I'm a lawyer. Quit shooting! I've already called the sheriff. He's on his way and will be here soon! Now be reasonable and leave," Michael finished weakly. He gritted his teeth and gingerly touched his left arm and shoulder. He'd been hit, but he wasn't sure if it were buckshot or roof shrapnel. Still, it hurt like hell; but he couldn't pack it in now. David's life, as well as Jana's and his own, were at stake.

"Hey, it's that black lawyer," Buck said. "Not that . . . that thing," he sounded both very relieved and a little disappointed.

"Oh, Michael Woods," Ernie slurred. "I don't know about this. I think I'll be going."

"Just another nigger," Jack said dryly. "All right, two for the price of one."

"We want David Matthewson! He killed two of my brothers, and he killed the Brookens boys!" Buck screamed. "He's dead meat! If you don't bring him out," Buck fired into the air, "then I'm goin' to—"

"He's sick and may be dying," Michael yelled weakly, beginning to grow dizzy.

"He can't die yet," Hank yelled, then spat. "I want to kill him myself."

"We don't care, lawyer man," Buck yelled, "you carry him out. Or let us in. Or . . ." he thought for a minute, then walked over to Kelly who was holding a torch, "Or we do this." Hank grabbed the firebrand, then ran out the gate toward the barn, the flames sputtering in the wind. He paused just in front of the barn, then hurled the torch. It streaked into the open hayloft. In seconds the fire was spreading, billowing out as though a dragon lived within.

"Heaven help us," Michael whispered, as he watched the barn rapidly become an inferno. This was going to be worse than what had happened to Carter. He'd thought those days were long gone, that times changed. Michael remembered how frightened his dad had been when he'd told that story to him as a child. And Michael was frightened now, and hurting badly. His shirt was soaked with blood, and he could see it run down his arm, but couldn't feel it.

Michael's head spun, the world threatening to tilt. What could have incited this? It was surreal, a flashback to the sixties, except that David was white. This was more like the Old West—an old-fashioned hanging. Even farther back in another black moment in American history, David might have been burned at the stake.

Hank came jogging back, stopping at Michael's Forerunner, and began blasting it with his shotgun. "Yee-haw!" He blew out the windows, reloaded, and shredded the grill. Michael held his ears. Laughing, Hank fired again, perforating the doors. Lastly, he obliterated the tires with a round. The blasts resounded and echoed. After a moment of silence, Hank yelled, "What you think now, mouthpiece? Is that brief enough for ya?"

"Listen . . ." Michael began, then nearly blacked out.

"Enough talk! It's showtime, put up or shut up!" Hank yelled. He took a lighter and ignited another brand. "Here you go!" He heaved the torch onto the front porch. "Just want you to know we left you a present at your doorstep." He chuckled. "A couple of gas cans!"

Inside, David finished the bottle of elixir and immediately felt a little better. He kissed Jana, then began moving toward the window. He had to do something to stop this! Michael might get killed.

In the distance, David could see the massive bonfire that was his barn. A giant hand of flame was reaching up to tear the roof apart. His animals! Did any of them get free? Murderers! Enraged, David began to climb out the window, then stopped. The night was alive and dead at the same time. Oh Lord, not now. Monique was here!

Sixteen

Calling Kin

Leaning against a tree for support, Monique waited in the ebony cover of the woods, untouched by the moonlight, but with her shadow at her side. "Dey are burning the barn! De house is probably next!" Between her fight with David and the beating she'd received from Grimm, Monique still wasn't feeling right; she was a mere shadow of her once-powerful self.

"Den we must stop dem!" Marlena replied. "Dey won't deny us the right of choice—de right of execution! Come with us, large one; breakfast is served, but work must be done first." Marlena moved lithely forward, then something followed, lumbering in her wake. Loose-jawed, Ross staggered out in the moonlight. His eyes were glazed and his shoulders stooped, arms limp and hanging, as if he were an ape. "Ah, de price for spying nowadays is very high!" Marlena laughed.

"I doubt David has changed his mind," Monique rasped, touching her throat as she glanced at her companion. She wished her other was not here. Things would have gone better without interference, but then one must abide by the Council or be destroyed. It was that simple.

"It matters not. If David doesn't want to feast on him,"

Marlena waved to Ross and laughed, "den I will. He is nicely fattened! Now come! I have been given free rein. We will resolve this tonight, one way or de other."

The two dashed forward, flashing across the moonlit spaces as though they were bolts of black lightning. They moved so similarly and in such close unison, that the two forms might have been one—one real and the other a reflection. Suddenly, Monique stopped, snarled quietly, and then moved away without a word to Marlena. Ross stopped, blank-faced.

Looking coldly beautiful, Marlena stepped from a shadow-gate right next to Stones, who didn't notice her. The reporter kept saying, "Great stuff. Great stuff! M-O-N-E-Y!"

Marlena's lips tightened into a silent snarl, then she grabbed Stones by the scruff of the neck and lifted him off his feet. He squawked, dropping his videocamera and flailing at her to no avail. Slowly, Marlena brought him to face her, nose to nose. Stones immediately panicked, trying to scream but unable to, his air cut off by her grip.

Marlena smiled. "Ah, I see you remember me from last night. I hope you told others, told dem to fear the dark. But alas, you didn't listen yourself, or you would not be here. And now, you are course number two." Marlena roughly switched her grip, moving from his neck to underneath his jaw, holding him high enough that the tip of his toes barely touched the ground. Desperation filled his eyes and fear his face, as the reporter stared into Marlena's eyes, his soul slowly becoming lost.

"You will walk around to the rear of de house and wait dere for me. Do not speak to anyone or do anything else," Marlena commanded. "Just wait quietly. I will come for you." Marlena checked his eyes, then let him go. Stiffly, Stones headed for the backyard. She motioned to Ross, and he followed the reporter.

Marlena slid forward, drifting like a patch of fog blown toward the cars in front of David's gate. They would not cheat her of her rights granted by the Council. Marlena surprised Ernie as he came bursting out the gate, running between cars. Marlena grabbed him and broke his neck in one easy, fluid motion. He would've tasted foul, old and rotted by alcohol. She dropped him and kept going, moving toward the rabble. It was time to have some fun!

Grimm sensed Monique before she arrived. Smiling, he slowly turned to greet her, still wielding the broken staff with which he'd beaten her earlier. "You, my dear, look like—pardon my French—shit. Truth be told, and I try not to, I am surprised to see you. Have you come back for more punishment? And do you like my new nightstick? I had to modify it since our last encounter." Grimm slapped the rod softly into the palm of his hand, to show he was ready to use it on her once more, and that he would enjoy doing it again.

She saw all in his eyes. "I owe you as I only owe David Matthewson," she briefly touched the bandage around her throat, "but at least he is an equal, not some primordial ooze that somehow learned to walk and talk. For you to live would be de-volution."

"That's a pretty complicated speech for a simple storage unit for a pussy," Grimm smiled.

Monique hissed and darted forward, moving more slowly because of her injuries. Grimm moved much faster than she expected, and Monique missed her lunge as he sidestepped. Chuckling, Grimm hammered her, connecting flush with the side of her head and driving her to the ground.

"You just ain't that tough a bitch anymore," Grimm laughed, and hit her again and again. The crosses burned, charring undead flesh where they struck. Monique tried to roll away from Grimm, but he moved lithely and drove the staff into her ribs. She doubled over and screamed. Grimm beat her unmercifully, cutting off her cries. "Now we know who the master is!" Grimm rolled her over and shoved the staff under her chin, then yanked back. The crosses seared her throat, unholy flesh bubbling, burning, and melting. "Why does it take longer for women to climax? Who gives a shit!" Grimm laughed madly.

Marlena saw one of the men hurl a torch onto the front porch. It bounced off the front wall, sparked, and landed by two metal jerrycans set on the porch. A wall of fire exploded with a mighty *whoosh* and leapt high, raking the ceiling.

Marlena cursed herself; they were too late, unless she killed them all, so that David could escape. It was the least she could do for kin. A cold wind, she blew through the gate and appeared behind the last of the mob, who was engrossed in loading his rifle. Marlena ran her chilly hands up his legs and squeezed him. He jumped and turned around. Smiling, she pulled him into her arms, kissed him, then quickly broke his neck. The sickening, snapping-grinding sound made a nearby man with a firebrand turn to watch his friend collapse. "Adam? Adam, you okay?" Jack rushed forward.

Marlena stepped out from a shadow. As she grasped the arm holding the firebrand, she heard her sister scream. She needed help! This was not like her at all. Something was terribly wrong, probably her brand, and if this were so, she would have to dispense the Council's justice: only the strong survive. With little effort, Marlena broke Jack's elbow, then jammed the torch into his chest. His clothing caught fire, and he screamed. "This is very appropriate, no?"

"Hey, Buck!" Hank whirled around to see Jack Huntington burning, now a human torch. "Something . . . that THING! That thing that got Rick is behind us!" Hank aimed and ripped off a blast. It tore through Jack and even hit several others in the crowd.

"HEY! Don't shoot at us!" Kelly screamed.

Marlena hurled the flaming body at those on the walkway. The Tubbs brothers fired again, then others joined in, firing at shadows, or anything they thought moved. One of the gas cans exploded, spewing burning liquid all over the front yard and some of the mob. They threw themselves to the ground and rolled about, trying to extinguish the flames.

"You don't put up much of a fight," Grimm said, as Monique slumped to the ground. "You know, I thought I might find you here, so I came prepared." He pulled a wooden spike from a nearby backpack and prepared to drive it home.

As Grimm lunged forward, the stake was forcefully struck from his hand and sent sailing into the woods. "What?" Grimm turned to see another Monique. "What the hell?" He'd been so focused on Monique, that he hadn't heard Marlena coming.

She grabbed Grimm by the ears. He tried to stop her, then break her hold, but she tightened her grip. "We meet again. I am Marlena," she said, then ripped off his ears. Grimm screamed and collapsed atop Monique. Marlena grabbed him once more by the head, and lifted him up so she could look him in the eyes.

"You are just a shade! I am a true mistress of darkness!" Ever so slowly, she swung him from side to side by his head. His feet flew left then right, each time he swung farther, all but his head and neck, which were held fast. "You can still die, while I cannot!" With a large sweep and twist, the vampire broke Grimm's neck and dropped him like a sack of potatoes. She stared at him for a moment, then at Monique, battered and beaten, lying exhausted on the ground.

"Come, sister, we must finish this." Marlena helped Monique to her feet. "You know, I am worried about you. Where is your will? Your desire!"

"I will be fine," Monique said unconvincingly.

"You had better be! Weakness is not acceptable. Come," Marlena told her. "We will go around back. Dose out front are distracted with killing each other."

Monique looked wearily at the ranch house. The porch was an open blast furnace, the flames devouring the front of the houses. Tendrils licked at the roof and reached around the corners, wanting more to eat. The house—probably the entire ranch—would not last long. Several nearby trees had caught fire, becoming towering pillars of flame. Below, running wildly about in the ruddy light, the mob was still shooting and screaming.

Monique heard the approach of another car racing down the gravel road toward the ranch house. She followed the sound and saw red and blue lights flashing. "Authorities! We must hurry!"

Monique and Marlena glided toward the rear of the conflagration. Suddenly, Marlena stopped, pausing to stare at the winding gravel driveway. Moments later, a second set of headlights appeared. "Worse dan the authorities. Another approaches dat I'd rather not face. Let us get on with it! We will either anoint a new brother, or execute de sentence of a rogue shade."

Seventeen

Firefight

Disregarding the danger, David crawled out the window and scrambled on all fours across the smoldering rooftop. The shingles were warm under his knees and hands; but they were still resisting the heat building from below, unlike the edges and framing of the porch, which were already ablaze. The wind suddenly gusted and shifted, sending tendrils of flame flicking across the roof and plucking at David's pants, threatening to ignite his clothing.

Gunfire and yelling continued from below, cutting through the crackling of the fire devouring his house. A bullet whined, digging into the roof nearby and coughing up debris that caught David in his chest and face. He flinched, but kept going, his attention focused on Michael. His friend wasn't moving, either because of paralysis, unconsciousness, or . . . he didn't want to think it!

David felt Monique close by . . . very close. And yet, she also felt somewhat distant, David was thoroughly confused. Another whizzing bullet pulled his attention back to his immediate problem, and he stopped next to Michael. David shook him gently. "Are you all right?" David glanced at his friend, then at the fire, which had finally ignited some of the fringe shingles and was slowly advancing across the roof. Between the fire and the firefight, they couldn't afford to stay here much longer.

"D . . . David, what are you doing out here?" Michael looked dazed, and sounded confused as well as drained. His shirt was blood-soaked, and he held his left arm as though it were lifeless. "I . . . I thought you were sick."

"I got better. Good medicine." David said, lying. He didn't feel well at all, just stronger thanks to the elixir, and driven by a combination of urgency and fear. His stomach still churned, twisting and knotting on itself, and his throat burned, but Michael looked worse—much worse. "You've been shot."

"Yes, I think you're right." Michael was in shock. "To tell the truth, I feel sort of numb."

"Hang in there, my friend," David moved closer and gently gathered up Michael. "I'll get us out of this." Easing him into a fireman's carry, David slowly moved in a crouch across the roof toward the window.

Ahead, Jana was biting her lower lip and waving them onward, encouraging them. On each side of the window, the flames had started to climb the walls, elemental termites of fire feasting, consuming everything they touched. As David reached the window, Jana moved to help him with Michael. She gasped at his bloody condition, as she took him in her arms. Staggering under the load, Jana still managed to gently lower Michael to the floor.

David climbed through the window and pulled the shutters closed, giving them an extra minute or two of protection. "He needs a doctor," David said, kneeling by his friend. "Hang in there, Michael, we may have to win this one at the buzzer." Michael managed to nod, his eyes threatening to roll back into his head.

"The phone is dead. We'll have to drive," Jana told him.

"We can't stay here. This place isn't going to last much

longer. Welcome to the Matthewson's tinderbox," he said sarcastically.

Jana gave him a pitying look, which David ignored as he ripped a strip from his shirt, then wound the torn cloth around Michael's wound. "Oh, David, I'm so sorry! I . . ." Jana began.

When David finished, he grasped her by the shoulders, "It'll be okay. We've already survived worse. We'll take Michael to Doc Katyu. Forget about the house. Surviving—the three of us—is all that counts!"

Outside there was a sudden burst of gunfire, then a loud crunching noise, as if several heavy metal objects had collided. "What was that?" Jana asked.

"Who cares! Let's get out of here, while the getting's good." Not wanting Jana to panic, David didn't tell her about Monique. "They sound occupied out front, shooting and burning things." Bitterness was heavy in his voice. "That's all that matters. Pray it's enough that we can sneak out and get to the Blazer without getting shot." David hefted Michael over his shoulder and headed into the hallway. David paused at the top of the steps, then said, "Wait here!" With Michael still over his shoulder, David disappeared into his bedroom.

"David! What?" Jana cried.

David quickly returned, tucking his silver cross and a Smith and Wesson into the waistband of his pants. "Now we're ready! There's a shotgun in the hall closet. We may need it. Come on!" He waved Jana down the stairs and moved to follow.

Just before he headed downstairs, David heard a noise and glanced into the front bedroom. The walls were beginning to blacken, and the shutters were smoldering, as though they'd been tossed into a wood stove. They were running out of time! David prayed nobody would be out back, then descended the steps into the smoky foyer. Flaming fingers were already clawing at the ceiling, and the entire front of the house was afire. The roar sounded as if a bellowing beast were trying to break in.

As David neared the bottom of the stairs, a bullet ripped through the front door and ricocheted off the steps, causing David to hop belatedly to one side. "Be careful!" David cried, then coughed. His head began to spin, and the world tilted, threatening to plunge him into a dark abyss. David almost lost his balance—Michael's weight was difficult to balance—but managed to grab the railing. It protested under David's grip, as he swayed unsteadily. Not now! Lord please! David stumbled down the last few steps, hoping that for once his luck would hold.

Jana had opened the closet and was frantically digging around in the back of it. "Forget the gun! Come on!" David urged, as he turned into the hallway and headed toward the kitchen. Coughing and wheezing, Jana jumped up and followed him. The smoke was growing thicker and heavier by the minute; it would soon be suffocating. A shot came through the front shuttered windows and broke a lamp. David ushered Jana past him. "Go on!" They ran down the hallway and into the kitchen.

"Grab the keys by the door."

"Which ones?" Jana asked, looking them over. There were several rings hanging from hooks on the wall.

"All of them!" David said, slipping by her and yanking the door open. "YOU!" David stopped short. "God, no!"

"Leaving?" Monique asked him, then coughed.

"I think not," another Monique—this one appearing healthy and coldly bewitching—said to him, as she moved next to the first. "Dis won't take long. Besides, depending on your choice, fire is a perfect ending. I've always liked the idea of a funeral pyre. It's so primeval."

"Meet my twin sister, Marlena," the sickly Monique waved to the other Monique. "You have met before, intimately, in a graveyard, I believe. As she said, we have come for your response to her ultimatum," Monique said, pushing her way inside. David quickly backed up, as did Jana, her eyes wide and face ashen. She reached for the crucifix hanging from her neck.

"And I have brought the first and second courses," Marlena laughed and waved. "Come in, my friends. You can roast dem, if you prefer your meal cooked," Marlena chuckled. Staring blindly forward and moving as though zombies, Ross and Stones stumbled into the house, following the two vampires. "I will have your choice now, David Matthewson. Either you feast on one of dese and accept your heritage, or we will destroy you. Which one is it?"

David gently placed Michael on the kitchen table, then faced the twin vampires. "I will never do as you wish! Never!" David cried defiantly. "You must be the ones to die!" David yanked his silver crucifix free and displayed it to the vampires.

"That is not the right choice," Marlena said, as the twins took a few quick steps back. Smoke was beginning to fill the room and obscure the ceiling. The crackling and popping of the hungry fire roamed down the hall, announcing that it was coming for them.

"I am not surprised," Monique managed a small smile. "He is very stubborn, very much in love with life." Suddenly she wobbled unsteadily and grabbed the nearby countertop.

As though the spell had been partly broken, Stones dropped to his knees, begging and pleading, "Don't kill me. Please!" Ross had backed against the cabinets, and was cringing like a dog who'd been beaten too many times.

"Stop that!" Marlena commanded. Ross and Stones grew quiet, their expressions lost and faraway. "Now, Jana, your decision!" With an irritated sweep, she wiped sweat from her brow.

Jana was at David's side, helping him guard Michael. Fear and stubbornness were mixed, playing across her face. They were trapped between hell and damnation, but at least they would go together. "Leave us alone! I want to live to the fullest! Not just exist, empty and soulless until the end of time!" Jana raised her crucifix, wielding it as though it were a warding shield. "Life is worth living and worth dying for!"

"You are throwing away the chance—the honor—of a lifetime," Marlena told her with a hint of sadness in her voice, but it was gone just as quickly as it had arrived. "Sister, attend me." The two vampires—healthy and ill—moved together. Marlena supported Monique as the two stared down David and Jana.

As though slapped, David could feel the physical effects of their psychic assault. Jana gasped and staggered back as the invisible attack assailed them, squeezing them in a vise and trying to seize their wills. Fighting the hypnotic effect, David held his crucifix higher, staring past it at the terrible twins. Both appeared less than confident—a bit disconcerted and annoyed. Could the painted verses be working?

Together, the twin sisters took a halting step forward. David felt more pressure and began to sweat, his muscles growing heavy and stiff, as though he'd been drugged. David knew he'd fought this battle before and lost. Yet he held the crucifix firmly with both hands as his strength quickly ebbed, draining away as if the evil sisters were sucking the life from him. David's arms began to waver and dip.

"David . . . I . . ." Jana began. Having lost to their will, she dropped her cross and crashed against the table.

"Jana, stay behind me," David gasped. He felt the weight of the world pressing on his shoulders.

"Get them!" Marlena suddenly commanded, and Ross and Stones rushed forward, slamming into David. The trio staggered together across the floor, then rammed into the pantry door, breaking it down and tumbling inside. The cross flew from David's hand, as he was buried under the mass of flesh. Dead weight, the huge deputy just lay there.

"Danka," Marlena said to her thralls. "Stay. I will finish this one off first." David heard a resounding slap.

"JANA!" They were killing her! David struggled futilely against the human mound piled atop him. Desperate, his hand dug for the pistol digging into his hip and stomach.

"Let him up!" Marlena told her thralls. David scrambled to his feet, pushing Ross and Stones aside. He started to go to Jana, but Marlena grabbed him. "You will listen to me," Marlena told David, jerking him around so that they were face to face, her gaze boring into his and trying to quash his defenses. Once again, he felt held by invisible hands. "You are a shade, caught between dying and being undead. Yes! You heard me! You are in the final stages of dying, more than simply sick. Now drink to your new health," she motioned to Ross, "drink of de blood of life, and accept your destiny! It is your very last chance!"

"Never! I AM NOT A VAMPIRE!" David gritted.

"He is stubborn. I have never met anyone like him," Monique said sadly. "You are right. He must be destroyed. Sad, because I will never learn how he managed to be caught by the camera." She glanced uneasily down the hall at the flames. "But time is short, and I have already been in one burning house too many. Let's finish it and leave. There is something," she shivered, "strange about this place." Monique came to David, leaned forward, and kissed him. Unable to move, David flinched. "We would have made an incredible couple, led a timeless existence unparalleled by any others. And I might have been a movie star, and you a great author. Alas, it is not to be."

"I AM NOT A VAMPIRE!" David managed to scream. If he must die, let it be known that he died a human, not a monster as some believed. "How can I be?" he finally managed, choking down his rage at the injustice of his life. "I am only just now dying, according to you. If I'd been bitten by Liselle a decade ago, wouldn't I have died long ago? Wouldn't the transformation already be complete?"

Marlena stared at him a long time, not even acknowledging the danger to them all. The hallway carpet was now afire, and something collapsed out front, hurling burning debris down the corridor toward them. "You are different, I admit, but it could be because you have not slaked your thirst. And yet, it is possible that Monique could have been mistaken. It would not be the first time. She has been failing quite a bit recently."

"What?" Monique reacted. As the twins glared at each other, they might as well have hurled daggers.

"But it doesn't matter. I have my orders from the Council; you must both must be destroyed!"

"What," Monique screamed, "are you talking about?"

"I have spoken with the Council. I will absorb your power, which will be divided among the members. You have grown too weak. This never should have become a fiasco." Marlena waved about her.

"But you're my sister!" Monique cried, backing away as though ready to flee. "And it's not my fault! I have been branded by the cross!" She jerked a scarf away from her neck, revealing the seared tattoo of a cross on her throat. "By you!" she shouted at David.

"I was your sister in flesh, until you transformed me so that you would not be lonely," Marlena said levelly, "but since then, never in spirit. You changed me, and I have never forgiven you. You know the code: only the strong survive. There must be no sign of weakness, no chinks in the armor of darkness." Marlena began advancing on Monique, who was now cowering. They were ignoring David, but he was still held fast. He fought on, struggling against the paralysis, and felt it ease a little.

"No," Monique pleaded. "It's not my fault. I will heal!"

"You know you aren't strong enough to stop me. It will be easier, if you relax," Marlena told her. "I will be gentle."

David looked around wildly, first at Jana—wishing she was all right—then searching for his cross. Finally he saw it in the hallway, where it must have bounced. David glanced at the twins, then tried to ease toward the hallway. He broke free for a moment, taking a couple of steps.

"Hold him!" Marlena commanded, glancing quickly toward Ross and David, then back to Monique. Suddenly, David was caught in a breath-denying bear hug, and lifted off his feet. His arms were pinned to his side, as his breath exploded from his mouth and nose. Gasping, he frantically attempted to wriggle free of Ross's grip.

Marlena backed Monique into the cabinets near the sink. "You couldn't handle dis situation, so I will finish it for you!" Marlena roughly grabbed her wasted twin, her fingernails digging into undead flesh. A chill swirled through the air and Monique's head rocked back as she screamed in plaintive agony, the horrible sound drowning out the roar of the oncoming fire.

Monique twisted, trying to pull away, and they both fell to the floor. Marlena landed on top. "You only make this more painful." She placed her legs on both sides of her twin, then worked her fingers ever deeper, searching for Monique's cursed spirit. A glow welled within Marlena's hands, then began to crawl up her arms. Giddy, she began to laugh.

As David fought for freedom and a breath, his head began to spin, and he felt himself growing weaker and weaker. He tried to flex his arms and drive them upward, but failed again. Frustrated, he slumped forward, gasping and choking on what little smoke-tainted air he could seize. Then he snapped his head back as hard as he could. His cranium smashed into Ross's face, crushing the big man's nose. The big deputy teetered, then, still holding onto David, fell backwards. As they hit the floor, Ross's grip finally loosened, and David wrenched himself free.

Suddenly David felt somebody—something else—enter

the kitchen. Through blurry eyes, he glanced toward the rear door and saw a pale shape quietly enter the kitchen. His head was held oddly, limply laying on his left shoulder, as though he were a puppet with some strings severed.

Earless, bloody, and looking like death warmed over, Kevin Grimm smiled at David knowingly. Grimm placed one finger to his lips, then opened his hand to reveal a wooden spike—a cross with the bottom sharpened. In the other hand, he still carried his broken staff.

Without a joke, Grimm stealthily approached Marlena, who was fully aglow and reveling in the ecstasy of absorption. She was laughing, while her sister's scream was slowly dying. Grimm reared back and jabbed the stake into Marlena's back. The vampire straightened, snatching her hands from Monique's undead flesh. The glow left Marlena and refilled Monique, who slumped to the floor. Laughing and snarling at the same time, Grimm drove the cross home, hammering it with the rod. Marlena screamed, rearing up and arching, then she, too collapsed on the floor.

Grimm stood over the two, examining them, then smiled and said, "What a pair of bitches. Hey, Marlena babe, do you know what Jesus said to Mary, while he was being crucified on the cross?"

David's faculties began to return, but he couldn't believe his eyes. Saved by Grimm, but to what grisly fate? He reached for his Smith and Wesson, and found it gone. It must have fallen out during his struggle with Monique's thralls. David looked around wildly, spotting it on the closet floor among cans and boxes.

"Can you get my flats! These spikes are killing me!" Grimm laughed. "I got one for you, too," he told Monique, and raised the rod.

David reacted. Diving and grabbing the gun, he twisted around in one motion and fired. He pulled the trigger, not once, but until the hammer clicked empty several times. The shells ripped at Grimm, and he danced backward, a crazed marionette. Finally, bleeding and tattered, he stopped, slumping against the oven door.

"Thank God," David gasped. Now they could escape before it all came down around them. He tried to climb to his feet, but his knees refused to comply and buckled. Determined, David began to crawl toward Jana, then the sound of movement stopped him. He glanced at Grimm, then stared as the body began to move.

Very slowly, and with a smile crawling onto his face, Grimm stood. "You know. I do believe I'm already dead. There can be only one top vampire in Temprance, so guess what? You're next." Grimm raised the rod and advanced on David.

Eighteen

Wild Dogs

"The place is being torched!" Logan exclaimed, as the ranch house and barn came into view. Bricker just frowned and grunted. Logan cursed, struggling to keep the Mustang under control as they sped along the rutted driveway, bouncing and skidding. Gravel pummeled the car as though they were being stoned by protectors. The Mustang hit a rut, hunkered low, then sprang skyward. As they landed, the wheel twisted in the deputy's hands.

Bricker hit his head on the ceiling. "Damn! Be careful!"

"I told you to put on your seat belt!" Logan admonished. He glanced ahead at the fire-ravaged barn, then at the house. Ripples of flame were crawling out from under the porch, and nipping at the roof. A sheet of flame wafted, then rippled across the entire front of the house, like a new coat of ethereal paint. "Damn nightmare. The Carter lynching all over again, but worse."

"Yep," Bricker said stoically. The sheriff unstrapped his holster and removed his .38. "Try not to—" The Mustang lurched.

"Damn, sorry," Logan struggled to right the car as it slid sideways again. He knew he was driving too fast, but he'd felt a sense of urgency ever since getting a phone call from Zane Harkness, and now he saw why. David was in mortal danger, and only the Lord knew who else—Penny, Carolyn, Jana, or Michael maybe? Anybody nearby was fair game, when the wild dogs were loose.

If only he'd received Zane's message earlier, Logan fumed; but there was so much going on, even urgent messages took time getting through. The barber had sounded frightened as he breathlessly repeated what Ernie had heard at the First Street Club, where the unruly of Temprance were gathering. He'd said that the Tubbs brothers would have been out earlier to lynch David, but it took them most of the previous night and day to cautiously round up enough men to feel the safety in numbers. Something about the place scared the boys. They'd armed themselves with all sorts of strange paraphernalia, including crucifixes, as well as guns and gasoline. Lastly, it seemed that Rick Tubbs was missing. Logan didn't know what to make of that. He'd raced to the club, but was too late; everybody had already gone. Unable to find Ross, Logan and Bricker had hopped in the car and raced into the countryside.

"Who's that behind us?" Logan asked, glancing in the rearview mirror. The sound of shots altered his attention, and he looked ahead as they finished the last curve leading to the house.

"Gunfire!" exclaimed Bricker, who had turned to look around, twisted back. A bullet crashed through the side window, shattering it. "I'm hit!" he gurgled, and clutched his chest. Another bullet ricocheted off the front windshield, cracking it in a thousand places and blinding Logan as it went opaque.

Flying glass stung Logan, and he spun the wheel. One hand slipped, and the car skidded sideways, its rear facing the house. Suddenly the front tire hit a rut. The Mustang jerked and jumped, gliding briefly, then crashing into the nearest parked car. Bricker was thrown through the side window, as though he'd been ejected.

Logan's belt snapped tight, holding him as he was twisted sideways, then recoiled as though he were a pretzel being shaped. Dizzy, he slumped against the wheel. The car stopped, rocking slightly. Logan heard more gunfire in the dim distance; shouting and the roaring of flames filled the night, as he slipped into unconsciousness.

Cooper drove much faster and more desperately than he believed wise, praying to God to guide his Camry and keep him safe. Following the sheriff's car, the reverend was on a mission to save lives and souls this time. He'd been on his way out to see David once more—since he wasn't answering his phone—when he saw the black and white Mustang speed by, its lights flashing, but no siren wailing. Immediately, Cooper Page felt that he knew where the sheriff was headed. Cooper prayed, hoping that all would be right—that cooler heads would prevail during this time of madness—then stomped on the gas and drove as though he were in a stockcar rally.

Cooper gasped when the ranch came into view; it appeared he was too late. The conflagration had devastated the barn. Billowing flames covered the front of the ranch house, now burned black, as more fire cavorted across the roofs.

The insanity continued as Cooper watched the sheriff's Mustang slide sideways, bounce, and then slam into a truck and a station wagon. What was he to do? This looked like a war zone. Cooper stomped on the brakes, his white Camry sliding to a stop.

Praying, the reverend jumped out and ran toward the front gate. He could hear shouting as well as gunfire. He paused next to the sheriff's car, wondering if he should help—if he could help—then he heard, "Oh my God! Buck's been shot! Speak to me, Buck!"

Logan heard the same thing as he regained consciousness. His vision had cleared much earlier than his head, and he still felt addled. Stiffly, as though all his joints had been welded, Logan undid his seat belt, opened the screeching door, and crawled out of the car. He was still so woozy that he wasn't sure what was going on. There was fire and shooting, but where was Donald? He'd been with him a minute ago. And who was that near the bushes? My God! It looked like the Reverend Page. What was he doing here?

"He's dead. Damn you all! He's dead! All my brothers are dead!" Blast after blast rocked the area, bullets going every which way.

Cooper ducked, scrambled on his knees to get to the front gate, and peered around the bushes. Crimson light played across Hank Tubbs's twisted face as he knelt, cradling his injured brother. Buck's chest was a mess of red cloth. Hank held a pistol in his free hand, firing into the air and sometimes over his shoulder. He appeared to be the only person left alive. There were at least a dozen dead around him. Cooper recognized most of them, many were in his congregation. So senseless and so many . . .

No, wait! Cooper saw one of them move, then another groaned and shifted. He was not too late, but something must be done quickly. "My son!" Cooper slowly stood, trying to calm his shaky legs. "It's not too late. Things can be worked out!" Hank pointed the muzzle of the pistol toward the reverend, but Cooper kept ministering. "God forgives all transgressions, but we must take the first step. Now is the time! Take that step! Save yourself and these others!"

"I don't give a fuck about the others," Hank moaned. "It's not my fault, ya know. It's really not. It's Matthewson's and that . . . that THING! They killed JJ, Rick, and now Buck! Now I'm all alone. But what the hell, I'm goin' ta hell anyway and I hate travelin' alone." Hank pulled the trigger.

Logan shoved Cooper aside and caught the bullet. He

screamed, twisting with the impact. There was a ringing in Logan's ears as he hit the ground hard and tumbled. Seconds passed and were lost. Logan thought he heard the crunching of footsteps, then, through blurred vision, he saw Hank standing over him, pistol pointed at his face.

"You know, I've always wanted to do this," Hank glanced over at the prone and motionless body of Bricker, and said, "I'm just sorry I won't be able to do this to him, too!"

"No more!" Cooper screamed. As though he were a linebacker in one of the Cowboy games he loved to watch, the Reverend threw himself at Hank Tubbs, striking him sideways in the knees. Hank yelped in pain and surprise as ligaments tore, and he went down in a heap. Cursing, he tried to rise and bring his pistol to bear.

Groggy and fading fast, Logan groped for his gun. Flashes of darkness threatened to overwhelm him and take away consciousness. After long moments his .38 just seemed to appear in his hand. Hoping he'd get lucky, he fired at Hank several times. Hank jerked backwards, hands going to his chest and face. Logan heard a scream, and smiled as the darkness buried him.

Stunned and aching, Cooper looked around. What was he to do? He glanced at Logan, then Hank, then at all the others. He'd never seen anything like this, not even during his tour of duty in Korea. And this wasn't even a war. Or was it? Fighting hate and prejudice was a relentless battle.

Cooper staggered to Logan's side and checked his pulse. Thank heavens, Logan was still alive! Cooper began to pray; then he knew what to do as surely as though he'd received a message.

The reverend tried the passenger door and found it stuck fast. Undeterred, he limped around and climbed into the battered Mustang and turned on the radio, hoping it still worked. The light came on. "Hello? Help, we need help! I'm at the Matthewson farm! Is anybody listening!" he shouted into the microphone. "Send help! Send—" Cooper stopped at the sound of more gunfire. Somebody was still up and about. Might it be David or other members of his family? Crawling out of the car, Cooper began his search, limping toward the rear of the house and the source of the noise.

Nineteen

Righteous Fire

"Hey, what do you do with a problem author?" Grimm asked, smiling as he approached David. The dark, oily smoke swirled around Grimm like a corrupt halo, but he didn't seem to notice. "Kick the script out of him!" Grimm reached behind him, then showed David a revolver. "Found this on a guy who didn't need it! Hey, how are you at shoot 'em up endings? I think this one is going to blow you away!"

Lying on the floor and unable to rise to his own defense, David couldn't believe it was going to end like this. Why wasn't Grimm dead? He looked dead, his neck apparently broken and his head partly caved in, revealing something shiny. He hadn't even slowed down, although he bled from both sides of his head, where his ears were missing, as well as a half-dozen scattered bullet wounds. David had not missed even once.

David tried to rise again, but his legs failed him once more. Frustrated and helpless, he knew they were all going to die, one way or another. The ceiling was now afire, and Grimm hadn't even noticed it. If David could keep him busy, then he'd also burn up . . . unless Grimm was a vampire. And what other explanation was there? Fire was nothing but an inconvenience to the undead. Monique had survived. And if Grimm and Monique survived, then David's death would be meaningless.

"You know, I think shoot 'em up endings have been beaten to death!" Grimm swung his rod and caught David across the knees. The pain was agonizingly riveting, and David screamed, instinctively curling up and clutching his legs. Grimm hit him across the back, and David straightened, crying out hoarsely. Laughing, Grimm struck him across the temple. Reeling, David saw stars.

"Uh . . . hey," David heard a voice. "What's going on here? Smoke? Hey, a fire! How'd I . . ."

There was a loud crack, followed by a sound that reminded David of a melon being struck. "Hey, you know the difference between a bucket of shit and a reporter, Mr. Stones?" Another blow landed. "No? Then I'll tell you. The bucket!" Again and again, David heard the sickening, wet smack of blow after blow. "Did you hear about the reporter who had body odor only on one side? He didn't know where to buy Left Guard!"

David thought this was his moment, time to do or die, but his legs continued to fail him. His only hope was to roll over to Grimm, pull him down, and slay him with his bare hands, if that were even possible.

"Hello?" came another voice. "Is someone alive in there? Do you need help?" David recognized the voice, but couldn't believe it. What was the Reverend Page doing here? David managed to roll over and look at Grimm.

Grimm quit beating Stones and turned toward the back door, which was completely obscured by choking smoke. "Hey, Reverend, what kind of meat does Pope Paul eat?" He raised his gun and fired. "Nun, but you can ask him yourself." There was a gasp, followed by the sound of a body hitting the ground. Chuckling, Grimm walked to the back door to check on his latest victim. "I guess this preacher found his perish all right!"

David cursed silently. Another had died, all because of him! It was his fault—his curse! If he'd gone away, or died, this never would have happened. Your death won't be wasted, David promised the Reverend Page. For the price of his life, Cooper had bought David time. Exhausted but dogged, David scrambled for the closet, hunting for his crucifix.

"Hey! None of that! No whiz bang endings!" Grimm shouted and fired at David. The bullet chipped the floor next to him, but it was not followed by a second, only the *click, click* of an empty chamber. "Oh, hell! A hands-on job! Well, I've always heard, give as good as you get, and I've gotten some pretty mean beatings! You can tell my dad I learned a lot from him, when you see him in Hell!" Grimm raised his modified nightstick and raced forward.

David spotted the crucifix and dove for it. He grabbed it and rolled away, just as Grimm struck. Grimm missed, but recoiled quickly and struck again. David twisted aside, receiving a sharp but glancing blow; David swiped at the weapon but missed. Grimm reared back once more. Desperate, David shoved his crucifix toward Grimm.

Grimm blanched, then shook it off, laughing and saying, "That ain't no salvation, and there ain't gonna be no sequel!"

Something moved behind Grimm. David couldn't believe his eyes! Could it be? Standing behind him was Tina's ghost! SHE WAS REAL!

There was a groaning noise—a protesting of wood, then the burning ceiling suddenly buckled and collapsed. Too surprised to react, Grimm was buried under the crush of debris. He crumpled, falling atop David and shielding him from the fiery avalanche. When his undead flesh touched the silver cross, Grimm screamed, kicking and writhing until he finally grew silent.

Barely able to breathe—smothered by Grimm and the pile of burning debris atop them both—David was thankful. He hadn't had time to cover up, if that would have been possible, and the sonuvabitch had protected him. Now David had to save Jana and Michael, if they were still alive. David felt totally pinned; the pressure on his chest was almost unbearable. Another smaller section of the ceiling collapsed nearby, throwing more flaming debris in his direction.

The sounds of the fire grew louder, as the heat increased. Things began to burst into flame without needing fire. Killing smoke continued to thicken, lowering to floor level and surrounding David. He tried to rise and didn't budge an inch. Groaning, he tried to slide out from underneath Grimm, and failed. His only hope, besides a miracle, was to try a combination of both, but the hand holding the cross was trapped under Grimm's body. Everything hurt so badly, David couldn't distinguish one pain from the next. Suddenly a searing pain rifled along his legs. His clothing was on fire!

Gasping and wiggling, David desperately tried to maneuver his left hand under Grimm's chest, and free his right. Grimm didn't move, but a few pieces of burning rubble fell upon David, burning his face and neck. David choked, then coughed, his body jerked. Grimm's inert form reacted to his heaving, moving just a little. Instinctively, David slipped his right hand out from under Grimm. With a strength born of desperation, David managed to lift Grimm's body a little. Twisting and shoving, David pushed the mayor's demented stepson aside and rolled free.

His clothing smoldering, David grabbed a burning wall, and, mindless of the pain, clawed his way to his feet. The heat and smoke struck him like a physical blow, staggering him, threatening to down him for the final time. David dropped to his knees, and gasping and wheezing, crawled across the kitchen. With blind luck, he bumped into Jana and Michael. With the superhuman strength of desperation and the belief they would die at any minute, David threw Michael over his shoulder, then tucked Jana under the other arm. Numb with pain and with eyes closed, he stumbled toward the door. Instead of finding it, he bumped into the cabinets and almost collapsed.

Where was he? Confused, David whirled around, almost losing his precious burdens. Which way was out? He coughed, then fell to his knees once more. His body cried out for him to relieve himself of the extra weight, but he feared he'd never be able to gather his friends again.

David thought he heard a movement ahead. He looked up and saw something moving only a few feet in front of him. He couldn't see what it was, but it didn't matter, so he prayed as he staggered to his feet and followed it. After only a few wobbly steps, he saw smoke swirling as though it were being sucked outside.

Stumbling and throwing himself forward, he pushed through the door and fell out into the night. He dropped Michael, but held onto Jana, trying to cushion her from the impact. For long moments, David laid there, gasping and sucking in clean air. He coughed several times, then rolled away from his friends and began to vomit black slime.

Finally, his heaving subsided, but tears continued to flow down his blackened cheeks. He glanced around, his face crestfallen as his gaze roamed over his fallen friends, the downed reverend, and his burning house. Was he the only one that was going to survive? Why was he so cursed? He'd trade his life for any of them if he could. David crawled to check on Jana. He thought he saw her chest rise and fall.

Suddenly, the door opened, smoke pouring free, and Monique stepped out, staring at David and saying, "Fire is just an annoyance, and I do not die so easily." She tried to smile, then slumped to the ground.

What about Marlena? David wondered. Was she already dead? And Grimm? It would take more than fire to destroy a vampire. As far as he knew, only sunlight or a wooden stake through the heart would kill a vampire. David managed to rise and staggered back to the house.

He paused at the back door, taking several deep breaths. He couldn't believe he was doing this, but he would not leave their deaths to fate. Fate had not been kind to him, and David didn't trust it.

With one final breath, he yanked open the door and rushed inside the inferno. It was so dark and noxious, he closed his eyes and went by feel and memory. He grabbed the car keys first, jamming them in his pocket, then began his search for Marlena. Surprisingly, he had no trouble finding the vampire, tripping right over her.

Blindly, he dragged her along the floor, using the counter for guidance in helping him find the door once more. He tossed her outside, stuck his head out and took several deep breaths, then returned for Grimm.

David dropped to his hands and knees, feeling his way across the searing kitchen floor. All around him parts of the house continued to crumble. Several times he was struck by falling debris, but he kept going.

David bumped into Grimm face first, grabbed him, and hauled him out. David tripped at the door and tumbled outside.

Almost through, David told himself, there were still two people—Monique's thralls—inside. As David rose once more, his home collapsed like a house of cards. He turned away as it seemed to somehow implode and explode at the same time, becoming compressed and yet spewing fiery shrapnel in all directions.

Quickly, David rushed to Cooper's side and pulled him farther away from the inferno. He was glad to find the reverend still alive, blood pouring from a crease along his temple. As David set him down, the reverend's eyes flickered; he opened them and stared at David. "David?"

"It's going to be all right, Reverend."

Page nodded, then said, "I've already radioed for help."

"This is all for naught," Monique wheezed. "If you kill us, dey will come hunting for you, hunting for us. Already, dey will believe that you killed Marlena, and dey will destroy everything in deir path for revenge. It is deir way," she finished and had a coughing fit.

David looked down at the reverend. His eyes were closed; he was unconscious again, trusting David to make things right. Gently, David laid him on the ground and went over to check on Jana.

Yes, she was alive! Her face was battered, and her nose and jaw appeared broken, but her pulse was strong. Such beauty destroyed, again. He'd almost lost another woman he loved . . . if it hadn't been for the woman he had loved coming back from the dead to save him. Or had she? As sick as he was, it could have been a delusion.

"You might as well kill her," Monique wheezed. "Do it quickly, for dey will do it slowly. Unless . . ." she coughed, "we flee, draw dem away from here. Together, with a head start, we might have a chance. We can still be together. Dere is much we can teach each other. With your strength of will and the power to wield the cross, we might be able to . . ."

Incredulous, David stared at her until she grew silent, then he looked down at Jana. What was the point of all this, if more vampires were going to come to Temprance, searching for him and destroying all he loved? David stroked Jana's dirty hair, looked at Michael and the reverend. He kissed Jana, then removed her crucifix. He stared at her for a moment, then stood, staring around with grim finality.

Pulling the keys from his pocket, David unlocked the rear door of the Blazer and opened the tailgate. He removed a wooden mallet and stake, searched for another, but couldn't find one. Moving like a man twice his age, he loaded Marlena into the rear. "What . . . what are you doing?" Monique asked, fear showing on her face. Without a word, David went to Cooper Page and removed his crucifix, then walked toward Grimm.

David wrapped the chain around Grimm's neck, then placed

the cross on his chest. Grimm twitched and spasmed, his eyes suddenly open. His mouth gaped, and his hands clenched, but he couldn't move. His hateful stare bored; his lips silently working on a joke. As David placed the stake over Grimm's heart, the vampire managed a defiant sneer. David raised the mallet, then struck, driving the stake deep into Grimm's chest. The neophyte vampire grunted, blood spitting from his mouth, then grew still. Expressionlessly, David loaded him into the Blazer, setting him next to Marlena.

Lastly, David approached Monique. "No! David! Please, after all we've meant to each other!"

David took Jana's chain and stuffed it under Monique's clothing. She was too weak to resist, and screamed as it burned, sinking into her flesh. David picked her up, then loaded her into the Blazer and slammed the tailgate shut. Looking at Michael, then longingly at Jana, David climbed into the Blazer, started the engine, and drove toward the lake.

Twenty

Last Rites

Stroke after stroke, David rowed farther away from the dock, toward the center of the lake. The fiery glow along the south shore had long since died, and it seemed as though he'd been rowing for hours, lost in the rhythm, and reveling in the gentle breeze and the soft slap of small waves against the bow.

A glance to the east made David realize that he had been rowing for a long time. The darkness was giving way to the flat pale gray of predawn light. A hint of pink, the telltale herald that the inevitable dawn was coming, touched the clouds that had gathered just above the horizon. David was surprised he hadn't noticed the change in the sky earlier, but then he'd been lost in thought. Had it really been Tina coming to his rescue? And was he—could he—really be a vampire?

David's gaze moved from the sky to the bow, where Monique sat silently. She was no longer bewitchingly beautiful, but emaciated, her face etched by agony and desperation. With burning eyes, she continued to stare silently at him, hoping she could somehow force her will upon him, since her cajoling words had already failed. Long ago, Monique's voice had failed her, causing her to cease in her persistent pleas for David to change his mind. Several times she had struggled against her invisible bonds, but the cross was welded to her flesh, and its holy power held her fast. At Monique's feet were the corpses of Grimm and Marlena, neither so much as twitching during the journey.

David hoped help had arrived, and that his friends were all right. Several times he had wondered if what he was doing was right. He fervently wished things could have been different, but knew that wishing didn't necessarily make them so. Living with Jana might have been wonderful—a way to shake the curse—but as long as he was near the ones he loved, he was a threat to them, bringing violence and death into their lives. David didn't see that he had much of a choice.

Still, if he hadn't grown tired of all the dying—all the violence that his presence seemed to attract—he might have forced himself onward, living for a miracle. If he were really living; Monique might be right—after all, she believed it.

In truth, David was no longer sure, but it no longer mattered. Now all he desired was to revel in the sunlight one last time, then hopefully join Timmy and Tina, as well as his father and sister in Heaven. Despite his failing of faith, his drunkenness and debauchery, surely destroying three vampires would wipe away enough of his sins to enable him to enter the Lord's eternal home.

"You're mad!" Monique croaked, finally finding her voice again.

David simply smiled. He shouldn't need to explain anything—she could read it in his eyes, as she'd often told him. Hopefully, his death and their true deaths would leave a legacy of tranquility after his wake of devastation.

"Uh . . . where?" Grimm suddenly sputtered, then looked up at David.

Surprised, David stared at Grimm. The stake still protruded from his chest. Had something gone wrong? This alone justified his current path of action.

"Missed me, now you have to kiss me," Grimm laughed,

tried to move, but couldn't, paralyzed by the power of the cross. "Hey! What the Hell's going on?" Grimm's eyes darted left and right, seeking. "I'm in a boat."

"We're surrounded by water," Monique wheezed, "trapped and waiting for the sun to rise."

"DAWN? How long?"

"You will not have to wait long, but it will seem longer for us, now that you're awake!"

Would he ever have peace, David wondered, glancing to the east. Hopefully soon, by the looks of the sky. It was lavender, and the clouds were brightening from soft pink to fuchsia. For some reason, the cloud formations reminded him of towering mountains, as they stretched to the north and south on the far side of the lake. A hint of orange crept along the bottom of each range, where there was a gap between them and the horizon.

"Hey, writer-dude! How come you ain't dead?" Grimm spat.

David ignored him, his attention staying on the horizon as his anticipation rose. He would get to see the sun in all its glory one more time. Peace was coming.

"I said, how come you ain't dead? I poisoned your precious home brew, man! Did you go cold turkey or something? That was good stuff man. Killer, in fact!" Grimm began cackling.

So that was why it had tasted bittersweet, David mused. Another mystery solved. But then why wasn't he dead already, instead of just now dying? And he was dying, he could feel it, just as surely as was his mother. Did it have something to do with the odd, but miraculous properties of the home remedy he'd found in that old book? Or was he really a vampire? He would know soon enough.

"Grimm, get serious for once!" Monique screeched. "We are going to die. Really die! David . . ."

"Hey, David" Grimm began, "you got guts, but you're a fool. This religious stuff is all crap. You got it all wrong, if

470

you think offing us will save your soul. Yeah, I see it in your eyes. There ain't no God, no Jesus, or Buddha, or Allah or anybody. Nobody gives a shit about us!"

"David, please," Monique continued, repeating herself. "It is not too late. I will heal, I can be beautiful again. All I must do is feed. You may be dying, but that can change. All you must do is feed on the living, then we can—"

"Mormons know that shit will happen all over again. And Moonies claim only happy shit really happens. You know Protestants have it together, because they let shit happen to someone else," Grimm continued laughing, tears rolling down his cheeks. "Oh man, I really crack myself up sometimes, ya know?" He started thrashing about, but did little more than mildly rock the boat.

"—Live together in ecstasy," Monique continued to plead, her voice cracking. "It was Marlena who wanted to destroy you, not I. David, look at me, please."

David knew better. He kept his eyes on the horizon, waiting for the sun and wishing for silence—for release and peace. "Monique, I'm tired of living . . . of being," David murmured finally in a weary voice. "Tired of being hunted and chased. What I want is peace, and to see the sunrise as a testament to the working of the Lord. Now, will you shut up!"

Monique's mouth worked; she didn't know what to say.

"Ah, here it comes now!" David said excitedly, as he watched the tip top of the blazing red orb peek over the horizon, further igniting the clouds and turning them fiery red. Some of the higher clouds, the pinnacles of the ranges, radiated a Day-glo orange. Above them the sky was pale blue, pushing at the retreating dome of purple and black.

"Ah yes," David sighed and sat back, feeling the light caress him. Suddenly, the world changed with the emergence of the sun. The texture, sounds, and smells were different. Nearby a fish jumped, and David could hear birds chirping. He dropped the oars and just let the boat float into the sunrise. A slight breeze rippled across the shining waters, the light dancing to and fro like faeries cavorting.

"David, please, it is not too late!" Monique pleaded. She struggled, seeming to vibrate as though ready to explode.

Grimm continued on, still struggling to no avail as he spoke, "Catholics say shit happens because you deserve it, while Jehovah's crew tell you that if you let them in, they'll tell you why shit happens."

David totally ignored them—out of sight and out of mind. More and more of the sun rose, freeing itself from the bonds of the horizon and rising to incandescence. A sense of awakening overwhelmed David, and he felt so alive and so happy, that he thought he might explode; then he began to feel weak. He didn't even try to shield his eyes, staring boldly into the brightening sphere; it was all right if he were blinded by the light. Sweat seemed to leap from his skin, as though he were trapped in a sauna. Dizziness assailed him, and he grabbed the gunwales. It wouldn't be long now. Despite the pain, David smiled broadly.

He glanced, then stared at Monique. Ever so slowly at first, then more rapidly, Monique began to decompose. The skin yellowed, then puffed and ruffled as she bloated. The eyes swelled, then popped, dry bubbles bursting. Her hair turned sickly white and mottled brown, as it fell from her wrinkled scalp. Once beautiful lips blackened and fell off as her nose imploded, leaving dark, gaping holes. As time caught up with her in a heartbeat, her flesh receded, melting away and leaving her clothes slumped as though set on a skull-faced scarecrow. Bleached bones quickly shrunk and withered under the power of the sun. An arm slipped out of its socket and fell away. Her skull lolled to the side, as bone began to flake and pit. With a mighty puff and a terrible smell of ancient tombs, suddenly all that was left of her was a pile of dust and the crucifix on a chain.

David glanced at Marlena and found that she was already long gone, the dust gently swirling as it finished settling.

The same was happening to Grimm but more slowly. His skin was the color of old parchment, and his hair that of a hundred-year-old man. His lips were dried and flecked, falling apart as he continued to rant, "Judaism asks why shit happens to *us*." Bloated eyes abruptly sank as though punctured, and his nose collapsed into the cavity. Flesh quivered, then began to slip away from bone moments before evaporating. Little more than a skeleton now, Grimm continued in his relentless joke-a-thon to the bitter end, his blackened teeth clacking together. "I've always wondered why shit happens for no apparent reason." His laughter was rattling and discordant. The bones began to pit, and his skull shrank smaller and smaller. Suddenly, he simply fell apart, the clothing piling up as dust puffed through the material. The stench was gone as quickly as it had come.

David managed a smile, then looked away. Peace and quiet at last. As he reveled in the sun and the wind, he had a strange sense of accomplishment.

In the distance, more birds were singing a glorious song and David began to hum "Morning Has Broken." The sun began to lose its red coloring, as it cleared the horizon and began to play hide-and-seek among the cloud towers. The lake shimmered golden all around him, as the world continued to come alive. He had almost forgotten how this looked, and how it felt. It was worth it. His friends and family would be safe now, and he was going to see Tina.

David no longer felt hot, but a strange combination of cold without and warm within. He began to shake and shudder, then suddenly, all went black, as though he were blind. David lost all sense of balance and thought that the boat pitched and lurched beneath him as though it had been struck by a swell. He felt as though he were falling, then all was cool and comfortable around him as he drifted, journeying to find peace.

Epilogue

Mysterious Ways

The funeral proceedings ended, and the mourners slowly moved away from the grave site. David's family, as well as Michael, Jana, and Logan, stayed behind to pay their last respects. Despite the gloominess of the occasion, the day was cloudlessly sunny with birds singing sweetly.

"Thank you, Reverend," Penny Matthewson said, dabbing at her tearstained cheeks as she moved to hug Cooper. "Those were beautiful words and well written. David would have approved."

"He was a good man and deserved better, but now his troubles are over," Cooper said. "He will find peace in the hands of the Lord."

"And with Tina," Penny said wistfully. Between her illness and the loss of her son, she was drawn and tired. "He missed her so. Even when David was with us, he seemed faraway, and now he's gone," David's mother sobbed. Carol and her children surrounded Penny, hugging her.

"Reverend, if the reporters hassle you when you leave," Logan began, "let me know. My arm may be in a sling, but I'm far from helpless. After dealing with Stones, I have no desire to be kind to big city reporters."

The reverend nodded sympathetically to the new sheriff. Cooper wanted to thank Logan one more time for saving his life, but now wasn't a good time. So Cooper simply said, "Thank you, I will." They shook hands, and Cooper moved to leave.

"Reverend," Michael called as he led Jana to Cooper. The lawyer's right arm was in a sling. "How's your head?"

Cooper turned and said, "The wound of flesh is minor compared to those of my spirit." Michael nodded, bitterness in his expression and despair prevalent in his eyes.

Jana moved into Page's arms, hugging him fiercely. Her bruises were healing, and although she was still a bit gaunt from grieving, her beauty was slowly returning—like a flower in springtime. After a minute of racking sobs, she finally sniffed and said, "Reverend, why did this have to happen? Hate killed David as surely as—" She couldn't finish and wept again.

"I don't know, Jana," Page said, gently stroking her hair. "Tests are part of the life experience; and oftentimes the Lord gives us examples to remind us that although we're made in his image, we are far from perfect. We must learn to live with ourselves as we are, and with others as they are."

Finally, Jana said, "I'd like to come talk with you soon."

"My door is always open," Page said. "You know that."

"Yes." With a faraway expression, Jana said "It's a magnificent day. David would've loved it. Besides Tina and Timmy, there wasn't anything he missed more than sunshine."

"Come see me soon," Cooper said, hugging her one last time. He slowly walked out of the Temprance cemetery, leaving the last of the grieving in the hands of God, and at the mercy of reporters. Those of the fourth estate still hovered around Temprance like flies in a barnyard. Cooper stoically ignored their questions and walked to his car. When the newsmen saw that he wasn't responding, the group flocked toward the gathering of anguished mourners, but Logan blocked their way.

As Cooper drove away, he was introspective. It was always a little disconcerting to deliver a eulogy over an empty grave, he mused. Despite the dead being just that during the funeral, there was definitely more than the body missing. It was as if the soul were also absent, somewhere else instead of saying goodbye one last time. In its place, the ambiance of the unknown hovered, whispering doubt and discord. Sometimes Cooper wondered if David were alive, fleeing Temprance for some place without prejudice—if there was such a place. Wherever your body may lie, David, rest in peace.

They could all certainly use a little peace. The last three weeks had been filled with chaos and death. Donald Bricker was dead, the Brookens brothers' bodies had finally been found, and the dozen killed at the ranch brought the total to nearly twenty. The authorities had done a thorough search of the smoking rubble, but no more bodies were discovered. David's Blazer was found at the dock, and a boat was missing. No one knew why. A day later it was washed ashore. After a week, David was finally assumed dead and a funeral was arranged—the last of all those who had died.

No one made such an assumption on the mayor's stepson, Kevin Grimm. APB's were out on him. Logan was confident that he would be found sooner or later. Cooper wasn't so sure. He had the feeling that somehow Kevin had perished in the house fire—he thought he remembered the boy's voice—but only the bodies of Bubba Ross and Corey Stones had been found.

Surprised to find himself already home, Cooper pulled to a stop in front of his house. He wearily trudged up the sidewalk. He'd been doing too many funerals for too many abrupt and senseless deaths. Those funerals, along with Patrick's condition, made him feel very old.

"Father!" came a yell, and suddenly Patrick was running down the steps to greet Cooper.

"PATRICK!" the reverend barely managed through his total surprise. Father and son hugged as the Missus watched from the door with a huge smile on her face. "You're all right. What happened?"

"I wasn't scared any longer!" Patrick said. "And I just spoke to Skeeter on the phone! He sounds good! Mom said I can I go see him tomorrow! Is that all right?"

"Of course, it is," Page said, taking his son in arm and heading up the steps. "I think it is definitely all right for the first time in a while."

PINNACLE BOOKS HAS SOMETHING FOR EVERYONE —

MAGICIANS, EXPLORERS, WITCHES AND CATS

THE HANDYMAN (377-3, $3.95/$4.95)
He is a magician who likes hands. He likes their comfortable shape and weight and size. He likes the portability of the hands once they are severed from the rest of the ponderous body. Detective Lanark must discover who The Handyman is before more handless bodies appear.

PASSAGE TO EDEN (538-5, $4.95/$5.95)
Set in a world of prehistoric beauty, here is the epic story of a courageous seafarer whose wanderings lead him to the ends of the old world — and to the discovery of a new world in the rugged, untamed wilderness of northwestern America.

BLACK BODY (505-9, $5.95/$6.95)
An extraordinary chronicle, this is the diary of a witch, a journal of the secrets of her race kept in return for not being burned for her "sin." It is the story of Alba, that rarest of creatures, a white witch: beautiful and able to walk in the human world undetected.

THE WHITE PUMA (532-6, $4.95/NCR)
The white puma has recognized the men who deprived him of his family. Now, like other predators before him, he has become a man-hater. This story is a fitting tribute to this magnificent animal that stands for all living creatures that have become, through man's carelessness, close to disappearing forever from the face of the earth.

Available wherever paperbacks are sold, or order direct from the Publisher. Send cover price plus 50¢ per copy for mailing and handling to Penguin USA, P.O. Box 999, c/o Dept. 17109, Bergenfield, NJ 07621. Residents of New York and Tennessee must include sales tax. DO NOT SEND CASH.

MAKE SURE YOUR DOORS AND WINDOWS ARE LOCKED!
SPINE-TINGLING SUSPENSE FROM PINNACLE

SILENT WITNESS (677, $4.50)
by Mary Germano
Katherine Hansen had been with The Information Warehouse too long to stand by and watch it be destroyed by sabotage. At first there were breaches in security, as well as computer malfunctions and unexplained power failures. But soon Katherine started receiving sinister phone calls, and she realized someone was stalking her, willing her to make one fatal mistake. And all Katherine could do was wait. . . .

BLOOD SECRETS (695, $4.50)
by Dale Ludwig
When orphaned Kirsten Walker turned thirty, she inherited her mother's secret diary—learning the shattering truth about her past. A deranged serial killer has been locked away for years but will soon be free. He knows all of Kirsten's secrets and will follow her to a house on the storm-tossed cape. Now she is trapped alone with a madman who wants something only Kirsten can give him!

CIRCLE OF FEAR (721, $4.50)
by Jim Norman
Psychiatrist Sarah Johnson has a new patient, Diana Smith. And something is very wrong with Diana . . . something Sarah has never seen before. For in the haunted recesses of Diana's tormented psyche a horrible secret is buried. As compassion turns into obsession, Sarah is drawn into Diana's chilling nightmare world. And now Sarah must fight with every weapon she possesses to save them both from the deadly danger that is closing in fast!

SUMMER OF FEAR (741, $4.50)
by Carolyn Haines
Connor Tremaine moves back east to take a dream job as a riding instructor. Soon she has fallen in love with and marries Clay Sumner, a local politician. Beginning with shocking stories about his first wife's death and culminating with a near-fatal attack on Connor, she realizes that someone most definitely does not want her in Clay's life. And now, Connor has two things to fear: a deranged killer, and the fact that her husband's winning charm may mask a most murderous nature . . .

Available wherever paperbacks are sold, or order direct from the Publisher. Send cover price plus 50¢ per copy for mailing and handling to Penguin USA, P.O. Box 999, c/o Dept. 17109, Bergenfield, NJ 07621. Residents of New York and Tennessee must include sales tax. DO NOT SEND CASH.

MAKE THE CONNECTION

WITH

Z-TALK *Online*

Come talk to your favorite authors and get the inside scoop on everything that's going on in the world of publishing, from the only online service that's designed exclusively for the publishing industry.

With Z-Talk Online Information Service, the most innovative and exciting computer bulletin board around, you can:

- ♥ CHAT "LIVE" WITH AUTHORS, FELLOW READERS, AND OTHER MEMBERS OF THE PUBLISHING COMMUNITY.
- ♥ FIND OUT ABOUT UPCOMING TITLES BEFORE THEY'RE RELEASED.
- ♥ DOWNLOAD THOUSANDS OF FILES AND GAMES.
- ♥ READ REVIEWS OF ROMANCE TITLES.
- ♥ HAVE UNLIMITED USE OF E-MAIL.
- ♥ POST MESSAGES ON OUR DOZENS OF TOPIC BOARDS.

All it takes is a computer and a modem to get online with Z-Talk. Set your modem to 8/N/1, and dial 212-545-1120. If you need help, call the System Operator, at 212-889-2299, ext. 260. There's a two week free trial period. After that, annual membership is only $ 60.00.

See you online!

KENSINGTON PUBLISHING CORP.